The Four Hundred

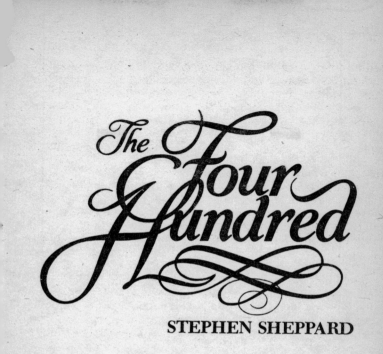

The Four Hundred

STEPHEN SHEPPARD

BERKLEY BOOKS, NEW YORK

THE FOUR HUNDRED

A Berkley Book / published by arrangement with
Summit Books

PRINTING HISTORY
Summit Books edition / October 1979
Berkley edition / November 1980

ISBN: 0-425-04665-6

A BERKLEY BOOK ® TM 757,375
Berkley Books are published by Berkley Publishing Corporation,
200 Madison Avenue, New York, New York 10016.
PRINTED IN THE UNITED STATES OF AMERICA

Text Designed by Michael Serrian

For WINKY and THE PEARL FISHERS

CONTENTS

MY home life was happy. My education minimal. For the battle of life I was equipped with phantom weapons. Unaware that at the first conflict of the fray they would shiver to fragments, my brother and I stepped into the world. Our parents cared little for this life and dwelt on the spiritual, where golden streets and the promised rest of heaven would give solace for the toils and pains of existence. But, boylike, we discounted all they said—we wanted some of this world before we knocked at the gates of the next. In life, the portals, to which only the crème de la crème had access, were guarded by those who would measure wealth, power and position before allowing entry. There could be no more than four hundred the world over, it was generally agreed, who could—with the confidence that heaven on earth was theirs as a fact, no future promise—stride into that land knowing that in life, at least, they were the chosen few.

From Delgraw Street, South Brooklyn, it was a long journey, but poverty and the bounding ambition of youth create a sustained resilience in some characters that can be broken by little less than total annihilation. My brother, George, and I determined to ourselves that we consisted of such "stuff" and would one day—no matter what—gain entrance at the gates of the Four Hundred.

AUSTIN BYRON BIDWELL

Winter

1872

George

BELCHING smoke and cinders, a huge consolidated four-four-oh engine was crossing the Buckeye State at forty miles an hour pulling carriages bound southeast for Norfolk, Virginia, out of Chicago, Illinois. A single beam of light from the lamp fixed in front of the engine's boiler swept ahead of the train as it roared into snow that whipped across the tracks out of surrounding darkness.

The face that peered from a window of the moving carriages saw only a frozen night landscape obliterated by the blizzard. Seen through snow-flecked glass it offered little hope.

George Bidwell wiped away condensation from his distorted image on the window of the railway car with both hands together. The dim light from oil burners in the carriage gave his head a cadaverous look, short dark hair and pale skin emphasized by shadows filling his hollow cheeks. As thoughts prompted a smile, George's deep-set eyes suddenly glittered.

"There ain't nothin' out there for you," said a familiar voice.

George turned from the window.

"That there's just snowy ol' Ohio," the voice finished.

George smiled slowly and put both hands back in his lap. Firstly, he thought, as he felt the metal on his wrists, the handcuffs were going to be a problem. Pender was the second. The powerful man opposite had his full attention on George—unwavering, impassive; he took his job seriously, proud of the shining badge he had stuck on his thick fur coat. Slowly, twin barrels of the shotgun came up until they were beneath George's nose, touching his moustache. Pender smiled viciously, in imitation, it occurred to George, of a dime-novel sheriff.

"You're goin' home, boy."

For George, "home" would be two—perhaps now three—more years of prison in Wheeling, West Virginia. The two he'd already spent had come near to being exorcised from his memory by the three months he'd been in Chicago. He'd sure as hell never get over the wall a second time. Five of the seven who had tried it the night he'd got out hadn't made it across the exercise yard.

George turned again to the window as Pender lowered his shotgun and settled back on the bench seat. His troubles had first begun more than two years back when he'd been taken in Norfolk—the result of a certain scheme for separating some of the Rebs from their money. On arrival in Norfolk, he had been taken into custody within a week, as if betrayed. That was now more than two years back. After his recent escape, fortune had seemed to change in George's favor. He had reached Chicago—where his luck had run out. George censored all other thoughts. He'd had enough time already to regret going South in the first place. His home was New York City. There he was protected: he knew the right people—first of all, the police. His mouth set in a hard line, and his eyes strayed momentarily to the hick Reb who had been entrusted with the safety of his prisoner until delivered back to custody in West Virginia. The money he'd made up North didn't count for a damn chicken down South, where they were still fighting a lost war; when the word had gone out that the hunt was on for George—a born Yankee—he hadn't had a chance—in peacetime, at least. During the civil conflict it had been— Well, George remembered, that was different.

George stared out into the darkness, seeing nothing but the past—people, places and mistakes. In Chicago he'd gone straight to a "safe house"; how in hell did he know that his friend Stoneman was being watched?

The group behind Pender bent over a makeshift table at the forward end of the long carriage let out a combined shout—the "Holy shit!" (and worse) heedless of the ladies and other passengers seated farther down the railway car. Pender, delving into some recess where manners were a fading memory, absorbed the obvious displeasure of the women and, recognizing his authority over the deputies, turned to chastise them.

"You ain't cleanin' pigpens now, Luke, Jake, Elisha; you cut that crap, now—you hear?"

Luke splayed out his cards for Pender to see: four aces and a deuce.

"You beat that, Sheriff?"

The three men burst out laughing. Jake waved a hand limply.

"Hey, Pender—come an' hold a hand over here."

Again laughter exploded amongst the group—coarse, high-pitched, inane, unintelligent; it went with a Rebel drawl never forgotten by George from the first time he'd heard it in battle. When was it, now? he asked himself. Could the War really be ten years back? He'd been not much more than a grown boy when he'd signed on. George probed the harsh night out-side—impassive, unmoved. He had no fondness for the green youth who now leaped into his mind, brash, confident and eager. That had been another person in another time. Through the window George watched as snow brushed against the glass, then was wind-borne back into the cold darkness. His eyes strayed once more to the window frame and realities. The shrouded land held no secrets for George Bidwell; he'd been out there before—he remembered it well: at the end of the war, in the chaos of victory. Now it seemed a whole world away.

The Civil War had changed many things. On April 9, 1865, after the final defeat of the Army of Northern Virginia, Robert E. Lee's flag of truce was accepted by the victorious Major General of Volunteers. The division had cheered their

young, yellow-haired commander and felt proud to be part of
this moment in history. It had been a long and bloody war for
the lucky few amongst the crowd who had survived it all, and
the swelling hearts of the Ohio-born went out to George
Armstrong Custer as he accepted the flag from a vanquished
foe. In the forefront of the photogravure of the occasion, to
the extreme left, posed with the others in unnatural
seriousness, George Bidwell gazes out into the future.

§

"Move a muscle and I'll blow off your ass—y'hear?"
Startled, George looked around quickly, then up at Pender,
who, already on his feet, emphasized his threat with the twin
barrels and a stony face. George nodded just sufficiently to
relax the lawman. Pender glanced over his shoulder at the
table where, as another hand was dealt, noise from his trio of
deputies vied with the steady roar of the train.

"Deal me in," he said.

They were golden words to George as, with a single backward look at his prisoner, Pender broke open the shotgun on
his arm and shuffled over to the bench seats to play poker.
Far from dreaming into the night through the cold glass,
George Bidwell had, as discreetly as was possible, been eyeing
the two press-down, flick-over catches at the base of the pull-
up window for just under seven hours and thirty-six minutes.

§

Their prisoner had for several days provided the four
Southern Lawmen with some amusement—needless to say, at
his expense. Once custody had been transferred to them, they
had taken every opportunity to humiliate the recaptured con-
vict. In charge of their very own "gentleman," they'd had a
good time. Cropped hair and coarse prison issue had quickly
replaced a barber's skill and conservative tailoring. In actual
fact, George was in no way a gentleman; he had assumed
everything he appeared to be. George had been born and bred
in South Brooklyn, New York City. Poverty on the streets had
shown him that the only way was up. Life had given him

sharpness and quick wits. Experience had taught him the power of money, which he'd learned to use well—and enjoy.

George glanced quickly across at the group, each one of them now concentrating on his first hand of the dealt cards. Had George been a killer, these men would probably have asked him to sit in; but because he used his mind to obtain money in not altogether legitimate ways and had proved successful with numerous coups in New York City—several of which had come to light during his trial in Norfolk—these men called him a "paper thief" and gave neither his reputation nor his physical appearance a second thought. George clenched his teeth. If any of them came within arm's length he would show them—when the time came. His compact, powerful body allowed him the grace of movement an athlete projects—smooth, controlled, disciplined. He had always been fit, and in his youth a feared street fighter. Despite the changing circumstances of his life, he had always made time to maintain his superb natural physical condition. George withheld welling anger and swore under his breath. At that precise moment, the huge front wheels of the four-four-oh engine hit the beginning of the incline George had been waiting for—an hour later than he had calculated. For that he thanked his stars: the difference in time had now removed the ever-vigilant Pender. His luck was changing.

"What the hell?" exclaimed Jake loudly from the table, alarmed at the train's slowing down. Unperturbed, Luke relieved his fellow deputy's consternation.

"We allus switches tracks top of the gradient. 'S about a mile up ahead. Stop only takes a minute—then it's a straight run into Cumberland; be there come mornin'."

"That where we left the horses outbound?" asked Jake.

" 'S right," answered Luke. He looked at his cards and grinned. "Now, you goin' to show what ya got?"

Pender glanced back at George as the reduction in speed momentarily ruffled the drowsy suffering of all in the third carriage from the caboose. He nodded as if to congratulate George on his obedience, then turned back to continue play. Outside in the cold night, wind blew, snow flurried and the huge engine's steady roar changed pitch as it began to strain against the incline. George conjured a silent prayer and leaned toward the push-up window of the carriage.

The press-down, flick-over metal window catch nearest George released its grip on the frame stud and went slack. A fine stream of cold air brushed George's shoulder as he cautiously took his gaze off the absorbed group of poker players and tested the window with his weight. It had not been easy to conceal his action, and he knew he would have to reach for the second catch.

It was at this moment, as George shifted to the exact position he would need to apply pressure to the other catch, that a child appeared, seemingly from nowhere. She stared at George with quiet concentration, then sat down on the seat opposite.

George remained absolutely still, feeling the cold air of freedom cutting into his shoulder, chilling him down to his prison-issue boots. He held the disconcerting stare of the child with a steady appraisal of her face and clothes. She looked at the catch, then into George's eyes again, and suddenly broke into a sweet smile. Over her shoulder, the final moments of a second poker hand were being played out in furious silence as the four had been induced to bet more than their pockets would safely allow. George tried a cautious grin and received from the child an immediate frozen face. If he could tell only one thing, this kid had a big scream and was looking for a valid reason to get herself a carriageload of attention.

At forty miles an hour George knew a fall would hurt, and if he lost an ankle he was done. He needed the gradient. He had to make his move now. They were down to about thirty, he calculated, with just over a half mile to go. At the poker table, all four men were engrossed. George glanced at the window and then looked at the child. With less than a minute remaining, he had no choice.

George snapped open the second catch and leaned back, now feeling cold air from the entire length of the window. Mesmerized, the child absorbed the loose metal piece disconnected from its stud. Slowly she looked from the stud into George's lap and at the handcuffs. She's obviously never seen them for real before, thought George. He felt another lurch as the train slowed again. A roar went up from the poker group.

The final cards were laid. Pender turned away in disgust and saw the child.

"Hey, kid—get the hell outta there."

As Pender began to rise, the child obeyed his shout and turned to him.

"Is he a bank robber?"

George clenched his teeth.

"Never mind that—get the hell outta there."

Jake and Luke snickered as Elisha nudged Pender heavily.

"That there's a lady, Sheriff, an' you ain't cleanin' no pigpens now, boy, remember?"

The child ignored Pender's coarseness and asked a second question as if a lawyer for the prosecution.

"Are you a sheriff?"

Pender cut in quickly, stifling any retorts already on the lips of his deputies.

"That's right. Now you git back there."

As he indicated the rear of the carriage with a gesture, the train lurched again. The kid remained composed.

"I think your bank robber's going to escape, Mr. Sheriff."

Pender ignored his deputies' laughter.

"Now, what the hell makes you think that, kid?"

Words influence history; action makes it. That night, in the next moment, the occupants of the third carriage from the caboose saw both.

"He's opened the window," said the child coolly. Then she turned her head to smile directly and sweetly at George.

With an oath, George wrenched at the window with all his power. As the child made three fast paces toward her mother, every excuse now available for the scream that was fully lubricated and ready to rip, George succeeded in pushing the window right up, half shattering it. Pender leaped across the space between them with surprising agility for one so large, fumbling with the shotgun, trying to lock it closed in a single action, but it caught in the fur of his coat, so he swung the barrels at George with a roar of anger. George ducked, then kicked Pender hard, between the legs. Immediately the large man fell to his knees in agony, his mouth wide, gasping with pain. The double-fisted blow George aimed at Pender's head whipped the face from right to left. Teeth snapped off; blood spattered across the compartment: handcuffs on bone at speed—a bad conjoining.

The second, equally vicious swing from above took Pender to the floor of the railway car as if poleaxed. The impact locked the shotgun, and it blasted from both barrels down the aisle of the car, raking the end door. Slow at the best of times, Elisha, Luke and Jake were only now struggling to their feet, pulling awkwardly for guns stuck in their belts, yelling all the while, more in fear for themselves than in consternation at Pender's predicament.

George took not a moment longer. The child screaming loudly, shouts from alarmed passengers, the roar of raw elements rushing into the carriage through the open window—the confusion George had ignited—all were left behind as the prisoner propelled himself into the darkness following a pair of handcuffs—which for every person remaining in the carriage took him out of their lives forever. . . .

§

Meteorological observations for this night during the third week of the New Year record that a great atmospheric wave of cold passed over the continent of North America. In Chicago, the mercury suddenly fell thirty-three degrees. The wave then passed southeast at the rate of twenty-five or thirty miles an hour. The thermometer dropped to fifteen degrees below zero, and the barometer rose as rapidly as the thermometer fell. For those who could see the moon it is recorded that the lunar coronae and halos existed with marked chromatic peripheries.

§

Tensed in anticipation of the rolling fall, George was already absorbing with his senses swirling snow, a shallow embankment and the luck of missing any protruding object before he hit the ground. Settled snow cushioned the impact. A moment later he slithered to a halt. George shook his head, cleared it and was immediately on his feet, oblivious as yet of

the battle royal his blood was engaged in with an atmosphere
fifteen degrees below zero, but fully conscious of the biting
wind that numbed his legs and feet. George stumbled up the
embankment onto the tracks as the caboose passed. Increasing his speed awkwardly, handicapped by wrists locked
together, George began to sprint after the train.

In the carriage, amidst confusion, consternation and shock,
Pender was helped to his feet by wide-eyed deputies. His
shouts were incomprehensible as broken teeth, welling blood
and obvious pain hindered all sense. Luke thought he identified "Stop the train" and looked uncomfortably at Elisha
and Jake, who were now staring at a large gentleman who was
attempting, with difficulty, to close the damaged window.
The prospect of "snowy ol' Ohio" that night was hardly
inviting.

"Aw, he ain't goin' nowhere, Pender." Luke appealed to
Elisha, whose mind had now grasped the situation, albeit tentatively.

"An' we got such a good game goin'," Elisha said, grinning at Pender.

"Aw, let him freeze his ass off," Jake said. "We can come
back come mornin' and pick up what's left of him in our own
good time," he declared reassuringly.

Jake forcibly sat Pender down on a bench seat. The sheriff
looked out into the raw dark night, at the plump gentleman
wrestling unaided with the window frame, then directly at
Jake. He was obviously perplexed.

"But he knows that too—so why the hell . . . ?"

"He jus' don' wanna do no more time—'s natural," Jake
said sympathetically. He pulled off his neckerchief and offered it to the sheriff.

"Here, wipe your face—you're bleedin' all over yer shirt."
The filthy kerchief changed hands as the gentleman with
considerable girth and now pink face surprised them all by
succeeding in slamming down the window—and completely
shattering the already damaged glass. As he turned shame-
faced to the other passengers with a helpless gesture, Pender's
exasperation reached its peak.

"We gotta stop!" he spluttered.

"We allus stops at the top of the gradient to switch tracks.

If you wanna stop, we're stoppin'." Jake looked quickly at
Elisha and Luke, then continued fast, "Look, if you wan' him
bad, we'll all get off at Cumberland and come back in the
mornin'—right?"

The pause was pregnant, but even Pender could see the
sense of remaining warm. Elisha flicked the cards still in his
hands.

"He's a damn fool's what I say."

Pender spat blood, and before wiping his face and wadding
the kerchief to bite on, he showed the insight that had
probably got him his star.

"No, 'Lisha. If there's one thing he ain't, it's that."

§

The last thirty yards to the caboose were the worst for
George, but he was helped by the decreasing speed of the
train. He couldn't afford to have inquisitive eyes find him
limping along the tracks when the stop was made. Running fit
to bust, he reached up with his hands, almost fell, then felt the
cold metal of the rear guardrail. He gripped securely, then
pulled so that his feet gratefully left the track and he was
suspended beneath the platform. He locked his aching
muscles and tried to remember the words of Stephen Foster's
"Oh! Susanna" to detract from the painful messages he was
receiving from all over his body.

George was making his third request to Susanna not to cry
as the train slowed, lips taut with the cold, his grip unfeeling,
his body assaulted by increasingly icy blasts of freezing wind.
Then, up front, the engine halted and a final lurch stopped the
carriages dead.

Above George, at the caboose guard's window, a face appeared briefly in the glow of a lamp. Distant shouts indicated
that the train was switching tracks.

George Bidwell lowered himself to the rails, then lay beside
the nearside wheel of the caboose. George knew about wheels
and rails, suspension bars, coachwork, bolts, axles and
generally the underwork mechanics of a carriage. The world
over they were much the same, and he'd learned the hard way.
Cut off behind Southern lines years before, he'd hung on

beneath the coachwork and above the wheels of a Reb train until it had carried him out of the town—eighteen miles. Had he relaxed once, he'd have been chewed up. He certainly knew all about the power of wheels on rail. His face had been inches away as tons of wheel and carriage ground dust to powder. He had made his escape then as he would have to do again—over rugged country, hunted in the cold—until he had managed to rejoin his division. His exploits had not gone unnoticed or unrecognized. George smiled fleetingly at the thought. This time it would be different; he was no longer the young hero.

A whistle sounded up front. George extended his freezing hands, placing the short chain of the handcuffs on the metal rail. Suddenly the coaches lurched and the wheels ground forward, biting into the chain links. George's hands were drawn toward the wheels as metal ground on metal. The handcuff bracelets cut deep into his wrists. The wheels rolled over the chain, and as he stifled a scream of pain, the links snapped.

The warm cocoon of the caboose guard's small compartment had lulled its occupant into a doze that after several more minutes, backed by the now steady rhythm of the train, formed the beginnings of a dream. One word destroyed it.

"Evenin'."

The guard could feel metal beneath his chin. He woke up and saw that his old Army Colt was firmly held by a bedraggled man in prison issue, leaning toward him and smiling, not without humor. As his eyes snapped open and translated the situation to his sluggish brain, the guard grimaced and replied, also with one word, more to himself at his own stupidity than for the benefit of the other who was beginning to settle against the cabin heater. "Shit!" the guard said.

That night the Civil War was fought and won by both North and South—the little whiskey the guard had produced going a long way. If brothers, sons and fathers, abolitionist politicians and plantation owners, glory-hunting generals and their later-to-be-lost regiments could have got together before hostilities and talked, as George and the guard did all the way to the dawn stop in Cumberland, they might well have ended the night much as these two did—asleep on each other's shoulders as first rays of sunlight in a brilliant clear sky penetrated condensation on the cabin windows.

The guard later contended publicly that, given the chance, he'd have somehow got the drop and delivered the prisoner. Fact was the guard liked George and was under no duress at all when he took in the steaming coffee and a loaf of bread from a little Negro boy and delayed for a moment to conceal George's quick look up the platform at Pender and the deputies. Clambering down with their saddles, they exchanged several insults with passengers still aboard the train, then dragged their way into the station house to begin their search for the escaped prisoner.

The four-four-oh engine's whistle blew long and shrill. The guard waved All clear, stretched, checked his watch, slipped it into his waistcoat pocket and came back into the cabin to the warmth of the stove, freshly poured hot coffee and new-baked bread. George settled back and began to pick the locks of his handcuffs with a long nail prised from the wooden floor. The rest of the day passed in conversation pertaining to all the problems men solve on long journeys.

George jumped the train a second time eight miles out of Norfolk and stood in the evening light brushing down his guard's uniform, then waved cheerfully back at the man in prison issue, standing arm aloft at the rear of the caboose.

That evening, as George turned north and threw away the bracelets of his handcuffs, he wondered at his fortune. He had just experienced the worst period of his life and given himself—a reprieve. Now he would know the best. George had determined that he would become, as he put it, one of the Four Hundred, and for that he needed one thing: money. He fingered the several silver dollars given to him willingly by the guard and remembered the man's address, also given, at George's insistence.

Twelve months later, five thousand dollars posted to this railway employee, from "a brother in Europe," became the talk of his small home town.

§

It was ten days before George Bidwell entered the restaurant upstairs at Delmonico's in New York City, plans

finalized, with a ticket to travel and ready for a last American
dinner. He sat down at his favorite corner table in this old
haunt, ordered, then accepted the greetings of the lad who
served cool wine brought directly from the cellar.

"Been a time, Mr. Bidwell, sir."

"You've grown," replied George.

"That I have, sir," said young Harry McCann proudly.

"Thinking lucky?" George asked with a twinkle in his eye.

"Like a Fenian man," the lad retorted with a grin, referring
to the Irish rebels of whom he was a direct offspring.

"So am I, Harry," said George, tipping him five whole
dollars; "so am I." On George's face a smile; in his mind, a
single thought which reconfirmed the decision he'd made: he
was going "to sea."

§

The open coach and four, horses foaming at the bit,
careened down a long colonnaded drive, reached the intersection of E Wharf and the dockside, turned sharply,
cleared the area of crane rails, rattled over a cobbled pathway,
then began to race along the waterfront toward the passenger
harbor. Standing braced at the reins was a uniformed driver
totally concentrated on his dangerous task; inside the coach,
three men in somber tailored clothes; on the polished walnut
coachwork, an emblazoned badge and lettering: NEW YORK
CITY POLICE DEPARTMENT.

Between barrels, bales and boxes stacked in every available
space, scattering complacent porters, dock laborers and the
few steerage passengers who sought frantically for their ship
amidst wandering crowds, the vehicle sped toward the
gangway of a distant vessel now making final preparations to
sail.

The driver began to haul at the reins with his entire weight
fifty yards before the coach finally skidded noisily to a halt.
The detectives were already up in their seats, doors open on
both sides, before the horses, neighing and plunging, understood that the six-mile chase from Central Police Headquarters was over. One of the men, stout, broad-shouldered,
red-faced, anxiety clear in the set of his features, jumped

down with an agility that surprised the waiting steward standing at a gangway on the pier. Indicating the gentleman already ascending the steps behind two porters, the policeman, breathing hard, shouted, "Hold it!"

The steward looked quickly from the anxious detective stumbling toward him to the gentleman who, unperturbed, took several more paces, then stopped and turned to look down on the commotion. The crowd of onlookers come to wave farewell parted, allowing access to the policeman. He reached the gangway, brushed the steward aside and slowed to take the steps with care.

The gentleman remained unperturbed. The detective appeared to find words difficult; although his eyes fixed the man before him, his attention was on regaining his breath.

"Hello, Irving," said George Bidwell calmly.

The basso profundo horn of the White Star Liner *Atlantic*, equipped for three classes and steerage, obliterated all other sound for a full ten seconds. Detective James Irving began to squeeze out his words.

"George—there was nothin' I could do—I swear." The sudden comparative silence made Irving turn quickly to see if words carried to the crowd. He softened his voice and continued in a harsh whisper.

"Listen, George, you know who I am and what I represent. Don't forget . . ."

"Two years and seven months in a Southern hole, where I was shown why Yankees fought, is what I don't forget, Irving."

"George, I tried . . ."

Irving began to finger the ostentatious diamond ring on his left hand beside the two others of gold. George's eyes discovered the diamond pin in the now sweat-stained pink cravat before him.

"And Irving, I don't forget the ten thousand dollars you've had from us to keep our noses clean—wherever!"

This hit Irving where it hurt most—in his handstitched pale gray pigskin wallet. He shouted down to the two waiting detectives, "Okay, boys, I'll be with you."

George turned to walk up the gangway to the deck. Irving followed, still breathless.

"I appreciate the relationship we've established, George. Hell, the three of you boys is like brothers to me. How can you think I've let you down? Why, when I heard you went down Norfolk I wired Virginia State personal just so's you'd have a friendly ear if any of your . . ."

He paused, uncertain of the correct euphemism.

". . . well, 'ventures'—went wrong."

George stopped at the twin rails that ran the length of the main deck; looked up at the clear February sky; then slowly, containing all the anger Irving could see as their eyes met, said quietly, "That, Irving, is how they found me."

"You mean those boys didn't take care of you?" Irving was transparently perplexed. "Why, I knew Brown six years afore he went South, and he's been juiced like the rest."

"Brown was shot two months before your wire arrived."

"Listen, George." Irving could see much of his income dwindling for several years as he fought to find words to console George Bidwell. A payoff protection racket, instituted by Irving in the mid-'sixties, had proved at first a lucrative bonus to his salary but had now been for several years an enjoyable necessity.

Irving had become wealthy. Initially he had hidden the fact; then, declaring a coup on the market, he began to show himself about the city as if he were one of the Four Hundred. Visions of early retirement and a mansion on Long Island had begun to evaporate when George had been caught in Norfolk, Virginia, by astute and honest police. The clerk who checked back with the New York police while Irving was away discovered George's record, and the prisoner, without protection, was convicted of fraud. Irving knew that George was in a position to finish him, so inspiration provided a diversion.

"How's Austin?" asked the policeman nervously.

George's brother, Austin, had come to Wheeling Prison to visit and had been identified as wanted, so he had been forced to take to his heels. It was Irving who had suggested Europe until the vigorous hunt—to which Irving had (commendably, George remembered) eventually put a stop—cooled off. Irving continued with confidence.

"And how is Mac?"

George MacDonald, known amongst friends as Mac, so as

not to be confused with George Bidwell, had been apprehended during the Chicago fire the previous year, actually helping some people escape the inferno of their hotel, but arrested on the grounds of "suspicion." Once his equally dubious record in New York City was discovered, he'd been accused of looting. Irving had provided a bribed judge, who had quashed the case with bureaucratic ease. George softened slightly at the thought of the trio's imminent reunion.

"Austin and Mac are in Europe," he said.

Bells began ringing loudly to signal the ship's departure. George stepped onto the deck as Irving, now satisfied that any breach between them was at least temporarily repaired, hesitated atop the gangway.

"Will you keep in touch, George?"

George nodded, noting the steward below on the pier gathering his papers and beginning to ascend the steps. Several ladies still aboard blew last kisses to their loved ones, giggled past the two men and ran squealing down the gangway.

"Just let me know, George. Anything—remember, anything." George remained impassive, thoughts of a new continent already stimulating his imagination. Last bells of warning sounded throughout the ship. Irving descended the gangway quickly, whereupon it was immediately disengaged from the White Star liner.

On the dockside, the Chief of New York detectives looked up and waved once. "Where exactly you goin', George?"

Although Irving's voice was raised, it was drowned by the ship's basso horn—deep and mournful.

Where was he going, exactly? He knew perfectly well, privately: Great Britain and, more especially, the greatest metropolis of the age—London. But publicly George would begin as he intended to continue, with caution and cunning. His mind was determined, and he was the product of rugged spirit in a raw country.

In England, to the various church and charity organizations established to rehabilitated prisoners released or on parole, an ex-convict represented a challenge. More especially, he represented both a government subsidy and a legitimate excuse for seeking private donations. Provided the prisoner remained respectably at large, the work of the organization was declared a success. If conditions forced him to crime once again and he was caught by the always vigilant police of that small island, the government withdrew its subsidy and private money became reluctant to continue patronage. Though each man got a pitifully small sum, the national total became impressively large as the number of ex-prisoners given aid increased. The problem was that each man actually received only a small proportion of the money officially due to him; with unemployment high, a return to crime was his only recourse.

Perhaps it had been a clergyman or perhaps a lady of good intentions over cress and salmon sandwiches in a drawing room of London's Belgravia. No matter, someone had come up with the idea of sending men, should they choose, to the great continent of North America.

Publicly it was stated that America was "an opportunity for the poor fellow to start anew"; privately—"a way to dispose of our problems abroad at minimum steerage fares; the men officially rehabilitated, *and* off our records." Unfortunately, criminals proved to be of resilient stock, and complaints were raised across the ocean; but both Britain's government and her society's charity continued to see the system as efficient and discreet. Thus it was that when a prisoner was interviewed in England on his release and asked the vital question, he was shushed to silence, should he mutter the word "America," and reminded that his public answer to the official question of a possible transatlantic fare should be merely that his wish was to go "to sea."

Thus, with his knowledge of the pre-eminent hypocrisy of an entire nation, gleaned from endless conversations with an English-born cellmate in Wheeling Prison, George Bidwell had decided to reverse the process.

George turned his head east as again a warning blast from the ship's horn sounded out over the great river.

Smoothly, the *Atlantic* departed the shores of the North American continent.

George Bidwell smiled in understanding of their implications as he mouthed words softly in reply to Irving's question.

"To sea," he said.

A fresh wind off the Hudson cleared George's head as first seeds of new ideas were sown into the fertile soil of his ambition.

Austin

AUSTIN Byron Bidwell lay back in the deep bath and, with the faintly pungent smell of warm sulphur in his nostrils, closed his eyes. Sounds filtered into the ornate bathroom as, outside, Wiesbaden prepared for another day. The Hotel Nassau stood opposite a park gate leading from the Spa to the Casino, so it was the murmur of early-morning strollers and leather on gravel that formed for Austin a background to memories of his late-night gambling. Dogs barked, carriages passed, a lady took herself into fits of laughter and the breeze wafted chintz draperies inward from an open window in the lounge that was the third room of his suite.

A cough, suddenly so near, so loud, went directly to Austin's heart before he allowed his eyes to register the intruder.

Austin's arms hung over either side of the bath, his head was back and the cigar in his mouth would certainly have fallen had his confidence not been restored by what his hand now found. Old habits, even in sophisticated environments, die hard.

The servant saw what was in fact a Smith & Wesson .32

rimfire pistol appear from behind the enamel bath and believed in that instant all he had heard about the wild continent of America. He thrust a cable at the man in the bath as if his life depended upon it. Austin took the paper. The servant clicked his heels in a rising motion, spun round and was gone before Austin had time to begin reading.

Too young for the Civil War, Austin had awaited his brother's return to New York and, together with George, had become a willing pupil in the art of making money. They had explored every illegitimate postwar avenue they encountered. Eventually, experience had given them influence, and natural intelligence had provided increasing success. Silver dollars, "green-issue bucks," bonds and bills had become their business. The two brothers had exploited to the full discovered "situations," as they called each potential hit. With various partners, utilizing what was stolen or forged, they had found ways to turn paper into dollars and cents, which they spent in a style to which they became accustomed. The few friends they had made remained loyal. The few men they had bought gave service proportionate to payment. They had accumulated if not substantial, then adequate funds for whatever enterprise they might decide upon next. As did many amongst their associates and friends, they dined at Delmonico's, were seen in many a theater lobby and seldom missed a charity or public occasion of the sort designed for the elite but, unbeknownst to most, attended only by the inconsequential. Life in New York had become, if not wealthy, pleasant. Then George had gone south to Norfolk, Virginia, with some scheme, whose details Austin had discovered much later as he sat looking at George through chicken wire stretched across iron bars. It was the nearest Austin had come to being "inside." His occasional nights, in the past, in the care of "New York's finest" were no comparison to the degradation and appalling conditions that George continued to endure. George was more miserable to have been caught than self-pitying at his surroundings. He was certainly resilient enough to want escape at the earliest opportunity—one that Austin immediately began to arrange. Then, on a tip-off by the very prison guard who was to ensure George's "release," Austin had found himself—not, as he had declared himself to be, a relative, but as a suspected associate of the prisoner's—a hunted man. Once he was back in New York, Chief of Detectives Irving, many times a guest at "their" table at Delmonico's, having heard of George's entrapment, had pointed Austin east. So to Europe he had gone, and there he remained.

Irving, months later, had informed Austin, via an agreed-on poste restante, that the pressure was off. In his own time, it was suggested, Austin, who was in no rush to repatriate himself, could now return to America assured of protection. Next, word had come from the same source that brother George had escaped from Wheeling Prison; then, in another cable, that he had been caught again; and yet a third message had conveyed to Austin the joyous information that Irving had met brother George at the New York harborside alive, well and traveling east.

The cable now in Austin's hand was the second to have arrived that same day: the first, Irving's last; *this* was also from America but directly from George. The words written in New York clearly set forth a rendezvous—in England.

Austin pulled the plug deftly with the chain around his toe; water began to gurgle away. As he stepped from the bath, he began making plans.

§

The city of Wiesbaden was the chief town of one of the numerous petty principalities scattered over the face of Europe at this time. Since Roman days the town had been famous for its hot springs, consequently its hot baths. Thus a good many people came to take the waters, hoping to benefit from the reputedly marvelous cure.

The daily routine of these throngs began with coffee in bed at eight; then, dressing gowns donned, either private or public baths were enjoyed in the hot mineral waters which were conducted directly to all the hotels.

Half an hour in the bath for the dedicated, less for those impatient to be up, out and at Society's throat, and no time at all for those who still considered a damp sponge their maximum concession to personal hygiene.

A light breakfast or the full *table du matin*, whichever will power dictated, prepared the now fully stimulated subject for the day's offerings. Sashaying along corridors, sweeping down staircases and sallying out of doors, ladies and gentlemen representing all the strata of European societies drank the water, meandered in the parks, listened to the band and saw or were seen.

At two in the afternoon a quartet played in the Musiksaal, and most of the idlers gathered there to listen and eat lunch. At four o'clock the Northern European version of siesta began; liaisons of the night, passing the scrutiny of daylight and encouraged by the chilled Hochheimer, retired to conjoin on soft quilts in large bedrooms. At seven P.M. was the ponderous *table d'hôte* dinner. At nine everyone flocked to the Casino, and the game, for which the entire day had been preparation, began.

§

The wheel was spinning as Austin reached a large roulette table in the center of the huge, ornate room. He joined the group around the green baize as the click-click of the ball on the number ridges brought several of them to their feet. The silence of the final moment after the ball dropped into place could have been broken by a pin falling onto velvet. Zero. Only one chip in the right place. But there were two winners. The young Prussian officer contained his jubilation in an undisguised look of great affection across the table. Austin saw the Countess once again. Her profile seemed molded out of porcelain; only her eyes glittered. As his winnings were thrust at the young officer, she smiled.

A hand barely touched the shoulder of this lovely woman, but it was enough to take away all joy. Austin saw her face—beautiful still, but now dead. He looked at the man behind her—the other winner. In old-fashioned spectacles and a seedy coat, "the man of ice," François Blanc looked more like a country advocate than the head of a great gambling establishment.

Vast as his ambition and achievements were, he was a man of the simplest tastes. Impervious to flattery, he was a hard-headed, silent man who kept a lavish table yet ate sparingly himself. He had a superb wine cellar yet was content to sip only mineral water. And he never gambled.

Blanc had only two passions. The first: money; accumulated from the "butterflies of society" who "scorched their wings in the flame of his casino"; its power interested him. His second passion, he adored. As he pulled back her chair and the lovely woman stood up before him, it was obvious he possessed and was possessed by her: the Countess, his wife.

Austin watched the Countess and her husband part, with barely a nod between them. Blanc toward the conservatory, the Countess toward the stairway.

Immediately, the young Prussian—with good sense, thought Austin—stood up, gathered his chips and began to cross toward the Caisse, presumably to cash his winnings. Austin hoped that Blanc was now alone. What he was about to do might well prove difficult; but quite simply, Austin needed the money.

§

With intense displeasure, François Blanc replaced the cutlery on his plate beside a piece of cold chicken and watched Austin Byron Bidwell close the conservatory door, turn and smile.

"Monsieur . . ." began Austin. Blanc wiped his mouth with the starched napkin, fixed Austin with a piercing look and interrupted.

"It is Count."

The gaze intensified; Austin swallowed. Blanc stared at him a moment longer, then dispensed with Austin as one might an unwanted thought. He began to eat once more. Austin—in brocade waistcoat and with a silk square in his top pocket, in contrast to Blanc's somber appearance—suddenly felt awkward.

"The bill of exchange," said Austin. He had introduced the idea to Blanc the day before; this was merely a reminder.

The Count looked up. When he spoke, it was decisively. "I will accept it at seventy per cent."

Austin's immediate indignation was obvious, but ignored by Blanc, who merely awaited his reply.

A bill of exchange was a convenient way of carrying money. Less interest paid to the issuing bank and a further commission to the purchaser, it provided, during an agreed-upon time period, substantial funds in a form acceptable internationally. But for Blanc to ask *thirty* per cent to cash Austin's bill was outrageous.

"It is a week's bank holiday we have here in Wiesbaden," said Blanc smoothly, "and, as no doubt you are aware, only my Casino carries such a sum as is in question."

Austin thought of his two-thousand-dollar bill of exchange and knew he had no choice.

"After my dinner," said the Count. Austin was dismissed.

"Wait for me outside," finished Blanc. Austin went.

François Blanc grimaced as he felt a pain in his chest and then unhurriedly belched—loudly.

§

Two pairs of hands pushed with equal passion at the top of tight breeches that stubbornly refused to give way. From the sides, panting with exertion, the young Prussian officer prised the cloth inch by inch from his skin; from behind, with less patience, two female hands pushed with a strength that during lovemaking comes from only one source.

Legs up, frills everywhere, her bodice undone, the Countess lay on the floor feeling the young flesh of the Prussian officer as bosom, stomach and bare limbs gratefully accepted all his grasping caresses. Groin to groin, mouth to mouth, on the carpet against the chaise-longue from which they'd fallen, oblivious of any world but that of passion, the two young people began to enjoy the primal exchange granted to male and female.

Had Countess Elizabeth known at that moment the immediate consequences of her actions, it must be assumed she would never have begun, or at least not continued; but as the breeches finally slipped completely off the smooth backside of the young Prussian, with a stifled scream of delicious pleasure, Elizabeth surrendered to the manhood pressed between her thighs.

§

François Blanc was quite a tall man, thought Austin, and extremely thin, but as Blanc stopped on the stairway to catch his breath, Austin remarked to himself on the man's unhealthy pallor. Below them they could see chandeliers which hung over each roulette wheel. For a moment, the expression Austin had heard proved correct; the people swirling about the tables did look exactly like moths around a flame. Recovered, Blanc quickened his pace, and the two men walked rapidly down the corridor to the large door at the end.

§

Her approaching orgasm forced the young Countess to take gasps of air between moans of ecstasy that were as rhythmic as were the thrusts the young Prussian made with the same expertise he had applied to mastering an altogether different sword—one that he would never, unfortunately, use again.

The door opened, and François Blanc stepped into the last chapter of two lives. Austin watched in astonishment. Blanc actually managed to close the door behind him. The key to the chest Blanc had been bound for was still in one hand as his fury began. Austin was mesmerized with the fascination of a blameless witness. The Countess certainly said, "François" twice. She called her husband's name once in question, as she tried to fathom from the deep waters of sexuality the image she saw as she surfaced; the second time, it was an exclamation at the action her husband had taken. Austin saw the young Prussian try vainly to extricate himself, but he was caught in several places, buttons to frills.

As Blanc raised the heavy chair in an astonishingly sweeping movement with the strength of rage, Austin watched the Countess break free and, legs apart, crablike, manage to push herself just beyond the head and shoulders of her young lover. The strangulated roar from Blanc was lost as a scream from the Countess and a shout from the Prussian fused into breaking bone and sinew. Definitely dead, was all Austin could think—and of course, the young Prussian was, in that moment and the few twitching seconds that followed, deprived of life.

François Blanc stood breathing heavily for several moments, then suddenly threw back his head and chest and began to stagger. His color changed from white to puce. Clawing at his heart as if to grasp it, François Blanc sank onto his knees; then, as spasms wracked his body, collapsed to the floor, convulsing twice until a dry, choking sound faded from his throat and blood-flecked bubbles popped and dribbled from his half-open mouth. Definitely dead.

Austin stood like a rabbit in a corner after two threatening cobras have miraculously vanished—disbelieving. Only his eyes moved, and they saw everything. The key on the floor; the Countess; the chest in the corner; the Countess Elizabeth; the young Prussian with the matted, bloody blond hair; the beautiful young Countess; François Blanc twitching still; the white porcelain face, bosom, stomach, thighs of the beautiful young Countess Elizabeth—widow.

Austin assessed the situation, as did the Countess. He grinned cautiously. She took a moment, then closed her legs; but not, Austin noted, without first the trace of a smile, then tears—tears and laughter.

For Austin, well, he had never seen so much of a woman before knowing more of her pedigree. No formal introductions.

"I don't know your name," the Countess had said as Austin took up the key to cross to the chest.

"Warren . . . Frederick Albert Warren," he had replied with swift invention—after all he had no idea how all this might turn out.

Unspoken decisions had already been made, both knew. The Countess had managed to dress herself without help, but the Prussian had proved a problem. Thus, again four hands had pulled at the stubborn breeches—this time, although with equal passion, in the reverse direction. The deft movement Elizabeth had made with her hand to tuck in the obvious protrusion had given Austin (made all too aware, by immediate events, of his own mortal coil) pause.

He made adjustments to the scene. The open and empty chest was the obvious reward—the objective of an intruder. The young man, an unfortunate victim. The great François Blanc, a sad but natural loss. His successors had buried him so quickly, the joke became that Blanc's demise had been effected with more speed than his birth. Nobody had liked him, and everyone soon forgot him. . . .

The long corridor to the other door at the top of the stairway overlooking the Casino had been hard on their nerves, but Austin and the Countess had made it—unobserved. By carriage with clothes and trunks thirty miles to a different town, its station and a train Austin and Elizabeth managed with the ease two parties achieve who are equally committed to the same course. Partners of a sort.

A whistle blew loud and long, startling Austin, who had settled among the furs, blankets and hastily stowed trunks in the first-class compartment with Elizabeth. She put her head on his shoulder, tears now abated. The train jerked into motion, and as its wheels gathered momentum to take this young couple away in the night, bright eyes exchanged a look of anticipation—the horror of the hours before already fading—to be consumed in a passion altogether more controlled—of declarations made, revealed intentions accepted. They had established a mutual respect. Their preamble to animal abandon had not been weeks of formalized posturing but—Austin smiled—well, rather unusual. The boy from South Brooklyn with the money *and* the girl. To stop a surge of laughter, he spoke to the soft, glittering eyes staring up at him.

"In America we have, courtesy of Mr. Pullman, what are known as sleeping cars. Should I get an opening, I would readily invest in such a venture here in Europe."

All the Countess Elizabeth said was "It would appear to be an idea with excellent prospects."

At which Austin pulled down the window blind and the train thundered out of the town into the dark night.

Mac

FEBRUARY 27, set apart as the National Thanksgiving for the recovery of His Royal Highness the Prince of Wales, was not only a national holiday but a brilliant and successful occasion. The celebration was at first intended as little more than a private service; it became the grandest outburst of unanimous popular emotion witnessed in England since the age of the Tudors. The deep sympathy of the nation during the painful, terrible days of the Prince of Wales's illness was acknowledged by the Queen, Victoria: "The remembrance of this day and of the remarkable order maintained throughout will forever be affectionately in our heart. Words are too weak to say how very deeply touched and gratified we have been by the immense enthusiasm and affection exhibited towards our dear son and ourself from the highest down to the lowest, on the long progress through the capital, and we would earnestly wish to convey our warmest and most heartfelt thanks to the whole nation for this great demonstration of loyalty."

The day dawned with weather that was all that could be desired. The crowds in the streets were denser than ever before, and the decorations along the royal route such as had never before been seen in London. Individual householders, each of the many guilds and every local council vied with the others in doing honor to the great event, more especially in the city proper; the spectacle, looking eastward from Temple Bar, was never to be forgotten by those who witnessed it.

Soon after twelve o'clock, the band in the inner court of Buckingham Palace struck up "God Save the Queen." At the same instant, the Speaker's coach was driven out to the semicircle in front of the Palace and placed in position to head the procession. The carriage of the Lord Chancellor followed, and in a few minutes the order to proceed was given. As the first of the royal carriages emerged from the central gate, the center window of the state room over the portico was opened. The exiled Emperor Napoleon III of France and his wife, the Empress Eugénie, stepped out onto the balcony.

When the carriage conveying the Queen and the Prince and Princess of Wales came out from the courtyard, the Emperor took off his hat; then both he and the Empress bowed, more than once, to her Majesty and Their Royal Highnesses. As the procession reached the Mall, the masses on either side of the line raised a cheer, which was instantly taken up by those who as yet could not get even a distant glimpse of the Queen or Prince. The cheering strengthened until an incessant roar from the vast gatherings, with cries of "God bless the Queen" and "God bless the Prince of Wales," enveloped the procession in a balm of loving emotion, stirring pride in every heart at being one and part of the greatest nation on earth. Turning from the Mall out to the front of St. James's Palace, the procession followed a route prescribed along Pall Mall and the Strand, through Temple Bar, to end at St. Paul's Cathedral.

At the Great West Entrance of the Cathedral had been erected a covered way of crimson cloth, ornamented with such devices as the royal arms and those of the Prince of Wales. Within the pavilion at the top of the steps, decorated in magenta relieved with vertical bands of white, was, above the entrance, the inscription which caused Victoria to stop just a moment and tightly grip the arm of the son her love had borne from the loins of her own Prince—her Albert, now dead. The

Prince of Wales looked into his mother's eyes, and for a
moment they were as ordinary mortals, aware only of their
love each for the other, of the great joy that surrounded them
and of the debt of thanks they must offer up to the divine
Lord in whose sight all men of any station were equal.

The inscription read:

I WAS GLAD WHEN THEY SAID TO ME, "WE WILL GO INTO THE
HOUSE OF THE LORD."

With unashamed tears in their eyes, a mother and her son
entered the portals at which all men are welcome.

§

For George MacDonald it had at first been an amusing day.
Sober citizens merely stared at him amidst their shouts and
cheering directed toward the procession, which the American
was following with a visitor's curiosity. But as the day
progressed, gin and ale released what natural reserve
remained in the now dispersing crowds, and Mac, as he was
called by his friends, became the object of unwelcome attention wherever he went. Elegant clothes, his top hat and a
square-cut, formal beard made the young man, for the common folk at least, a very acceptable facsimile of the person for
whom they had officially been asked to give thanks. The fact
was (even though his accent belied the impression) that Mac
looked remarkably like the Prince of Wales.

Only evening and the illuminations had brought him peace,
and he had returned along the processional route by Ludgate
Hill, the Holborn Viaduct, Oxford Street, Hyde Park and
Constitution Hill. Even from the hotel entrance he could see
three rows of colored lights which studded the vast roof of the
dome of St. Paul's like gems; they were composed of ships'
lanterns fitted with the most powerful lenses, calculated to be
visible at a distance of more than five miles. Even the yellow
fog seemed to respect the day's events and only swirled about
over the Thames, which at low water had stranded many
boats, whose skippers (drunk with the excuse of celebration)
beached their craft and began intermittently to sound fog-

horns, sirens and bells as a tribute to the occasion and release of their spirits.

Mac was fatigued but determined, after being part of such a moment in Britain's history, to enjoy a fine dinner. He crossed the foyer of the Terminus Hotel as the servants turned up gas lamps on the walls. He had come back to change quickly and once again venture out into the mass of humanity that crammed the streets. He took off his gloves, accepted a key and proffered telegram from the clerk at Reception.

"From some place in Germany, sir."

The clerk squinted across at the open telegram. Mac conveyed to the man, with a steely look which never failed, that his interest was unwanted. The clerk fumbled with papers behind the counter and sat down. Mac read the wire. It was from Austin, with the news that George's arrival was imminent. Plans were afoot, and the three of them would shortly again be together.

"Will you be needing a bed warmer, sir?"

The clerk's head had emerged from behind the counter and inquired with the faint hint of a second meaning. Mac ignored the question and strode toward the stairway. But before he took the stairs, two at a time, to the first floor, it was first "the Prince of Wales" who answered the clerk with a wink; then, English style, Mac replied in the affirmative. "If I may," he added.

§

In England at this time, barmaids were a great institution. There was seldom more than one man behind a bar, and the station counters of the developing railway system were attended exclusively by females. A more efficient source of ruin for both male customers and female bar staff it would be difficult to imagine. The girls were chosen for their beauty and attractiveness; an excellent inducement to enter, they offered continuous enticement to slake, quench, then drown a thirst.

The fascination in the gin palace of its lovely (but officially untouchable) women for the youth of the great metropolis could be relieved only by alcoholic excess. Especially for the lower classes, long working days in unpleasant surroundings ended with few alternatives for the hours before sleep. A sweet smile of welcome from a woman at a bar, made increasingly more alluring by cheap alcohol, was the obvious choice for the majority without vocation or future.

On the corner where the Strand meets Bow Street was a place known as the Gaiety, a famous saloon flooded with light—gas inside, naked torches over the pavement. Mac had seen earlier that to coincide with the great celebration, the annual "Beautiful Barmaid Show" was to be held that very night.

The beauty contest—a bar-top parade of the final selection amongst London's taverns—gave some of the women a prospect of better things: high salaries in aristocratic circles, often serving their betters more than alcohol. For many others it merely confirmed their fall from grace and indicated that henceforth it would continue more rapidly.

The Master of Ceremonies, in a glittering sequined frock coat, was brash, loud and enthusiastic. His strong voice commanded the attention of the large smoke-filled room, packed to capacity. The portly figure strutted on top of the long bar. On its mahogany surface was laid a red carpet that ended at some hastily assembled steps leading from the floor. Directly behind them was an open door, beyond which was only darkness. The hush from the crowd was one of anticipation.

At the end of his speech, in a pause for breath, as the M.C. made ready for a grand finale, the atmosphere suddenly seemed to Mac too thick, too rancid, stale and decadent. It represented all that he sought to escape from. He knew it well and hated his familiarity with the coarse and commonplace. He began to edge his way past the Cockney faces drink-ruined and life-scarred, sweating and leering—figures in a nightmare.

"Nah, come on, ladies and gents, if there be any among ya."

A humorous roar from the crowd startled Mac. He pushed nearer to the main doors.

"Let's 'ave yer votes. The Gin Palace Queen o' London Town she'll be, an' on to 'igher things. They've all a number, so cast yer one an' only. Bets on the side finishes now, folks, so once again a big 'and."

The roar of the crowd, coupled with applause, heralded eight young women. From behind the bar they stumbled up the steps, and giggling, they paraded down the red carpet. Rouged faces, bared bosoms and certainly, for Victorian England, an astonishing amount of exposed leg thrusting out of a dress held to a height that left only one further question begging—one that some of the crowd now took up. An exchange began between the crowd and several of the girls, who aggressively gave as good as they got.

Mac slipped out the entrance between the two doors with colored glass panes. As they closed behind him, a further roar went up from the crowd, indicating that voting had commenced. The cold air was a relief, and Mac's burning cheeks responded gratefully. As he pulled his coat about him, he looked up into the dark night sky, the flanking torches crackling with flames that leaped up and away from the building as if, Mac thought morbidly, they were the Hell-bound spirits of the crowd within.

"Lookin' for a star, sir?"

The small voice surprised Mac as if it had come from his own mind; he turned and saw beside him a wan-faced, hollow-eyed young woman who could have been little more than twenty.

"You'd have to stand in the dark for that, sir."

She indicated the torches. It was the first time Mac had thought of light's obscuring anything. He looked at the woman with interest.

"I knows a great deal of stars, sir."

She was obviously starving, but the transparency of her skin enhanced her large pale green eyes; her red lips were so delicately etched, framing regular white teeth, that Mac could do nothing but watch them shape words. She had a girlish figure and long, dark hair. She wore a simple smock and dull brown half coat, but the impression she made above all was wholesome—clean—not at all like most of the poor Mac had encountered in England. She smiled sadly, continuing:

" 'S all I've got, sir—them there stars and this here city. 'S what me father used to tell me."

She looked up again for emphasis, coughed, then gazed directly and winningly at Mac, who was already a willing subject. The obvious quality she had was a real and unassumed pride.

"I likes t' think of stars as bein' people now an' again—'cause it makes 'em seem beautiful—for a time —like."

There was an innocence in her expression that gave delicacy to the pause between them.

Her eyes, Mac saw, were as yet unscarred with the frightful understanding of the life for which she was destined. How she had survived Mac suddenly wanted to know; who she was; her name. . . .

The doorman's voice contained none of Mac's curiosity.

"Gar 'n' be off wi' ya."

His hand swept out to strike, but catlike, the girl was out of range, into the darkness and gone. Mac strained after her with his eyes.

"Cab, sir?" asked the doorman.

He touched his cap as Mac absently gave him a coin, shook his head and began to walk.

"Keep a look out, sir."

The doorman understood one thing: money; his job was to recognize where to get it, and sharp eyes had taught him to appreciate Americans, who were already establishing a reputation for generosity.

"You ain't been over here long enough to know the way afoot."

Mac had gone only a few steps into the darkness when the woman's voice came to him again.

"Would you 'ave a shillin', sir?"

She fell into step with him and stopped as Mac turned to her.

"How old are you?" he asked gently.

"Twenty. Why?"

Mac guessed how this young woman had been treated by others in a city and a country where amongst the rich he'd seen dogs eating from tables and cats fed morsels whose taste would have amazed this lovely creature.

"Have you eaten?"

She hesitated for only a moment. Just long enough for pride to construct the lie.

"Oh, yes, sir—I've 'ad a very large dinner."

Mac's frown forced her to details.

"First there was oysters, sir."

"Then I 'ad a large piece of steak an' kidney with boiled carrots an'—brocc'li."

She ended lamely, unable to pronounce the exotic vegetable, let alone conceive of its taste.

Mac didn't believe a word of it.

A hint of color appeared in her cheeks, and the look of indignation caused Mac to laugh spontaneously. She pointed quickly back to the Gaiety and continued fast:

"I was one o' them afore I got took ill. I 'ave gen'lemen friends, sir. An' proper they are, too."

She paused a moment to allow Mac time to absorb and be impressed with her connections.

"I'm only out on the streets 'cause I wouldn't do what they wanted. I was tol' I was to look pretty an' serve—no more 'n that. But some o' them gen'lemen . . ."

She didn't have to go on. The only surprise in her story was that she had not succumbed to the temptation of the " 'igher things" that had obviously been offered.

Mac stared at her, warming to this woman chance had chosen to throw to him.

"It ain't a story."

Misinterpreting Mac's gaze, the woman was again on the defensive.

"What's your name?" he asked firmly.

"May," she replied.

He had no time to savor the word. She again fought back, it occurred to Mac, rather like a child.

"What's yours?"

"George MacDonald."

She assimilated the name, then smiled, proving instinct right.

"I bet your friends call you Mac?"

"Call me Mac," said the American.

Now they were both smiling.

"You reminds me of a doctor," said May suddenly, her head cocked to one side, looking Mac up and down with sharp eyes.

"Why is that?" questioned Mac. May hesitated.

"You've the air about ya."

"I almost was," Mac said quietly, "once." For a moment he sank into the dangerous world of lost possibilities.

"See, I knew ya was somethin' special," said May innocently.

"At a place called Harvard," Mac went on absently.

"You ain't like those I've come across," said May quickly; "gentlemen I'm meanin'. Somehow," she stated, looking directly into Mac's eyes, "you're different."

Mac focused on the young woman before him, and his course of action was decided. For his amusement—her pleasure or amazement, depending on how she would cope.

"May—for tonight—you do have one gentleman friend, and that meal you haven't seen for at least a week . . ."

She dropped her eyes at this last, and Mac finished softly:

". . . shall be yours tonight also."

Defiantly she looked up, mood changed, hackles risen.

"I ain't bein' bought."

"No," Mac stated, "you ain't."

"I ain't bein' thought no dolly-mop, no five-penn'orth 'ore."

"Indeed not, May."

Mac was all understanding.

"To me you are every bit a lady."

At this Mac raised his arm and hailed the cab he had seen approaching. The horse reined in and the cabbie leaned down.

"Where to, sir?"

Mac opened the door and indicated to the astonished May that she should enter.

"Claridge's."

The cabbie looked May up and down. "With '*er*, sir?"

Mac looked at May's face turned up to him. She knew that she was entirely in his hands.

When Mac spoke, he did so in a manner that the Prince of Wales himself would have envied. "Yes, cabbie . . . with 'er."

May climbed into the cab like a lady. Mac followed, slamming the door. The cabbie, made fully aware of his status as a public servant, cracked a whip and drove his hansom into the darkness, west toward Piccadilly, Berkeley Square and the corner of Davies and Brook streets.

§

In 1815 a French chef of proved ability, Jacques Mivart, had taken over a house where he created sumptuous accommodation to match his excellent table. In time success allowed him expansion, and four adjacent houses became the sizable property of Mivart's de luxe establishment. Visiting royalty added to the hotel's reputation, and the Prince Regent, by reserving a permanent suite on the first floor, turned the exceptional into the exclusive.

In 1851 the hotel was bought and became known for a while as ''late'' Mivart's, but a continuing high standard maintained by the new owners allowed their name that rare privilege, the same connotations ''Mivart's'' had given the city, an empire and indeed the world; Mr. and Mr. Claridge began to create a legend.

The ladies' room at Claridge's was all pink and mirrors. At Mac's insistence, May had been ushered in by an attendant, whose disapproval was made obvious in a permanently frozen stare. Wiping smudges from her face with the white, soft towels, May surveyed features that shone back at her. The pale green eyes were wide with wonder. In the background a lady of some distinction, all flounced dress and corset, waited impatiently, unwilling to allow herself near the natural beauty her beady eyes perceived. She had assumed the contrived look of disgust perfected over the years for such as May.

Rising to the occasion, May began to enjoy herself. As she strode to the door she thrust the towel at the lady, who automatically took it and was left gasping in indignation. May crossed the foyer, entered the lounge and looked nervously for Mac, already at table in the large and crowded dining room.

If Mac had ordered tripe and onions served in his top hat, the waiters at Claridge's would have obliged the whim without a murmur. To them, May was a similar aberration, an obvious night's adventure for the gentleman, so they maintained

their standard—superb efficiency, seen and not heard—which
served to relax May's nervousness, as did the Krug champagne which Mac poured without waiting for the wine waiter,
who hovered elsewhere. Food arrived, and May, unable to
contain herself, fell upon it, engaging in conversation only, it
seemed to Mac, when her mouth was quite full.

"You got business 'ere?" May asked, enchanting Mac immediately.

"Perhaps," he replied, "when my friends arrive."

She cocked her head to one side.

"Nice to 'ave—'ard to keep."

The wistful philosophy struck home to Mac.

"True 'uns is rare," she finished sadly.

"Yes, May, they are," Mac said thoughtfully. He was
already thinking of George and Austin, impatient to see them.

May took a large gulp of the champagne to clear her throat.

"Do you pray, sir?"

"I go to church," said Mac. "Do you?"

May spluttered at the thought, coughed, calmed herself and
replied, "I ain't fit."

"You're wrong, May. You should."

"Oh, sir—I couldn't."

She was most perplexed at the idea of brushing shoulders
with what she thought of as respectable people.

Mac knew that most of them treated church as they might
theater or Rotten Row on a Sunday afternoon: a show place
each for the others. Where mothers began matchmaking;
where others were merely easing consciences disturbed by
clandestine afternoons with mistresses or lovers.

May was drunk. She leaned forward to convey an intimate
thought to Mac and in so doing knocked over onto the table
and into her lap the newly filled glass of champagne. Immediately, blushing like a rose, aghast at her clumsiness, she
leaped up. Mac calmed her, and a waiter replaced her chair.
Carefully this time, May again leaned forward to whisper
gravely about church.

"To tell the truth, Mac, I gets the giggles." She hiccuped
loudly. Mac burst into laughter.

The effect of the evening, the delights of the meal and the
joy of them both must all have contributed to the look in both

pairs of eyes as they met across the table despite tears of laughter.

"So," answered Mac, "I think," he went on, "must God."

§

Mac took May home. A single basement room beneath a public house next to its damp cellar was "chez May," as Mac said, forcing a smile at the squalor.

"What's that?" May had inquired.

"French," Mac had replied.

May attempted to tidy the few objects assembled in the room that illustrated it was inhabited by beings other than rats. She showed Mac the pump faucet in a corner—an indication, Mac noted, that this had probably once been a washroom: this it was that kept the lovely young woman so clean.

"The water's cold," May said, "but it's as fresh as . . ." She sought a word and received only a kiss from Mac. Then he left.

In the hansom cab he eventually hailed, some way from the Holborn pub, he determined to enter the life of this woman. Her tenacity in the face of a horrifying present and terrifying future was astonishing. He smiled at the thoughts his sympathy had elicited.

"May," he said aloud.

George MacDonald had failed to become a doctor—only just. The lure of a more sybaritic life style at Harvard had destroyed his concentration more effectively than cancer does tissue. After which—no second chance. So his sharp eye and dextrous fingers had turned to other means of satisfying a brilliant mind. But his sense of humanity had remained—as had his need for adventure. He was determined to actually hurt no one—and if he failed at that too, then it would be only because the victim was himself.

Behind the locked doors of his rooms at the Terminus Hotel, Mac persevered, despite the late hour, at his task, bent over a table scrutinizing several sheets of paper glowing beneath an oil lamp. He shifted his chair, took up a pen, dipped it into a phial of pale blue ink, made his hand comfortable, then wrote a signature quickly and accurately. It was not his own. He repeated the procedure on a second rectangle of paper. He put down the pen, breathed deeply, then examined both signatures against what was in fact—on a third sheet—the name of a London bank manager. He had issued to Mac a bill of exchange; now Mac had created two facsimiles. The signature was the penultimate step; more enjoyable, to Mac's mind, was the "process of figures," as he called it. The date the bill had been acquired and the sum to be drawn. He watched the ink drying slowly; remembered the cheroots he'd bought during the day and took one from the slim leather holder in his pocket.

Mac stood up, stretched, then crossed to the long windows. He opened them and stepped over the low sill out into the cold air onto a small balcony. Leaning against an ornate cast-iron railing, Mac peered up into the murky sky hoping to find even a single star—and did, eventually. He lit his cheroot from a box of Lucifers and threw away the match, which arced toward the gutter. Whether star or gutter he never afterward remembered, but some association brought into focus the image of a lovely woman as she might become; and the figures in Mac's mind with which he was toying dissolved. Mac was content to think only of May.

Noyes

WHEN Edwin Noyes stepped out of the gates of New Jersey's State Prison at ten minutes past nine on the morning of March 3, 1872, he had lost three years and two months of his existence.

He had been at home several weeks when a telegram arrived for him from England. It was from Mac and stated simply, "Wait." Thus, as winter weather moved toward spring and Connecticut assumed all the life he had not seen since January 1869, although his appreciation of the world outside four walls was still intense, his anticipation for the future elsewhere increased daily, as did his impatience. On his knees in Sunday church, Edwin could think only of England, Great Britain and an Empire; he had read nothing but English history since the Atlantic cable which had recharged his imagination. The congregation rose, sang a hymn, sat down and prepared for the sermon. The preacher's every word of divine wrath seemed to Edwin aimed directly at the only surviving male Noyes in Hartford. His mother and two sisters were part of a small-town life that for him had palled. New York had stimulated his ambition; he had wanted more of

43

everything until he had entered the bank on his last day of freedom, more than three years before. . . .

Edwin Noyes had been persuaded to present a forged check, together with stolen bonds; it was a calculated risk, which he might well have pulled off—but had not. Sharp eyes at the bank recognized the imperfect imitation, then double-checked against serial numbers already in circulation from the police, immediately discovering the bonds for what they were. Edwin Noyes was apprehended and charged. He had been able to say little of import. Names he knew meant nothing to the detectives who questioned him. Had he been less impulsive and taken advice from Mac never to become involved with men he did not know well enough to trust, things would have been different. His friends had been abroad, out of touch and therefore unable to help; and thus Edwin's reward for his efforts was not a large share of the spoils but incarceration.

The sentence he received quite obviously changed his life. Eventually poor health, the loss of flesh on bone, a raw, dark-eyed look he had assumed, his catatonic depressions served finally to convince the authorities that they should release him. He had returned "home" to endure the nightmare of disgrace, shame amongst his family and hypocrisy from the community. Only, it seemed, in church were all men equal.

The sermon finished with fire and brimstone being flung at the vast majority of the world's population, past, present and future. The congregation stood up and, as the preacher regained his breath, found the appropriate number for the final hymn. A small organ ended the service, playing a background dirge for Edwin's thoughts as he filed out of church with the crowd, some lingering to brush shoulders and exchange time and place for assignations that evening.

The general gossip outside in the clear air allowed Edwin Noyes pause to look up at the empty blue sky falling to a crisp horizon of trees still bare from Connecticut's harsh winter. But the faint warmth of March sunlight was almost intoxicating, and what few birds braved the cold air chirped enthusiastically. All around Edwin, the congregation continued to enjoy one another's company. Only Edwin remained silent, in a world of his own—oblivious to the gay conversation that conveyed the small talk of small minds.

As he waited for his mother and sisters—sitting on the buckboard that would take them back to the Noyes homestead—Edwin thought fondly of Mac, Austin and George. He breathed deeply at the idea of possibly joining them. His memory found a moment when they—all four—had shared the same passion to have whole what they had, as yet, only tasted. Delmonico's had been a heady place that evening, and New York had seemed to be made only for the whims of the four of them. Whatever was decided could be accomplished. They drank a toast—glasses brimming, as were their eyes with the shared fire of youthful ambition.

Now, more than three years later, Edwin Noyes smiled to himself as the memory reached a crescendo of proposed intentions and the laughter of comradeship obliterated the hell that had followed. This time he would be sure to heed Mac's advice. Instructions would come eventually; he would wait.

His gaze wandered across the fields to the forest edge. Why, there, in the distance, where the four first stood out in the sunlight, he could almost see the portals themselves, and he heard again Austin speak the words as glasses met in a toast to "the Four Hundred."

The Bank of England

IN 1872, the world crown rested squarely on English velvet. The foreign trade of the United Kingdom was more than that of France, Germany and Italy put together and nearly four times that of the United States. There were five dollars to the English pound sterling. Income tax was down to fourpence in a pound, which then consisted of two hundred and forty penny units.

The population had risen astronomically, and although agriculture was still Britain's largest industry, the country exodus to the cities allowed textiles to flourish beyond expectation. Three quarters of a million people were engaged as domestic servants, half a million in the mines and quarries. Exports exceeded two hundred million pounds per year—a staggering sum.

Wages rose sharply at the beginning of the 'seventies, and with the price of food almost constant, even the poorer classes were able to save. The records of the decade-old Post Office Savings Bank reveal accounts totaling eighteen million pounds.

Sterling, anchored to the gold standard for nearly thirty years, guaranteed that the five-pound note could be exchanged for five gold sovereigns and had become the currency of international finance as English was already the language. Other national currencies were bought and sold at fixed rates, which created stability. The custodian of the standard of sterling was the Stock Exchange.

Within sight of St. Paul's Cathedral, this Exchange was centered in what is known in London as "the City." This was ultimately controlled by the guardian of Britain's, and hence the Empire's, entire financial reserve—the Bank of England.

§

"Gentlemen, the Old Lady of Threadneedle Street, the 'eart of an empire . . ."

The driver of the open carriage doffed his hat and looked over with obvious respect at the huge and imposing building. Greek columns ended in Corinthian capitals which supported a long architrave, above and behind which were two further stories. In the center of the base of huge stones which gave the impression of might and solidity was the entrance, guarded by uniformed doormen who observed the melee passing to and fro as the city bartered toward its lunchtime crescendo.

Three passengers in the open carriage followed the driver's example and slowly removed their hats as he turned toward them to continue his speech. He was displeased with the attitude of at least the one whose rejoinder to his last remark had been the facetious " 'eart of gold" in mimicry of his Cockney accent. More so because he resembled the Prince of Wales. He knew quite well that words from Jenny Lind's current song had no place here before these hallowed portals. Even as the three appeared formidable by their wealth, he gave them a long stare of appraisal before speaking.

"You gentlemen be Yankees, no doubt?"

The reply of "Indeed we are, sir" from the other American who was attending to him was, therefore, no surprise. Only the arrogance was irritating: after all, rich or poor, cab driver though he might be, he was still British.

"You should 'a' stayed in the Empire."

The driver smiled in open sympathy with the sentiment felt by all who were loyal to Victoria's England.

"We chose to take our leave," said the third man absently. This shocked the driver, and the grin and nudge one man gave to the other, sprawled there on the seat, angered him.

"You'll regret it one day, without a doubt—you mark my . . ."

He was about to finish when the hypnotic eyes of the third man turned for a moment from contemplating the Bank and all its worth to dwell on the driver at the reins, who was immediately subdued.

". . . if you'll pardon me sayin' so," he finished lamely.

The third man stared a moment longer, then back at the Bank—seemingly in deep thought. The driver was unable to speak—"taken, as it were," he said afterward, "as if a demon was lookin' up at me." But that was long afterward, when the entire world knew what those first glimmering ideas had sparked off in that man's brain.

Before the driver cracked his reins over the backs of both horses, he said, "It's pride what I'm speakin' with, sirs—pride." He remembered the tears that came welling up, proof of his wife's loving opinion of him as an old softie, and as he was to relate in many a bar, he would always remember, in that last glance he took at the three before he drove off to other sights, "Two was laughin', 'appy-go-lucky like, but the other . . ."

Here he learned to pause knowingly, as if prior insight had given him an edge over the forces of the entire world's law and order.

"The other," he would repeat, "was lookin' at 'the Old Lady' as if . . ." And here again his story, polished through the years, would halt before a mesmerized audience. Looking about him to see if any women were present and assuring himself that what few there were would appreciate his ending, he would finish, ". . . as if he was gonna have down her drawers, pay for 'is whistle an' gap-stop 'er minge."

The twist in the tale never failed to bring hoots of laughter. Even George Bidwell smiled at it years later when it had become a standard, if bawdy, joke, and when he too thought back and remembered his first sight of the Bank, he had to admit that coarse as the driver's analogy had been, he was not far wrong.

§

"So I left her in Calais with most of the proceeds. No doubt if a scandal has developed they'll all want it hushed up."

"And how much of it do you have left?" asked Mac.

"Of Blanc's money?" Austin replied. "After I'd paid our bills—little enough." He smiled to himself. "But memories I have aplenty."

Austin thought fondly of Elizabeth as he told Mac his story, ending with a passable imitation of her pronunciation of his hastily concocted alias "Frederick Albert Warren"— "as she knows me still," Austin finished with a grin. The Countess had decided to return to Wiesbaden slowly via the Casino at Monte Carlo, where Blanc had also established an interest. By the time she was in Wiesbaden again, the world would have turned; money and influence could, without too much trouble, quell diligent investigation, she believed. Then perhaps they could meet again. For a moment Austin was lost in thought and hardly heard Mac's own accounting.

"Well, my little waif May thinks the fripperies I've bought her are all kinds of finery. You shall see her smile—worth a bagful of British sovereigns."

Leaning on the rail of the river steamer, Mac too had succumbed to a private world and thought affectionately of the young woman to whom he'd developed an attachment. The River Thames sluiced by, and the other seventy or so passengers made as merry as was possible aboard the long, low steamboat as it chugged upriver toward Hampton Court.

George Bidwell concentrated more on the brown water, the swirls, eddies and tide lines, than he did on the riverside habitations. Watching the flotsam pass, he established the boat's speed. Then, as he counted absently, a figure came to him. It made sense. "One hundred thousand."

Standing on either side of George, Austin and Mac were disturbed by the softly spoken words, almost lost in sound from the out-of-tune piano playing in the saloon behind them.

It was the first phrase George had uttered since Tower Bridge. Austin looked at his brother.

"What's that?" he asked.

"George?" questioned Mac, concerned at his friend's introspection.

George looked slowly into Mac's face, his eyes probing.

"Five hundred thousand dollars, Mac—each."

Austin began to laugh and clapped his brother warmly on the shoulder.

"See, Mac, the woman for George is 'the Old Lady of Threadneedle Street'!"

At that moment the seemingly drunk pianist started up a barely recognizable version of "Barbara Allen." It interrupted them.

The second verse began, with voices joining in the well-known lyrics. Mac and Austin exchanged a glance and saw in each other's eyes the same disturbing sign of fear. Perhaps their initial reaction, had they discussed it, would have put an end to the scheme then and there; but arrival at an unfamiliar destination is always distracting.

" 'Ampton Court, ladies and gentlemen" from the boatman and a shuddering reversal of the twin screws as the boat drew alongside the jetty caused them both to look away and, under a blue sky filled with swiftly passing clouds, establish their first impressions of the Palace.

"Think on it, boys," said George Bidwell quietly.

§

Garraway's had been established on a corner of Exchange Alley, in the City, as a convivial meeting house in which to discuss prospective business.

George, Austin and Mac settled into one of the private alcoves ranged along a side of the large main *salle de maison*. They ate a light dinner. It was over coffee and brandy, as the waiter cleared their table and carried his tray through the crowd across to the serving hatch in the oak-paneled wall near the bar, that George signaled to Mac.

"Pull the curtain," he said. Mac did as instructed.

Shut off from the crowds in the secure privacy of what was now a small room, George savored his plan.

"Come, George—let's have it," said Austin. He leaned back in his seat and gave his brother full attention.

"Money, boys," George began.

Austin absorbed the almost tangible atmosphere George had created in the alcove.

"George, we're here abroad. Time is ours, and we've money enough, so . . . ?"

He was ignored by his brother.

"What would you say was enough, Mac?"

Mac took the idea seriously. "Well—as you were saying —maybe—well, one hundred thousand," he replied.

"Dollars or pounds?" Austin asked with a laugh. He was vainly attempting to steer the conversation's course away from where he knew it was now headed.

"Pounds sterling," said George. Austin swallowed.

"Austin's right, George," said Mac quickly. "We all have plenty of money on us right now—and ways of making more."

Austin pulled out the bill of exchange he had meant to discount in Blanc's Casino.

"I've still got Mac's bill—undrawn," he said smiling, "which my lady Countess insisted I keep."

Mac leaned over and took it from Austin.

"Let's see it again," he said.

Mac examined the bill.

"I could do better—now. The clarity of the circles and depth of ink here is not . . ."

George took the bill from Mac and looked at the figure printed on it.

"Two thousand dollars is only four hundred pounds, Mac," he said.

"Bigger bills are a risk, George," began Austin. "The larger amounts are always checked more thoroughly—you know that."

"Then you need the letter of introduction, especially if you travel," interrupted Mac, "*and* a letter of credit. If they don't know you, George, they are going to be suspicious. If they do

. . ." Mac paused and shrugged. "You get caught with a forged bill."

"Then" George said, "we must think of other ways."

"How?" Austin's voice was not firm.

"With confidence, expertise . . ."

At this, George looked at Mac; then, smiling, ". . . and imagination."

Austin took out from his waistcoat pocket a large wad of money and threw it down on top of the bill of exchange.

"That ain't imagination."

Seeing the challenge, Mac tossed a second roll of notes onto the impressive pile.

"Nor that." Mac grinned at Austin.

George paused, looked at both of them, took out his own smaller roll of notes and placed it on the pile. He gauged the amount, then slowly settled back into the seat with his brandy.

"No, boys," he said, "it's a start."

George raised his eyebrows and lifted the brandy glass. Austin remembered that toast as the most reluctant he ever made. But they all drank to it.

§

The two children should have been in bed. Why was the nanny pushing a third in a pram, obviously newborn, four hours before midnight? These, Austin always remembered, were the first thoughts that had struck him.

The fact that the pompous, fat, swaggering epitome of Victorian middle-class society was parading with his wife so late, along with the incident he prompted, was part of what created in all three Americans the resolution that was to put them into history. Having strolled down Lombard Street, George, Austin and Mac paused before the Bank of England. Stars glittered from a night sky that framed the building clearly. Torches burned on either side of the entrance. The doors were open still. It was late, Mac thought, for what was about to happen, but they had come in the hope, now proved correct, that they would see it. The man and his small entourage mounted the large center island between the two roads that met in front of the Bank, and they too now waited with the patience that knowledge gives to the well-timed arrival at an event.

The man, leaning on his cane; the wife, a puppet on his arm; and the nanny and children obediently behind these two, turned their heads toward the regular marching noise now discernible to all ears. Around the corner in the distance, lit by the city gaslights, in perfect order, a platoon of Coldstream Guards marching with the precision of discipline came into sight. The traditional night guardians of the Bank of England were about to take up their duties.

The red tunics and gold buttons caught the light as the column ordered ranks and began to pass along the Bank's façade. The officer in charge reached the entrance as his sergeant barked out a command. A final tread, the stamp of boots on cobbled stones, then only the roar of torch flames sounded out against distant noises from the West End of London. In a moment the Ceremony of Keys took place, and in loose order the guards mounted the steps, fur glowing as each busby passed between the torches. The last man in allowed the Bank watchman to close the doors. The deep, resounding note of tons of metal fitting together ended the spectacle.

George, Austin and Mac were impressed. The "toy" soldiers outside Buckingham Palace had looked like pretty statues, but the way these men moved left little doubt in all their minds that the fathers of their fathers' fathers could not have had too easy a time of it against Burgoyne.

The family group was already on the move as a little urchin boy ran up to the fat gentleman. Without even breaking his stride the man lifted his cane and hit the boy such a blow that he staggered and fell. George's anger was instant. Austin and Mac were forced to take hold of him.

With only a cursory glance the gentleman looked at the three Americans, sensing commotion. Recognizing no threat in the distraction that had prompted him to turn his head, he took his wife, nanny and children off into the darkness.

George, watching the small boy rise, whistled across at him. Mac threw a sovereign, which was well caught, bitten, tossed and pocketed. With a grin, the boy ran off, leaving three

Americans, two flickering torches and the entire fortune of an empire before them, behind massive sealed doors.

As Austin remembered later, Mac had said, "How?" He himself had spoken knowingly, looking first at George, as if the plot were fathomed and the ploy fully understood. In fact Austin had known nothing when he said, "Like a ladder at a window, Mac. You know where you're goin', but you concentrates every rung of the way."

What they all remembered was the way George put out his hands and took Mac's and Austin's warm and firm. The grip communicated a passionate hatred of the bureaucracy and traditions of the country that had bled nations dry, subjugated continents and destroyed cultures.

Looking at the Bank of England that night, George had become quiet and calm. His American voice spoke softly.

"We'll take her," he said.

Spring

1872

Golden Cross

SPRING had settled in England with the quirkiness particular to that country. Equatorial winds and sharp rainstorms shared each day as if competing for dominance of the season.

The morning Austin Bidwell stood opposite the entrance to the Bank of England, heavy rain fell from a dark, lowering April sky for several hours. Then, as the clouds parted, sun burst through, drying up quagmire streets and pavements awash from the blocked gutters; this created, from the dampness and heat, noxious odors so intense that Austin decided to lunch and return at two o-clock to wait and watch again.

That was how he met Mr. Green. Not in the small restaurant behind the Scots Bank, but as he sauntered back to his vantage point and saw the fussing figure, patting his pockets and peering at his deposit book through rimless glasses. The smile, as Mr. Green found the new total, beamed its way across the road. Austin immediately sensed that he had found his man.

What had happened for several days was this: Austin had waited at the same vantage point until he saw someone he felt might be the one he wanted. Four out of five depositors, he discovered, when they took money to the Bank, came out examining their passbooks. He had followed several, using the same cab each time. The cabbie established Austin's identity early on, and thereafter he gave Austin the respect he felt due to his fare. Austin had not argued and now just continued to smile knowingly.

The previous morning the cabbie had looked inquisitive as Austin rejected a third possibility on instinct and walked out of the East India importing house leaving a costly white shawl, bought but not paid for, resting on the counter within, awaiting a customer who would never return. Austin had been curt to the cabbie, disgruntled by another false lead. The man inside the import house had been totally unimpressed by the hundred-pound note. For the scheme in Austin's mind, money was the key.

"Nothin' you wanted, sir?" the cabbie had asked.

Austin had shaken his head at the driver's question and climbed into the open vehicle.

"Where now, sir?" the cabbie had asked, concealing badly that he had already guessed the answer.

"The Bank," Austin said, knowing his driver knew.

"Again, sir?"

It became for a moment a game between them.

"Yep."

Austin drew deeply on his long cigar and took off the large Stetson, donned every time he entered an establishment to which a "possibility" led him. He had brought the hat with him, from across the Atlantic. In the United States, Stetsons were commonplace but admired. In Europe they represented the wealth of a new world and, in consequence, were impressive.

The English at that time still had absurd ideas concerning Americans. The stage version of the American Silver King they took for the genuine article and devoutly believed that the pavements in America were crowded with "millionaires in silver" marching around with rolls of thousand-dollar bills in their pockets ready for whimsical distribution to bootblacks and bartenders. In England it was cobbled streets of gold and Dick Whittington's London. Every country has a similar myth, and Austin was playing on his.

The cabbie said the obvious. "That's three times, sir."

Austin grinned. "Superstitious!" he stated, as if it were a confidence.

The cabbie and he were now eye to eye. Austin gave away nothing, preferring speculation to fact. Instantly the cabbie's suspicions were confirmed. He winked knowingly.

"Are you a detective, sir?"

The thought had not occurred to Austin, but as a cover it was not bad, and it would be a good enough reason to keep the man on until he was successful in his quest. Austin puffed the long cigar, winked back at the cabbie and replied, "I ain't sayin'."

The cabbie straightened up, proud of his intuition.

"I knew it, sir, the minute I saw you, sir—I ain't never wrong."

"You don't say." Austin swallowed alternative responses.

"Mum's the word, sir."

"What?" Austin didn't understand.

"I'll not say anything, sir."

Again the cabbie winked, touched his cap and, Austin remembered, had been distinctly cocky in the way he made the reins flip their message to the two horses. Austin had bought his man with better than currency. Silence creates enigma, and assumption was always international exchange. Austin made a mental note not to forget this discovery about the English. It might well prove valuable.

The cab had driven Austin back to the Bank, where he waited once more. He followed two further possibilities, buying an expensive opera glass from an optician and promising financial involvement in a producer's play. Austin rejected both men, as instinct dictated, but time was passing and he had made no progress.

So it was with acute anxiety that Austin waited for and then, thankfully, saw the cabbie returning from watering his horses on the afternoon Mr. Green turned the corner of Threadneedle Street to begin his brisk constitutional back to the West End.

§

A doorbell rang as Mr. Green entered the shop. His assistants had already seen the familiar figure through the window and had ample time to engage in their various tasks with heightened fervor, to create for the old gentleman the correct impression and conceal the real. For nearly a century, Green's of Savile Row, fathers and sons, had followed tradition almost to the minute and, apart from holidays, the Crimea emergency, news of Waterloo and the Trafalgar victory, had returned from the Bank on a Friday afternoon, entered the shop to survey and absorb the level of activity, check the same pocket watch, snap it closed, then walk through without another glance to the rear office.

Austin Bidwell, arriving outside in the open cab with white Stetson and long cigar, momentarily disturbed the habit of almost a century.

"Mr. Green, sir!"

The assistant was already pointing out the window, where the family name in reverse obscured a clear view for Mr. Green.

"What is it?" asked Mr. Green.

He was irritated. He liked to sit in his office and think of his accruing account, alone and in silence, before engaging further in the afternoon's problem of running a high-class tailor's establishment.

"Money!" replied his assistant.

The one word stopped the entire shop. Mr. Green's reflexes to it were faster than those of his staff. Although his reaction was a mere flicker of the eyes, he saw, as did the others, the white Stetson, large cigar and ebony cane climbing down from the cab now pulled up onto the pavement of Savile Row.

"Go about your work," he commanded.

The staff immediately scurried as Mr. Green began to retrace his steps to the door.

The bell rang again as the door opened inward. Mr. Green stopped in mid-step to avoid the heavy oak and glass as it swung past him to reveal Austin Bidwell, poised at the threshold, radiating a confidence born of wealth. Sounds of the street invaded the large room. Smoke from a long Havana cigar curled past Mr. Green. The American stood where he was and said nothing.

Cloth talks—to a tailor. Although the cut of Austin's clothes left much to be desired in Mr. Green's English eyes, the material he wore was of undoubted quality. Austin had chosen it, fine gray worsted wool, mindful of the impression it would make in the practiced eye of tradesmen. Here it found its mark more truly than he had ever hoped.

Silence held sway in the shop as each assistant calculated the potential customer's spending power. But even Mr. Green was far off the mark, though years in business had taught him to estimate the worth of a client at a glance. But then, Austin was not playing by the rules. Given the opportunity, Austin veered almost always toward the ostentatious—a word discovered by George to lightly remind his brother of a natural flamboyance that must not be allowed out of control. The rhyme with Austin's name George used with merciless humor, much to Austin's irritation. But in the English tailor's shop this aspect of Austin's personality gave a fillip to his imposing character. The tailor was already convinced of Austin's importance and the American had yet to speak.

He stepped down into the shop and the door was closed by a respectful assistant, who took the Stetson from Austin almost with reverence and immediately (as an excuse for a professional examination) began to brush it down.

"Can I be of assistance, sir?" asked Mr. Green. The tentative question ended in a cough.

Austin raised his eyebrows. He was obviously going to ask to whom he was addressing himself, Mr. Green realized, so he spoke quickly and smoothly.

"Green, sir. Mr. Green, tailors hereabouts for almost one hundred years."

"Indeed," Austin replied languidly, but he speedily calculated the wealth that must be amassed in the vaults of "the Old Lady" from these fathers and sons whose charge was probably more for reputation than for the fit of their garments.

"A suit, sir?"

The suggestion was made by Mr. Green with the winning smile of one who believes he has guessed correctly, wants the answer corroborated and is then immediately able to continue with proposals already formed.

Austin savored the moment and continued a slow march between the arrays of cloth. Not so much scuttling, but decidedly at Austin's heels, Mr. Green had time to prepare the idea of a topcoat as well, and his hands came together in an automatic family gesture almost a century old. The words from Austin, who had now stopped and turned to Green, drove palm against palm with some force.

"Ten suits, Mr. Green—or thereabouts." Austin wafted a hand airily. "Three from that," he pointed. "Two of that—cut hacking and long."

An assistant began to scribble even before Mr. Green's gesture showed that he had absorbed the fact that here was money indeed. Austin continued:

"A topcoat from that, another suit from the check tweed, another from that."

He pointed swiftly to each roll of cloth, number and mark taken immediately by the efficient assistant.

"Another from that, from that; that." He spun on his heel. "And that, with gold buttons and braid for ceremonial occasions." He smiled. "Not a uniform, Mr. Green, but a dress reminder of my military past in the Americas, of course."

Mr. Green answered warmly, "Of course, sir."

"Now show me some dressing gowns," Austin continued.

Mr. Green was already moving.

"Oh, and tell the cabbie I shall be a short while." Austin turned and walked toward a young man who had bowed the moment the word "gowns" had left his lips.

"Williams!" Mr. Green called to his other assistant and indicated to him that a message was to be conveyed outside. Reluctantly, the young tailor's assistant put down the white Stetson beside his brush on the shining mahogany work top.

Williams had a mind of his own. He was, he thought, no errand boy, but the look in Green's eye was formidable enough to remind him who paid the meager salary he took home, so he made do with a youthful scowl, and—deciding to slam the door, outgoing and incoming—he went.

§

Lounging in imitation of his fare and smoking a long cigar

(a gift from Austin), the cabbie replied to Williams, "Thankee, me man. Tell me fare I 'as the message and will conduct meself accordin'."

His toothless Cockney grin stretched ear to ear. The cabbie had observed the scene within through the window and now had a question to ask this haughty youth before him.

§

"Frederick Albert Warren," said Austin, enunciating his invented name slowly, allowing Mr. Green ample time to spell it out for himself. If it was good enough for a countess, it would do well enough for a tailor.

"Address, sir?"

For a moment Austin's face went blank. The address! of course. Hell, he thought—he was so pleased at the alias he'd forgotten a damn address. He put down his cane, took off a glove quite unhurriedly and reached into his pocket to find the newly acquired English diary. He used a pencil from the spine of the small book to flip the pages.

"I've not been here long, Mr. Green, and always seem to forget your English names."

"Of course, sir."

Mr. Green waited patiently. Austin ran out of pages and imagination. Where the devil could he say?—he couldn't make up a name or mention a place he wasn't able to find. At that moment Williams entered and slammed the door. Distracted, Mr. Green turned to the approaching figure to chide him, but Williams spoke first. He addressed Austin, who was grateful for the delay.

He said, " 'Ave you found your man, sir?"

Deeper and deeper, thought Austin. The last thing he had expected was conversation between the damn cabbie and this obviously inquisitive assistant. What was his name?

"Indeed, Williams," said Mr. Green.

"It seems that Mr. Warren has indeed 'found his man,' as the cabbie puts it; a suitable tailor would be more like." He turned to Austin.

"You will find, sir, that we shall do our utmost to please."

Austin nodded his thanks and found on the last page of his

diary an advertisement for a small hotel—family, intimate, aiming, as it stated, like Mr. Green, to do its utmost to please.

"The Golden Cross, Mr. Green, at, ah—Charing Cross? Would that be it?"

"No doubt, sir." Mr. Green took it down.

From Austin's wallet came two one-hundred-pound notes. Williams swallowed. Green accepted them, respectfully. He paused only to glare at Williams.

"Hundreds? Why, thank you, sir. Now if we could have your basic measurements?"

Austin raised his arms to allow the tape measure around his chest and felt, in that moment, not the exuberance of a quest accomplished, but the depression of a man surrendering to the machinery of a plot he had now activated and whose momentum might well prove difficult to control.

Fear or premonition? He could not decide. A moment later, as the two, Green and Williams, bustled about him, his dismal thoughts were replaced with the high excitement he had anticipated. He had to wait until he was in the street to actually laugh, and then he covered his emotion with a cheery wave back to the faces at the window of the shop. He climbed into the cab knowing all eyes were on him still.

"No arrest, sir?" The cabbie was obviously interested.

"Not yet." Austin lit another cigar.

"Ah." The cabbie winked knowingly, already Watson to Holmes. "Where to now, sir—the Bank?" He tapped his nose as they did in music-hall acts.

"The Golden Cross Hotel," said Austin clearly so as not to repeat himself.

"Where's that?" asked the cabbie perplexed.

"I don't know," replied Austin. He took a last look at the faces in the shop window. "But find it—and quick."

The cabbie thought a moment longer, then cracked his whip and took Austin down Savile Row into Burlington's Vigo Street, then Regent Street and on into the melee of Piccadilly.

§

A cane was a cane, ebony was quality and silver made it unusual; but to Williams, when silver and ebony were combined with the initials A.B. (they were delicately inscribed amidst a floral pattern on the crook), a cane became something special.

Williams moved the bale of cloth that almost concealed it, took up the object of his desire from the mahogany table and fell in love.

In an instant he could see himself striding down the Mall "of a Sunday," twirling the shiny beauty, then stopping before some acquaintances listening to the band on the steps of Waterloo Place.

"An' 'ow's young Williams?" one of them might say.

" 'e's as fine as punch," Williams would reply.

"That there's a fine-lookin' object." The speaker would point at the cane.

"An' 'ere it is to view close." Williams would flip the crook in the air for inspection.

"Why, there's even initials 'ere on the—silver is it?"

"Indeed it is, my man." Williams' pride would swell, but he would affect nonchalance.

"A.B." The speaker, if literate, would read out the letters.

"Why, Williams!" The speaker would be impressed, knowing now that the cane was no cheap acquisition, but "tailor-made," as it were—Williams might even use that as a pun. "Why, Williams," the speaker would repeat. "Them's yours!"

Twirling the cane and turning with a grin to continue beyond the music toward Buckingham Palace, Williams would finish: "Arthur Byron's me given names, an' them's the one's I had writ down." Silver would shine, ebony flash, and Williams would walk away with a swagger.

Words dispelled the image.

"Oh—gracious!" Mr. Green had arrived beside Williams, aghast at the discovery.

"Williams, run at once to the Golden Cross and deliver that cane personally to Mr. Warren. . . . Williams? Do you 'ear?"

Reverie broken, a disconsolate Williams had only the walk to look forward to. Still, he thought, consolation is better than no reward at all. He took his hat and ambled to the door.

"An' be quick about it!" Mr. Green had a good customer and wished to impress.

"Yes, sir." Williams went. The door slammed hard.

§

By the time Williams reached Trafalgar Square, the cane
and he had grown accustomed to each other and his stride had
indeed acquired a bounce that those of his acquaintance
would have envied had they seen him. Beyond the Savoy
Palace Hotel, where he took the steps down from the Strand
to the Embankment, he, and the cane, had become one. The
detour from the more obvious direct route down Northumberland Avenue had been made to test himself against the
swells outside the Grand Hotel. One day, he thought, he too
would have rooms in the Savoy Palace overlooking the
river—like all them toffs. Williams crossed the road and entered Villiers Street. Moments later he was at the entrance of
the Golden Cross Hotel.

Had Williams cared not a fig for canes, he would have gone
direct to Charing Cross, found the hotel, entered and
discovered that no one had heard of Mr. Frederick Albert
Warren. A mystery would have turned into an inquiry. But
history writes itself; and as Wellington's victory at Waterloo
was aided by a French general's whim for a second plate of
breakfast strawberries, delaying his start to the battlefield by
vital minutes, so Austin unknowingly had gained time to
emerge from the thick traffic in the Strand and reach the
Golden Cross while Arthur Byron Williams was turning from
the river to walk up the slight incline of Savoy Place.

Austin Bidwell's fifty-pound note had been gratefully taken
and the signature, *F. A. Warren*, blotted when, from behind,
he heard a quiet voice.

"Them's the wrong initials."

Austin froze. What thought at that moment raced in his
head Austin never revealed. He turned slowly to confront—he
knew not what.

Williams stood looking at Mr. Green's customer. Austin
said nothing.

"On the cane, sir—A.B." He held it up to illustrate the
point.

"You'm an F.A."

Austin pursed his lips and swallowed. He'd bought the cane and had it monogrammed in Germany some months before.

"Looks new," said Williams.

"Well cared for," replied Austin.

"It's a fine piece of work," said Williams, referring to the floral pattern in silver. "The initials is well picked out." He finished scrutinizing the crook.

Austin needed inspiration. The two men looked at each other in silence. The receptionist watched with curiosity.

"The initials represent my uncle's name, Mr. Williams," Austin said coolly.

"Oh?" said the tailor's assistant.

"He has recently passed on," Austin stated softly. Williams immediately took off his black bowler. Austin had found an audience. Even the receptionist had raised a lavender handkerchief as a reflex to the euphemism of death.

"When my true father left this world, my mother's brother was all a young boy could wish for." Austin's imagination was prodigious. "From the great plains of the Midwest, he returned to be at his sister's side in her hour of need. . . ."

"Oh, Mr. Warren, sir," began Williams. The receptionist opened her mouth, eyes already moist. Austin would not be stopped.

"My brother and I," he went on, "were raised by that man." Austin paused. "And all I am today, as I stand before you, I owe to him." There Austin decided to finish. Both Williams and the receptionist (now tearful) shook their heads in sympathy. Austin pointed at the cane in Williams' hand.

"An inheritance," he said.

"I *am* sorry, sir." Williams spoke with feeling. Austin merely nodded. Williams, Austin noted, continued to grasp the cane tightly.

"Well, 'e 'ad good taste in 'ats as well, sir," said Williams suddenly, "if you don't mind my sayin'." Austin was perplexed only a moment; then, with horror, he was stricken by a realization.

"What?" he managed to say.

"An' you'm lucky to have the same 'ead size," continued Williams.

Austin—heroically—was trying to frown: *his* names were

clearly printed inside the Stetson!

"Personalized property for custom-made wearables," Williams went on, "is an essential, I'm thinkin', but now he's dead perhaps you should change his names to your'n, sir—for safekeepin' like." Williams paused, a glint in his eye. " 'Course, the cane you ain't able to do anythin' about, sir." Austin remembered his discovery about the English—*their* assumption maintained by *his* silence. He said nothing, cursing his carelessness. The receptionist continued to watch, enthralled. Tears now abated, she nodded agreement to the young man's obvious sense. Williams stood absolutely still, hands together holding his hat, still clutching Austin's ebony and silver.

"Thank you," Austin said, "for returning my cane."

He took out a coin and gave it to the tailor's assistant.

Williams put his black bowler back on his head and accepted the money, then nodded—but did not move. Austin stared inquiringly. Williams shifted uncomfortably—then smiled.

"Williams—sir."

"Thank you again—Williams."

"Arthur Byron—sir."

No one could say Austin was not quick. He realized immediately how attractive the cane must be to a "Williams, A. B." He smiled back at the youth.

"I shall remember your—promptness—Mr. Williams."

Austin held out his hand for the cane. Silently the exchange took place. Williams didn't actually wince, but he did, Austin observed, depart rather quickly.

"Will you be staying long, Mr. Warren, sir?" Emotions stimulated, the receptionist spoke almost as a confidante. Austin spoke only to himself—even *his* nerves frayed.

"Yes," he said, "I hope so." And took off the white Stetson.

He never wore it again.

Introduction

TWO trunks and a large portmanteau arrived some weeks later at the Golden Cross. Complying with her instructions, the receptionist paid the carriage fee and had the luggage deposited in Mr. Warren's room. He occasionally came to take tea, but never appeared to use the room for the night. Money had suppressed any questions she was tempted to ask. The generous advance had secured his room for as long as Mr. Warren cared to use it—and for whatever purpose.

The portmanteau had clearly printed on it, GREEN AND SONS, SAVILE ROW, and F. A. WARREN. Embossed in gold against the dark leather, it was very fetching. A day later Mr. Warren arrived and checked that all was in order. Obviously, the receptionist thought, as she watched the attractive young man wave a cheery adieu that brought a blush to her cheeks, it was.

§

Austin had agreed to remain in England alone. There was little that his partners could do as yet, and they had thus both

69

decided upon a European tour. Having landed at Lisbon, in Portugal, Mac and George were now making their way to Spain and France from city to city: San Sebastián to Biarritz; then, after a journey to Bordeaux, the return passage to Southampton.

Austin, meanwhile, enjoyed London. He went to Bath once to take the waters; to Dorchester, in Dorset; then to Weymouth and the great Naval Dockyard at Portland; to Norwich, in Norfolk, to see the meandering streams and flatlands; finally on a late-spring tour of the Southern Counties, Hampshire, Sussex and Kent, which gave him a familiarity with England that he was to cherish for many years to come.

A brief return to London had allowed him to check that Green had delivered at the Golden Cross Hotel. That done, Austin had gone once more to the Savile Row shop.

"Savile Row tailoring at its best, Mr. Green," he had said. The owner had come out to the street, where Austin remained in his brougham. "Duplicate the order—I must have more garments."

At this, Mr. Green changed color rapidly and, taking the advance (once more given in hundred notes), had waved to Frederick Albert Warren until Burlington Vigo Street, at the end of Savile Row, swallowed him up in the noisy horse traffic.

Fourteen days had been prescribed for completion this time, and with much diligence and not a little agitation (although the quality of the clothes was in no way affected), the job was done. Mr. Green awaited his customer with an open bottle of port on the day Austin had stated he would collect, knowing all was well.

§

Mac and George had arrived the night before, and after Austin revealed the success of his first moves in their agreed-upon plan, they treated him to a grand dinner that ended in laughter and good wishes for the morrow and Mr. Warren's appointment in Savile Row. That night they all stayed at the Grosvenor.

Newly built, the hotel was adjacent to Victoria Station, which served all points south—the Channel ports and the Continent. Thus, not only convenient but with the constant traffic of foreigners, it provided for its clientele considerable anonymity.

§

Six five-hundred-pound notes; five one-hundred- and fifty five-pound notes were bound in a roll, deftly secured by a thin cord and placed in the side pocket of Austin's coat. He resettled himself in the corner seat at the table, accepted a cup of coffee from Mac and went on with his story of the tailor and the cane.

George was impatient. "Ready?" he asked.

George looked across at Austin—young, exuberant, with confidence to spare and completely unaware of the nerves that George was unable to conceal. For George, experience created—always—hidden qualms.

Age, George thought. He would have been a lot less excited and far more apprehensive faced with the responsibility of the next hour.

If there was a difference between them, the older Bidwell mused as he heard Austin (ignoring George's question) continue his revelations of Mr. Green's shop to Mac, it was this seeming innocence, coupled with his obvious intelligence, a certain arrogance and infectious enthusiasm. This apparent vulnerability gave exceptional dimension to a personality that became at times magnetic. People listened, trusted, believed. Austin had a natural, rather than assumed, authority which created a power he wielded delicately and with immense charm. It was a quality all three of them shared, but less sensitive than Mac, and less wise than his brother, Austin had it to excess.

The more sober of the two Bidwells waited until Austin paused to laugh at Mac's reaction to his story. George repeated his question.

"I asked if you were ready," he said.

Austin relieved his brother's obvious consternation with a grin.

"Ready—*absolument*!"

Mac had gone back to *The Times*, which he was trying to read whilst keeping an eye on all others in the lounge of the hotel.

"Market's on the up," he said, now fully absorbed in the business pages. "U.S. Bonds are doing briskly."

"Mac, be serious; today is make or break. The guy is only a tailor."

Mac looked up. "Exactly," he stated.

"That doesn't make it any easier," said George. "I'd say, the reverse."

"Well, at least we'll have clothes enough to share," said Austin brightly. George did not respond.

Austin began to feel his brother's concern and spoke out.

"Look, maybe we could still get a solicitor to set us up—"

George interrupted.

"A solicitor is law, and that means references. You want me to write to Pender in Wheeling Prison, or will *you*, Austin, write to Blanc's Casino? Or you, Mac—you want to write to Irving in New York for a list of avoided convictions?" George paused, his point made.

Mac grinned. "I could write us the best references possible. Give me their signatures and I'll give you letters of introduction, credit, recommendations. Who'd you like?"

George's serious expression caused the two younger men to laugh. For a moment at least, Mac broke the tension which had risen with George's fear that the next hour would see only the failure of carefully laid plans.

"Okay, brother," George went on, unresponsive to the others' levity. "Remember that you may be here at the Grosvenor as Mr. Bidwell, but Mr. Warren resides at the Golden Cross. Keep your cover tight, and no slips—this time."

George was recalling Austin's lighthearted story—his version of the " 'at and cane."

Austin tapped his forehead with two fingers. "How could I forget, George?" he replied, his eyes twinkling. "Mr. Bidwell is just your poor loving kin, but Mr. Warren is about to become our benefactor."

"Perhaps," George said, apprehensive at his brother's overconfidence.

"*I* know him," replied Austin.

"Then, good luck!" said George. He looked long at Austin. A judge was never more stern.

Austin stood up, adjusted his coat and began to walk across the lounge and through the reception hall to the entrance. Outside, a cab was waiting, fully loaded with the trunks and portmanteaux of Mr. Green's first order—Austin's English wardrobe.

Mac turned his head after the retreating figure. Softly, almost to himself, but still heard by George, who swallowed and then finished his coffee, Mac said, "See you outside the Bank."

§

Austin completed the necessary task—and task it was—of trying on all the suits. The sessions he had had with Mr. Green measuring his figure with practiced accuracy (insisted upon even with the repeat order) ensured that the clothes were a perfect fit.

In Savile Row the cab awaited its fare, pulled over, up onto the pavement, to allow other traffic passage. Austin, having supervised placement of the first and pointed out where, when ready, the second portmanteau was to go, turned to Mr. Green, who ushered him back into the shop.

Inside, Williams was packing this second large, dark leather-covered portmanteau as other assistants handed him the garments. Some clothes Williams hung; others he folded and put into compartments he was then able to close, securing the garments against rough travel. The portmanteau was a beautiful piece of craftsmanship in itself, specially made for Green's, and with wealthy customers was always a complimentary gift of the establishment.

Austin and Green toasted, once to a good journey, a second time to good business and a third to better customer-craftsman relations. The port was excellent.

Williams closed the upright portmanteau, secured the locks

and, with a quick wipe (using an old rag) of the gold lettering—GREEN AND SONS, SAVILE ROW, AND F. A. WARREN—stood back to survey the beauty of the dark leather and imagine an inscription with his *own* name in gold.

The five-hundred note came to Williams from the hand of Mr. Green, who had accepted it with a bow from his customer, Mr. Warren.

"Williams, give Mr. Warren change."

Mr. Green smiled at his customer, happy that in anticipation of so large a note, he had seen to it that the safe of Green and Sons was today full of smaller bills with which to return the change. Even so, for a tailor's assistant who earned barely sixty-five pounds a year, it was a moment to linger over. Williams stared at the note in awe, before moving into the small office.

The American gentleman leaned against the polished wood counter and smiled back contentedly at Mr. Green, whose own pleasure at the completed transaction was equally apparent. Another satisfied customer, the tailor thought, and what a client this Mr. Warren was; he sipped his port from the elegant glass—part of an heirloom family set.

"Are you going away again, sir?" he asked.

The reply, "Pleasure, not business," started the course Austin had decided upon.

Williams caught only snatches of the conversation that followed, but heard, he remembered later, the words "shooting" and "Lord Clancarty's in Ireland." Mr. Green was cooing with appreciation of his client's acquaintances.

"Then the hacking jacket will be—"

"Perfect," Austin cut in. "As are all the others, Mr. Green."

At that moment the cabbie entered the shop and stood wiping his nose and brow with alternate sleeves of his dirty jacket. He remained waiting for the portmanteau, as were his instructions.

"See to it, Williams," Mr. Green commanded loudly.

"I'm doing the change, sir!" the young man shouted back from the office. Williams had decided he would not be forced into the flurry all who knew him associated with Mr. Green.

"Then get the others!" were the words that came out tartly,

aimed straight as an arrow at Williams, who yet again wondered, on sheer instinct, why his employer was unmarried.

"Thank you, Mr. Green," Austin said, "for everything." He watched the portmanteau being manhandled out by the cabbie and two assistants.

"I'll be on my way."

Williams arrived with the change.

"Here we are, sir—all correct."

"Prompt as usual, Mr. Williams." Austin looked at young Arthur Byron. Outside on the pavement, to anguished shouts, the portmanteau slipped from the grasp of three pairs of hands.

"See to it, Williams," Mr. Green said.

Reluctantly, Williams went out to help.

"Oh!" said Austin. "I almost forgot." He smiled with great charm at Mr. Green. "I've more money on me than I like to travel with—in a vest pocket, at least. I'd like, if I may to leave it with you." Austin took out the roll of money.

"Certainly sir. How much is it, Mr. Warren? May I be so bold as to ask?"

Austin casually looked at the roll.

"Only four thousand pounds—it may be five . . ."

Green was astounded. Money was money. Big money was hundreds. But thousands . . . !

"Oh, sir." He hesitated. "I would be afraid to take charge of so much. . . ."

Displeasure clouded Austin's countenance, conveying precisely what was intended.

"Well, I really don't know what to do. . . ."

Mr. Green was upset as he heard *his* Mr. Warren speak this last. What could he do? He thought hard, then spoke.

"What about your bank, sir—surely . . . ?"

Austin kept his tone casual.

"Truth to tell, Mr. Green, I've no introductions here. Didn't think I'd be staying long in your country, and I suppose I just 'plain ain't bothered' about banks and the like." The impression struck home.

"But so much, sir . . . ?" Mr. Green said.

"I didn't expect to accumulate 'so much' whilst here in England," Austin replied.

Mr. Green hesitated and said nothing. Austin was silent.

"Well, sir, I'm sorry but I couldn't . . ." began Mr. Green eventually. His face was all anguish. He just could not take the responsibility of such a large amount.

The shop bell rang, and Williams entered.

"All shipshape, sir!" he said to Austin as he arrived. "Loaded and ready." He grinned with an openness he reserved for the wealthy. Manufactured charm met concocted helpfulness in a look between Austin and Williams that lasted barely a second but was enough to give "Mr. Warren" an edge on the situation. What came next was an extraordinary finesse.

"Here," Austin said. "I am sure you will cherish it." He handed the cane, ebony and silver, to Williams, Arthur Byron.

"I have many others," finished Austin "—of my own." He winked at the young tailor's assistant. There was magic in the moment as Williams took the cane lovingly. Words came eventually.

"Oh, sir! I . . . I couldn't . . . I mean . . . I could . . . I will . . . oh!" The cane was more important immediately than words of thanks, so Williams gaped still whilst his hands, having none of the inaction of his halting gratitude, tested the weight, then twirled the cane.

Mr. Green breathed deeply—partly with instinctive jealousy at the transfer of affection from himself to a mere assistant.

"How very generous, Mr. Warren," he said.

"To stave off footpads, Mr. Williams," Austin suggested.

"Thank you, sir," Williams said, looking at the inscribed initials A.B. "But *I* ain't worth knockin' over." Austin laughed, Williams smiled at the success of his joke and Mr. Green was suddenly given visions of his best customer beaten to the ground in some back alley and deprived of this large sum of money still evident on the polished wood counter.

Austin remembered that silence at the correct time says far more, influences more effectively and lures action more surely than words, no matter how well put together. Even to Williams it seemed like an eternity before Green spoke; but when he did, for Mr. Warren they were the precise words he had expected.

"Look, sir," Mr. Green began. "If'n you'll permit me—I'm going to introduce you to my bank."

Austin affected surprise and gratitude,

"Why thank you, Mr. Green." He took up the roll of notes. "Where would that be?"

"Why," said Mr. Green, his decision made, "if we can take your brougham, sir, it is not too long a drive from here." Mr. Green took up his own hat and indicated to Williams he should get Mr. Warren's.

"I can return afoot," Mr. Green concluded. He looked at Austin.

"And which is it, Mr. Green?" Austin said. "Your bank?"

"Why, sir," said Mr. Green. "The Bank of England, sir!" It was said with pride.

In his imagination, Austin had rehearsed every aspect of the crucial meeting. Now what remained was mere formality. Austin indicated the door.

"Then shall we?" It was said with the relief, after weeks of waiting, that success brings to a mind tense with the prospect of possible failure. But to Mr. Green and young Arthur Byron Williams, who was oblivious of everything but ebony and silver, the three words had only the charm of a well-mannered reply and were quite obviously entirely spontaneous.

Garraway's

―――――――――――――――――――――

"GENTLEMEN," Austin said, "John Bull." Three glasses met in a toast across a table in the alcove of what had now become, for the three Americans, a familiar rendezvous— Garraway's.

George sipped his champagne, then looked down at the crisp new checkbook on the table, BANK OF ENGLAND clearly marked on the cover. His smile faded. He stared thoughtfully and was stern when he spoke.

"I think we should now take care. If we're to come out of this clean, we've got to be seen together only in a public place so we are just part of the crowd."

Mac leaned back, exuberant still; he spread his arms.

"Then let it be here in Garraway's." He looked out at the masses in the large dining room. "There's such a business throng around us, most times we'll be lost faces."

"It reminds me of Delmonico's, off Broadway," said George, following Mac's gaze.

"You're right!" said Mac with a smile, remembering their favorite haunt in New York. Austin interrupted the reminiscence: "Then we have to remain living separately?"

George nodded. "I've yet to work it out, but come the time—as yours is the face that's been seen . . ." He paused and looked hard at his brother, sobering them all with his voice. ". . . you have to be far away when we make our final play."

Mac exchanged a glance with Austin, then stared at George. It was inconceivable—were they crazy? Mac coughed, then voiced his thoughts.

"How do you mean, George? If Austin's far away and he's the only one actually involved, it's not possible."

George had a plan, quite obviously. Mac was confused, although Austin appeared to understand. George went on, now spelling it out for Mac: "Austin will have to take on a clerk to conduct our business."

"Edwin Noyes," said Austin.

Suddenly Mac began to see the plot.

"George, you've a mind and a half!" He looked at Austin and shook his head in admiration.

George smiled wryly and sipped more of his drink—remembering at that moment less favorable times.

"When there's nothing before you but walls an' silence for two years, you've got nothin' else but . . ." He stopped, recalling all too vividly Wheeling Prison and the hell of time lost. He paused, then went on.

"We must pool our funds, and Austin can then use our account at the Bank to maximum effect. We'll begin with, say, four thousand in, two thousand out; then six thousand pounds in, five out; convert that to U.S. Bonds, then, reconverted to cash, put two thousand back in. Then repeat it. To the inquisitive eye it'll seem we're conducting quite brisk business."

"So we're looking for an opening?" asked Mac.

"No, establishing a reputation," replied George.

"But it may take—" Austin was interrupted by Mac.

"As long as it does." Mac paused. "Until we find a flaw in the system," he finished, "we wait."

George smiled knowingly to himself, but Austin appeared to be decidedly unhappy. George looked out at the dining room, where the hubbub drowned the half whispers in which they were conducting their conversation. He nodded at Mac, who leaned back and, with his long arms, pulled closed the curtain. Only then did George speak—softly.

"We're taking on a giant to whom details, which we don't yet know anything about, are everyday fare. If we end up with our two million, we've done all the work we'll ever need. After . . ." Here he paused a moment for effect. ". . . we've only our whims and pleasures to satisfy. It's worth some time to pave the way—wouldn't you say?"

Thoughts raced in Mac's mind, but Austin spoke impatiently.

"And what do we do meantime?" he asked.

"Try our skills elsewhere," replied George.

"After all I've done so far! We'll lose the chance here," said Austin.

"When a chance is offered, we'll take it," said George firmly.

"And what if we don't . . . succeed elsewhere?" Austin's anger was growing.

Mac smiled and said confidently, "No one can fault my work, Austin. I've a fine hand and a good eye. I was taught by masters."

George sighed and looked hard at his brother. They had known the worst and the best; survival without bequeathed material advantages had been, to put it mildly, extremely difficult. But, thought George, here they were, as they were, and not too badly off at that. He gazed in silence as Austin calmed himself.

"If we fail—elsewhere," said George, " 'the Old Lady' will be the last of our problems, Austin." His point made firmly, George watched his brother sink back into his seat, apologetic but stubbornly silent.

George turned to Mac. "We are not hunting small game—there's none bigger." George let this last sink in. Mac was a willing audience. "The old lady with a heart of gold," he said grinning.

George nodded. "We've got to get exchange-bill paper and have a whole heap of blocks made. We'll give ourselves thirty days, I'd say, to do our business and show ourselves. If we make time bills of three months—ninety days—then we've left ourselves sixty days to get lost."

"It's a lot of work," said Mac quietly.

Austin shook his head.

"But George, the bills we make, no matter how good, are going to be declared fake when they go for clearance," he said.

"They don't . . ." replied George, ". . . go."

Mac was stunned momentarily. "What?"

George grinned and continued.

"That's the flaw in the system, Mac."

"I don't believe it," Austin said emphatically.

George leaned across the table. His eyes were hypnotic, authoritative.

"I spent the best part of two years with a defraudin' clerk from this John Bull island who had gone 'to sea'—shipped out in the 'sixties and he was caught again in Virginia for forging." George looked steadily at his brother. "In this country, the best banks simply assume that their valued customers who present bills have already checked that they're the genuine article; why should the bank trouble a second time? This, I'm told, has always been the practice, and as here in England tradition is the rule, I'm betting things are the same now as one hundred years past—certainly as ten years ago."

Austin would not be turned; he believed he was right and stuck to his point. For the first time in quite a while he thought his brother had overstepped the line of credibility.

"George, in a nine-by-nine in Wheeling Prison, that may be a fact—but it sure ain't living proof!"

George, knowing he had them both—Mac and Austin—holding on to his every word, lit up a cigar slowly.

A time bill was a form of credit, created by the banks for the convenience of businessmen traveling abroad, for whom these bills of exchange were as good as currency. Irrevocable once endorsed by the issuing bank, they became known as acceptances, which could be traded at any bank. At the end of a prescribed period of, say, ninety days, the bills matured and were returned to the issuing house to be withdrawn from circulation.

Between European countries, in fact throughout the world, this trade in bills was common practice and, indeed, con-

venient business. London merchants dealing with Paris could
buy bills issued at Parisian sources and give these to French
merchants as payment, thus negotiating their purchases
without the need to ship large sums of gold or currency across
the Channel.

As the bills passed from person to person, endorsement
marks were stamped on them by the banks through which they
passed, often accumulating until they covered the back of a
bill of exchange. To safeguard each transaction, every bill was
supposed to be checked at the issuing house or with its
representative in the city where it was presented before
payment was made. Only occasionally was this formality
waived. Then the account of a known customer of substance
would be credited at once, the endorsement stamp thus
establishing the validity of the bill. The issuing bank would
not be notified until the time had run out and the bill was
finally returned. So for a few valued customers, this time-
saving exception was made, simultaneously creating in the
system, hitherto regarded as impregnable, a fatal weakness.

Lighting his cigar, George concentrated on every move—
cutting the end, warming the tip with a lit taper, then slowly
puffing against the flame. Austin remained dubious, but
Mac's optimism was as aglow as George's cigar. He whistled.
"But if that was . . ." Mac said, ". . . why, we could . . ." He
stopped, not caring to finish the sentence. Austin bit his lip,
then looked at George steadily.

The older Bidwell went on. "We need only one thing," said
George. "Money."

"Money we have," answered Austin.

George blew out smoke from his Havana. "Not enough,"
he replied.

Exasperated, Mac interrupted the calm silence.

"What exactly are you planning, George?"

The older Bidwell smiled. "No-risk capital," he said. Mac
caught Austin's eye, and the latter looked back at his brother.

"Say it all," he said, sympathetic with Mac's mood.

"Mac," said George, "supposing we were to be sure the
bills could not be presented."

Mac shook his head. "I can't really believe it's possible,
George. Why, even in the U.S. a cable would be used to check

on them. From the bank discounting back to the bank issuing.''

"Think . . ." George said, ". . . farther south, Mac."

"Where?" asked Mac.

"Brazil," said Austin.

"Rio," said George. He paused and smiled.

"They have no telegraph."

Austin looked at Mac and finished: "Twenty days to and twenty days from, and then by fast boat."

Mac understood immediately. "George, you're a genius!"

Austin in that moment was proud to be of the same blood. George sobered him.

"We have yet to do it!"

Austin smiled.

"Perhaps, then, we say only 'low-risk capital.' "

Enthusiasm now raged at the table, champagne aiding excitement.

Mac began: "Then we'll need letters of credit and introduction." He paused, his mind racing. "I'll get some bill-of-exchange paper and have blocks made up that we can print from. I can copy the best bills we have—given time.

"George, I have to make only one contact in the city to get the addresses of all the engravers I can use. The detailed work—scrolls, bank lettering and the like—I can farm out to different shops. It's always suspicious if one man does all the work I need for the same bill."

"Maybe I can help," suggested Austin.

"I doubt it," answered Mac. His tone of voice had a sharpness prompted only by pride in his abilities. Austin was hurt, Mac could see, and immediately he softened toward his friend.

"I'll print the money," he said smiling; "you cash it." Mac put a hand on Austin's shoulder, and they both laughed.

"Then I," said George, "will book our passage for the tropics."

Austin's face fell. "And the John Bull Bank?" he asked.

"Austin," answered George calmly, "when we come back from South America we'll have our pockets full and our heads brimmin' over with experience—so when we hit 'the Old Lady,' we do it right with only need for the once—which is all the chance we'll get."

"But . . ." Austin paused. ". . . Rio's one thing, but here . . ." He looked at Mac. ". . . we still are not sure, George. Sight payment on a bill, or a credited account . . . I can't believe it."

"When we return," George said, "we have only to assure 'the Old Lady' that you are a valuable customer—and that is what will take time and our money."

Austin remained stubborn, but after all, it was he who, for the trio, had fronted the operation—at least, to date. He drank more champagne while George and Mac watched.

"Okay," he said, "I accept that in Rio it's not a physical possibility to have a time bill initialed and cleared from the issuing house before payment: forty days there and back—okay; but here in London a messenger has only to walk—well, sometimes it's only a hundred yards, and the bill is checked *and* verified—or not," he finished ominously. He looked at his brother. "It can't be a fact, George."

"It is not . . ." said George firmly, ". . . done."

"It's an oversight, Austin," Mac said, his desire that it should be aiding belief.

"Hoping . . ." said Austin, ". . . ain't knowing."

Mac looked at Austin and grinned.

"Well, so as we know what we're coming back to, Austin, there's only one way to find out—for certain."

George surveyed his brother a moment longer, then made his proposition.

"Then the day before we leave, *you* buy a real bill, and you go to the Bank of England and try it."

Austin swallowed at the thought.

"But what if—if it doesn't work—if it *is* sent off straightaway to be checked; if the bill is cleared, initialed and sent back?"

"Then, Austin, we and 'the Old Lady' will not do business," George said.

"If the bill is genuine," Mac said, "there's nothing to fear."

Austin remained only partially convinced. After all, it was he who had gone into the Bank with the tailor. It was he who had met the Assistant Manager. It was he who had felt the tradition of centuries and the might of Empire in the great rooms of the Bank.

George softened as he looked at his brother and smiled, realizing that now even he had been taught caution by experience. The greatest bank in the world had made its impression. It had taken the biggest to do it, but it had happened.

"Austin," George said. "If I am wrong, there'll be no need to return—so I'll buy one-way tickets."

A pause held as eyes met across the table; then the combined laughter of the trio, tensions gone, was enough to summon the waiter, who opened the curtain to the alcove, emptied the champagne bottle into the half-filled glasses and went off to find another Krug '61—chilled. He made his way across to the door leading down to the wine cellar.

Garraway's, the waiter thought as he weaved between the crowded tables, avoided elbows, legs, feet and table edges, where several port bottles were now precariously perched; Garraway's, he thought, as he absorbed the scene around him and caught yet again a glimpse of the display above the door before going through it; Garraway's is becoming its old self again.

Above the lintel of the wine-cellar door was a large, framed old poster advertising South Sea shares, offering fantastic dividends for modest investments. On either side of the poster were two small newspaper clippings, also framed. Both had barely discernible headlines: SOUTH SEA BUBBLE—BURST.

Bills of Exchange

THE year 1872, in England, was known chiefly, by those who survived it, as the most remarkable weather year of the century. The first week of January had brought shocks of earthquake, fearful thunderstorms and a hurricane with snow and hail. The precedent thus set was faithfully followed throughout succeeding months.

Steady rains and cold were prolonged far into the summer, to be followed by "an amount of electrical disturbance" unparalleled in living memory. Gales caused disastrous wrecks at sea. Thunder and lightning of destructive violence raged, which, with the accompanying polar winds and snow, greatly retarded the crops and vegetables, destroying those which were early. Throughout the month of May, heavy thunderclouds often overspread the whole heavens, and only occasionally was the sky clear, even then checkered by a canopy of wispy silver.

Cirro-stratus or nimbus?—Mac could not remember. He saw, as he looked up, St. Paul's Cathedral framed by the high cloud diffusing against a pale blue sky. But the morning was fresh, and he had enjoyed the long walk from Victoria along the riverside to Blackfriars. The rattling traffic—horses and carts, drays, high-stepping four-in-hand, ponies in traps and cabbies cracking whips at urchins—and messenger boys who darted across the roads: all this was a background to thought as his regular stride ate up the several miles to his destination in the City.

Barges passed on the river as eventually, fractionally faster than his pace, they overtook him, disappearing with hoots from the tug to which they were attached as it pulled them beneath bridges straddling the River Thames.

Mac turned up Puddle Dock, entered Queen Victoria, then Godliman Street and crossed into St. Paul's Churchyard. Here he paused only to ask the way of a little girl selling flowers. He gave her enough to buy a pair of shoes, then, entering Cannon Street, recognized the area from his previous walks, some time before, during the celebrations for the Prince of Wales's recovery. He strode briskly up New Change until he reached the corner of Paternoster Row.

The sign THOMAS STRAKER, ENGRAVER AND PRINTER hung outside the premises. Mac had a list. Straker was on it. He entered and closed the door behind him, shutting off the noise of the city. Smells of ink, fresh-carved wood and burnished metal—copper and brass—along with oil from machinery, thick and heavy; also light, almost sweet aromas from the lubricating liquids were the first things Mac absorbed. All were familiar. He was a master at what, he could say honestly, was an art, not a craft. Forgery was a word for Law. Mac never used it. He took a deep breath, absorbing the rich mixture in the air—filling his lungs in a way that was almost sensual.

"Yes, sir?"

The voice was helpful, polite; it recognized quality. Mac turned to face the speaker as he emerged from the workshop at the back. Ink-stained hands, a magnifying glass pressed to his eye, a filthy apron about his waist, the proprietor shuffled toward his gentleman client.

"Straker?" said Mac.

The man nodded, brushing back thin white hair.

"Do you do copperplate work?" asked Mac.

"Indeed I do, sir," Straker replied.

Mac had brought with him several blank bills of exchange
of the type used in London by the major financial houses and
banks. They were accessible on order from any reputable
stationery manufacturer.

For Mac, Straker had one use. Provided he stuck to
precisely what was asked of him, he would be none the wiser.
Mac represented himself as the member of a firm who
traveled the world—Straker would soon see where. Mac put
his prepared list on the counter, then took out his purse.
Ignoring further attempts at conversation, he watched Straker
fumble with his reading glasses.

"Here is a list of city names I wish prepared, in the precise
style of these bills, each separate," said Mac. He offered a
sovereign to Straker whilst the engraver was still putting on
his spectacles. He accepted the coin, then took up the list,
referring to one of Mac's bills. Mac put away the leather
purse, watched Straker copy out the list and took it back.

"I shall call in seven days," he said. "Good-bye."

Straker looked up as Mac began to go, confused at the
speed with which his customer had conducted what ordinarily
would be a leisurely exchange and eventual agreement. He
was a man who did not like the way the century was going.
Now it was all rush; time was . . . He interrupted his thoughts.
"Your name, sir?"

Mac paused imperceptibly and spoke as he reached the
door.

"Brooks."

In the comparative silence within the shop, Straker began to
read his handwriting slowly, aloud to himself. "Cairo; Bom-
bay; Hong Kong; Val-pa-raiso; Yoko-hama; Con-stanti-nople
. . ." The list was long.

§

The area Mac wanted had a perimeter bounded by
Moorgate, Liverpool Street, Fenchurch Street, Cannon Street
and Blackfriars: all railway stations; all serving the City,
whose daily exodus to the suburbs was rapidly increasing. The
word "commuter" had just been coined to describe the daily

journey many took to City jobs as urban development swallowed the outlying villages and work was transferred into London itself. To live within one's means was becoming an equation of time, distance and skill at husbandry.

Mr. Arthur Mitchell lived in Hackney Wick and as a young man had walked to and from the City each day. Now he took the omnibus to save his legs. Horse-drawn and crowded, it took some time to reach Throgmorton Street, but it was worth it. Weather changes were always telegraphed to Arthur Mitchell's legs, translated by arthritis or rheumatism, he still didn't know which, then conveyed to his awareness by varying degrees of pain and discomfort—to be relayed throughout the day to his customers.

As Mac entered, Mitchell thought he saw a man good for several sovereigns and some advice on how the English weather was to settle after the miserable year to date.

A foreigner he is, thought Mitchell, and American it has to be, as Mac sat down on the stool at the counter and made his introduction with two printed bills of exchange laid flat on the counter top beside his gloves. The first attempts Mitchell made to elucidate the elemental disturbances were greeted with a polite smile, silence and a firm indication that the speaker should pay attention to business and leave the atmosphere to God. Having perused the first bills with care, Mitchell took a third bill of exchange from Mac and held it to the light.

"Observe closely, Mr. . . . ?" Mac paused.

"Mitchell, sir," said the tradesman without disturbing his concentration.

"It is different from the others in one respect and one respect alone," continued Mac.

Well, of course it is, thought Mitchell; it has been endorsed.

"Can you make me a seal and holder that will provide an accurate copy of that endorsement mark?" asked the American gentleman.

"I see, sir," said Mitchell, observing—as he had been instructed—closely.

"Can you do it?" asked Mac.

"Well, sir . . ." Mitchell began a twenty-year-old practice

of "procrastination for profit," as he described it to his wife. "Do a favor," he'd say, "and you gets no thanks—but give 'em the wait-an'-see an' you 'ave 'em eatin' out yer 'and."

"Difficult," said Mitchell. He looked at his customer and raised his eyebrows.

Mac had heard enough of Mitchell in his inquiries to persevere. He took out the answer to all tradesmen's problems and laid it on the counter. Mr. Mitchell smiled at the two sovereigns.

"How long, Mr. Mitchell?" Mac's patience had an edge to it.

Mitchell scratched his head and began. "Well, it's an . . . unusual request like . . . sir. . . ."

Mac swiftly took out from his purse two more sovereigns, placed one in each of Mitchell's hands forcefully, then took from his pocket a carefully written list.

"Read it," Mac said.

Mitchell read it—willingly.

"Well?" asked Mac.

Mitchell grinned and replied, "No trouble at all, sir, I'm sure. Now let me just get this down."

Mac watched patiently as Mitchell finished his own version of the list, reading aloud as he wrote it down. "Hamburg Banking Company—Smith, Payne and Smith—Bank of Belgium and Holland—The London and Westminster."

Mac then took out four drafts on those companies listed, handed them to the engraver and indicated the endorsement marks on each. Mac and Mitchell looked at each other a moment in silence. It was the hat and the cut of clothes that kept Mitchell's mouth closed. He confirmed for himself the only justifiable story acceptable: a gentleman of business he was, this American, and questions don't get sovereigns.

Mitchell grinned, remembering he had already been "crossed with gold." "You want exact copies in the same lettering?"

"As each differs, Mr. Mitchell, copy it to precision—if you are able."

"Indeed I am, sir," Mitchell stated proudly. "No doubt you'll be wantin' these seals with 'andles?" He paused as his customer nodded.

Mac remained impassive and was about to go when Mitchell referred again to the bills on the counter.

"All marked 'accepted,' sir—right?"

"No, Mr. Mitchell," Mac said firmly. "As it states on each of these bills"—he indicated the examples in front of the tradesman—"the word printed is 'endorsed.'" The man nodded, took up one of the bills and held it to the light.

"'Accepted' is written, if you observe, by the guarantor in his own handwriting," continued Mac.

Mitchell no longer bothered to hide the fact that without a magnifying glass he was becoming quite positively long-sighted, and although his reputation remained beyond reproach, he had begun to notice, in his work, small mistakes, before he spotted them and made corrections. He concentrated, squinting hard.

"Endorsed . . ." He began to spell it out as he read. Mac frowned and glanced at the bill; one of them was wrong, and he could see that Mitchell was squinting.

"With a C," Mac said.

Mitchell referred to the bill. "It says here quite clearly . . ." He held it out to be examined by Mac.

But Mitchell had exhausted Mac's patience; he was experienced, and Mac had given him adequate information and excessive payment.

"I will be back in one week," he said brusquely.

Mitchell watched Mac step to the door before asking the name of his customer.

"Morris," Mac replied.

Squinting still, Mitchell started to write it down. He began speaking before he looked up.

"Morris, sir—with an S?" But Mac was gone.

§

Mac had a solitary lunch amidst the furor of Garraway's, then walked out and down Exchange Alley to begin the afternoon's business. He had hoped the list of engravers would prove sufficient halfway through, but inquisitive eyes and probing questions had forced him farther down it all morning, until only six names remained.

It was important that what work he required be done with
diligence and skill, but most of all without the necessity for
credentials that, firstly, he was unable to produce and
secondly, he knew, if asked for, indicated immediately that
the craftsman concerned was likely to be "on" to the
authorities.

Mac was being doubly careful. If the tradesman was
prepared to do the job asked of him for the princely sum Mac
paid—no further information solicited—all well and good.
Mac scrutinized the examples on display each time he entered
a shop; only then did he watch the craftsman, his eyes, the
hands, the way he talked of his work. Above all Mac
respected pride. Mac, utilizing *his* particular skills, intended
himself to put together the work bought from the craftsmen.
He would then be able to make very passable facsimiles of accepted and endorsed bills of exchange, each one missing but
two things: the sum to be drawn and the date issued. This,
along with signature and, indeed, handwriting of any sort,
Mac felt confident, would prove no problem for him.

Now he had only two more calls to complete the list.

Mr. Chaloner had all the abilities Mac required. His
specimen books of scrollwork were beautifully done, and Mac
did not hesitate to show admiration. Flattered, Chaloner went
on to pull out other books, which Mac looked at but which
were unnecessary to his choice.

It was a good move; Chaloner beamed at Mac, who had
shown his complete understanding of the difficulties intricate
patterns presented when made into a printing stamp. Mac
listened and waited. He was tired; it was becoming a long day.

"Good day, sir," Chaloner said, eventually.

"In a week, Mr. Chaloner," Mac replied. He went out of
the shop and closed the door slowly.

At the bottom of Mac's formidable list was a Mr. Dalton.
Although he was very tired, Mac was sustained by the fact
that this was the last name and there were still rules and ink to
buy. Afterward he knew where he would go. Mac entered
Dalton's shop.

Somewhere bells chimed six o'clock. Mac stood quietly
waiting for the man before him (hunched over a workbench)
to turn and give him attention.

"Sir?" Mac maintained his charm, even though the edges were frayed. The man continued his task, oblivious of his customer.

"Sir?" Mac began again, his voice hardening. "Sir, if your name is Dalton, you have a customer."

Still the man remained at his work, his concentration total.

The long day welled up inside Mac, and raising his cane, he determined to speak only a few words before giving Dalton the edge of it.

"Be damned, you ill-mannered navvy!"

It was the shadow of the cane that Dalton saw as the evening sunlight outside, slanting across the workbench, was split in two for a moment. He spun round with surprising speed.

"So, you've ears, at least," Mac said. "If you have a mouth, you might make an apology before I take my leave of you!"

Dalton could read the discontent in Mac's face and realized what had taken place—unlike Mac. Slowly Dalton grinned and then shook his head. Pointing first to his mouth, then to his ears, he covered his eyes with both hands; then, opening two fingers, he peered out at Mac with the humor of a goblin.

Mac later remembered this as an apt description, when relating the story to George and Austin, and even, in the telling, laughed all over again, much as he began to do at the very moment he loosened his tie and sat down heavily beside Dalton, on a second stool, at the bench. He clapped the man on the back and shed the strain of the day in loud, unconfined laughter, accompanied by the soundless convulsions of the deaf-and-dumb craftsman.

The two men remained together for an hour.

§

As Mac stepped into the Red Lion Public House in Holborn, after the brisk walk from St. Paul's, he knew there were two things he wanted badly. The first was a drink, so he crossed to the bar, amidst the jocular crowd shuffling around on the sawdust floor, and asked the barmaid for whiskey. His voice spoke teasingly, as if he were a stranger, but his eyes betrayed the feeling inside.

She looked enchanting as her face fell at the tone of his voice, but as her intuition caught the look in Mac's eye, May's face broke into the smile he would not have exchanged for a bagful of sovereigns.

"Well," she said, exuberant, glowing with pleasure, "my gentleman friend!" She held a pause that Mac dictated with his own smile—one of appraisal—as he saw what a little money and his confidence in her had done for his waif.

May leaned over the bar top, pushing the whiskey glass toward Mac. She softened.

"Where've you been?"

Mac took the glass, then said pointedly, "What would you recommend to revitalize a tired man after a hard day's business, May?"

May looked first at the whiskey, then into Mac's eyes, which glittered, as hers did, at the thought.

"I ain't thanked you properly," she said.

"That's 'cause I ain't let ya," Mac replied, mimicking her accent.

May pursed her lips and cast her eyes at the ceiling without thinking.

"They've been good to me since I was able to pay me way. I got two rooms now"—she paused and smiled beautifully—"upstairs."

To date Mac had been only a kindly benefactor, giving May time to re-establish her confidence and spirit. He respected her pride and recognized the quality, inherited from some past conjoining, that created in her a unique spark. She was the woman he had known he would always recognize when the time came. She was not what he had thought she would be—not overly intelligent, fine, mannered, cultured, knowledgeable or the thousand other prerequisites society concocts as the amalgam of the perfect mate. She was just May, and he loved her.

"I tol' you they'd take me back if'n I was presentable," May said.

"Well, you certainly are that," Mac replied.

Farther down the bar, the owner of the public house turned

and shouted for May; then, seeing Mac, tipped his hat and went off to do the job he had been about to delegate.

Mac's money had spoken well at the Red Lion, securing May as permanently as she wished. The proprietor's financial problems had been partly resolved by Mac; and in consequence, the freehold establishment had acquired a barmaid with a small percentage of the profit.

"A part share in the business . . ." May trailed off, her voice unable to convey thoughts newly implanted of a life now stretching ahead without worry or care.

"I didn't never think . . ." She looked at Mac with gratitude that filled her eyes with tears.

"Before I leave," said Mac quickly, "I'll buy it for you, lock, stock and barrel."

May impulsively stretched over the bar top, encircled Mac's neck with her arms and kissed him in full view of the largely unheeding crowd about them. She whispered in Mac's ear, "I'd rather be havin' you."

After that, with the key in his hand, the steps upstairs, through the side door, were only minutes away for Mac. He had undressed and been asleep an hour before he heard the door close softly in the outer room and saw May come to him through moonlight streaming in from the soft night outside. A light breeze stirred lace curtains at the bedroom window as the woman shed her clothes. Nervous now, and not yet naked, she stood by the bed awaiting the invitation to an initiation.

As Mac's hand went out to this suddenly fragile creature, he knew that the second thing he wanted badly that evening would be found not in the taking of a woman in a moment of passion, but somewhere during the night in the ephemeral exchange two people add to the making of love by the precious knowledge of feeling a part of it.

§

The following morning, Mac took his breakfast privately in the small outer room of lodgings three floors up, above the Red Lion in Holborn. The lovely young woman who sat opposite him was attentive, loving and, with newly stimulated feelings, astonishingly accurate in her reading of Mac's behavior. It was with more than intuition that she guessed correctly.

"When you goin' away?" she asked.

"I didn't say," he replied.

"When?" she asked again.

"Not immediately," Mac said lightly.

"When?" she repeated.

Mac paused, drank his coffee, looked into May's eyes and spoke. "A week, maybe—ten days, perhaps."

The statement created a silence. Outside, below in the street, shouts of ragamuffins, cries of traders and the rattle of passing carriages indicated the day already under way. The sun intermittently shone into the room. The air was fresh, borne on a wind that swirled between the roof tops. The morning smelled of a summer already come.

"Where?" May asked.

Mac paused, stretching with a yawn before leaning across the table to look into May's face lovingly. Softly he said, "If I told you, would you believe me?"

"Yes," May said, wide-eyed at the thought that Mac might think for a moment she would not.

"Then," answered Mac, making a joke of it, "I ain't sayin'." The kiss he gave her reminded them both of the night that had passed, and they were content then to be just two lovers seeking nothing more than the silent pleasure of each other's company.

Fenwick

MAY 29 was Derby Day. At ten forty-five, George, Austin and Mac were sitting in the lounge of the Grosvenor Hotel drinking coffee.

"I fancy Cremorne at three to one against," Austin said. "He's the favorite."

Mac's thoughts turned to the line-up of the Derby in a paper George now thrust at him.

"Queen's Messenger for me," said George.

The two brothers looked at Mac, who had already made his decision. Mr. J. Astley's horse was being ridden by a jockey named Chaloner, which was coincidence enough to bring luck. Of the commissions now collected, it was he, in Mac's opinion, who had done the best job. The scrollwork was perfect.

"Brother to Flurry," Mac said. "I'll do a late bet and check the odds for us all."

Mac looked at his pocket watch. It was approaching eleven o'clock.

"Make or break, boys," he said.

Mac and George looked at Austin. He took out the bill of

exchange, purchased several days before, and placed it on the table.

"How much is it for?" George asked.

"A thousand pounds," Austin said. "On Blydenstein and Sons—ninety days to come due."

George dropped an envelope beside the bill and settled back in his seat with a grin. All three observed the illustration of a ship afloat at full steam to the left of the name *Wilson* that George had used to book passage.

"I'll tell you," Mac said. "I'm ready for the tropic sun." He was about to develop the thought when Austin cut in seriously.

"I tell you—I'm not sure about this."

"I am not wrong," George said firmly.

Austin slowly took up the bill, studied it vacantly for a moment, then looked at the envelope on the table.

George saw his brother's worry and winked at Mac, indicating the envelope.

"Tickets for Brazil."

"Round trip?" Austin asked.

"You want to look?" asked George.

Austin stood up. He put the bill of exchange into his wallet, knowing that upon the next hour would hang their entire scheme. They would, all of them, soon know if the impossible that George had described was a fact.

Referring to the tickets as he took his hat to go, Austin said to George, "I don't have to look at them. I dropped into the shipping agent's early this morning."

The laughter of Mac and George disturbed two ladies by the door who were taking morning tea in the sedate, mannered English way the unattractive of that species do. Their momentary consternation served only to relax Austin as he jauntily tipped his hat to the two women and strode out to his waiting cab.

§

Mr. Fenwick was not too fat or too thin. He was neither too short nor too tall. His color did not have the pallor of the unhealthy or the ruddiness of robust overindulgence. He was certainly not well off, but then, he was not poor. He dressed not without taste, but decidedly was not ostentatious. He observed Sundays with respect, but was not overly religious, preferring Hampstead Heath of an afternoon to church of a morning. He was not a stern man, but then, no one could say he was lax or did not command the respect of his staff. He was not married, but then, he was not altogether what it was thought a bachelor ought to be—and even he disputed that definition (after all, he was not a priest); his preference was the occasional liaison with an eligible Englishwoman approaching her prime, as he graciously put it.

He was not teetotal, but he drank sparingly. He enjoyed his work and appreciated the responsible position he held; his zealousness was always directed toward productivity in the younger employees. Eventually he made them all aware of the position of trust they held, exalted amongst men and women, gracing, as they did, the very corridors that were like arteries of the Empire itself. Even if the job was merely to carry tea, it was one in which to take pride, Mr. Fenwick would say, since it was within the portals of the greatest banking institution of this world or any other.

Mr. Fenwick liked his tea. Very much, in fact. But then, that spoke more of his patriotism and embellished his obvious loyalty. The conditions of the workers who dropped like flies in the Colonies, picking leaves that months later found their way into Mr. Fenwick's cup, were of no concern to him. Tea aided concentration, and his job was important. His concern was only for the realm to which he gave his all. Reputation, Fenwick mused: that was what gave dignity to a man's life. Then a thought struck him. Why, someday even the little Queen Victoria herself might know of him by name.

The very idea caused Mr. Fenwick to pause mid-sip, so he put down his teacup into its saucer for a moment. Fenwick of the Bank. Good heavens, he thought: now, that would be a mark hit for a man's ambition. Thirty years' work since boyhood had made him what he was and put him where he sat at this desk, in his own office at the bottom of a long corridor—the wrong end as yet, but time would perhaps solve that, he vaguely hoped.

In fact, for the likes of Mr. Fenwick, ambition would

always stop here. Beyond, at the top of the corridor, lay a larger office, a greater responsibility and the weight of it that a figurehead of society must accept with a job representing a peak, respected by all in the world of finance. One would have to be born to different circumstances than those which had surrounded Fenwick's first blow, breath and cry in this world to be even considered for the post. In his heart, Fenwick knew he had arrived and would go no further. All in all, he was basically content. This made Fenwick a most perfect Assistant Bank Manager.

§

At eleven fifteen, Farley, Mr. Fenwick's assistant, brought in three files for Mr. Fenwick's attention and took out the empty cup and saucer, drained to the last few leaves of the tea remaining. At eleven twenty-five, Fenwick had familiarized himself with the recent transactions of all three clients he would see before lunch. At eleven thirty he stood up as the wall clock struck the half, checked his pocket watch and crossed to the window.

Fenwick was in this position, looking down at the horse traffic below, when his first appointment was ushered in by Farley.

"Mr. Warren, Mr. Fenwick."

"Thank you, Farley."

Fenwick gestured to Farley to leave, crossed to the young man standing relaxed behind the chair opposite his desk, shook hands, indicated that he should sit, then made his way around to his own seat. Fenwick and the young man looked at each other a moment, and both smiled.

"Well"—Fenwick spoke first—"you've been doing brisk business these past weeks, Mr. Warren."

He looked down at the top file, more for effect than to substantiate the remark with figures that he could anyway not see without his glasses. With clients he seldom wore them, thinking his image better served with a clear eye and firm stare.

"Quite substantial business at that, if I may say so," Fenwick concluded.

"Thank you, Mr. Fenwick," said the young man.

"Our Manager," continued the Assistant Manager, "will be with us again soon, and he is, I know, most anxious to meet you."

A pause held as Fenwick awaited a courteous response to this last. The young man remained relaxed and silent, his clear eyes and firm stare appearing to Fenwick much as Fenwick hoped his own eyes and stare appeared to his customer—impressive. Mr. Warren took his time. He removed his gloves and placed them on his lap as he crossed his legs.

Mr. Fenwick was almost mesmerized. He was about to speak when the young man began:

"That mutual pleasure must wait."

"Oh?" said Mr. Fenwick.

"I shall be away and gone some while, shortly," said Mr. Warren.

"I hope business does not tempt you abroad," said Mr. Fenwick. Then, realizing that it probably did, he continued: "If so, for not too long an absence from us?"

Mr. Warren merely smiled at the obvious and seemed, to Mr. Fenwick, to be in no mood to discuss his travel plans. Fenwick coughed and decided, not for the first time, to stick to business and cut the pleasantries. The trouble was that he liked people, and the fact that people might not have a complimentary opinion of him never entered his head.

"I shall need substantial funds," said the young man, "so in addition to my balance, I shall put through this bill." He paused a moment.

Fenwick saw only the open smile of the mouth. He should have watched the glint in the eye.

"I hope there will be no delay?" finished Austin.

Mr. Fenwick was charmed. He took the bill from Mr. Warren, stretching across the desk to do so, resettled himself and looked at it. He smiled back at the pleasant young man. It was nice to see youth with money—a gentleman, that was—even if he was American. Well, that was the way of the world; we can't all be British, he thought.

"A century of service," Mr. Fenwick began, "can discount that fear as it will this bill."

Good, that, he thought. Somehow he managed to use the

sentence every day, but always it came out as if new. Now he would laugh and pardon the expression.

"If you will excuse my levity." Here Fenwick giggled a little, as if he and Warren were mortals sharing a secret in trepidation of omnipresent gods somewhere in the large room.

The young man's attempt at a smile was dismal.

"Must it be cleared?" he asked firmly.

Fenwick coughed again and repeated to himself, Stick to business; cut the pleasantry.

"Why, no," he said; "you are obviously as good as *it* is." Here he referred to the bill again. "Thus one journey will be sufficient for the bill, Mr. Warren . . ."

The young man, Mr. Fenwick noted was now quite immobile; for a moment it seemed he was carved from rock. Even his color appeared to fade.

". . . the journey which takes it to the finance house—ah"—he looked at the bill—"Blydenstein, in—ah, yes—ninety days."

Austin Bidwell looked across at Mr. Fenwick and could hardly believe his ears. By God—George was right. He saw the man before him at the desk speak, his face seemingly perplexed at something.

"Mr. Warren?" Mr. Fenwick said.

"Why, yes, Mr. Fenwick." Austin recovered and became quite animated. He stood up.

"If you will then, credit me for withdrawal, and I shall be off."

"You will leave a sufficient sum to maintain your account, of course?" Fenwick asked.

"Of course," smiled Austin.

"You will be using us again on your return, I hope?"

Until the following year—in March, to be exact—Mr. Fenwick would not know the import of the words Austin now spoke in reply to his question.

"Of that," he said, "you may be quite sure."

"Then," said Mr. Fenwick, as he came around the desk to his young client, "I will say only, as they do across the Channel—*au revoir?*"

Austin only smiled. They walked to the door.

"Where does your business take you, Mr. Warren, if I may be so bold?"

"Oh," said Austin. He turned to Mr. Fenwick so that they were face to face. Quite blatantly, and with a cool eye, Mr. Fenwick remembered, Austin Bidwell said, "Why, St. Petersburg, Mr. Fenwick, then on to southern Russia."

"How interesting," Mr. Fenwick replied.

"As you say," said Austin, "*au revoir.*"

Putting on his gloves and waving a cursory good-bye to the Assistant Manager, Austin was led out of the Bank to the large foyer by Farley. He took back his hat and cane and thanked Mr. Fenwick's assistant for his aid. He breathed deep.

"Are you a betting man, Mr. . . . ?"

"Farley, sir—Oh, no, sir."

"It is Derby Day, is it not, Farley?"

"Indeed, sir, I believe so."

"Then take a tip, boy," said Austin: "the favorite."

The boy nodded his thanks and watched Mr. Warren walk out, down the steps and into the crowd outside the great open doors of the Bank.

§

Austin crossed the road onto the island pavement between Threadneedle Street and Cornhill, and stood stock-still a moment—a man in a dream. Now he had only to walk in and collect from the cashier. It was unbelievable. Two familiar faces appeared in the crowd, and the solitary figure standing amidst the rush and bustle of the city became a group of three.

Only the beggars and trinket sellers noticed the sudden jubilation of the trio as a few words were spoken by the man who had stepped out of the Bank.

The more active of two beggars dragged his limbless mate toward a better site in Lombard Street. They'd already had a shilling apiece from the two men who had been watching the Bank half an hour, pacing up and down Finch Lane. And what did they care for the feelings of others? Their welfare was of consequence only to themselves. Life was a pain, joy a myth, and happiness a lie. Almost in unison, both creatures spat into the gutter.

The three Americans were in a different world.

"Rio, boys." said Austin.

"*Return*," said George.

Mac only smiled.

That afternoon, Mr. Savile's horse, Cremorne, the favorite, ridden by Maidment, won the Derby at odds of three to one in a time, recorded by Dent's chronometer, of two minutes forty-five seconds. The issue hung in the balance until the last stride, but the verdict of the judge was adamant. Brother to Flurry came second, and Queen's Messenger was third.

Many said it was a fluke and, as the race had been hard run, just pure luck; but then, most winners are accused by the less fortunate of one thing or the other. At the end of it, generally, the opinion was that it had been a good day for all.

Summer

1872

Plot

MORNING of the twenty-second day from their European embarkation brought landfall for all aboard the good ship *Lusitania*. As the cry "Land ho!" circulated amongst the passengers, all those who were able found some vantage point to see the horizon and the land that was appearing.

In a state of high excitement, the three Americans, only half-shaved, in shirt sleeves, already damp under the arms, looked from the railing of A deck outside their cabins and absorbed first impressions.

George had a guidebook with maps and gave names to the vision of hills, peaks and ravines now in the distance: Urca, Leme, Cantagello, Formiga, Nova Cintra, Novo Mundo. The curious aspect of the stone giant all three Americans could see clearly: a colossal human body lying on its back—morning haze affording a soft mattress; the face composed from the highest elevations of Gávea and Tijuca mountains, the body and legs by those of Corcovado, the feet by the thrusting pinnacle of Pão de Açúcar.

Islands began to emerge from the land mass, and before them George, Austin and Mac could now see the Dedo de

Deus, a slender elevation of the Organ Mountains; the lower part resembling a clenched hand; the upper, the shape of a huge finger pointing to the sky. Mac wiped his brow as the first effects of the tropics made their mark.

"Know what I'm thinking of, Mac?" said Austin.

He stopped a moment, shut his eyes and saw the vision clearly. "Cold snow, a closed carriage and my cozy Countess all snuggled up in furs and rugs."

George grinned. "Let's go inside; I want to see our letters of credit. Did you finish them?"

"The ink's still wet," answered Mac.

"Dry now," George retorted. He turned brusquely and went into the cabin behind them.

Mac lifted a loose shirt sleeve to his face once more. "Well," he said, "I'm not."

Only Austin remained on deck as the ship's bow cut into a smooth sea and nosed toward the majestic panorama.

At the mouth of the channel into the Great Bay is the Island of Lage, dividing it into two passages. Austin heard bells sounding out all over the ship as speed was cut by half and the readiness of the crew was signaled by their sudden appearance on the decks—at winches, davits and guardrails, each to his station. More bells clanged; then a long blast from the ship's horn sounded out over the bay as the *Lusitania*'s prow entered the broader western channel, almost a thousand yards wide, close by Pão de Açúcar, the almost barren Sugar Loaf rock.

The South Atlantic was now behind as Austin took a last quick look, then turned to survey the distant town—revealed more clearly, as the mist lifted, as a large, picturesque colonial city, spread out along the shore beneath a brilliant sun in a cloudless sky. Two more miles at half ahead slow; then, with a juddering of engines, the ship lost all momentum and rattling anchor chains told all aboard they had arrived safely at their destination below the Equator, just inside the Tropic of Capricorn—Rio de Janeiro.

Austin leaned against the rail and watched activity below on the foredeck: preparations to receive the many small boats coming out from docks called the Cais Pharoux to off-load passengers and cargo. Suddenly the peace of ocean travel was over and here were the exuberance, noise, squalor, pleasure and excitement of South America.

Like Mac, Austin too now felt the heat and humidity. He wiped his brow. Voices from boats all around shouted up at the sailors aboard, who let down ropes and ladders toward a glittering sea. To Austin, all appeared confusion, and he watched a moment longer as loud exchanges in an unfamiliar language floated back and forth over the water. As other passengers now crowded out onto the deck, Austin went inside to prepare for disembarkation.

The trio went ashore onto the Cais Pharoux and saw beyond the customhouse an extraordinary labyrinth of narrow streets. Already their senses were assaulted, overwhelmed by an aroma, even as they stood on the wharf: coming from sacks, bags, boxes; on trays, in cups; ground or in original form—the beans were undeniably coffee.

From sixteenth-century Cairo, *kahwah* found its way to Europe and thence, in 1723, from France to the tropics. The plant, brought to Rio by Judge João Alberto Castello Branco, thrived in its new habitat; a Dutchman, John Hopman, was first to export what was to be the basis of Brazil's wealth, rescuing a trade which had almost exhausted the gold and precious stones that had created the prosperity enjoyed by the Portuguese colony.

As coffee consumption in the Old World rose, so productivity in the New increased. Fortunes were made and reinvested for further expansion. Financing was readily available should loans be required. The banks and business firms dealt in large sums and were unperturbed by the arrival of foreigners, willing to invest, with money drawn on letters of credit or bills of exchange: provided the papers were in order, cash was immediately forthcoming.

Maua and Company was the most considerable firm in all South America. George, Austin and Mac knew this much. Utilizing the work he'd had done by the London engravers, Mac had concocted their introductions to this company. He had painstakingly prepared letters and, having surveyed them minutely aboard the *Lusitania*, felt they could not be faulted: a letter of introduction from the very respectable London and

Westminster Bank in England, which had dealings with Maua and Company; a letter of credit stating that the holder was a man of considerable means and several bills of exchange, apparently issued from different British banks but copied to precision by Mac—the first of many from genuine originals.

§

The English engineer Charles Neate and Brazilians André Rebonças and Borja Castro had begun the year before, in 1871, to construct a Customs area with its own dock fully equipped for the growing commercial trade into and out of the city. It took time to complete, as things do in South America; so unfortunately, it was into this semioperational area of the Cais Pharoux that the passengers of the *Lusitania* had been thrust on arrival.

The aplomb of first class melted quickly. When Customs and Police had finished their inquisition, all were free to go. Never had all men been so equal. Brows glistened, faces glowed and even the women would attest to the fact—perhaps months later, when the embarrassment wore off—that as they all plunged on into the city proper, even they had physically declined the verb to sweat.

Exceptionally, in that year of 1872, the climate remained unkind. Gentlemen in chaos, Austin thought as they walked into the crowded streets of the city from a square beside the wharf called the Praça Maua. Disheveled by the sun's heat and the heavy atmosphere, all three Americans looked as if they were in a Turkish bath. The chilled claret of the voyage emerged in continuous perspiration.

Coats slung, baggage carried by Negro slaves, they followed a guide provided by the shipping line who indicated the route ahead through a market ablaze with color from a variety of fruit. An occasional carriage made an attempt to pass amidst the throngs of multicolored "Cariocas"—white, black, yellow, red and all the half-caste variations thereof—but it was almost impossible to gain headway, as the trio could well see. Whilst they were not altogether content to walk, they knew their destination would at least be achieved sooner on foot, as the guide had explained.

Mac, out of the corner of his eye, saw Austin reaching for a large apple amongst the rainbow of fruit displayed.

"Austin—the Purser warned us about fresh fruit."

Austin rubbed the apple.

"Mac," he said, "I ain't so long in the tooth I can't take myself an apple when I choose."

Mac saw that George was now beckoning from the distance, and as he moved off he prayed his hotel would have the cool spring water and the large ceiling fans newly installed and run by electricity that he'd heard talk of aboard the ship. Mac took his friend by the arm, but Austin tossed the stall holder a coin, put the apple to his lips and said—partly to Mac, partly to the dark eyes of the Negro clutching his silver piece, who stared blankly back at him—"I've the digestion of a goat." He took a deep, hard bite.

Two hotels served for accommodation. The International in Santa Theresa, near the Central Station, was the place George chose, whilst Mac and Austin checked in separately at the New Hotel Estrangeiros, behind the ocean frontage of Avenida Beira Mar.

George arrived to visit before dinner and discuss plans for the following day, but found only Mac, bright and fresh from a long bath, relaxing in Austin's suite. George greeted Mac, who continued engrossed reading of a financial paper, then he crossed to the long French windows leading onto a balcony.

As he stood watching the evening breeze stir the palms, George heard what may well have been a first intimation of the unforeseen events to come: dry vomiting. Mac spoke from behind his paper.

"Exchange rate is goin' up."

George flashed a look at Mac, who winked and nodded toward the bathroom. George closed his eyes and shook his head helplessly.

"Hey!" shouted Mac. "Goat!" There was no answer. "George is here!" Mac waited for a reply from Austin. It came—loudly, as before.

George crossed the ornate, high-ceilinged room and sat opposite Mac, who put down the paper.

"It better be me tomorrow, George."

"Well, we've taken the precaution of separate registration

in our hotels," said George, "so if anything should happen to one of us, at least we're able to count on each other for help."

In the bathroom, Austin vomited once more, then pulled the flush. George stood up.

"Let's take another look," he said.

Mac joined George at the wide table where letters and bills were laid out. Mac had added last-minute touches to several of the letters, having yet again compared them with the originals.

"They look all right to me," George said.

He took up and scrutinized the letter of credit.

"Here's the original," said Mac, "from the London and Westminster."

George looked and saw several figures that had been changed in the copy—namely, a one hundred to ten thousand, and the date. Mac's letter was made out to a Mr. Morrison.

"But," said George, "the original is nine months old?"

"Well, I needed a real one to copy—it was all I could get," said Mac. "It's on Maua and Company, at least. They have the biggest turnover here in Rio, so I'm thinking no questions will be asked when we put in for large sums—cash."

George might well have argued the point that paper, design, wording or even procedure can change during a nine-month period and it would have been safer to copy a more up-to-date letter issued for credit—perhaps even relinquishing the idea of Maua and Company. But as thoughts assembled themselves in his mind, Austin came into the lounge—white, shaken and altogether alarming in his appearance.

George pointed at the bathroom and grinned quickly.

"Mac's goin' tomorrow, brother," he said, "so you just go back about your business."

"I'm going to be all right," whispered Austin hoarsely.

"We were just talking," said George, "of tropical prisons where they throw lawbreakers, then chuck away the key."

"Look," said Austin, as well as he was able, "I said I'll be . . . Jesus!" He broke off, unable to finish, the renewed spasms racking his body as he stumbled back toward the bathroom. Mac and George could see him as he collapsed beside the toilet seat once more. Mac was genuinely worried.

"Should we get a doctor, George?"

George's opinion of the local aid available was not encouraging.

"In these parts," he said, "they'd only take a fat fee, then recommend an apple a day."

In the bathroom, Austin, now angry, shouted an obscenity, then pulled hard at the flush in an attempt to be rid of the residue of his own stupidity.

§

The streets of old Rio were narrow, with here and there a small square called a *praça*. The one wide street was the Primeiro de Marco. Here the kaleidoscopic charm of Cairo or Constantinople was emphasized by the bright and gaudy apparel. People bustled about their business, bartering with the joyous temperament strong sunlight and extreme warmth seem always to elicit.

Above Mac, as he strode toward Maua and Company on the morning arranged to present himself, was the other aspect of street life—the lookers on. The Carioca girls at the windows, Rio wives and Brazilian widows, perched on a balcony or leaning over the sill, with or without baby, were future, present and past in the marriage market, eyeing all movement below, to dream or sorrow if their gaze should linger on such as Mac.

He plunged on into the melee, despite the heat quite enjoying himself. Street vendors competed with staccato or dolorous cries above the level of noise; fish, fruit, wine, old bottles, wickerwork, sweets, clothing, laundry, bread, flour, ice water—all were declared loudly amidst the jostling multitudes.

Eventually, Mac reached the square surrounded by palm trees. He was exhausted but lighthearted, and he sat down on a bench beyond which some old men were playing a game of bowls on a sandy area. Mac looked at his pocket watch as George appeared, a few minutes late.

The building across the way was imposing enough to sober them both. George took the bench; Mac crossed the cobbled street, narrowly avoiding a carriage and pair, then stepped onto the mosaic-patterned pavement. In front of him, steps led up to a large portico.

A clock chimed eleven. In the square, George checked his watch. Mac entered Maua and Company.

§

The old men at bowls finished their game. Starting another, they paused for ice water from a vendor. Hitching up their trousers once more, the two men began a third game. At that precise moment, Mac stepped out of Maua and Company across the way and stood atop the flight of steps. George saw Mac give the signal of a doffed hat. All was well. Beneath Mac's arm was a package.

Mac entered the square at a leisurely pace and paused only momentarily beside the bench.

"We've ten thousand pounds in Brazilian notes, George," he whispered excitedly as his friend took the parcel. "They were only too pleased to do business."

"Then," said George, "we'll go again tomorrow."

Ploy

ON the afternoon of July 1, 1872, May stood in Hyde Park and waited with the rest of a gathered crowd for the Queen of England to arrive. Sun shone intermittently from a sky that threatened thunder. May had walked from the Red Lion in Holborn to the Serpentine Lake where she had watched the horses in Rotten Row parade their riders past each other.

The royal carriage reached Hyde Park Corner, turned west in front of the Duke of Wellington's mansion and slowly completed the distance to Prince Albert's Gate. May cheered with the crowd as their little Queen climbed down from her carriage. Accompanied by the Duke of Edinburgh, Princess Louise, Princess Beatrice and Prince Leopold, she mounted the pyramid of beautifully chiseled gray granite steps of what was to be a Memorial.

At the top, she entered the barricaded area beyond which the gathered Londoners were unable to see. The official opening was to be the following day; this was merely an inspection for approval. The decoration was superb, it was agreed by the elite within the hoarding; everything was as it should be, the Queen remarked. The builders congratulated

115

themselves silently. It was then that the Queen noticed an omission which caused immediate consternation. Her entourage assumed the stiff faces of disapproval.

"Where," asked the Queen, "is the object for which this entire structure has been conceived?"

"Mr. Foley," it was explained, "is the sculptor. His health," she was told, "is not of the best."

"It is unfortunate," the architect, Sir Gilbert Scott, said.

"The date set for the official opening can be postponed," it was suggested.

"There will be no delay," the little Queen said determinedly; then left, it was noted by the cheering crowd, a little more rapidly than she had come.

The following day, all the country knew what Society agreed was something of a farce: the statue of the Queen's late husband, Prince Albert, was missing.

§

As May walked away from the scene that afternoon, lightning flashed across the sky, heavy with black rain clouds; a rumble of thunder, and first drops began to fall. May saw an empty hansom cab and thought of the authoritative shout with which Mac would have hailed it. She put up a hand, and to her astonishment the vehicle stopped; the cabbie leaned down with a smile and asked her destination. She got in, as if she took cabs everywhere. In fact, it was the first time in her life, without Mac.

She lay back in the seat and thought fondly of her gentleman friend. Silently she blessed him, wherever he was. Perhaps, if indeed God was not at that moment preoccupied with falling sparrows, it was that heartfelt honest blessing which saved Mac—just.

At the moment May's eyes closed to conjure a vision of her love, eight thousand miles away in South America, on what, in Rio, was only the morning of July 1, Mac mounted the steps of Maua and Company a second time and walked through the imposing doorway into deep and totally unexpected trouble.

§

Mac was ushered down the long corridor. An immediate relief from the heat outside; cool air lingering from the night before, stirred by several lazily revolving fans beneath the high ceiling, wafted gently toward a thick-carpeted floor.

All sound seemed to be absorbed by the surroundings; Mac felt for a moment that he was penetrating a sanctum. Involuntarily, he shivered suddenly, then was into the familiar anteroom where the previous day he had remained patiently ten minutes before entering the Manager's office. Today Mac saw the oak door already open. He was taken straight through to two men waiting for him. One he knew: this was Braga, with whom he had so successfully concluded his first transaction. His size and shape were tailored to the richly furnished room. Stout, but tall, the man bore himself well; the assumed pomposity and slow smile, merely necessities of his job as Manager of Maua and Company. He seated himself once again behind his enormous mahogany desk.

His assistant was a grim-faced little man, whose eyes slithered about beneath glasses that were thick, tinted and gold-framed. The assistant's clothes were dull and poorly tailored, Mac noted, ill-fitting a figure that was as spare as was possible in a healthy human being. His mouth was wide, his lips narrow; in a large, sallow face his features appeared disproportionately small. He was almost bald on the crown of his head, with overlong sideburns to compensate. His eyes did not leave Mac for one instant. Mac sat down.

"Well, Senhor Morrison?" Braga said. He paused as Mac smiled in return. "What is it we are able to do for you?"

Mac thankfully felt cool air from the ceiling fan and was pleased to see shutters on the sun side of the building closed. These Portuguese coped well in the tropics, he thought. Nonchalantly, he said, "I wish to purchase some additional exchange."

"I see." Braga smiled slowly. "May I, then, once again see the letters—both of credit and of introduction—please?" Braga's smile left his face as he went on, "A formality, of course. Banking, as you must know, is full of them."

Mac felt no premonition of trouble. He knew how well his letters had been copied and had the success of the previous day to justify his confidence. But small things are clues to great disasters, and it was the eagerness with which the grim-faced assistant took the letters that put Mac on his guard. He became suddenly very alert. The assistant did not pass either letter to the Manager, but examined them himself. He stiffened and looked slowly first at Mac, then at his superior. He shook his head. Braga pursed his lips, weighing possibilities. Seconds passed.

"Is something amiss?" Mac asked.

Braga spoke slowly and firmly. "I am afraid so, Mr. Morrison."

Mac's body underwent an immediate change. Even in the cool room, the rush of blood could not be prevented from forming a film of sweat on his brow. Mac swallowed, smiled and awaited explanations.

"Communications," Braga began, "between ourselves and Europe, even in this age of wonders, remain, unfortunately, at the pace of the fastest steamship."

Mac could not yet even guess the nature of the suspicion that had been aroused. The Manager droned on. Mac felt as if he were fading from the scene; already he wished himself away and out of the situation. A sudden silence and look of suspicion from both Braga and the assistant brought Mac to his senses.

"The name of Mr. . . . ." Braga hesitated.

"Bradshaw," prompted the assistant.

"*Sim*—Bradshaw," said Braga. "He is the Manager of the London and Westminster Bank issuing your credit; his name is on the letters."

Mac relaxed slightly, now perplexed.

"But," continued Braga, "as our new instructions indicate"—he paused for breath—"the name of the sub-manager—the necessary requirement; now essential these six months past—is missing—from both the letter of credit and the letter of introduction: a Senhor . . ." again he paused.

"J. P. Shipp," said the assistant acidly.

"*Sim*—Senhor Shipp," said Braga.

"With two P's for Pedro." The assistant made his point, thought Mac, with one P for impossible.

There was no answer. He knew it. And already the silence had grown to six seconds. Two pairs of eyes fixed him unwaveringly. Mac felt clammy and knew his brow was giving away far too much. It felt decidedly damp. He shifted in his seat a little and said the only thing possible.

"Well, I wonder how the omission could have occurred." He tried a smile. "Accident, perhaps?"

Suddenly Braga represented a huge, ponderous society that would come crashing upon Mac's head at any moment.

"I can think," said Braga "of no other reason." Grimly he looked at Mac. "Can you, senhor?"

Mac just wanted to be out—of the room, the corridor, the huge portico, the city, the country, the continent. He hoped still that it was a dream.

Braga continued, his voice firm: "For us, you see, it is important, as you already have ten thousand pounds sterling in Brazilian currency, and the paper I have here"—he indicated the letter of credit—"is worthless without the corroborating signature."

Mac knew they were truly finished. Or more precisely— George and Austin being unknown to either Braga or the authorities—he was finished.

If he left the bank, he would be unable to leave the country. If he remained more than forty or so days, as of course he would be forced to do, proof would return from England, by steamer, of the transaction already made, indicating that the bank had been deceived. Strictly enforced passport control, which the trio had already experienced at the Cais Pharoux, made Brazil a "difficult" country to leave without official sanction. So even if Mac was allowed to go to his hotel, he knew that he would have to return and, at Maua and Company, placate suspicion. But how? He did not even know what the signature of Shipp was like!

He remembered George's indicating the age of the original letter he had obtained in London and cursed himself.

§

Sparrows may fall, and God may see every little one—but all the same, they fall. There is no divine providence, only happenstance, or so Mac believed. In a conversation with May many months later, he was to revise his opinion. As people the world over share that most precious of all things, time, in their respective parts of the same day, at that very moment in England, in the hansom cab she had hailed to take her home, May was emitting thoughts of love and blessing with the power of faith in creation, in its various divinities and, more especially, in Mac.

Prior to his departure he had kept his promise and given her the security of which she had never before dared dream. In Braga's office, Mac suddenly had a picture of himself signing the lease of May's rooms, using a blotter to dry the ink.

"Have you," he asked, "an original example of the letter—as it should now look?"

Braga and his assistant were momentarily surprised. Mac became indignant. "I have with me other letters, and substantial bills of exchange, and most certainly to have the mistakes of others affect my credit so far from home would be more than inconvenient." Mac's brow was not yet dry, but he knew that it was considerably less damp.

"May I make," he said, "one further request?"

The eyebrows of Braga responded. He was still confused by the renewed confidence of the man before him.

"Some more of your excellent Brazilian coffee?" Mac's trump card was played. He had, the previous day, made a fuss in appreciation of the coffee presented him by the Manager at their first meeting. This request, Mac knew, would not be denied.

The assistant had given the original letter to Mac and was returning to the Manager's side. The timing was perfect. As the Manager turned to the assistant, who immediately gave full attention to his superior, Mac casually wiped his brow, then laid a damp finger across the signature he saw before him, written boldly in black ink. He quickly turned the paper over so that it was face down on other letters and bills he had now taken out of his pocket and that lay on his lap.

"Milk or cream, senhor?—I forget," asked Braga, turning to Mac.

"If it is fresh, senhor," said Mac, "cream."

The Manager's gaze shifted momentarily to the assistant, long enough for Mac to put pressure on the form along the back of the signature of J. P. Shipp.

"May I . . . ?" requested the Manager, Braga, extending an arm.

"Of course," smiled Mac. The paper was taken quickly from his hand by the assistant, who placed it on the desk.

"My assistant has indicated to me that coffee will take some moments to prepare, so perhaps if you would like to . . ." the Manager did not finish.

"Then perhaps I will forgo it; I do not wish to disturb you in any way," Mac said.

"Indeed, sir"—Braga's face was without expression—"it is *I* who appear to have disturbed *you*."

"That," said Mac, attempting a wry smile, "I will not contradict." He stood up decisively. Braga was immediately on his feet.

"I have a luncheon appointment," said Mac, with as much calm as he could muster. "Immediately after which I shall return to my hotel." He paused. "You have the address?"

Braga nodded warily.

"Good," Mac went on, his speech betraying not one shred of the terror he was suppressing. "This afternoon I will survey the documents I have with me. Those relevant to Maua and Company I will, of course, bring back for your inspection."

Braga was about to speak, but Mac took the words from his mouth.

"Should I discover further—omissions—all the relevant papers must, of course, be returned to London."

Braga nodded. "Exactly so, Mr. Morrison."

The assistant was silent, but his gaze remained unwaveringly upon Mac's every move. For a moment, nothing happened; then Mac found the words that got him out of the bank. They were strangely simple.

"Would eleven tomorrow be convenient?" he asked.

The Manager glanced at his assistant. A pause held.

"I hope then," finished Mac with a magnificent smile, "to be able to continue our business, which will, I have no doubt, prove mutually profitable."

"You have every confidence, it seems," began the Manager.

"In the London and Westminster," interrupted Mac as he moved smoothly toward the door.

"Why is that?" asked the assistant suddenly, his voice harsh, by no means sympathetic.

"Because," continued Mac, finding charm from he knew not where, "I cannot believe that so excellent a system as that bank operates can allow more than one mistake to pass its scrutiny." Mac was already home—but not, as yet, dry.

"Eleven," said Braga. "Tomorrow," the Manager went on, the trace of a smile on his lips, "I shall have coffee waiting."

Mac shook hands with Braga, ignored the assistant until he had opened the door, then followed him through into the anteroom. Outside, an attendant escorted Mac along the cool corridor to the main entrance. Mac took his hat and cane, nodded his thanks and stepped into sunlight. He stood a moment and breathed deeply of the welcome air. Hot and humid as it was, to Mac it felt delicious.

George, watching a second game of bowls the two old men were playing in the sand of the small square, looked up to see Mac emerge from the Maua and Company offices, then put on his hat, remaining at the top of the steps. Perplexed, George watched Mac take papers from his pocket and look closely at them. In the strong sunlight, Mac found the faint impression of a signature, resembling what a mirror might well, he sincerely hoped, reveal as that of a British assistant manager by the name of Shipp. Mac, giving no signal of any kind—in fact, without even glancing at the square—descended the steps two at a time, reached the pavement, turned directly toward the city center and was, in the next moment, lost in the crowd.

George, now sensing something wrong, was already on his feet when a first shout went up from the several old men and women come to watch and judge the return bowls match between the two players of the day before. The winner of the previous day had lost this decisive and most public confrontation. A combination of nerves, heat, humidity and wine of the night before had taken its toll of aging flesh.

The defeated old man staggered, then fell heavily into the sand. George, already at the gate leading onto the road, was unaware of anything but his own alarm. Shouts of consternation and the rasping breath of the fallen player were of no concern to George, for the day appeared to have taken an altogether unexpected turn.

Persuasion

"DISTANT thunder," said *The Times*, reviewing July, "was a frequent occurrence throughout the month, which as a whole may be said," it continued, "to have consisted of one grand prolonged demonstration of the vast powers that elemental storms of the nature witnessed, illustrate to even the most exalted among us." The weather in England became sultry, the sky the color of ink.

In the late evening of that first day of the seventh month, threatened rain which fell in light showers during the afternoon became torrential the moment a simultaneous flash of lightning and crack of thunder denoted the eye of the storm directly over Westminster.

Streets were submerged, houses flooded; reservoirs burst and rivers overflowed. The great storm became a minor cyclone, and what was thought to be fearful enough became fearful indeed. Brilliant shafts of light illuminated horizon to horizon; the sharp and reverberating thunder rose in volume, as did the wind in strength. On such a night, man could believe in the fantastic.

As May looked out the upper window of her rooms, unable to sleep, she was struck with awe at the sight presented to her—unleashed fury which before she had only cowered against in some alley or night lodging crowded with vaga-bonds, gin-drunk and beer-swilling. She had survived the cholera that had claimed her family and left her destitute. Now, it seemed, as she gazed out from her own rooms at the great storm, she was to survive the hell of poverty on the streets that claimed the body and ruined the soul. She con-jured visions of a future which now held promise and ex-citement. Her imagination was fanciful, nurtured by a father whose compositor status had provided sufficient earnings to buy what he had loved most—books. As a child May had listened to her father, enraptured by the stories he read her before going to his night employment. She often recalled his voice. Now May thought of Mac, who for a time had re-created the atmosphere she loved, reading to her words from a mind of the past. Immortality within her cozy rooms and ob-vious reminders of mortality outside, Mac had said. She sighed and wished him back soon.

Torrential rain lashed at the glass; the wind moaned; somewhere below in the building, doors creaked; May pulled the newly acquired robe about her. Lying in a chair, as she was now, warm and snug, she thought, without looking at them, of the books on two of the walls behind her, in shelves put up by Mac: books that were full of information, ideas, the imaginings of man; books of words—magic letters that put together could make whoever understood them laugh or cry. She had seen it in her father and had felt it herself when he, or Mac, had spoken the words as written. She still hoped that one day perhaps she too would be able to read.

Accustomed to the noise now, even as it roared louder, May allowed her eyes to close, allowed herself to dream of love and lands beyond the great ocean. This way she saw Mac clearly, and with his smile came words difficult for her to remember, given to her in childhood: "Mighty winds that skirt the bounds of some far-spreading wood of ancient growth, make music not unlike the dash of ocean on his winding shore. . . ." Her memory faltered. That was it, she thought: it

was all, all the furor outside, like some great symphony Mac
always talked of. ". . . that lull the spirit," she knew the poem
finished, ". . . and fill the mind."

The candle on the table beside May was suddenly ex-
tinguished, but for the lovely woman, now asleep, darkness
no longer was fear. Tortured nightmares of the past had
received a balm that healed the wounds opened up in her by
the raw existence she had led before Mac and she had chanced
to meet. She was now flying high over a roaring sea and could
see beyond the horizon where a land of sunlight beckoned.
Mac seemed to appear and blow a kiss; then all was suddenly
instant darkness, and for the first time in many months,
horrors of the world she had known surrounded her.

Although she was asleep still, May's brow furrowed with
inexplicable anguish. The roaring elements had now become a
threat, and her position in the dream on the wind, high above
a now black ocean, was perilous. She could no longer fly, and
as her momentum ceased, the bird or creature shape she had
assumed dissolved, to leave her naked in the nightmare, about
to experience what only Icarus could have told her of—but
then it was too late. She screamed all the way down. That
night God was busy. Sparrows fell in abundance.

§

Mac put down a large brandy and wished himself, not for
the first time that evening, in two small rooms with a loving
woman of his acquaintance—most importantly, eight
thousand miles away. He looked again at papers on the table
before him and extended his hand once more. It was not
steady; again he tried to put out of his mind the prospect of
the following day. Angry at himself, he dropped his pen and
shouted an obscenity.

George and Austin had come to Mac's rooms at the Hotel
Estrangeiros, to be more of comfort than of assistance. Only
Mac could relieve the situation in which they now found themselves. He, as they did, knew it all too well, and that didn't
help.

Mac took another sip of brandy, then finished what

remained in one swallow. He had transposed the faint signature of J. P. Shipp so that it was at least legible. The difficult part was in finding the right flow to re-create what would pass as an authentic specimen. This to be put on two further letters that it had taken him hours to re-create.

Outside, it poured; rumbling thunder over Rio's Guanabara Bay followed occasional flashes of lightning that momentarily lit all the peaks and islands. Open French doors allowed some rain to splash into the room, but the humidity was so oppressive that Mac had demanded a circulation of air when Austin went to close the shutters. Now Mac just sat still, obviously nervous and distraught.

"It was an old letter I copied, George. You pointed that out when you saw it." Mac spoke almost in a whisper.

"We should have checked on current procedure," said Austin.

"I should," replied Mac. He was now staring out into the approaching night; George could see that he was exhausted and depressed.

Thunder rumbled long and loud from one side of the bay to the other. The day's afterglow added to dark clouds and the black sky, a diffused red and deep orange that seemed to build mountains on mountains beyond the true land mass; vast phantom ranges stretching away to an horizon lost in a murkiness that the rain made of twilight.

Nature dominated the room, and for a moment all three men felt their danger. Mac, at least, had the preoccupation of his immediate problem. Austin, dulled by the understanding of what had happened, was glum, but at least his confidence and natural optimism buoyed him up, and he merely reflected on possible solutions and potential escape plans. George—intelligent, imaginative and now pessimistic—was in another world where he stood answering to divine judges. He shook his head, seeing amidst his gloomy philosophizing the ludicrous aspect of their predicament. He then did what has saved many a life and often rescued a situation. He began to laugh. His laughter was infectious; soon all three were in paroxysms.

"George," Mac began, unable to control his laughter, "it's

up with us—with me, anyway—tomorrow if I can't . . ." His eyes filled with tears. Mac was unable to finish as his laugh became a suppressed roar.

"Keep cool, Mac," George coughed amidst laughter. "Have another brandy."

"George, I . . ." Mac couldn't finish. He looked at Austin and was silently racked. He held his stomach and pointed, speechless. Below, on the terrace, under an awning, the evening music began as several violins struck up. This only set the trio off into further peals of laughter. Austin stood up and, staggering to the table, managed to splutter out a few words.

"What you write in the next moments," he said, tears streaming down his face, "decides what we do the next twenty years."

A flash of lightning and crack of thunder effectively curtailed the trio's fragile euphoria. As the prolonged fading rumble raced off toward the horizon, they were left with their own silence, the pouring rain, badly played violins below and, with a return to reality, an agony of speculation. Hard-eyed and cold sober, Mac took up the pen.

"Give me," he said, "another brandy."

§

Rain fell on Rio out of the pitch-black heavens. It was already midnight; standing alone at the open doors to the balcony, despite the humidity and distant city sounds Mac felt cold and isolated. The oil lamp behind him on the table flickered as a gust of wind brought rain into the room. Mac's face and shirt were spattered with wet drops that ran down his cheeks and soaked into his skin. He saw himself as an adventurer presented with a crisis and hoped he could face calmly the dangers of the day to come.

Despair offers discipline thereafter to whosoever conquers challenge to the spirit, or defeat to those others who succumb to their weakness. Sieges are broken by heroes created by a resilience that sustains their passion to overcome. Difficult voyages are completed by captains whose ambition denies them the alternative of return. The insurmountable is

achieved, the unassailable breached, by men who banish all
from their minds but the objective.

Mac blew smoke out into the night rain, then threw away
his black cheroot. He had done his best, and on the table was
the result. The signatures were by no means perfect to his
mind, but they needs must do—there was no alternative. He
turned away from the balcony and went back to a large armchair, into which he slumped. He could think of nothing but
his fears for the unknown day ahead. He took up an old copy
of *The Times* lying next to his empty brandy glass on the small
desk; he began to read. It was going to be a long night. The
syndicated article became interesting, and it might take his
mind off the time: Six hours to dawn, God, he thought—six
hours.

§

The news startled us all. "A white man?" we asked. "Is he
young or old? How is he dressed? Where has he come from?"
we asked.

"From a very far country," we were told, "a long time
ago."

On November 10th, 1871, the broad African waters of the
Tanganyika were sighted, and with guns firing and the Stars
and Stripes flying, we descended the hill and entered Ujiji. The
news of a caravan had flown through the town, and principal
Arab merchants were already discussing the matter with the
white man I saw, on what appeared to be the verandah of his
habitation.

I pushed back the crowds and, passing from the rear, walked
down a living avenue of people until I came in front of the
semicircle of Arabs, before which stood the white man with
grey beard. As I advanced slowly towards him, I noticed he was
pale; wore a bluish cap with a faded gold band around it; had
on a red-sleeved waistcoat and a pair of grey tweed trousers.

Two hundred and thirty six days out of Bagamoyo, I felt my
quest was at an end. I would have run to him, only I was a
coward in the presence of such a mob—would have embraced
him, only being an Englishman, I did not know how he would
receive me; so I did what cowardice and false pride suggested
was the best thing—walked deliberately to him, took off my
hat and said . . .

Mac stopped reading and lay back in the chair. Tears ac-

companied silent laughter as he shook his head in disbelief. By
God, he thought, if another American, after two hundred and
thirty-six days, could control his emotions to that extent, he
could damn well show these pompous, backwater, half-
civilized natives of another wilderness continent that he was
certainly a match for them.

Mac, now in a better frame of mind, stood up and stretched
his limbs, lit another long black South American cheroot,
then went to the open doors and stepped out onto the balcony.
The rain had stopped; he saw stars appearing as black clouds
moved slowly east, taking with them the distant thunder over
a far horizon. He smiled to himself and quoted the famous
greeting in imitation of the *New York Herald* journalist
Henry Morton Stanley:

"Dr. Livingstone, I presume?"

Children's shouts and raw city sounds engulfed Mac's calm
for only a moment as he isolated the chimes of a nearby clock
tower, striking eleven A.M. In strong sunlight Mac climbed the
steps to the open portico, strode into shadow and entered
Maua and Company.

Outside, Austin blinked against the day's brightness and sat
down once more beside George, who wondered idly where the
two old men were; the square looked naked without them.
Austin spoke quietly even though they were alone. "The
steamship *Ebro* leaves for Liverpool tomorrow."

"Then," said George, "Mac better be on it. When he
comes out, you watch him to be sure he's not followed. I'll go
to the port and get a ticket. I've got the passport Mac made
me in the name of Wilson. We still have the exit-visa
procedure and what the hell else to go through before we can
get out of this damn country." George paused. "But leave all
that to me." He breathed deeply. "Now," he said, "we
wait."

The chimes for eleven o'clock finished. Two men on a
bench in the palm-fringed sandy square of a tropical city.
Hot, heavy and peaceful without, the atmosphere within the
Maua and Company building was cool, quiet and dangerous.

§

The Manager of Maua and Company, Senhor Braga, stood up the moment Mac entered his large office. Braga nodded, and the door was closed behind the visitor. Mac was aghast: the office was crowded. A chair was presented. Mac sat down. Four other men stood up. Mac stood up. All bowed. All sat down. A moment passed, and only Braga smiled—slowly.

"Senhor Morrison," he said, "these are associates of mine who unfortunately do not speak English but appreciate my taste, as you do, in one thing—coffee."

Mac managed a hoarse whisper. "Good morning," he said.

"Now," stated Braga, "you have news for me." It was said with the certainty that Mr. Morrison, or whoever he was, did not in fact have news. Braga was wrong.

"See for yourself," said Mac. He took out the letters, which were almost snatched from his hands by the Assistant Manager, who appeared from behind. The grim little man had been waiting by the door. Do they think I am going to run? thought Mac.

"A singular omission," he said, "only, it seems, on those first two letters which you have, of course, seen."

The Manager looked to the men at either side and murmured in Portuguese. The bank's originals and Mac's newly presented letters of credit and introduction passed around from hand to hand in a silence broken only by the shuffling of papers. Mac nonchalantly chewed imaginary gum and wished himself dead.

Two minutes passed. Eventually the Manager took back the letters, placed them on the desk, removed his glasses and lay back in his chair. He smiled slowly.

"We have a difficulty, it seems," he said.

Coffee arrived.

§

Austin saw the fast-moving carriage before his brother did, but George was first to realize that its destination was Maua and Company. The carriage stopped. One man stepped down; two remained seated.

"A Hebrew," said George.

"Do you think it concerns Mac?" asked Austin.

"What concerns Mac," George answered, "concerns us, Austin; don't forget it." Austin swallowed.

"You better be ready," George finished, looking across at the small, sprightly, middle-aged man with a hooked nose, as he mounted the steps of Maua and Company.

"Ready for what?" asked Austin, confused.

To George, the day seemed suddenly dark and quite definitely sinister.

"Ready for damn near anything," George replied. The Hebrew disappeared through the large doorway. The carriage slowly moved across to the shade of palm trees. The two men stepped down, tethered their mules and crossed into the square; they found a shaded bench and sat down. To George it appeared that they were prepared for a considerable wait.

§

A servant poured steaming coffee from a large, solid silver pot, into a delicate porcelain cup. The Manager indicated his client.

"Cream for Senhor Morrison," he said.

Mac held his cup steady and accepted cream, which was also taken by two of the associates and the grim little assistant.

Braga waited until the servant had gone and the door firmly closed, then spoke.

"We, Maua and Company, wish to deal no further in foreign exchange at this time."

"Oh," said Mac. "Why?"

"We have enough," answered Braga abruptly. He looked at his associates, then deliberately sipped his coffee—his gaze fixed, as were all the others, on Mac. It was a game. The reward was freedom, but if Mac made one false move . . . Incarceration was, Mac knew, a poor euphemism for what faced lawbreakers in the tropics; so he moved not a muscle and said not a word.

"Tomorrow," Braga began eventually, "a ship leaves for Liverpool. All bills of exchange accepted, and sums paid out on letters of credit issued from England—these, including your first transaction with us, will return for our reimbursement. Perhaps, if you could wait—something more than a month, but less than six weeks?''

"I am afraid," said Mac, "I am unable to do that." He did not think that his statement would surprise anyone. It didn't. What happened then filled Mac with sheer terror for a split second, as Braga suddenly sprang to his feet and, behind Mac, the door burst open.

Mac stood up slowly, then turned to greet this new arrival.

"Mr. Morrison," said Braga, "Senhor Meyers, our broker on the Exchange."

Mac extended a hand and tried a smile. Neither worked. Meyers merely bowed quickly, crossed the room and sat down on a chair hurriedly vacated by one of the associates. Meyers donned glasses and looked for a moment at this Senhor Morrison. Mac sat down.

"To business," said Meyers. "Where are the letters?"

The Assistant Manager was already moving.

§

In the hot city square, two men sat on one bench, two on another. Both in the shade. Forty yards apart, it seemed as if they were oblivious of each other. A clock chimed the quarter. Austin lost his composure.

"I'm goin' in."

"Don't be a damn fool," George whispered forcefully. But it was too late: Austin was already moving.

§

Comparing the two signatures, Mac's with the original, was, for Meyers, not a lengthy business. He looked up—first to Mac, then across at the Manager.

"Do they appear to be in order, Senhor Meyers?" asked Braga.

"They have," replied Meyers, "that appearance."

Everyone in the room seemed to relax. Meyers and Mac for a second looked at each other in mutual appraisal.

"Then, Mr. Morrison," said Braga, "although I feel we

cannot offer you further credit, if you wish it Senhor Meyers will sell your bills on the Exchange. This, I think, is a small service we can supply, as your letters of introduction appear . . ." Here Braga shrugged and again looked at Meyers, whose eyes had narrowed; but Braga finished first:

". . . that is, of course, provided Senhor Meyers is satisfied. All is in order?" He addressed himself to Meyers.

"All is as it should be," said Meyers. But he paused. Then:

"May I see the other letters again, with the originals?"

The Manager handed him the whole sheaf. Instinct or experience, Mac never knew, but his throat promptly went bone-dry.

§

In the public banking section of Maua and Company, customers, depositing or drawing, walked from counter to cash teller, queued in ragged lines or came and went with smiles or long faces, depending on their balances.

Austin stepped from the long corridor into this busy but hushed scene and sat on an upholstered sofa with a view out into the corridor and down to the Manager's office. He wiped his brow with a colored handkerchief and murmured nervously to himself, "Come on, Mac!"

§

Meyers was seated directly beneath the lazy fan in the Manager's office. Distant cries from the city penetrated the closed shutters but did not disturb his concentration. All eyes were fixed on the papers in Meyers' hands as they were shuffled, read and shuffled again.

Mac was immobile, his toes curled, throat tight, face frozen. Slowly Meyers stiffened; put down the papers on his lap, still rereading what he had found; then, taking off his glasses, he focused on Mac and, it seemed to his prey, poised like a snake about to strike.

"There is here, a word, Mr. Morrison," Meyers began, "that I cannot understand."

Mac's eyebrows toyed with the unexpected for a moment, then transferred a message to his mouth. It wasn't received.

" 'All sums,' and I quote," continued Meyers, looking quickly at the others, " 'all sums drawn against this credit please endorce on the back and notify the London and Westminster Bank at once.' " He paused.

"Why, sir," said Mac confidently, "that is the normal practice, is it not?"

"Why, sir," said Meyers, uneven teeth showing, "indeed it is, and being so it makes me wonder at the education of London clerks, which hitherto I have never had cause to question."

Mac could only say, "I don't follow you."

"Then you shall," said Meyers with relish, "you shall." He turned to the Manager and indicated two points on both letters. The assistant made the transfer smoothly, taking a quick look himself.

Braga looked at the letters and made a comparison. He murmured something in Portuguese to the associates on either side of him, then looked at Mac, as now did all in the room.

"It is essential in international business that common parlance be uniform, would you agree?" Meyers said to Mac.

"I would," said Mac.

"Then can you explain," asked Meyers grimly, "why in your letters—and in my experience, in your letters only—the word 'endorse' is misspelled with, instead of an S—a C?"

Porcelain china is delicate. It breaks easily. If a cup is correctly placed in a saucer and is firmly held, there is no danger, but age or nerves are often culprits—causes of a chip or hairline crack. After that, the set is less than perfect, and the value is obviously diminished.

For this reason the Manager of Maua and Company, Senhor Braga, would always have a reminder of Mr. Morrison. But on that Tuesday at the beginning of July 1872, he heard the only sound that broke a sudden complete silence, as did all the others in the large cool office: the rattle of bone china in a hand somewhat less than steady.

To Mac, it was uncontrollable—and he tried. His other hand did the only thing possible: he took the cup from the saucer in the hope that it would find his mouth.

§

During a lull in the morning's business, a teller at a counter in the banking section of Maua and Company saw a young man of foreign dress seated in the corner on a sofa, looking in a quite concentrated way out into the corridor that led in two directions—to the main entrance, or along to the Manager's office. The teller's curiosity was only fleeting. It was not an unusual sight. To Austin it was detection and discovery—for a moment. He calmed his nervous fear, smiled weakly at the teller, who looked back at the figures before him, and thought only of luncheon. Austin crossed his legs. God in heaven, he thought, I need a drink.

§

In the square—the *praça*—outside Maua and Company, George breathed deeply and stood up to stretch. The clock in the tower struck the half, and perhaps by coincidence, the two other men forty yards distant stood up also. George now felt for sure something was wrong. The gnarling fear that had knotted his stomach was now suddenly confirmation to instinct. His immediate, suppressed reaction could be summed up in a single word . . .

. . . Panic

<hr style="border-top: 3px double;">

THE room at Maua and Company, was still. Meyers, staring at "this Mr. Morrison," knew for certain that he had a victim.

Mac strove valiantly to control the welling fear of a situation that, disastrous as it was, could become catastrophic at a gesture. He took the entire minute to look from each face to the other, as if a trial lawyer paused before concluding his case, surveying a hostile jury.

Mac was on pure reflexes. Quelling obscenities directed at the group in front of him—Meyers in particular—and his own stupidity, he delved deep into experience and instinct. Even the city outside, it seemed to him, was hushed and expectant. He slowly put down the cup and saucer on a small table beside his chair and stood up. He was Jesus before Pilate. Joan at her inquisition. Hancock declaring Independence. Lincoln addressing the North. His feet were firm, his eyes hard, his voice strong—and his back ran with perspiration.

"Gentlemen . . ." he began, ". . . a neglected procedure and a clerical error have been imputed to my charge as if it were I to blame. This . . ." He paused, looking from Braga,

137

who turned away his eyes, to Meyers, who did not. ". . . behavior to arouse suspicion of my honor persuades me to deal elsewhere."

Mac looked directly at the grim little assistant, who was not unimpressed and, extending a hand, snapped his fingers loudly. Mac's right index pointed at the papers on the desk. The assistant took them up as if compelled and, open-mouthed, handed them across to Mac. Slowly, without looking at the letters and bills, Mac folded them, then put them in his pocket. He held the group successfully a moment longer as he calculated the distance to the door behind him. Quiet and decisive, another voice spoke.

"Mr. Morrison," Meyers began, not at all cowed, as were the others, by Mac's demeanor, "I would prefer it if you would remain, to explain—"

Ignoring Meyers, Mac turned, walked to the door, then spun round to interrupt.

"Your veiled accusations put you, sir"—Mac's voice was low, harsh and venomous—"within an ace of a bullet at tomorrow's dawn."

He paused with a meaning that communicated itself in any language.

"Should you utter a single word more before I leave this"—Mac looked about him, affecting mild disgust —"place," he stared into Meyers' eyes "you shall have it!"

Mac turned, opened the door smoothly and stepped out into the corridor. The room remained mesmerized as the large oak door slammed shut.

Mac strode purposefully toward the main entrance, where he could see sunlight streaming across the hall. Halfway down the corridor, a face and figure appeared at an open doorway. Mac had eight paces, a turn, three more and at least he'd make the steps; after that . . .

Austin was relieved, then astonished as Mac, without a glance, strode by.

"Mac!"

"The pack is behind me, boy," Mac replied. "Run while you can."

§

George watched Mac take the steps two at a time, reach the mosaic pavement, then turn quickly toward the city center and the nearest crowd. George also saw, as Mac did not, the group of men appear at the portico—hesitant, it seemed; half in, half out of the sun. The gesture one of them made was directly toward him—or so, for a moment, George thought. The Hebrew was beckoning.

The two men in the square responded to Meyers and from their bench covered forty yards, to be at the vehicle opposite the company entrance in admirable time. The carriage spun round; with the crack of a whip, the two men urged the mules in the direction Mac had taken.

The group remained at the top of the steps, now talking excitedly; only Meyers looked all around—as if instinct told him Mac would not venture alone to such a meeting.

George, masked by the palm trees, crossed to where Austin now stood breathless.

"It's all up, George!"

Seeing, through the drooping palms, that some of the group were halfway down the steps, George pushed Austin from him.

"Okay," he said, "let's get out of here. You follow Mac. I'll organize the tickets and convert our cash to gold. We've got less than twenty-four hours."

They left the square separately to mingle quickly with crowds in the labyrinth of streets.

Passage "Home"

FROM a well-bred combination of Irish and Scots, the second generation of American MacDonalds had produced a son capable of a Harvard education that had failed to teach him the spelling of a simple word. Lolling in the armchair of his hotel rooms, slapping at the small *bichos*—the insects—that were flying around, Mac cursed himself loudly once again. He stood up, remembered his lit cheroot, walked once more to the open shutters and stepped onto the balcony with half a bottle of imported Irish whiskey in his stomach and a glass in hand. He was fast becoming drunk.

Below the gaslights on the terrace, where, as was usual each evening, violins played sweet romantic melodies, the large, dark-featured Rio citizen sat, as he had since one o'clock that afternoon, looking up at Mac's windows.

Tonight the sky was clear, and the Southern Hemisphere offered its stars embedded in a deepening purple heaven. At any other time, Mac would have enjoyed naming those he knew, but now his mood was almost black; not in despair—Mac was angry. His temperament would not allow inefficiency as an excuse of any kind.

Here he was, the focus of the biggest blunder he'd ever made. He was, he decided, becoming one of the fly-by-night idiots who were snapped up in New York streets almost as the ink dried on their first attempt at forgery. By God, he thought, I'd better face the word now, because I'll soon be hearing it resound in some courtroom before my incarceration behind bars or down some pit on a work island, a prisoner—guest of the Brazilian regime, detained at its pleasure.

He had never been unaware of the risks he ran. In fact, that was a part of the excitement he sought. It made him the man he was, fighting a bureaucratic system he knew well, and despised for its hypocrisy. When a man understood the power of money, he knew the machinery of human motivation. To Mac, money was like the counters of a game. What would he do with vast sums, anyway? He enjoyed what he did. He was good. The best—or had been. The first bill had been without fault, as the transaction at Mauá proved, but the letters . . .

Omissions were worse than a heavy stamp, poor-quality paper or too light an ink; to an omission found, there was no answer. But to be faulted on a spelling! Dear God in heaven, Mac thought, as he looked up to the night sky's zenith, is this why you brought me to this sleazy little tropical city? Am I to end here? Mac's thoughts were interrupted by a quiet knock at the door. He shouted, "Come in!"

Austin entered, closed the door and crossed to Mac gingerly. Insensitively, he ignored his friend's mood.

"They're in the lobby, the hall and outside—front and back."

To Mac's ears it was said with relish, and he turned to his so-called friend, who was actually smiling.

"Terrific," said Mac.

"Bags all packed?" Austin continued to grin.

"What do you think?" asked Mac sarcastically.

"Three weeks from now we'll be laughing at all this." Austin gestured, as if to take in not only the hotel but the entire city.

"Let's," said Mac emphatically, "talk about *now*."

"Okay." Austin moved away. "Let's go."

"You mean," asked Mac, as if Austin were an idiot, "just walk out of here?"

"That's right," grinned Austin. "George is at the station."

Uncomprehending, Mac remained at the balcony, incredulous.

"Look," Austin continued, "they still don't have proof for certain. The only thing they can do is wait the forty days till the word comes back from England for them to be sure. So you can travel around." Austin paused, understanding the strain his friend was under.

"Wonderful," said Mac sarcastically.

"They won't arrest you."

"Even better."

"They know you can't leave the country!"

Mac turned on Austin, who finished lamely, "So . . ."

"So . . . ?" questioned Mac. He opened his arms in answer, a gesture indicating that he had no choice.

"In an hour," Austin now went on quickly, "you're going downstairs, telling the clerk where you're off to—and then taking the train a thousand miles up the Amazon."

"What?" Mac was more than confused.

"Well," said Austin, withholding laughter, "they've a great opera house in Manaus; you can sit and swill with the rubber barons—they're goin' bust too!"

"Now, listen, Bidwell," began Mac ominously.

"Only," finished Austin, "you'll be Liverpool-bound."

Mac frowned and sardonically started, "How in hell am I—" He was cut off as outside a firecracker exploded and loud, fast music from the streets drowned even Austin's laughter. He began to shout over the noise, details of a plan he and George had conceived for Mac.

§

Bem inglês is a Brazilian expression meaning "quite English." It was used most often to describe an Englishman in his cups, in a public place. Eventually the term became one that was applicable to white, English-speaking Anglo-Saxons en masse.

It was the expression laughingly exchanged by two porters and the receptionist at the Hotel Extrangeiros as Mac strode boldly out of the main lobby and tripped down the steps toward his waiting carriage. Austin, in the marble foyer, seated to one side under the potted palms, made a note, despite the grimness of the situation, to remind Mac exactly of his very public exit as all others in the lobby attempted to understand a tune the seemingly drunk American was bellowing to the ceiling, floor, walls, pillars and any willing face that turned in his direction.

Austin watched the large Portuguese detective fold his paper slowly; then, rising from the corner sofa, cross to the main entrance. Outside, Mac climbed into the carriage already loaded with his luggage and made the first of what were to be several departures.

§

Although the holiday on the Eve of St. John was over, the excitement created by great beach fires, lit to observe the event, still lingered. Dancing processions in conga lines or maxixe groups continued in the streets.

To Mac it seemed that the lascivious nature of the people, their languid movements with strong sexual overtones instinctively responding to a fast background rhythm, created dance forms that illustrated their unrepressed pleasure in obvious abilities frowned on by the more cloistered spirits of Rio society.

Thus it was that the poor quarters of Rio remained alive, with a throng reluctant to relinquish this festival spirit. So when Mac arrived at the Estacão Dom Pedro II, ostensibly to take the train north, the streets were alive with lights, music and dancing figures in brilliant costumes and masks. The immediate future, Mac knew, would be decisive; if he failed, the two "tails" would know he was on the run, and he would, without doubt, be taken by the authorities. But he had no alternative.

Mac walked into the station. At the ticket office he booked a first-class journey, far from direct, that would end eventually at Manaus, then turned to supervise his luggage, now being carried onto the platform.

Mac could see George outside the entrance, according to plan, seated in the rear of a mule-drawn brougham. Fireworks

illuminated the night behind him, and then the silhouette that
George had become for a moment lost its edge and once more
Mac saw only a pale face, patient, impassive, awaiting the
agreed-upon signal.

Mac took off his hat, hit the crown once, replaced it, turned
and walked through the crowd assembled outside the station's
barrier, to gain access to the second platform and a train that
would take him north into the nighttime oblivion of a vast
jungle.

George watched the two detectives—one apparently Portuguese, the other a dark-featured Brazilian, both too large to
be inconspicuous—speak a few moments with the office
through an open hatchway; then, having purchased tickets,
they followed in the direction in which Mac had gone.

The harsh shriek of a double whistle startled all the gaslit
faces of a predominantly mulatto crowd on the platform.
Those who were traveling, hastily disengaged from their well-
wishers to board the long train. Railways were still something
of a novelty in South America, and the many who had not
traveled before made no attempt to conceal their wonder, joy
or fear at the adventure they were about to undertake.

At the rear of the train, Mac supervised the loading of his
luggage. He now knew the faces of both detectives quite well.
They tried hard to merge into the bustle and panic of the platform, but were too obviously calm and sure of their task,
shadowing Mac; consequently, perhaps only to Mac, they
stood out—one nearby reading a paper, the other farther up
the platform. Mac was boxed in.

Overhead, the large station clock dropped its minute hand
to sixty seconds from the half hour, and again a whistle
echoed beneath the high, galleried station roof. The last of
Mac's bags were aboard the baggage car. The porter stood
grinning at the long sliding door.

A railway official aboard had checked each piece and
stacked them together against the opposite side of the railway
car; he now joined the porter. Forty seconds to go. Mac
looked quickly behind him at the guard with his whistle and
green flag. Quickly Mac reached up and gave the porter what,
when it was counted minutes later, was a huge tip.

Thirty seconds. The Portuguese detective watched the

porter shake hands briefly with the railway official, then climb down from the baggage car onto the platform. He became lost in the crowd. The railway official shook hands with the American; then the two men parted and the sliding door was pulled across. The American began to walk beside the train. The Portuguese detective folded his paper; remembered the directive from his employer, Senhor Braga, to "follow this Morrison" wherever; thought of the advance in his office safe and began to make his way up the platform after the tall American.

Twenty seconds. Mac passed each carriage of third and second class, looking through the compartments beyond the figures at each window crowding forward for a last farewell. Each compartment was self-contained, with its own door. Farther ahead the first-class section shone—fine wood polished to a reflection.

Fifteen seconds. Another blast from the engine's whistle, and Mac increased his pace. Ahead, the Brazilian detective was walking with a firm stride; one behind, one in front, the two "tails" kept pace with Mac until all three could see the engine in front pouring out steam onto the platform and, above, smoke into the great space beneath the high glass and metal-grid roof. A long moaning blast sounded out. The engineer looked to the rear. The guard waved a flag.

Five seconds. A piercing cry called out by the guard provoked last embraces, kisses, the reluctant tears and arms aloft that a departure always elicits from those who must stay. Mac walked on, still nonchalant. Suddenly the great engine jerked forward, and tremors passed through each carriage. Six massive wheels bit into the iron rail and began to pull their huge load with slowly mounting speed.

The three men were now walking faster through the waving relatives and friends. The Brazilian in front anxiously turned, to see that his quarry seemed not to care whether he boarded or remained in the station. The large Portuguese detective behind was struggling to keep up. He cursed. What the hell was the American playing at?

Mac timed it perfectly. The moment before the trio would have had to break into a run to stay with the moving train, he turned in mid-stride, reached out for a handle, opened the door of what he knew to be a first-class compartment and hoisted himself in.´ Immediately, front and rear, the two detectives followed suit; then both, pushing away others in the compartments they had entered, leaned out the windows—in second class, where the Portuguese found himself, and a mere gap in third class, where the Brazilian had boarded—to ensure that Mac was ensconced for the night.

Smoke and steam obliterated much of the crowd and platform, but both men assured themselves that their quarry lay between them. They sat down in their compartments, satisfied to wait until the first stop, two hours away.

The Rio businessman and his wife were both astonished by the late arrival of a tall American, but that was nothing to his exit. Mac, on entering the first-class compartment, oblivious of any occupants, crossed two paces to a corresponding door on the other side, leaned through the open window into the steam and smoke, released the lock and leaped out.

Mac rolled painfully on the gravel, then lay absolutely still as the wheels of fifteen carriages passed him. He looked up only as the baggage car went by, now traveling with considerable speed. The railway official was sliding shut the car's off-side door. A brief salute from the man could have been to Mac, or across to another colleague: Mac never knew; he just felt a surge of gratitude that finally something of which he was a part had worked.

A distant cry into the night, as if from a lost wolf cub, and the train was only a memory. Steam and smoke settled in the station. Crowds dispersed to fondly cherish whatever images they retained of their loved ones. Few people looked at Mac as he stood shakily, then brushed himself down.

The porter appeared and pointed down the line to what, even from forty yards, looked to Mac like a pile of luggage—his. They reached the bags and cases; the porter grinned.

"In one side, senhor, and out the other."

Mac knew enough Portuguese to understand. He smiled ruefully, bruises taking the edge off his immediate pleasure.

"Senhor," said another voice.

Mac looked up and saw George. He closed his eyes in

disbelief at the success of their plan. George finished in the same mock South American accent.

"Your carriage awaits."

The ride into the night streets of Rio was, as Mac would always recall, like a strange dream; figures appeared, torches flickered, fire was in the sky and fast music seemed to come out of the very walls of buildings that flashed by at a speed George continually urged from the brougham's driver.

The whiskey Mac had since taken to relieve the pain of his bruises had released again what he'd already consumed. His intoxication this time was euphoric; a silent grin and lolling eyes showed George that Mac's tension was ebbing away. George offered the whiskey once more. They had been lucky—so far; now there was only the one hurdle remaining. The Cais Pharoux.

The brougham emerged from the labyrinth of streets into the Praça Maua, where at the center a great fire blazed and costumed crowds circled slowly, moving to a rhythm created by maracas, drums, tins, instruments of every kind, manufactured or improvised. The colors, light, movement and noise against a background of darkness gave George the feeling that he was a witness to ritual with origins in prehistory. Those crowds, masked and bedecked, were as if Hades-bound; the conjured imaginings of a priest at vigil. George was not superstitious, but that night in Rio, he swore that his shoulders had brushed with ghosts, and the entrance to the hereafter —Heaven or Hell—had not been far from that square. Of course, this conviction might also have been attributed to the whiskey Mac had been unable to finish. Truth to say, George was himself partially drunk, but not without a purpose.

§

The two boatmen had been well paid and were in no hurry when they saw the Senhor and Senhorita come out of the small café on the Pharoux docks. The Senhor had already indicated the luggage in the carriage, and it had been duly loaded onto the boat. The brougham paid off, the Senhor, with a sizable valise which he insisted he must retain, had gone back to the half-built customhouse to sign his exit visa and find his companion. One of the boatmen nodded to the other; as they well understood, tonight was for pleasure—or money.

The Senhorita on the Senhor's arm was no surprise to the boatmen. They decided that as soon as they returned from the long row out to the ship *Ebro* they would acquire their own equivalent of this vision before them. George, returning from the Port and Customs office, sensed the boatmen's reaction and played to it. Police on the Cais Pharoux were walking in pairs everywhere.

The last thirty minutes had not been easy for George. Half drunk in reality, he had appeared completely *bem inglês* to the port police, and with a sympathetic amusement they reserved for the wealthy Anglo-Saxon, the formal exit of a Mr. Wilson from Rio de Janeiro had been documented. George smiled his thanks and took back the stamped passport; he had left the office as easily as they all would, he hoped, leave Rio.

The Senhorita was a blind. For George it would mean, in the state he continued to assume, that he would, to the boatmen, be just another *inglês*—or *americano* if they were sharp-eared—who wished a final night of joy from the female wealth of South America. "What women we have, eh?" they exclaimed to the prostrate form of George, propped with the Senhorita at the rear of the boat as they rode away from the hell of Rio behind them.

What big feet they have, thought George as he looked at the not altogether attractive company he had the misfortune to accompany aboard ship.

With much nudging and winking up at the quite obviously drunken port officer above, on deck of the *Ebro*, the two boatmen helped the Senhor and his Senhorita onto the floating platform and thence, by gangway, on board. Face to face, George and the port officer—who could barely see the passport or ticket George proffered—were, to all who cared to observe, brothers in their cups. Both swayed a little, George trying to keep time.

"A night's entertainment, senhor," he said. "A last taste of Latin beauty."

"*Sim*, Senhor Wilson," the port officer managed to get out, squinting at the Senhorita. He belched, then remembered. "But," he went on thickly, "you have another visitor below."

For a moment George became utterly sober; then whiskey determined him to now accept whatever or whomever fate threw up.

"Oh?" he replied. "Then I shall have to get rid of him." He smiled long and slow and clasped his fellow drunk.

"*Boa noite*," said the official, "senhor"; he tipped his hat. "Senhorita"; he bowed slightly.

George and his liaison of the night went across the moonlit deck, where peace predominated, broken only by muted sounds and distant fire flashes from the city, several miles across the water. Feeling, for a moment, a tranquillity in the tropic night, George allowed the sobering effect to penetrate deep before accompanying the obviously eager Senhorita below.

The facetious behavior of the two boatmen with the port official, as the luggage Mac had brought with him to the Cais Pharoux, was unloaded, could have entertained a theater audience quite successfully. The sight of a burly laborer of indeterminate parentage carrying heavy luggage up, and waltzing down, the suspended gangway, in imitation of a bawdy Portuguese female, eventually took all three to their backsides on deck, leaning against the ship's rail to share the contents of a gallon drum of liquor with a broken seal that had already incapacitated the port official.

In the end, more than an hour later, all three went overboard to compete for the best dive; sobered sufficiently to want more pleasures of the flesh; then went ashore to the Pharoux, where, arm in arm, the three crossed the *praça*, still surging with life, and entered a labyrinth of delights that liquor can make of the most squalid brothel, if money can buy.

Belowdecks in his cabin on the *Ebro*, George was not so lucky.

"And now, my angel," George said. He reached for the Senhorita's veil.

"I could kiss you," said Mac, and lifted the veil for himself.

George was about to roar with well-earned laughter when

he saw the two large black bags on either side of what was the back of a deep leather armchair. The man slumped in the seat was concealed by the wide wings connected by a high, studded arch in the English style. He suddenly stood up, turned round and surprised them both. Mac gasped; George was only momentarily startled. The figure was, of course, Austin. He kicked open one of the black bags and began uncorking several of the bottles of claret he had cradled for two hours.

George took from one of the bags several of the ten small but heavy sacks. He shook them: gold.

"You'll never know how difficult—" began Austin.

George interrupted. "Perhaps you might have preferred to buy the Senhorita's clothes?" They all burst into laughter and then the now united trio began to drink.

Three separate splashes outside the cabin, and the subsequent boisterous Portuguese as the boatmen and port official clambered into the vessel that was to take them to their sexual destinations that night, were heard some time later only by Mac, whose eyes flickered, seeing his companions, as exhausted as he was, sprawled asleep on the two brass beds. Lying in a leather armchair, Mac wiped the red paint from his lips and rouge from his cheeks. George was right—he could never have done it sober. If they could get through the next twelve hours to a clanging of bells and the midday sailing time, they would be, this time at least, tantamount to being home and dry.

Mac was never quite sure whether it was reality, a phantom or a vision of the future, but through the open porthole, in a flash of light, as a firework silently exploded in the distance, he saw on the peak of the mountain Corcovado a great silhouette of Christ, arms spread—beneficent. Before he faded into sleep that night, Mac said a little prayer.

§

The sparkling waters of Guanabara Bay glistened as the hot tropic sun beat down without mercy. Already much of the morning had passed, and aboard the *Ebro* preparations had almost been completed to depart. The small boat in the distance meant very little to most of the passengers, who were taking their last look at South America.

But to George, who was settled in a chair at the bow, the approaching vessel was trouble. An elderly Portuguese with whom George had struck up acquaintance lent him a telescopic eyeglass that confirmed his worst suspicions. The boat, seen more fully, was by no means small. It was a Customs launch with an engine—a steam pinnace. Several faces were turned toward the *Ebro* as its speed of eight knots brought the craft nearer.

George identified Braga, Maua and Company's Manager; his assistant, seen only briefly by George on the steps of the company building before Mac's pursuit, and—worse— Senhor Meyers, broker on the Exchange. George suddenly felt the heat. The elderly Portuguese excitedly, but politely, asked for the glass as the small boat began to flash a light. The little Morse code George had picked up in the Army was enough to confirm his fears. Sweat began to bead his brow. He broke open his collar. So near and yet so far.

They were coming to search the ship. For Mac, the police uniforms and port officials on the craft were too numerous to hope that they might escape a cursory check; this was to be thorough. George bowed to the Portuguese and left as the old man stood up to peer at the small boat, which had already disappeared beneath the high bow.

As George reached the steps to go below, he heard engines cut and voices shouting orders, directed at the other craft offloading final supplies, to clear a path to the floating platform and gangway.

§

"They're gonna check the ship, boys!" said George grimly.

Mac sat down slowly—now ashen. "My God, George . . ." he began.

Austin looked quickly at George. "What are we going to do?"

George was looking over the large room of his cabin with a thoroughness that even Meyers would have envied. Austin,

George could explain, was merely a friend come to bid "Mr. Wilson" farewell. Then they both might question their interrogators for a more accurate description of this suspected blackguard, for if they should catch a mere glimpse of him in the future, they could immediately inform the relevant authorities—that, at least, was the way the conversation should go. In point of fact, Austin had not bought a ticket at that time because, should the unexpected occur, as indeed it was at that very moment, he would at least be on hand, and anonymous, to attempt some aid should Mac require it—if he were unavoidably detained in the tropics.

George looked at Mac. Now he was really shaken. It was eleven o'clock precisely.

§

"Where is the ticket agent?" Braga's voice was authoritative and brought the man running over between boxes and cartons. Slaves, merchants, officials, officers and sailors milled about on deck as cargo was stowed away down the foreward hatch, and bags ported to the individual cabins of first and second class. Third and steerage had a separate gangway to the rear of the ship and enjoyed accommodation on a par with the sacks of coffee now filling the cargo holds.

"I am here, senhores, I am here," said the agent as he arrived at the group. It was unnecessary, but he saluted. The group was imposing, to say the least.

"We wish to see the passports." The voice that said this was quiet and incisive. Meyers seldom became agitated. Beneath the hot sun, he, as the others did not, looked decidedly cool and was sure that this Mr. Morrison was aboard and theirs for the taking.

The port official, now again on duty, was suffering from the night that had finished only three hours before. He clicked his heels, bowed, then led the dignitaries to his superior in the makeshift office of the Purser's cabin.

§

At eleven o'clock, all who were sailing on the *Ebro* were

aboard—but not all who were aboard were necessarily sailing. At the hatches and below in the hold, dock workers who had been rowed out to complete final loading of cargo and provisions would be taken off immediately prior to departure.

On deck, in the corridors and staterooms that led off them, leaning against the rail outside the open doors of their cabins, passengers conversed with family and friends until the last moment, when (as they knew) warning bells were rung indicating that visitors must be put ashore, either on the large steam pinnace or by the myriad rowboats that lay round about the *Ebro*.

In the Purser's Office, the passenger manifest was scrutinized by the group of dignitaries, who were aware that, once at sea aboard the British ship, their man would have effectively escaped them. All likely names and descriptions presented by the agent were questioned by Braga. Meyers referred directly to the passports.

Time was running out for the group, as Meyers well knew: the Captain had been adamant that his ship would sail on the stroke of twelve or Maua and Company would answer for it. No proof existed, only suspicion, which was insufficient to delay the *Ebro*'s schedule; therefore, prompt action had to be taken by Braga, on Meyers' advice—action that was appearing, every minute, more fruitless. Suddenly Meyers was up and moving.

"The ship is not so large, and the reason to inquire not so inadequate, that we cannot, Senhor Braga, request a tour of the cabins and rooms in first and second class." He paused as all in the small, hot Purser's Office understood that this man was not to be satisfied by mere talk. It was eleven twenty-three.

"I am sure the agent will comply with our request, Senhor Braga," said Meyers, looking first at the chief police officer, then at the agent.

The port official, regretting his debauched night, coughed, loosened his collar and thought of the heat belowdecks from which there was no respite until the ship was under way and ventilated by a sea breeze.

Had the agent lived in Liverpool, he might well have argued successfully that he had done all that was in his power, and to

disturb his passengers at the outset of a long voyage was out
of the question. But he lived in Rio de Janeiro, and the men
before him were powerful figures of that city. It was difficult.
He gestured helplessly.

"If it is your wish, senhores."

"As I hope it is yours, senhor," said Meyers pointedly, "in
the interest of justice."

"Of course," said the agent.

The men left the room in order of importance. The duty
port official, who now felt sick, was last.

The *Ebro* was not so big that the procession, snakelike now
as it moved down the corridors, could not manage to
scrutinize all in first and second class. The agent had reassembled his charm, and a succession of "only a formality,
senhor, senhorita, my apologies," et cetera, issued forth,
ignored by Meyers and Braga, who, as they inspected the occupants of cabins and rooms, merely nodded and passed on.

At eleven forty the first bells sounded out above, startling
most of the police, who were basically of landlubber mentality
and had no desire to be trapped aboard ship. The procession
continued. Passports and tickets were produced, when called
for by Meyers, from a box carried behind the agent. All, ex-
cept Meyers, were now sweating profusely. At the rear, the
port official, who was counting the minutes fervently, felt as
bad as a human being is allowed to this side of the grave.

The inevitable rap on the door heralded the group outside
number 8. A stateroom, said the agent, occupied by
one—Wilson. Yes, he did know the man. Indeed he was
American, but by no means was he the type, he emphasized,
described by the honorable Senhor Braga; nor did he fit the
description.

George had seen to it that the ticket agent and Mr. Wilson
knew each other well. He had plagued the man with
questions—reductions on his ticket, the seaworthiness of
Ebro, the inadequacies and unreliability of steam power, the
expense of modern sea travel; all these had served to
exasperate the agent, who looked forward to going ashore to
an office where he would be certain to find peace—Mr.
Wilson being Liverpool-bound far out into the ocean. Nevertheless, the door of number 8 was opened by Meyers, who

stood at the threshold and looked in.

Two men, disheveled by the heat, coats flung on a bunk below the porthole, were drinking iced claret—shirt sleeves rolled, ties undone.

George and Austin turned to see their "unexpected" guest, Senhor Meyers. Both smiled in polite question at their visitor.

"A formality . . ." began the agent.

"We are searching, gentlemen," said Meyers, "for a suspected criminal."

"Oh!" said Austin.

"Indeed!" said George.

"Are you both traveling?" asked Meyers.

"Mr. Wilson is Liverpool-bound," said the agent.

"And this gentleman," said George, indicating Austin, "has come to bid me farewell."

Meyers looked long and hard about the room, then entered and walked to a spot where he could see through into the adjoining *chambre à coucher*. The bath area was to one side behind a partition. All was neat, prepared for the voyage.

Meyers' eyes sought for a single clue. He saw nothing but luggage and souvenirs.

"Is all that your baggage, sir?" he asked.

"Any excess can be stored as cargo until required on the voyage, Senhor Meyers," interjected the agent.

Bells again sounded above. This time longer, in double peals.

"I see," said Meyers. George smiled.

"You do not travel light, Mr. Wilson," said Meyers.

"I do not," said George. He smiled again. Silence held the room.

A final double peal of bells faded.

"You will miss the boat back to Rio, senhor," said Meyers to Austin.

"I sincerely hope not," said Austin. "Your beautiful city is one I hope to enjoy further before I replace it with fond memories."

"You are a poet?" asked Meyers, with more than a trace of sarcasm.

"A businessman," said Austin.

"Oh?" said Meyers. "In what do you deal?"

Austin took a long draw on the cheroot he had in his hand
and saw at that moment the veil and shawl Mac had worn the
night before, lying between his own white and pale gray check
and George's dark frock coat on the bunk. He became aware
of a prickling sensation that was growing by the second as
Meyers persisted. Bells again rang—now throughout the ship.

"Senhor Meyers," said Braga, "it is fifteen minutes before
twelve. . . . I fear we must . . ." He did not finish.

"Gentlemen," said Austin decisively, "my partner and I
must conclude our conversation, which pertains to private
matters. I am sure you understand."

Meyers did not move, but the others nodded and began to
leave. Meyers saw the veil.

"Are you married, senhor?" he said quickly to George.

Austin saw that George was taken aback and had no idea
how important his reply would be.

"He hopes, senhor," Austin said quickly, "to be."

"Oh?" said Meyers.

"To my sister," replied Austin.

George was wide-eyed at the tack his brother had taken.
Shouts in Portuguese from the waiting boats outside now interrupted the moment's silence.

"It is an excellent institution, as you say," said Meyers,
"provided you find the right woman."

"We, senhor, in America," replied Austin firmly, "say
'lady.' "

"Of course," said Meyers, looking George up and down.
He bowed slightly, making his opinion of the two men obvious. He was unimpressed. Meyers backed to the door.

"I hope she enjoys the gift." He indicated the bunk.

George turned quickly, saw the veil and shawl, absorbed
the shock, then recovered to reply smoothly, "I hope you find
your man."

"We will," said Meyers. He paused, then suddenly with
forced pleasantry he asked, "What is beneath your bunk, Mr.
Wilson?"

As if stunned, George was unable to think; he froze.

"Oranges," said Austin.

Meyers raised his brows. With a smile Austin stood up,
crossed to the bunk, knelt and opened the end two-foot-

square panel door. He thrust in his hand, found the bag and grasped a single orange, withdrew his arm, closed the panel, stood up and smiled at Meyers.

"Fresh," he said, and offered it.

Irritated by the young man's impudence, Meyers shook his head, bowed quickly and went, followed by the entourage.

Austin was about to close the stateroom door when the port official, who was just managing to remain on his feet, appeared and looked into the cabin. His cursory glance was mere curiosity, but he saw the veil immediately. He pointed. George swallowed. Austin blanched, then offered him the orange. The official took it, nodded his thanks, then winked hugely. He left to join the others on deck.

Bells clanging were drowned by the ship's horn as *Ebro* gave out to the entire bay that she was about to sail. The group at the top of the gangway to the floating platform halted. Austin watched; he had come on deck to ensure that they went and, should Meyers be observant still, to show that he too was about to embark for the shore. One by one the group descended to the waiting Customs pinnace.

Austin wiped sweat from his face and took a last look around at the clear sky above peaks that rose from a haze over the city in the distance. The water sparkled, offering instant relief from the heat. Austin longed for the bath he had promised himself immediately the *Ebro* weighed anchor.

Meyers turned a moment, squinted against the sun and watched Austin, in his white and pale gray check suit, cross to the other side of the ship, where a smaller gangway led down to rowboats that would take last visitors ashore.

Three blasts from the ship resounded over Guanabara Bay and gave dreams to young men ashore, who gazed longingly at the distant vessel. The deep note of engines, coal-fed and steam-driven, was absorbed by the tons of sea churned to foam. *Ebro* slowly turned on an axis, then settled her hull into the water at half ahead slow, as she nosed toward the thousand-yard passage between the Island of Lage and Pão de Açúcar.

Around the mooring, in their small boats which now bobbed up and down, boatmen along with their fares waved farewells to the crowded rails of *Ebro* as her wake increased

and the city began to fall away. All aboard the Customs pinnace were anxious now to be back ashore, sipping cool wine
and, after luncheon, to take their *siesta*, the tropics' relief
from intense midday heat.

Only Meyers searched the small craft now pulling for the
Pharoux. He wanted to find the visitor from Wilson's cabin.
The English-cut white coat with the pale gray check on it
would not be difficult to spot with a telescope. He surveyed
each small boat in turn as it dropped behind the swift-moving
pinnace, and there—in a longboat pulled by two Negroes
—there was the coat, thrown on a sack, beside which lay a
man whose face was hidden.

Meyers put down the telescope and resolved, after the
pinnace had docked, to await the longboat with its several
passengers. It would be only half an hour at most. After all,
fellow Americans abroad normally stuck together; perhaps a
clue . . . something, at least. He looked at the Manager of
Maua and Company. Braga was oblivious of everything but
his unaccustomed discomfort. He, Meyers thought, would
deal with this matter—as he did most things—himself.

§

Of the three two-foot-square panels beneath the berth in
Mr. Wilson's cabin, only the two end ones opened for small
stowage. The bunk was not particularly comfortable, being
just six feet long: for a maid, perhaps ideal—not a man.

George opened the end panel; oranges tumbled everywhere.
Mac could not fall out, as he dearly wished; instead he again
had to crawl painfully, inching his way, body contorted, now
out of the black hole and into sight of George, who aided him
as best he could, pulling, pushing and generally easing the
pain Mac had endured.

Extricated, Mac lay in a pool of sweat on the floor,
breathing heavily.

"Where's Austin?" he wheezed.

"I hope," replied George, "on deck."

"Jesus! George," said Mac, "what the hell else do I have to
do?"

Neither man laughed. It had been too damned near, and

both knew it. Instead, they listened to the sound of freedom: steam horsepower. A deep background note that would be with them for twenty-one days.

On deck, Austin felt a first breeze from the open sea caress his face and leaned back gratefully. Sugar Loaf Mountain was to starboard of the ship, towering above—barren but imposing. For Austin, Páo de Açúcar represented Rio perfectly: a city, he reflected, he would never forget. Clearing the channel, *Ebro* went to half ahead both. As the bow wave lifted and the ship's wake widened, her twin funnels began to trail thick smoke.

§

Even Meyers was hot before the longboat drew into the Cais Pharoux. *Ebro* was out of sight, having left only a smudge of smoke in the sky where she had rounded Açúcar. Meyers watched the well-wishers helped ashore. Two Brazilian women, servants no doubt; a young Portuguese male and . . . Meyers swore . . . only the two Negro rowers. Where was . . . ?

The American had not come ashore, obviously. The Negro rowers were fighting for the white and pale-check English coat, using very basic language. He saw that the young Portuguese was about the same height and shape, and from a distance could well be mistaken for the American.

For a moment, Meyers, astute as ever, toyed with the idea of examining the coat, checking the label, referring to the name and beginning a lengthy process of investigation based only on instinct; but suspicion of this nature was insufficient. Meyers suddenly felt tired. Proof was required to initiate such steps, and he had nothing but unanswered questions. The search would, no doubt, continue in the city. As he walked slowly toward his carriage in the hot square of Praça Maua, he thought to himself, Thank God the responsibility of the ten thousand is not mine.

§

Like an animal catching a scent, the *Ebro* seemed to leap

forward when the open sea appeared ahead—smooth and
calm as the bay behind. Her engines went to full ahead both,
creating a passage of air that swept through the ship, reviving
the packed crowd in steerage, sweltering in their particular
hell.

In the humid corridors of second and first, where on either
side the exhausted passengers sprawled in their cabins, it was
the first reminder of a temperate climate.

To those on deck, heads turned to see the South American
continent recede, cool air soothed the hurt of parting, was a
first consolation for the end of tropical adventure or became a
stimulus for thought of the immediate future—either aboard
and of the hope-for romance at sea or of a destination in
Europe and the continuance of life there. Such a wind, the
first at sea commencing a voyage, is a philosopher's wind.
Even children pause after the excitement of departure to
speculate and wonder.

George, Austin and Mac stood together on deck isolated by
their own private thoughts. Having bathed in Mr. Wilson's
cabin, they were refreshed; their one remaining problem
money could solve.

"I am your Purser for the voyage, gentlemen. Welcome
aboard."

The British voice was a wonderful thing to hear as they
turned to greet the smartly dressed officer in whites.

"And I," said George, "am Mr. Wilson."

"Ah, yes, sir," said the Purser; "the ticket agent in Rio advised me to be sure of your welfare aboard."

"Then," said George, "he put it very well."

He handed the Purser the unheard-of sum of one hundred
pounds, in a single note. Unabashed, the Purser merely said,
"Thank you, sir."

"Now," said George, "these two friends of mine were in
fact awaiting tickets from the agent. Unfortunately, he
was"—George paused and looked at both Austin and
Mac—"not to be found."

"I see, sir," said the Purser. "Then they have a problem."

"*We*," said George meaningfully, "have a problem."

"Quite," said the Purser, looking at his accommodation
list. He continued.

"I take it, sir—money—is not an obstacle?"

"You may so take it, Officer," said George with a twinkle in his eye.

"Good," said the Purser. "Then there will indeed be no problem at all; I have several unoccupied staterooms." He stopped himself and looked up from his clip file. "Will you be taking luncheon?"

"Indeed we shall, Officer," said George.

"For three, then, Mr. Wilson," said the Purser.

"Mr. Morrison," said Mac. The Purser wrote it down.

"Mr. Warren," said Austin. The Purser wrote it down.

"Thank you," said George.

"A pleasure, sirs," said the Purser. "Perhaps I can persuade you . . ." The Purser turned to the young waiter hovering behind him with a tray of full champagne glasses. "A custom for first-class passengers, you understand."

"Of course," said George. Austin and Mac each took a glass. The Purser handed one to George, wished them a pleasant voyage and continued to the port side and a railing where several unaccompanied Portuguese ladies were giggling together.

Mac, exhausted still, but thankful he was literally out from under, said quietly, "That's as near as I ever want to get."

"We're ten thousand in gold better off," began Austin, reminding his friend of the reason for their now successful expedition.

"An' our heads are brimmin' over with experience," Mac finished.

Both men looked at George, who smiled slowly. They raised glasses.

Champagne sparkling in the tropic light, sea gulls wheeling overhead, pale blue sky bleached by the hot sun, indigo sea and the creaming wake of the ship: all these things were to be often recalled by the trio years later—separately.

But at that moment, as the gong sounded out in the dining room for the *haute cuisine* luncheon, they wanted only words to bless their union of glasses and spirit. Three young men with the future before them, and George had to go and say:

"The Bank of England."

Autumn

1872

Edwin Noyes—Recruited

THE Noyes family were taking tea with God. His earthly representative was the Reverend Mr. Evans, who smiled occasionally at Mrs. Noyes and her daughters between sips of the warm beverage which he drank delicately from a china cup with a glazed bottom. He disliked glazed bottoms to his cups—at least, those of the people it was his duty to visit. Glazed bottoms clink; and cups, saucers, clink; tea and sandwiches had become something of a nightmare to him.

Conversations in small communities tended to repeat themselves, and as a catalyst, the Reverend Mr. Evans was not so much running out of subject matter as he was of the need to convey what he had already taken out, hung up and beaten to death at least twice already during each day that passed. Always he encountered sincerity in his flock. As they were not with each other, they were almost without exception with him; they would lean forward dewy-eyed, obliging, respectful, hearts bared to reveal innermost thoughts.

The Reverend Mr. Evans was unmarried. Mrs. Noyes was as aware of this fact as she was that her daughters were eligible and provided for, albeit in a small way, by what her husband had left to them all. Her apportioning of the money available had not favored her son, but then, as she constantly reminded herself, he was a man and should take care of himself.

Her praise of Dora's qualities as a cook and Claris' excellent husbandry about the house (a term she was careful to define, with a smile, not unaware of its ambiguous reference) was interrupted by her son, Edwin Noyes—sprawled in a corner chair turning several pages of the paper he was reading.

Although Edwin still sensed shame amongst his family privately, time had eased the attitude of the local community toward his prison record. He had allowed himself to relax—but his mother, ever vigilant of his manners since her son's fall from grace, would have none of it.

"Edwin," she began, authoritatively, "it ain't manners to sit readin' when a man o' God is a-takin' tea with the family."

"Your occupation with the material world, Edwin," said the Reverend Mr. Evans, "seems to afford you little time to think o' the next."

"The Reverend's speakin' to you," said Mrs. Noyes. Edwin put down the paper, looked at the clergyman, revealed a cigar and began to chew off the end.

"You ain't gonna smoke that in here," Mrs. Noyes said. "Like I tol' your father a thousand times, you got a choice!" She paused emphatically.

The grandfather clock chimed five. As all eyes eventually fell on Edwin, he stood up.

"Edwin!" exclaimed his mother.

He moved to the door, taking out matches.

"Come back here," said Mrs. Noyes. It was an imperious command, but her son was already out of the room.

"He's smokin' it, Ma!" cried Dora, whose vantage point allowed her to see Edwin lighting up. From outside, Edwin kicked the door shut.

Ambition destroys many fine things in a man, and Edwin had been sucked into the whirlpool of New York like so many others. Unprotected, he had been vulnerable, and he had been sacrificed to protect others more powerful than he. Now money sent from Mac and the quiet life he led, waiting as Mac had instructed, kept him, if not buoyant, at least afloat.

Months had passed since the cable from Mac. A brief letter from South America, unsigned and evasive in content, obviously concealed a great deal. Edwin was most intrigued and for some time now had grown more impatient. He hid this in sullen moods, uncooperative behavior and a general lack of communication with anyone but the clerk at the office of The Western Union Telegraph Company. Every day but Sunday, he'd walk to town to make inquiries. His faith was strong—in Mac.

§

In the late afternoon of a day that was to become memorable in his history, Edwin Noyes entered town at the end of his five-mile walk from home. He made his way to the Western Union office, where the clerk was just closing.

"Something for me today?" Edwin asked, crossing to the counter in the office.

"Yes, sir, Mr. Noyes," said the clerk. "Just come in. A cable."

Edwin turned away, opened the sealed message and read it with mounting excitement.

"Gonna be a reply?" asked the clerk.

Edwin was rereading the magic, stilted sentences.

" 'Cause I wanna close up," finished the clerk.

Edwin Noyes looked at the familiar face behind the counter—one he had seen, day in, day out, for months, when the same reply of "Nothin' " had thrown him once again into a dejection that deepened as he made his way across the fields back to the small property he called home. Today he had everything to thank that face for: it had given him the world. The cable was from Mac.

"What's the address say, Luke?" Edwin grinned.

"Why"—the clerk looked at it—"Great Britain." He looked closer. "London."

Edwin took out of his pocket the last from his cherished box of Havanas and gave it to the clerk.

"Then, Luke," said Edwin, "have a cigar."

Peregrine Madgewick

INNOVATIONS throughout the seventh decade of the nineteenth century had added greatly to the comfort of passengers at sea. Steam heat, electric bells and gas lighting had all been instituted by 1871. The ornate, spacious salons, coal-burning fireplaces, heavy furniture and sweeping stairways provided for the traveler, at least in first class, a cocoon, creating confidence—as if, even during a growing storm, he were merely in a large room, perhaps on a Scottish estate, defying elements angered by a successful day's hunt. The "seeming," of course, lost all credence when "weather" was encountered.

In fact, when the sea "got up," there was little anyone could do but pray—as even the most sophisticated devices of Victorian ingenuity still fell far short of those required to guarantee complete safety. Ships sank, were rent upon rocks, became helpless in storms, grounded in uncharted shallows. But still, sea travel grew.

In the Atlantic, commuting began for businessmen, emigrant trade escalated in the packed compartments of steerage, and trips abroad began with a "sea cure": damaged emotions were provided with the antidote of "a change"—lovesickness replaced by seasickness. But many were of the view that the voyage "across" should not be numbered amongst the pleasures of a trip abroad.

"When I hear people who profess to enjoy the steamer passage to Liverpool," said a contemporary traveler, "I always think how unhappy they must have been at home." Opinions were divided. "Ship-shape and Bristol fashion, the massive hull glides over the quiet waters, when one can observe the sheen from shining brasses, of glistening air-ports glazed white and lacquered black."

Publicity slowly reversed the fears of sea travel, still regarded as somewhat of an "enterprise"; not to be taken unless necessary. Ships became palaces afloat—segments of society one could enter for a fee, something more than mere conveyances. Even steerage, "the cellar on an ocean," packed and stacked as it was in most cases, provided better accommodation (and at least regular meals) than the slums from which the emigrants had escaped.

International travelers were divided largely into two categories: the well-off and the destitute. "Passengers of First and Second class," it was stated, "are requested not to throw money or eatables to the steerage passengers, thereby creating disturbance and annoyance."

Even more bleak were the deep unknown regions down by the keelson of the ship where passengers seldom ventured; descending levels of winding stairs led to the glare of opening and closing furnace doors where lived and toiled a body of grim, blackened and oily stokers, machinists, coal carriers, fire feeders and machine tenders, who knew as little of the upper ship as it knew of them. In these subterranean recesses of the hull between brick and iron walls, amidst the deafening sounds; pitch-black, with only fiery glimpses of these poor creatures at work, all sense of being at sea was lost as if the watcher were at a coal face or in a vast night factory of the new Industrial Age.

The *Ebro* was delayed for a week in Lisbon—her voyage interrupted by equatorial winds, slowly bearing northward weather that eventually became destructive thunderstorms. They broke over a wide area of Great Britain on the first and second, then sixth and seventh of August, causing much damage to life, limb and property. The ensuing floods George, Austin and Mac witnessed, through pouring rain, on the train journey south from their port of arrival—Liverpool.

The spirits of the three Americans fell as each mile the *London Express* traveled brought them nearer England's capital. Perhaps it was the different climate or the familiar language; certainly the euphoria of their escape from Rio was replaced by depression as they looked out the carriage windows at the dull countryside fading into an early rain-misted twilight.

"Mr. Warren" was to stay the night at the Golden Cross, where Austin still retained rooms. "Mr. Morrison" would reside at the Grosvenor, Victoria, which Mac preferred, until he found a set of rooms, which he did later in the month at number 7 St. James's Place; George, in the name of Wilson, decided on Durrant's in George Street, as it was quite central and whimsically apt. As they came into the station where they were to split up and go separate ways, until a rendezvous several days later in Garraway's, George read aloud, from the American volume he carried with him, words of Henry James.

Six years before, he too had entered London on such a wet, black Sunday after dark. George stopped a moment, seeing the others silently observing the very same arrival into Euston, "miles of house-tops and viaducts, the complications of junctions and signals through which the train had made its way to the station, gave some scale of its immensity, this City—London."

George decided for the trio there and then that they would first cable, then await Edwin Noyes and, should this mood persist, shake it off with a week or more in Paris before Austin, now too disconsolate to create a good impression, made the next move in their plan. Although the three men parted, each in his own cab, off into the wet night to the selected destination, they shared one thing, which came with an awareness of the enormous task that lay before them: utter misery.

§

Brilliant sunshine on a clear morning gave zest to that day at the end of the second week of September when Austin Bidwell walked briskly along Threadneedle Street to the Bank of England. Autumn weather at its best: the temperature was cool enough to be bracing, the moving air stirring, then sweeping away fumes that seemed always to hang upon the City in still weather—the bane of industrial expansion.

Austin crossed confidently to the other side of the street, avoiding the noisy horse traffic as wagons, broughams, cabs and carts jostled with riders, messengers and the ever-present destitute element, selling, shouting, quarreling and begging. Seeing the uniformed attendants at the great entrance of the Bank, Austin paused in mid-stride to throw away his cigar—half smoked. Auspicious day, he thought, as he nodded to the two smartly dressed men. They recognized him, even after the long interval away, and smiled a greeting. He entered the Bank at one minute to eleven.

§

Farley escorted Mr. Warren not to his immediate superior's office, but along the corridor to the anteroom set to one side at the end near the Manager's door. He had not taken the advice given to him at the last meeting and merely shook his head when asked if he had laid a bet on the horse that won the '72 Derby. Austin had expected nothing more, but it made polite conversation and reminded Farley that he was not wholly unforgettable.

In the anteroom, Mr. Fenwick stood as he did mostly, without company or immediate work to occupy his attention, at the window observing the horse traffic of the City outside.

"Oh, welcome back, Mr. Warren," he began enthusiastically as Farley ushered the customer into the room. Fenwick crossed to Austin and shook him warmly by the hand.

"I hope the caviar was sufficient consolation for what I hear are dreadful conditions even under such an illustrious Czar?"

A warm smile from the perfect assistant bathed Austin in its glow so that, for a moment, Mr. Warren did not exist. The man was so damned nice, Austin thought; he *said*, "What?"

"Why," said Fenwick, allowing only the shadow of a frown to cloud his countenance, "Wussia, Mr. Warren—Wussia!"

The mispronunciation was at first faintly amusing. Then Austin concentrated on the man he was supposed to be. What the hell was it in Russia? He began to think hard.

"Why, yes, Mr. Fenwick," he started, "caviar and—Schnapps . . ." He stopped immediately as the face before him questioned, first with its eyes, then with its mouth.

"Wodka, in Wussia?—surely, Mr. Warren."

Austin realized now how precarious his situation had become. He knew nothing about Russia and would certainly not survive questioning from one who knew even a little of the place. He cursed himself for ignoring the importance of his whimsical farewell.

To Austin, Russia was only a word. Worse was to come.

"As you say"—Austin tried to curtail the conversation—"wodka, Mr. Fenwick." The light laughter and imitation of the pronounciation he attempted merely wiped the smile from the nice man's face.

"We, at the Bank," Fenwick continued, "know of Wussia in the extreme, Mr. Warren. Thank you, Farley."

The young assistant bowed out but left the door open.

"Our dealings, shall I say," Fenwick went on, "with 'that country' have been more than—'one-sided' is perhaps the right phrase?"

Austin was perplexed by the pause when it was obvious a reply was expected. Fenwick sniffed and continued.

"The Crimea, Mr. Warren, bled us here in England from our pockets as well as our veins."

"The war?" Austin asked thankfully, remembering the conflict, two decades past, of several years' duration.

"Indeed so, Mr. Warren. Our reputation . . ." Here Fenwick paused, the word he was forming obviously distasteful to him. ". . . suffered."

"The charge of the Light Brigade surely regained what was lost, Mr. Fenwick?" Austin was now proud of himself. In his boyhood it had been news; now, in history, it had become a somewhat colored legend.

"A glorious chapter," said Fenwick, once more aglow with the pride of being English.

"And," said Austin, "perhaps foolhardy?"

Fenwick's expression froze at this mild criticism.

"As I remember it," finished Austin.

"As you say, Mr. Warren—as *you* remember it."

The atmosphere had lost its cordiality—a reminder to Austin to tread warily where criticism of the British was concerned.

"Our Civil War in the intervening years . . ." Austin desperately sought the right words to placate this neither too short nor too tall, too fat nor too thin Britisher. ". . . has filled our American minds, Mr. Fenwick, with the idea that there is nothing in war that can be deemed glorious."

The Assistant Manager softened, remembering the horrifying weekly reports from the United States during those terrible years. He put out of his mind the jubilation of many of his customers as their bank balances grew large—the result of increased revenue after the collapse of American competition, together with the clandestine export trade of "goods" to both North and South (despite the international ruling of European neutrality, officially strictly enforced by the British themselves). Fenwick had been counseled to ignore certain facts along with the word "munitions"; thus he reminded himself to forget and assumed the appropriate emotion of sympathy.

"Indeed, Mr. Warren, indeed—we have all suffered."

Austin charted the change in Fenwick—transparent enough to be graphed. He swallowed some anger and made his request. "My appointment was at eleven."

"I am quite selfish, Mr. Warren. I apologize, of course. Come through; you shall meet Colonel Francis." Fenwick indicated the door. Both men stepped into the hallway and took the four paces to a large door, and as Fenwick heard the word "Come" from within, he turned the brass knob, made in the shape of a lion roaring.

§

In 1872, Britain and the United States could well have gone

to war against each other. The Prime Minister, Gladstone, averted any final declaration by acceding to demands that were, to say the least, unpopular in Britain. So much so that, without doubt, the *Alabama* Affair, as it was called, did much to oust Gladstone in favor of Disraeli.

The British contended that throughout the American Civil War they had remained strictly neutral. The Americans claimed that because Britain had allowed the Southern privateers *Alabama, Georgia, Florida* and *Shenandoah* to be refitted in British colonial ports, then to "escape" (the Southern sympathies of Britain were not entirely secret), she was directly responsible for (a) the direct damage resulting from the destruction of vessels and cargoes by these Confederate privateers, (b) the losses occasioned by the transfer of the American shipping trade to the British flag, (c) the considerable expenses imposed on the United States by the necessity of chasing the privateers, (d) the losses from the increase of insurance premiums, (e) the enlarged war expenditure caused by the prolongation of hostilities.

Arbitration was delayed but finally convened on June 15, 1872, at the Hôtel de Ville in Geneva, Switzerland. The august body was august indeed: Her Britannic Majesty's Sir Alexander James Edmund Cockburn, Baronet, a member of Her Majesty's Privy Council, Lord Chief Justice of England; His Majesty the King of Italy; His Excellency Count Federigo Sclopis de Salerano, a Knight of the Order of the Annunciata, Minister of State, Senator of the kingdom of Italy; His Majesty, the Emperor of Brazil; His Excellency Marcos Antonio d'Aranjo; Viscount d'Itajuba, a Grandee of the Empire of Brazil, Member of the Council of His Majesty the Emperor of Brazil and his Envoy Extraordinary and Minister Plenipotentiary in France; Her Britannic Majesty's Charles Stuart Aubrey, Lord Tenterden, a Peer of the United Kingdom, Companion of the Most Honourable Order of the Bath, Assistant Under-Secretary of State for Foreign Affairs; M. Jacques Staempfli of Switzerland.

Charles Francis Adams, Esquire, represented the United States, together with J. C. Bancroft Davis, Esquire.

Britain ended up paying. Three million—pounds sterling.

§

"Good morning, Fenwick—and thank you."

The voice was firm, well modulated, and indicated, without effort, authority—difficult to achieve unless its owner was to the manner born.

Mr. Fenwick thanked his Manager as if even words from him were to be cherished. He left the room and closed the door without any further communication with Austin. Now he was on his own. The two men looked at each other, the one seated at his desk—a heavy antique, surrounded by what was familiar: the ostentatious agglomeration of Victorian taste, everything that was supposed to impress, as it did the majority.

Large windows, long draperies, Persian carpets, Louis Quinze cabinets, Reynolds paintings. Austin smiled. The Colonel, as Fenwick had declared him to be, remained seated and indicated the comfortable chair to his client. Austin took it and relaxed. Eyes absorbed first impressions.

"Mr. Warren," said Austin; "F. A."

"Colonel Francis," said the Manager of the Bank of England; "P.M."

"Frederick Albert," said Austin.

"Peregrine Madgewick," said the Colonel.

The Manager lay back in his seat and touched fingertips.

"Well, Mr. Warren—Russia!"

Austin became alert instantly.

"Did you go to St. Petersburg?" asked the Colonel.

"Austin nodded and spoke. "Indeed I did."

"And how . . ." said Peregrine Madgewick with some curiosity ". . . was it?"

Austin was about to invent a series of opinions when some instinct stopped him. He smiled in question.

"Have you been?" he asked.

"Indeed I have," said Colonel Francis.

With a small—almost involuntary gesture, Austin pinched his nose and thanked his lucky stars.

"Then I am probably unable to add anything to what you yourself know of the place," he said.

"Most interesting, didn't you think?" asked Madgewick.

"Most interesting," affirmed Austin.

Seemingly satisfied with this exchange, the Manager referred to some papers on his desk.

"You have," he began, "an excellent record of business." He paused as if unable to continue. He looked up at Austin and changed the conversation. Austin could see that the man's mind was racing.

"I unfortunately," he went on, "when you came to us —that is, were brought—I was—"

"Vacationing, I gather," finished Austin.

Colonel Francis nodded absently, directly at Austin. He again referred to the papers a moment. Silence held, interrupted eventually by the Manager's drumming fingers. Then he sat up in his chair and with a firm voice asked, "What is it exactly—your business?"

Austin knew how to handle direct questions from normally indirect people, so now he relaxed: his advantage.

"I have been looking for an opportunity some while, and now"—Austin paused to light the cigar he had taken from his pocket—"by courtesy of Mr. Pullman"—he struck a match —"I think"—he took the first puff—"I have found"—he puffed again—"one"—the cigar was lit; he shook the match out—"for which my experience well equips me."

"And that is . . .?" questioned the Manager.

"Sleeping cars," said Austin, and leaned back, blowing out the first delicious taste of fine Havana.

"I see," said Peregrine Madgewick. He did not.

"My brother," Austin went on, "has been in and out of railroad carriages in America, and what I've picked up I've learned from him." He took another puff of his cigar, savored the smoke and blew it out. "Distance," he said, "that's what we have in America, and"—he paused and drew on the cigar again—"comfort"—the word came out wreathed in smoke—"that's what you have in Europe."

"In Great Britain also, Mr. Warren," said Colonel Francis with an admonishing smile.

"I meant this Island—also," said Austin, temporarily thrown from his train of thought.

"The one word," the Manager began, deciding that now

was the time to reveal to this American just exactly what he, Francis, represented, "is insufficient; Europe," he continued with growing relish, "is a—place. Great Britain is—an Empire"—the word seemed to spark and glow the way he said it—"upon which the sun never sets, Mr. Warren." The express was on the straightaway now and would not be stopped. Austin attended.

"We, in Great Britain, are guardians of nations. Millions of our subjects need our help, seek our advice, owe fealty and give loyalty. This—*Island*"—he emphasized the word Austin had used, sardonically—"is the cornerstone of that Empire, and I like to think, I believe not incorrectly, that this Bank is the cornerstone of our Island; more than that . . ." Colonel Francis made a note that today he was inspired, galvanized by this arrogant American ". . . inasmuch as this Bank houses the wealth of generations of world-wide trade and fruitful business, attracting to it the inventive, the industrious, the honest and the successful, all of which"—Francis had decided to personalize these attributes to flatter, if not accurately describe—"I gather, you are, Mr. Warren."

Austin was unable even to mutter an affirmative noise. Francis continued immediately.

"Inasmuch as we, the Bank of England, do that, I like to think of us as the . . . the . . ." Peregrine paused only to enjoy the thought to be pronounced. ". . . heart of the Empire, Mr. Warren."

The speech was over. Austin had the measure of his man. He smiled, as now did the Manager.

"Hearts," said Austin, "stop."

Colonel Francis was John Bull—tailor-made by time, heritage and experience to sit just exactly where he sat. Normally the cat with the cream. This American seemed not to understand the might and pride of this paragon of civilizations. Perplexed and not a little irritated, Madgewick got down to business.

"Distance and comfort, Mr. Warren," he said.

"Yes," said Austin, "and large sums of money required to combine the two and conquer the one."

Every aspect, angle and attitude to money Colonel Francis understood. He relaxed again: his advantage.

"At five dollars to our single pound sterling, Mr. Warren,"
he said patronizingly, "you in America may be used to
dealing with larger figures, but I feel we"—and with this he
made it quite certain Austin was not a part—"*we* here in
Britain are used to transacting greater values."

"Then it appears," said Austin concisely, suppressing all
emotional reaction, "that I should have little trouble in my
business should I decide to base myself here in England."

"You are a gentleman of obvious acumen," said Francis.
"Should the vestige of a problem arise, do not hesitate to call
upon our experience."

"You are most hospitable, Colonel Francis," said Austin.
He meant it.

"You in America, sir," began Francis—determined to
beguile this American (Austin was aware only that this man
was cosseting)—"are, to my way of thinking, our 'country
cousins,' as it were, to whom we are indebted inasmuch as you
reminded us, almost a century ago now, that generosity from
the father is an attribute as worthy as quiet counsel . . ." He
paused, knowing Mr. Warren would interrupt. On cue Austin
spoke, irritated still.

"I don't follow you, sir."

Colonel Francis knew his speech from repetition and enjoyed leading initiates through its changes.

"When our dear King George," the Royalist said,
"gave"—he emphasized the word—"to you the seaboard
States of the American continent and said, 'There, they are
yours, I relinquish them,' the world must have taken great
note at that time of his magnificent gesture."

All that Austin knew of his history had been swept away in
a sentence. General Burgoyne's beleaguered army had been
decimated, left with no course but to surrender; words read in
his boyhood had imprinted that much upon Austin's memory.
They had leaped from the pages of his books, conveying the
pain, agony, exhilaration and final victory of the ragged
representatives of a new people over the colonial tenacity of
an old nation. This man was rewriting facts fought and won
with blood, not paid for with money.

"Gave . . . ?" Austin actually spoke the word.

Catching the reference, Francis smiled, "Yes—gave."

"And the War of Independence?" It was Austin who blurted it out, not F. A. Warren. The moment was dangerous.

Colonel Francis laughed at what was, to him, the obvious.

"The formality of honor, Mr. Warren," he said. "As a master might play at swords with an arrogant pupil, so we—"

Austin interrupted, now firmly Mr. Warren; he no longer trusted himself.

"Do you," he said, "perhaps"—he breathed deeply —"have some coffee?"

"Indeed, Mr. Warren," said the Manager smoothly, quite unperturbed at the flushed gills of the young man before him and the quite obviously angry eyes flashing with indignation. "We *may* have coffee; but I feel sure we have *tea*."

Tea was a British tradition, as the world knew. His finger went to the button of the newly installed electric bell to summon the beverage and as if to declare "game" in the mild confrontation.

"Tea," said Austin, "would be most agreeable."

"Good," said Peregrine Madgewick, finger poised.

"If," finished Austin between gritted teeth, "it is from Boston."

Austin's cigar went out, as did the patronizing glint in the eye of the Manager of the Bank of England.

Austin smiled generously. Francis said something like "Yes, quite." Fenwick arrived moments after the button was released and, outside, the bell stopped ringing. Austin pressed out his cigar in the ash tray on the desk in the Manager's office. It was not Havana ash that he could smell as he lay back in his chair to present further financial details to Colonel Francis; it was the contents of broken boxes a century before, thrown into a harbor with patriotic fervor. The history read in childhood was indelible and still conveyed to him the smell of what his mother had called civilized afternoons.

Fenwick had brought papers into the office and was obviously going to join his superior and the customer, Mr. Warren. Austin blessed his mother silently as he recalled her saying with that wan smile of hers, "Tea for one in drinking, tea for two is two for tea, but tea for three is a party!" Only then would she pour the contents of an old china pot for herself and her two young sons.

To the momentary consternation of both Fenwick and Francis, Mr. Frederick Albert Warren actually began to laugh out loud. He never told them why; they would find out themselves—eventually.

§

Mac and George were waiting for Austin when he arrived outside Garraway's for lunch at one o'clock. Austin was brusque and to his companions appeared offhand.

"Is Noyes here?" Austin asked.

"We're all to dine this evening," said Mac slowly.

"Austin?" questioned George. "You all right?"

The walk from Threadneedle Street, and in fact for almost an hour, through the business City's maze had calmed Austin from his explosive mood on leaving the Bank. He pursed his lips, collected spittle in his mouth then spat on the cobbled way.

"Boys," said Austin, "this is going to be a pleasure."

George frowned. Mac was quizzical. He asked, "What was he like?"

"Well," Austin said, "he made me think." He looked long and hard at both Mac and George.

"But for a signature on a piece of paper declaring peace, what we're about to do would make out of us heroes, not criminals."

"You mean," said Mac, "if we were still at war with John Bull?"

"Yes," Austin replied.

"Well"—George grinned—"I ain't heard o' no peace treaty, boys."

"Safe as the Bank"

DINNER at Garraway's was a celebration. Noyes made a quartet, and old stories, adventures and escapades were repeated until they had all become a little less than sober. The three men, George, Austin and Mac, had been putting on weight. They had lived regularly, eaten well, drunk good wine and lacked for nothing but exercise. Even George had become lax in his discipline. Mac had been the first to create measures of control. Perhaps his excellent upbringing in genteel circumstances had had something to do with his new regimen; whatever, he had cut out drinking alcohol and ate only half of what he now carefully chose.

His example had been followed by both Bidwell brothers, who after some harmless ridicule of their friend had only to look at their waists to see the sense of Mac's discipline. Edwin Noyes had no such qualms, and his immediate influence was to revert the trio to bad habits. But for the one night at least, their pleasure at seeing again a friend after so long a time apart banished conscience.

Edwin Noyes was wide-eyed, not only at being in Europe, or more especially in Great Britain (as Austin reminded them with a casual imitation of Colonel Francis), but at the concept George now outlined to him. The meal over, curtains drawn in the alcove, the group around the table, now cleared of all but brandy glasses and coffee, waited for Edwin to speak.

In the main dining room, noise continued; in the alcove only the gas lamps hissed. Edwin was sitting absolutely still as if in a state of shock. He looked at his friends—incredulous.

"The Bank of England?" His voice wavered as he spoke the words slowly.

"In or out?" asked George.

"Well . . ." Noyes hesitated, looking at Austin, who said nothing.

"But . . ." he continued.

"Ed!" Mac's voice was low—dictating the answer.

Noyes paused long; he remembered the thousand dollars the trio had sent to him in New York, the ten-day voyage to arrive in England; saw in Mac's eyes the friendship he valued and felt the spirit of camaraderie that prevailed around him.

"In," he said.

"Three and four," said Austin quietly.

"Are we set, George?" he asked.

George Bidwell leaned into the table, as did the others; he began to spell out the details.

"We'll introduce 'Mr. Noyes' to the Continental Bank as your clerk, Austin." George looked at the newly arrived friend. "There Austin's to be known as Horton, Ed." Noyes concentrated harder. "We'll then spend until Christmas buying as many bills of exchange as we can afford; putting them in the Bank of England through Frederick Albert Warren's account. Only Austin is to be seen there at 'the Old Lady,' Ed, and known only by that name—Warren. We get the bills credited, all bona fide. Time bills, all of them—short and long periods up to ninety days. They'll all come due eventually and give the right impression. Big business. All the while, Mac will make copies of each one. When Mr. F. A. Warren has built his way into the confidence of Colonel P. M. Francis, you, Ed, me and Mac will conduct the business from there on."

George looked at Austin a moment.

"Where did we decide to say the factory was to be built?" he asked his brother.

"Birmingham," said Austin.

"Then Mr. Warren goes to Birmingham," said George, for Edwin's benefit.

"What factory?" asked Noyes.

"There won't be any factory," replied Mac.

"I don't understand," said Noyes.

"Austin," continued George, explaining patiently, "will actually leave the country. He'll be gone."

"What?" said Noyes, "but how—?"

"Mac and myself," said George, "will go to Birmingham and send in the bills we've prepared ourselves, by mail."

"Can that be done?" asked Noyes.

"When the time comes—yes," said Austin firmly.

"Mac and I will remain unknown," said George; "only you, Ed, in your own name, as Horton's clerk at the Continental Bank, and Austin at 'the Old Lady,' in the name of Warren, will have been seen."

Edwin Noyes shook his head. He was still behind. "After Austin has gone, Mac will copy Austin's handwriting on 'the Old Lady's' checks with the Warren signature, made payable to Mr. C. J. Horton."

"And I'm to cash them?" asked Edwin as the plan began to come clear.

"Exactly," said Austin.

"The bills Mac makes, that we both send from Birmingham," said George, "will mount up in Warren's Bank of England account. Horton's credit will rise as he receives checks regularly from Mr. F. A. Warren. You, Ed, will put them in and draw out cash at the same time. To the eye it'll seem they've a business going on between them, Mr. Warren and Mr. Horton."

George grinned. Edwin's mouth fell open.

"But," he said, "they're both you—Austin."

Austin nodded humorously. "But we live apart, Ed. Mr. Warren's at the Golden Cross. Mr. Horton is at the Terminus Hotel, London Bridge."

"Where the hell are *you*, then?" asked Edwin.

"I'll be at the Grosvenor, Victoria," Austin replied.

Edwin Noyes shook his head again, looking for a flaw.

He couldn't find one—immediately.

"The Bank of England will never see you, Ed. They won't even know you exist—like Mac and myself," said George.

"So when do we start to use my bills?" asked Mac.

"We'll decide—exactly—later," answered George. "After months of good bills coming due, we won't get questions asked when the forged ones start arriving in batches. Ninety-day bills, Ed"—George looked at Edwin—"take the full three months to get cleared."

"How long do we play it?" asked Edwin. "I mean, after we start sendin' in the forged bills?"

"Thirty days," answered George.

A pause held in the alcove, and brandy was sipped by all.

"That isn't enough time," said Austin. "We can't sent them every day—and if we're after big money . . ." He paused and looked at Mac.

"We don't have bills bigger than a thousand pounds, George. More than that is—well—unusual; so—"

Mac was interrupted.

"Then if it looks good," said George, "we'll play it sixty days."

"So that leaves us only thirty days to get away before the first bill comes due and is declared a fraud," said Mac, thinking aloud. "It's not a lot of time, George."

Edwin drank his coffee. All eyes were on George.

"Look, Mac," he said, "if"—he emphasized the word and repeated it—"if things went wrong—and they aren't going to—Ed will be the only one around whom anyone can recognize. And that at the Continental! The bills come due at the Bank of England!"

The point was clear, but Edwin was decidedly unhappy —the flaw found.

"Terrific," he said.

George looked at Noyes, his patience strained.

"Ed . . ." He paused as Edwin looked up at him, sullen now. ". . . if"—again he repeated the word—"if the untoward occurred, you'd only have to say you were employed by a Mr. Horton, to be his clerk. You know nothing about

Mr. Warren. All you do know, Ed, is that money is building in Horton's account, an' that from Warren's Bank of England account, which is what Mac and I will be concerned with."

"Where do I say Mr. Horton is?" asked Edwin.

"You've only been left instructions," said Austin. "If there's trouble, that's what you say—and that you think Mr. Horton's 'gone off' for a while. You play the innocent, Ed, and they won't have a shred of proof against you."

"It won't be necessary, because it isn't going wrong," said George, confidently.

"There's no way any authority could make anything stick, Ed," Mac repeated the point.

"Well,"—Edwin Noyes hesitated—"you sure *seem* to have it worked out."

The tension of explanation and inquiry drained from George, he relaxed.

"And remember, we're only to meet in public, here at Garraway's," he said.

"Why?" asked Edwin.

"Well," George went on, "it's packed full of City business every day of the week. Everyone here is concerned only with food, drink or each other. Curious as the English may be, they need an introduction before being interested. It's the best country in the world, it seems to me: where you can remain a stranger in the crowd."

"But what if I was recognized?" asked Edwin plaintively.

"By whom?" George was harsh.

"Clerks?" suggested Edwin.

"Those with whom you deal," answered George emphatically, "would find this place above their station."

Edwin frowned.

"It's too expensive," Mac said.

"Austin," George went on, "is in the world of solid business"—he winked at his brother—"not the kind of rash speculation that is conducted here." He paused. "You'll get to know Garraway's, Ed. It has history and a certain— reputation." George grinned reassuringly.

"It's too 'fast,' " said Mac euphemistically, "for the respectable establishment."

Edwin shook his head, still unconvinced.

"Besides," George finished, "you'd only be seen with your employer, Mr. Horton, who was talking with two other men unknown to *whomsoever*." George emphasized the word.

"Relax, Ed," said Austin, clasping his friend's arm, "and think of the Four Hundred."

"Five hundred," said Mac. All eyes turned to him as he looked at the new arrival. "In thousands of dollars—each."

Edwin lay back in the bench seat, slowly, his mouth agape. "It's not possible." Edwin was astonished at the large sum.

"Here," said Austin, "that's only one hundred thousand pounds."

"We're after the 'four hundred,' Ed," said George.

"When this is over, we'll be free to do just about anything that comes to mind," said Mac.

For a moment they were each lost in dreams—speculating on what could be done with such a vast sum which now appeared to be a definite possibility.

"You know?" said Edwin Noyes with the first smile since dinner, "I think I'm beginning to enjoy this."

"Good; then you start tomorrow," said George.

"What?" Edwin was surprised, misunderstanding.

"A job, Ed, with Mr. Horton," George clarified.

"Then I'm declaring!" said Austin. The three others looked at him.

"Up, boys," said Austin, and stood. The others followed.

"Our sovereign independence," said Austin.

Despite the humor of the mock toast, all four men drank what brandy they had left, quite solemnly. It was not a small thing they had agreed upon.

Continental Introductions

DURRANT'S Hotel was created from a terraced row of town houses just off Marylebone High Street, on George Street, opposite Manchester Square. A brick façade with brilliant white stucco pillars made it an attractive building, added to by thick clinging Virginia creeper growing from the basement to the second-floor windows, behind protective street railings. The interior was fashionable. Wood paneling, polished brass and thick carpet. The hotel had a sedate atmosphere—the norm for an excellent version in the middle category of London hostelries.

Nevertheless, to Edwin Noyes it was grand. The ninety-dollar passage on the White Star Liner *Atlantic*, the journey from home had created many changes in the young man. His confidence remained basically unshaken, but his nerves were still not what they became after the several brandies he took at the end of dinner each night with his three friends. In a short time he would be as they, relaxed but alert, confident but wary, sharp but charming. Now, as the Manager bowed to gain his attention, then crossed toward him in the small foyer, Edwin Noyes's fears leaped graphically before him.

"Ah, Mr. Noyes is it, sir?" the Manager asked pleasantly.

"Yes," Edwin said, committing himself to nothing but his family name.

"An omission, sir." The Manager, portly with success, smiled with a face that was honest, but experienced in the gamut, hotel trade offers sweated labor.

"I'm sorry?" could have been a statement from Edwin, it was so devoid of expression. His entire nervous system had become a chaos of haywire communication.

"The book, sir." The Manager indicated the receptionist offering the registry. "You didn't sign for us," he finished with a gesture and smile.

Edwin coughed to cover dissolving fear.

"Will you be staying long at Durrant's?" asked the Manager.

Edwin signed the book in his own name. "Some time—yes," he said.

The Manager looked at the registry and again at Edwin. "A clerk is it, sir?" he said. "May I be so bold as to ask for whom—sir?"

Austin Bidwell had never made a better-timed arrival. Edwin Noyes was again stumbling through the hell of hesitancy when a concise reply to the inquisitive Manager, true, false or indifferent, would have ended the conversation there and then. He was saying, "Well . . . I actually . . ." when Austin entered the hotel with all the brashness of a young blood, bored with life and late for another rendezvous.

"You, I take it, are staff?" Austin lazily addressed the Manager as he crossed to reception.

"I, sir, am the Manager," said the Manager, verifying that Austin was indeed "money."

"My sympathies," said Austin, taking off his gloves. "Do you have an E. Noyer staying here with you?"

The Manager had the man next to him, and the difference of one letter was an easy mistake.

"Ah, this is Mr. Noyes, sir," said the Manager, looking at Edwin.

Austin betrayed not the slightest hint of recognition.

"Mm," he mused, "you must be the one—advertisement—yes?"

"Yes," answered Edwin—flustered.

"Let's look at you," said Austin. "Tall, eh? Are you honest?"

"Are you Horton?" asked Edwin, looking askance a moment at the Manager.

"I am *Mr.* Horton"—Austin emphasized the term of respect—"if you are Noyer."

"I am *Noyes*, sir—with an S."

"I see," said Austin. "Well, sir"—he indicated some armchairs around a small table—"let us sit."

Speaking to the Manager over his shoulder, Austin began to usher Edwin toward the table.

"Bring us some coffee, my good man. I can't conduct an interview without beverage, and I am not used to being in a hotel without being asked." Austin made his point; the Manager became immediately a willing servant.

"Coffee for myself—and you, Mr. Noyes?" Austin pronounced the word as if for the first time. "Or would you prefer alcohol?"

Edwin would have liked nothing better than a stiff brandy, but he said, "Oh, no, sir."

"Good," said Austin. "I like abstinence in my employ."

The manager continued to hover as if awaiting dismissal.

"Well, off with you, sir," Austin said; "coffee it's to be."

"At once, sir," said the Manager, and walked quickly into the dining room, where waiters were preparing the table for luncheon.

One of them would be dispatched to the kitchen with a snap of the fingers and a curt command. He would receive coffee from a boy at the huge brass urn, who in turn would be snapped at by the "stillroom chef" as he emerged from the steam to pour the hot beverage into silver-plated pots. Later in the day, the boy might kick a cat. Authority was like passing ice: somebody ended up with none.

The two men in the foyer sat down in armchairs. Austin whispered to Edwin Noyes, "*The Times* spelled your damn name wrong."

"Is all this necessary?" asked Edwin, referring to the subterfuge of the public roles they were now playing.

Austin knew exactly how necessary. If things did go wrong

later, Edwin would need all the details that could be mustered
to establish him as the innocent dupe.

"For you, Ed—only for you," whispered Austin. "It's
your cast-iron alibi." He saw the Manager out of the corner
of his eye emerge between the dining-room doors. "Now play
up," said Austin.

As the Manager of Durrant's was to recall, the interview
between a Mr. Horton and Mr. Noyes lasted perhaps half an
hour, after which time, by what he observed—handshaking
and a general respectful *ambience* between the two men—Mr.
Noyes had, it appeared, been accepted in the employ of the
gentleman who had arrived. This was later corroborated, after the meeting, when the first money was received for Mr.
Noyes's room. It was paid by Mr. Horton on a check made
out from the Continental Bank.

The public meeting between Austin Bidwell, alias Charles
Johnson Horton, and Edwin Noyes finished some moments
after midday. The two men rose, left a substantial tip for the
waiter, then went out into the street. The sky clear, the day
cold, but a fresh wind blowing, the two men decided to stroll
before taking a cab into the City. They walked down George
Street, paused on the corner of Baker Street to allow the many
passing carriages time to thin out from the stream going both
north and south, then, walking to Gloucester Place, turned
into Portman Square.

Austin remembered a pub he preferred above those they
had already seen (too full of jostling drinkers to be pleasant),
so he took Edwin's arm and directed him along Wigmore
Street to Mandeville Place, across Hinde Street to Thayer,
then into Marylebone High Street, until at the top, near the
Euston Road, they entered the fashionable Prince Regent.

In August 1872, Lord Kimberley had caused great excitement throughout the country with the introduction of his
Licensing Bill. It was directed at the repression of excess, of
disorder and of adulteration—a preventive measure against
abuses of the public- and beer-house system. The various
descriptions of license, as they then stood, were complicated,
difficult to understand and reluctantly enforced.

The bill regulated new licenses and, more importantly,
apart from doubling the penalty for drunkenness from five

shillings to ten shillings, restricted the hours of opening. Within four miles of Charing Cross, public houses would not be allowed to open before seven A.M., the bill stated, and must close at midnight. Elsewhere in the metropolitan district, and in towns of not less than ten thousand, they must close an hour earlier. In other towns and districts the same opening time applied, but closing was at ten P.M. Special police inspectors were to enforce these laws.

Riots in Exeter, Taunton and Leicester proved the initial unpopularity of the bill; but eventually, as the British do always, the population became accustomed to regulation. Their drinking hours, in company with the weather, became a springboard of all conversation.

Mr. Horton and his new employee engaged in far more consequential talk as they shouldered their way from the bar toward a space in the lounge of the Prince Regent.

"Ed, you just got to relax," said Austin as the two men each grasped a pint of ale. "I've been to the Continental before—they know me well. I opened an account with a check on the Bank of England, paid to Mr. Horton from a Mr. Warren." Austin smiled and sipped his beer.

"Are they expecting me?" asked Edwin.

"Us both," said Austin.

Edwin sipped his beer.

"The Continental Bank," said Austin, "has an excellent reputation, as I have with them. More than a thousand pounds in Bank of England notes silenced any discussion about references thereafter, together with my pleasure at their attractive interest rates. Mr. Stanton, whom you'll meet, will know you as my confidential clerk to whom all my business may be entrusted." Edwin nodded. "Then," continued Austin, "we go to Jay Cooke, McCulloch and Company, where you'll meet Alfred Joseph Baker."

"For what purpose?" questioned Edwin.

"He's a pompous little clerk from whom you will buy U.S. Bonds, when the time comes."

Edwin shivered involuntarily.

"Ed?" said Austin, anxious at his friend's suddenly pale face.

"I'm right as can be," said Edwin; "just thinking of all the money, that's all." He looked about him in the pub at the ordinary mortals; many of the women were gin-drunk already, and the men, talking loudly at each other, had no interest in these two Americans. Edwin spoke the figure out: "One hundred thousand."

Austin had downed his beer. "Each," he said. The two men left the Prince Regent quite unhurriedly.

§

The meeting between Austin, Mr. Stanton and Edwin Noyes went well. Austin smiled a great deal. Stanton continually smoothed his thinning hair, was excessively polite and respectful; Edwin responded with confidence but stuttered occasionally.

Finally they all emerged from the Manager's office into the area "behind the gate," as Stanton had referred to the Bank proper. Where the work was actually done, filing cabinets were crowded together amidst the staff. Beyond the counter and the hinged half door—locked from within—was the public area. Stanton stood on his toes a moment, leaning against an open file drawer for balance. He sought the teller to whom he referred. He pointed him out to both Austin and Edwin: Mr. Richard Amery—the man with whom he had decided the Continental's esteemed client Mr. Horton, and now of course his confidential clerk Mr. Noyes, should conduct business. Hands were shaken, smiles exchanged.

"Your contentment with our bank is assured," Mr. Stanton ventured as a parting shot, and suddenly Edwin and Austin were walking down the long counter past the queuing customers at various grilles, then out through the great doors and, with a salutation to the guard, into the street. Edwin took a deep breath, slowly responding to Austin's scrutiny.

"Easier than I thought," he said.

"So far," replied Austin.

§

As at the Continental so at Jay Cooke, McCulloch and Company, the U.S. Bond brokers in St. Swithin's Lane:

Austin and Edwin emerged "content." Both men realized the importance of the paper Mr. Alfred Joseph Baker sold —paper that Edwin would buy in increasing quantities when the time came, once their scheme was under way. U.S. Bonds were international currency: payment upon presentation was to bearer, who, should it be his wish, could of course remain anonymous.

Edwin shook his head in wonder at the ease with which Austin had introduced his confidential clerk—"who," Mr. Horton had continued, "will of course conduct my business should I be absent abroad for any length of time."

Baker, who indeed had a touch of the traditional British pompous reserve about him, agreed without question. He extricated his plump frame from behind the desk and ushered both client and clerk to the door, where he bade them good day.

Outside in the busy street, Austin took out two Havanas; he handed one to Edwin.

"Have a cigar," he said with a grin.

§

Good bills, hard currency. George and Austin, with their increased resources (Brazilian gold—as the three Americans referred to their capital, privately), procured bills upon first-rate financial houses so that these could be examined and copied by Mac. The flow of genuine bills bought, presented and discounted would eventually end with the batch of forged copies being submitted; but first the confidence of the Bank of England must be ensured absolutely, so—good bills, hard currency.

Mr. Stanton, at the Continental, was extremely happy to have such a good customer as Mr. Horton. Checks were paid in regularly to his account from a Mr. Warren, who in turn was a customer at the Bank of England. Mr. Stanton was doubly pleased—good business with excellent connections. Mr. Noyes now drew the money on behalf of Mr. Horton, as it appeared the latter was mostly abroad on some business errand or other.

CONTENT WITH THE CONTINENTAL was the sign that had

begun to confront Edwin as several times a week he approached the teller at that bank to deposit and withdraw. Two Warren checks were to go in and one thousand pounds was to be withdrawn to buy bills, once more to be submitted at the Bank of England, thereby increasing the balance from which Mr. Horton would again benefit.

"Do you wish to see your employer's account, Mr. Noyes?" the teller would ask occasionally.

"There is within it sufficient funds, I hope?" Edwin Noyes would reply.

"Oh, indeed, sir," the bank teller affirmed each time.

"Then, good morning," Edwin would finish, tipping his hat and going.

September became November. Austin continued to show himself at the Bank of England, presenting his bills and buying foreign currency for his several trips abroad to purchase on foreign houses. All the while, as each new bill arrived Mac would study it well and copy it to perfection, leaving out only the date and the amount for which it was valued. The ground-floor front room of 7 St. James's Place became a hive of almost silent industry as Mac, with the gaslight turned to full and the shutters drawn even during the day, examined the paper, scrutinized scroll and lettering and tested the inks, color and consistency of each bill of exchange George or Austin brought round.

It was not an easy time for Mac. But Edwin Noyes had relaxed and begun to absorb the confidence of his friends. He also began to enjoy London. Austin maintained his quite separate roles superbly. Now a decidedly infrequent visitor at the Continental and no longer at all in the offices of Jay Cooke, McCulloch and Company, Austin did maintain a relationship with Fenwick at "the Old Lady."

"Afternoon, Mr. Warren" might well begin one of several opening gambits from Fenwick. "Brisk trading of late, I see."

"Indeed, Mr. Fenwick," Austin would reply. "My regards to Colonel Francis."

"I shall convey them, sir," answered Fenwick.

Thus Austin had the best possible ambassador, who, seeing the large bills and knowing the regular flow of money to be consistent in both directions (a happy event for any manager), would keep his superior informed on the odd occasions conversation was struck up regarding valued clients.

As August had been, so was November Lord Kimberley's month. A grand banquet was given at the Cannon Street Hotel to celebrate the opening of telegraphic communications with Australia on the fifteenth of the month. The telegraph wires were brought into the room and placed in connection with the wires to Australia. During the speech at dinner from Lord Kimberley, replies were received from Adelaide, New South Wales and Victoria.

Six retransmissions were necessary to further the message either way. "The Company," Lord Kimberley had stated, "on the occasion of the telegraphic dinner, join me in drinking prosperity to the Colonies, and in rejoicing at this great bond of union between different members of the Empire."

Amongst distinguished guests were the Manager of the Bank of England and Mr. J. Stanton, one of the financiers of the project. Directly after the Lord's speech, the latter went downstairs to relieve himself of a half pint of claret. Had Colonel Francis, who was at that time unacquainted with Mr. Stanton, decided also to walk down the stairs to the gentlemen's toilet, the two men would have been shoulder to shoulder with Austin Bidwell and Edwin Noyes, who had taken a quick supper together in the Cannon Street Hotel dining room, paid for by Mr. Horton.

Had Mr. Stanton seen them, coincidence would have been named and smiles have resulted from the meeting; had only Colonel Francis seen them, the same would probably have happened as perhaps Mr. Warren would have introduced his friend in some fictitious name or other; but had both Mr. Stanton and Colonel Francis entered the gentlemen's "cloakroom" and encountered the two, Austin and Edwin, who now buttoned up and turned to leave—what might have been the story thereafter?

As it was, Mr. Stanton paused at the foot of the stairs to greet a colleague. Taking their overcoats, unaware of imminent possibilities, Austin and Edwin were out the main door before the conversation finished. That night, absently checking his overcoat pockets at the Grosvenor, Austin came across the guest list of the grand dinner, which he'd idly picked up while awaiting the cloakroom attendant.

Outside his hotel, November-night rain spattered the windows, and even a large gas fire in the grate of his bedroom was inadequate against the cold. As things were going so well, Austin had decided to go to Germany and rendezvous with the Countess, with whom he had remained in contact. So far so good, he said to himself. Then he saw the two names on the guest list. It aged him considerably.

Intimate Relations

MISS Agnes B. Green kept a private hotel at 7 St. James's Place. Captain MacDonald had become a valued tenant. Her manager, Franz Anton Herold, was, to a degree, jealous of Miss Green's affections for the admittedly handsome young American, but he did his duties with the panache he had perfected, a charm that was matched only by the young Captain's.

As the weather worsened, the young American appeared to remain in his rooms far more. Herold was asked, on several occasions, to build up the fires, as the young Captain obviously seemed to feel the cold. The gas lamps on the wall appeared to the Manager always to be in use; the globes were cracked from the pressure of the gas, and the ceiling above the burners had become very black.

The man's health began to suffer toward the end of November, and Miss Green invited the young gentleman one night to her rooms to advise him to rest. Whatever he was doing, writing or illustrating, he must be careful not to neglect himself: that was the drift of her conversation. All else was in reference to his friends and, of course, herself. Here she dwelt some while, so that the candlelight, wine and pale green dress she wore, provocatively low-cut, mesmerized the exhausted Mac, who was saved only by the timely arrival of Franz Anton declaring that Captain MacDonald's acquaintance was at the door, despite the late hour.

Mac descended with Franz and greeted George, who was waiting in the hallway. Flakes of snow lay on his shoulders, and his pale face seemed even whiter with cold.

"Come in. I've a good fire burning still, George," said Mac. "Thank you, Franz," he finished.

The Manager took the finely made topcoat from the visitor and watched the two men go into Captain MacDonald's rooms. The label of the coat was Savile Row. Franz Anton hung it up to dry.

"Is it snowing?" Mac asked.

"Damn near trying." George paused as he took off his gloves. "He called you Captain."

"The Civil War gave us all something," Mac replied sardonically.

"I just got wounds and busted to private," said George, unbuttoning his suit jacket.

"For what?" asked Mac, genuinely inquisitive.

"Which?" replied George with a grin.

"Both," said Mac.

"Playing . . ." George smiled. Mac didn't follow. ". . . hero," George went on, "and with officers' ladies."

Mac shook his head and laughed.

They both crossed to the large table covered with a white sheet. Mac lifted it off and turned to George. He watched as his visitor slowly studied the paper; he was careful to touch nothing.

"Mac—you're an artist," George said eventually.

Mac walked to the open fire, stoked it noisily, then flopped into the armchair on one side of the grate. He spread out his legs and sighed.

"I hope I wasn't interrupting anything?" George began.

Mac opened one eye. George indicated the floor above.

"She's pretty," he said, smiling.

"For a landlady," said Mac flatly.

George sat down opposite his friend and took out a

cheroot. He lit it from the fire with a taper. The fire roared in the grate, throwing out flames as logs crackled; outside, the wind blew against the windows. The snow made no sound, but it was there—early this year: it was not quite December. Mac looked long at George, his eyes only half open with a combination of wine and fatigue.

"We need," said Mac, "a big bill, George. On an important house."

"Like what, Mac?" questioned George.

"Rothschilds'," said Mac.

The one word fell heavily in the room.

"Now, listen, boy," George began.

"It's too much work, George," interrupted Mac.

A pause held once again between the two men. Mac shifted his feet and reached out for some of the port in a decanter on the small table beside his chair. He poured two glasses.

"Mac—look . . ." George remained calm, recognizing the strain in his friend. "We're almost ready."

"If we put in a bill to 'the Old Lady' on Rothschilds' that is real and has been accepted here first as proof, I think *then* we'll be ready," said Mac.

"Mac," said George, taking the proffered glass of port, "Rothschilds' is no different from Baring's or Blydenstein."

"I'll tell you just how different they are," said Mac. He took up the newspaper beside him, which he then threw at George, who caught part of it. "Read that." He pointed.

"Mac, you're tired."

"One hundred thousand pounds," said Mac, "is one hundred bills, George. You know the amount of work in only one?"

"Mac, for two months now you've . . ." George faltered; he could see Mac's mind was set.

"Sixty thousand on Rothschild could be only ten bills, George." Mac spoke it quietly, making the implication obvious. George could add up.

"A bill for six thousand pounds is not possible, Mac—you know that," he said.

"What we're doin' isn't possible," replied Mac. His eyes glittered in the firelight as he looked at George. He sipped his port slowly. George took up the copy of *The Times* and looked again at the picture and article Mac had referred to.

"Sir Antony de Rothschild is not only head of the London House and therefore the acceptor here—he's a director of the Bank of England," stated Mac. Then he grinned.

"You need a rest," said George. Now he was worried. Mac would not be dissuaded. He'd thought it all out.

"But in Paris on London," Mac began; "say you don't want to carry six bills—tell them anything; play the Silver King—anything; but what we have is an impression, George, that we have established 'intimate relations' with the Rothschilds."

George looked at Mac patiently. "It's never been done," he said, eventually.

"Exactly," said Mac.

George could hear demand in his companion's tone of voice. A lot depended on Mac now that the setup had been created, so the question had to be asked.

"You're saying that you want this bill—a time bill of six thousand on Rothschilds'—or you are going to stop; is that it?"

Mac didn't even have to think.

"Exactly," he said.

"How's May?" asked George.

"How's Ellen?" retorted Mac, quite a match for his friend in any confrontation.

Ellen was a young woman whom George had taken up with during the past month. Obviously attractive, she seemed to Mac too shrewish to be considered for more than a night's liaison; she was the marrying kind and had little more than a sort of peasant beauty to recommend her. May too . . . Mac stopped the thought. She was altogether different. But then, so men think always—the eye and the heart. Mac smiled, then began to laugh as George answered, "She's ridin' round in the area with the cabbie."

"In the snow?" said Mac.

It was hardly funny to think of his woman suffering in the cold, albeit under rugs, but George laughed all the same. The atmosphere lost some of the charge that was building up.

"I want to be sure," said Mac softly.

"I am already," George stated confidently.

"We've got credit," Mac began, "but a Rothschild bill for six makes us rock-solid."

"I'm sure," George said quietly.

"I am not." Mac was firm.

The two men retired to private thoughts. George drew on his cheroot. Mac sipped more port. There could be no argument if Mac remained adamant—that was obvious. A knock sounded on the door. Mac looked up a moment. Franz Anton Herold's voice came through the oak:

"Miss Green has retired, sir."

He paused for a reaction. There was none. "She said to tell you, sir . . ." Franz's voice trailed off. "Good night," he finished.

Both men heard his footsteps recede in the large hallway. The fire crackled and roared still. The sash windows shook in the wind. It was late.

"Austin can't do it," said George.

"Why?" asked Mac.

"He's gone to Germany to see his woman—the Countess." George faltered.

"He told us Paris, George," said Mac harshly.

"He won't be in Paris for several days," answered George sharply.

"Where?"

"The Grand Hotel."

Mac listened to this last reply of George's, then smiled almost viciously.

"Then *you* go," he said.

"But that's not possible . . ." began George.

"Why?" asked Mac sarcastically.

"Austin is Warren, and the bill would have to be made out to—"

"Then go as Warren," interrupted Mac. "Austin is traveling in Europe as Horton—as you well know."

This last struck home. George took several moments to answer. "It'll take time."

"One week," said Mac. He softened toward his friend, smiled, stood up, stretched and walked to the door.

"Where you goin'?" asked George, rising from the armchair.

"To bed," grinned Mac. "For a week."

"Wait, and I'll come with you," said George.

"You have to check the bills," said Mac, "and you already have a cab—remember?" Mac took his coat and put it on, hugging it to him as he reached for his hat.

"Take care of yourself," said George.

"Let yourself out," Mac smiled.

The two men shook hands warmly—comrades without a doubt.

"Give May my love," said George.

"Give Paris mine," replied Mac, and went.

George turned the key in the lock, then pocketed it. He heard the outer door slam shut and looked across at the table and its bills. If Mac was going to be away for a week, he would need to cover them all with the sheet before he left; turn off the gas and dampen the fire; then lock the door from inquisitive eyes. Mac had assured him no one entered unless requested. He hoped Mac was right and decided to hide the made-up blocks and seals at least.

A delicate knock on the door froze George on the spot.

"George," the voice said.

George remained silent.

"George?" the voice repeated.

Silence again; then a key went into the lock and the door slowly opened. Miss Green stood against the strong hall light, lit from in front by the fire in the large room, in all her glory. A very daring nightdress concealed relatively little of her bosom and accentuated her well-kept Victorian shapeliness.

"Has he gone, George?" she asked, squinting into the comparative darkness within the room.

George realized full well, as he emerged from the shadow, that she was addressing George MacDonald, but he stood before her all the same. She knew him by sight if not name, and her passion was already aroused.

"Oh—it's you," she said—but didn't move.

"Mac has gone out," said George.

"And what do I call *you*?" said Miss Green, mischievously and not a little drunk.

"George," said George.

"Well, that won't be difficult to remember," she slurred.

"Would you like a drink, George—upstairs?"

George said yes, and Miss Green giggled. She went upstairs slowly, looking back twice, coyly.

George said, "Don't catch cold," and Miss Green was out of sight through a doorway that glowed with a soft red light from within. George closed Mac's polished oak door and gathered up all the bills. He put them carefully into a small case by the sideboard, then locked it. He put all the engraved work into a trunk in Mac's bedroom and locked that too. Only pens, ink, rules and glass squares he left on the table. He looked around him, then opened the door again.

"George" came a whisper from upstairs. Damn the woman, he thought. He locked the door and was about to leave, worried now about his lady in the cab outside, negotiating the small streets in a circular route as he had instructed, when the thought occurred to him of the other key the landlady had upstairs. Without a doubt she would be inquisitive if Mac was truly absent for a week.

If he could get that other key whilst Mac was away!

Damn Mac. He might well jeopardize the whole plan, especially if he, George, was going to Paris. With Austin away, no one would be around; Ed was not known to them here. George looked up the stairs and saw the soft, warm red light glowing onto the first landing. Perhaps he could say Mac had lost his own key and needed the master—something; or, as Mac had said—anything.

George took a quick look around at the front door and thought of Ellen. He decided then and there that one of these women would have to wait. George cursed Mac again. Now he was in a real quandary. He began to mount the stairs slowly. He could at least take Ellen with him to Paris.

George climbed into bed in November and eased himself out, two hours later, in December. He put back on what clothes he had taken off and, lifting his topcoat from the hall stand, quietly left 7 St. James's Place. The cab was directly outside the large house. The cabbie had fallen asleep up top, as had Ellen beneath the rugs in the cab itself. The two empty gin bottles and a half smile on both faces told its own story.

The snow had stopped, and the night sky had been cleared of cloud by a warmer equatorial wind that was now blowing.

Suddenly George's spirits rose despite the soporific effect of a considerable amount of port and lemon.

He slapped the cabbie's boot to wake the man and climbed into the hansom beside the still-sleeping woman. If Paris went as well as the last two hours, he'd have little problem even with Rothschilds'. He felt both keys in his palm. At least they were safeguarded for a week, thought George. All he needed now was luck for—as Mac had said—"intimate relations."

Winter

1872

Off the Rails

═══════════════════════════════════════

RAILWAY expansion divided the nineteenth century into two different worlds. In one generation, English life and landscape were transformed.

The canal system of Britain had been dug by laborers known as navigators; this word became corrupted to "navvy" and was applied to the individuals who worked on the expanding railroads. Well paid and largely unskilled, these men—rough, tough, often drunk, always at odds with either each other, their employers or the elements—dug the cuts, created embankments and excavated tunnels that allowed access to most parts of the country.

Thirty miles an hour by coach and three pairs of horses had been fast until the railway. By the middle of the century, a mile a minute was the standard for an express. But people did not immediately realize the dangers of speed. They fell out of and off the carriages; they jumped down to retrieve hats or lost lace and constantly attempted to board the train whilst it was moving, oblivious of the consequences. If the increase in population was, as one wit put it, to be attributed to the in-

208   WINTER 1872

vention of the bicycle, then it was a truth that the railway prepared people's minds for the idea of the journey.

By the early 1870s, over five million passengers were being transported by the railways of England, and rail transport gave to everyone who could afford the basic fare what now became a magic word: travel. To which was added a new Victorian invention, initiated by a few, catering to the masses now on the move, replacing the old, more personal coaching inns. At first there was a reluctance to see them go, a part of English tradition—but they were soon forgotten as comfort and good cuisine became synonymous with the new edifices (largely financed by the new railway companies) called hotels.

George Bidwell (as Mr. Wilson) had moved to the Terminus Hotel, London Bridge, to make sure all went smoothly when the several checks arrived from Mr. Warren for Mr. Horton, who was also registered there. Mr. Horton's clerk, Mr. Noyes, the receptionist noted, was always courteous and charming when he arrived to collect the odd letter that came for his employer. Mr. C. J. Horton's rooms, although paid for, were nearly always unoccupied. In fact, Austin only occasionally showed himself to allay suspicion and create the impression that business kept him on the move, especially abroad.

After all, it was not unusual, in Victorian England, for a gentleman to have "rooms" where what he did was no one's business. Money could not quell curiosity, but it could buy a knowing smile and loyal silence. To the receptionist of the Terminus Hotel, Austin was an attractive young man in this category. George had been the same, in her mind, bearing some resemblance to her "Mr. Horton," although the two were clearly not acquainted. Now her vague idea of making an introduction, one to the other, was dispelled. "Mr. Wilson" had found a woman. Ellen moved into the large suite, registered in the name of Wilson, and they had shown themselves, even in the dining room, as the receptionist had noted, to be obvious lovers.

No longer did George and the receptionist, pink-cheeked and red-haired, exchange the same twinkle of the eye. Now, for the receptionist, when George was with the dark-haired, admittedly (she would sigh to herself in honest moments) beautiful "other woman," as she liked to privately refer to Ellen, it was back to "key on the counter" and "proper talk."

Ellen was possessive in love and clearly suspected most women whom George encountered. She was not yet, but might easily become, a shrew. Her anger at the long night in St. James's dissipated with George's announcement of the Paris trip. What this Mr. Wilson of her affection did, Ellen knew vaguely, had something to do with business. What she saw, appreciated and spent without question was his money. An American, no less, and "hers," she would remind herself with pleasure—"for now," thought the receptionist each time the two of them, arm in arm, left the hotel.

Ellen was equally aware of the "for now" aspect of the relationship she had with George, but knew him to be in love, and this strengthened her resolve to make of the man a permanent fixture.

Ellen and George ate a leisurely early dinner before proceeding, unhurriedly, into the foyer of the Terminus Hotel and out to a waiting brougham, hired for the occasion to take them along the river-embankment roadway to Victoria Station, which served all points south and the Continent.

§

Mr. Williams stuck the pin into his cravat, gazed a moment longer into the mirror, took a last look around his small lodgings (a single room in Kensington), picked up his traveling bag and briefcase, then crossed to the door beside which, on a chair, lay his hat and cherished cane.

The young tailor's assistant was on his way to Berlin, via Paris—on business. It was his second such trip, and he blessed the day God had given Mr. Green rheumatics. Williams had risen to a place of some trust and thus was sent on such errands as now: a fitting for the British Consul in Berlin and two members of the British Arbitration Council in Paris. Very important business, he reflected. If only he could be seen to be a very important person. Williams sighed, then locked the door of room number 8 and descended three flights of stairs to the street and an omnibus that would take him to Victoria Station.

§

To Ellen the night station was most impressive: smoke,
steam and the noise of bustling crowds, greased pistons and
grinding wheels carried upward into the huge space above, en-
closed by girders and glass. To George it was familiar. Their
luggage was piled high and trailed behind them on a trolley,
pushed by a porter. Ellen, staring all about her at this great innovation of the century, walked along the platform with
"her" George until they reached the first-class section and
selected a compartment.

"Paris, madame?" inquired the ticket inspector who approached this imposing entourage with haste.

Ellen, playing the lady (as she did at every opportunity),
said nothing, but gave the man a superior look as ladies
did—in the music hall. The inspector had her measure immediately, but the gentleman was different. He turned to
George Bidwell as Ellen climbed aboard.

"Mr. Warren, sir?" he asked, looking at his reservation
list.

"Yes," George replied quickly.

"Oh!" the inspector went on, "then that'll be Mrs., will
it?"

"See that the luggage is boarded," said George, and gave
the inspector a sovereign, effectively curtailing any further exchange.

George climbed aboard the carriage after his "wife."

The reason for the name was simply that for George to succeed in his attempt on Rothschilds', it was essential that all
bills issued be made payable to the respected customer of "the
Old Lady"—Mr. Warren.

Since Austin was already traveling in Europe under the
name Horton, George felt (as Mac had suggested) that the
temporary—and most necessary—assumption of his brother's
alias was without danger. As the authorities could well check
back on George's exit from England, should Rothschild "accept" him, he (ever cautious) had begun as he intended to continue—yet instinct did not allow him to relax his constant
vigilance. In a word, he was, although it did not show, uncomfortable.

George looked through the corridor window at the pompous railway employee gazing up at him, still fingering the sovereign; the man smiled. George nodded, then went into his compartment.

The ticket inspector turned and, before moving briskly along the train, beckoned imperiously to the porter now lounging beside the trunks and cases. The man spat and slowly responded to the gesture.

§

The tip of a cane touched the porter's right arm just as he was about to make the dexterous movement of swinging a second portmanteau onto his shoulders. Had it been the Prime Minister himself, the porter's exasperation would have shown clearly and it was not Mr. Gladstone.

"An' 'oo is the howner of this 'ere fair luggage?" asked the cane with a voice.

The porter came out from under the portmanteau and stood straight. He saw the young buck standing beside a single traveling bag and briefcase—long coat, check trousers, cravat and pin, soiled shirt and rakishly tilted top hat.

" 'Is business an' none o' yorn," said the porter emphatically. To his mind this "little nothing-very-much" looked like a tradesman's assistant.

"The portmanteau a-comes from me own shop, my man!" exclaimed Mr. Williams sonorously.

Arms akimbo, the porter faced off this so-called "gent."

"Oh, really now—an' 'oo be you, then?" The sarcasm at the apparition before him playing the toff was concealed as badly as was the class difference between even Williams and this porter.

"My name," said Williams, "is Mr. Williams."

"Master, more like," said the porter quickly, sharp enough to see the double edge of the retort.

"I am a tailor of Savile Row, you ruffian," said Williams, irritated by this inconsequential piece of humanity.

"Then trade in your own name. It says 'ere quite clear marked, 'Green and Sons,' see!" the porter indicated. "Now g'orn—be off."

Williams swallowed and was preparing a scathing explanation when the ticket inspector returned.

"Come on, James," he said, "get Mr. Warren's luggage aboard—we're off in two shakes."

"I wonder if you might help me . . ." began Williams pleasantly to the inspector.

The man looked Williams up and down in a glance and hardly checked his stride as he began to walk to the rear. "Third class is at the back—this way." He pointed as he said it. "And be quick about it," he finished—then was gone.

The porter was already at the carriage's open door with the portmanteau. The newly made corridors of these carriages made for more work, but in first class they did provide access to friends' compartments en route—and of course, a welcome innovation, an available toilet. Once on board, luggage (usually at the insistence of the owner) had to be lugged to the occupied compartment. In England, unlike the Continent, the windows were too small to allow baggage to be passed through.

As the porter mounted the steps of the open door, Williams took his briefcase and traveling bag from the platform; the cane tucked under his arm, in a hurried, undignified manner he made his way back to the third-class compartments.

§

In Holborn, above the Red Lion, Mac lay in comfort on a chaise longue, looking out the window at the night sky. The day had been cloudless and calm, the temperature just below freezing, but in the early evening the wind, which had veered from northwest to south-southwest, rose steadily in gusts until—in London, at least—a moderate gale was blowing, accompanied by squalls; rain fell from clouds that scudded across the stars, massed a moment, then dispersed to leave again a clear, if wind-swept, night.

The gas fire of the improvised dining room hissed steadily, filling the room with enough heat to have allowed Mac to lie back in only shirt sleeves and a waistcoat. Wind shook at the window, and the net curtains inside, responding to a draft, billowed slightly with each gust. Mac turned from the rain-flecked glass and watched May go back into the small kitchen. The lounge–cum–dining area was candlelit, a table laid perfectly with an excess of new cutlery and glass. A delicious aroma from the kitchen described to Mac's sense of smell good plain cooking—a relief from the interminable over-sauced hotel *table d'hôte*.

The room pervaded love and care; flowers—from only God knew where, thought Mac—were in three vases around the room, blooming in the protective warmth, their colors muted by two very low gaslights on the wall and flickering candles. Mac smiled, then sighed deeply in utter contentment and drew long, once more, on his cheroot. May was humming a Jenny Lind song when she brought in the soup tureen, "all proper china," placed it in the middle of the table and looked at Mac affectionately.

" 'S almost ready," she said.

"Where did you get the flowers?" asked Mac.

"The Market," May replied. "I knows a number of 'em in Covent Garden, and now I've money I gets pretty well what I wants." She smiled at Mac, who was shaking his head.

"If you take the S off your verbs, you'll be nearer to talking 'proper,' " he said.

The lovely woman frowned.

"I forgot."

May had been seriously attempting a transformation for months. Beginning soon after meeting Mac, she had studiously attempted to improve her grasp of the spoken word. Her father's job as a newspaper compositor had given her a foundation, at least, to understand what she was about.

New clothes and soap "used regular," now with the luxury of warm water had changed the woman into the beauty she really was—as Mac had seen that first night.

" 'Fore we fell on 'ard—*h*ard," she corrected herself, "times, me mother taught me *h*ow to do it just *sh*-o," she finished with a giggle, the last word causing Mac to laugh loudly. "Oh, Mac," she said, and crossed into his open arms, "I knows they was alwus 'ard times, but I likes—like—to dream they wasn't—weren't, once," she finished softly, then looked down into Mac's eyes, warm and protective.

"They ain't now," she whispered, and leaned toward Mac's

face, her lips parted to give a kiss that would have sold a
thousand times, at a circus fair, at a farthing a go. (With no
other prospects, provincial Victorian beauties often found
this a way to make a stake to go to "town.")

"Is it alwus—always—goin' to be like this—now?" May
asked Mac quietly, half-listening to the cold wind howling
outside.

"Perhaps," said Mac honestly, his expression sincere.

May sank to her knees and leaned against Mac, ₋₋ooking out
at the night. She fell in with his mood.

"What about dinner?" asked Mac eventually, reminded by
the wafting aromas.

May barely managed to withhold tears of sheer happiness
when she looked up at Mac and said, with a touch of her old
defiance, "There's more important things."

No other sounds in the room added to the wind outside ex-
cept gas hissing on the wall and the cooker perfecting what
would be a late dinner, but the two people in each other's
arms on the chaise longue shook with a shared laughter that
was at once joyous and silent but also contained the fears all
lovers have that what is most delicious is often most
perishable.

§

Stepping into the corridor of their first-class carriage in
Calais Station was a totally different experience for George's
Ellen. The stormy late-night crossing to France had been
made from Dover with little consideration for the passengers
of the *paquet*. In fact, the short, rough voyage had been attempted only because the ship's Captain was French and was
to have a holiday the next day.

The train waiting for the ferry had been held two hours, so
it was at one in the morning that the exhausted group made
their way from the docks to the harbor platform to board the
French carriages. George watched Ellen shakily reach their
assigned compartment.

"Once more the unwilling victim," he began lightly. "Once
more the fitful note of Triton's breathing shell," he finished,
smiling.

"George, I feel sick," said Ellen thickly.

"My dear," said George, sitting beside her, "if you *will* attempt to eat a hearty supper in a gale, then 'alight on foreign soil amidst strange sounds and smells,' "—here George paused, embellishing his countenance with the wide-eyed look of an impassioned doctor—"it is not startling."

"Do you think this is a good idea?" asked Ellen as she looked about her at the luggage and carefully stowed dark leather portmanteaux.

"Going to Paris?" George suggested.

"Together," Ellen said, implying that their relationship had already suffered through George's resilience to the waves' motion whilst she succumbed.

"We'll know," replied George (an inkling of reality sinking home to him) "when we get back!"

Ellen reclined into the wide, armless seat. George unfolded a newspaper. Whistles blew outside, and the train began to move away, southbound for Paris.

§

The usual third-class throng impeded Williams as he forced his way along a narrow central aisle toward the second-class carriages. At a first stop before Boulogne, he was able to step out onto the platform and jump several carriages before departure. At some speed the train began to sway; Williams, thrown from shoulder to shoulder against the corridor sides, squeezed past people with an "*Excuse*" or "*Pardon*," assuming all to be French.

"*Billet*?" a voice asked harshly.

Williams became immediately alert; before him suddenly emerged, from one of the compartments, a mustachioed giant of a French ticket inspector.

"Ah," began Williams, "I'm in third. *But*," he went on quickly, "I've a friend up first."

"*Allez*," shouted the inspector.

"Look." The tailor's assistant reached into his pocket; he took out a coin. "Here." He offered it.

The ticket inspector took one look at the small coin. "*Allez*," he repeated loudly.

Williams went at the first push.

§

"Why," asked Ellen, "did the guard call you 'Mr. Warren'?"

George looked up from his paper, then down at Ellen. Her eyes were open; she had apparently been thinking.

"What?" George replied.

"At Victoria," said Ellen.

"Did he?" asked George.

"An' you've a portmanteau with the same name."

George bought time and looked up at the object referred to. Ellen had certainly been observing.

"It's a business name," stated George calmly.

"Oh," said Ellen. She closed her eyes—curiosity satisfied and suspicion dispelled. He was "her" Mr. Wilson; his business meant money, and that she understood. The train began to sway more as its speed increased.

§

Mr. Williams was nothing if not tenacious. At the end of the corridor in which he had had his only (he hoped) confrontation with the ticket inspector, he had waited until the man was in the last compartment. This was all a new system—access doors between carriages, corridors and inspectors on trains—so perhaps Williams was the first of many.

He whisked by the compartment and was gone, up the corridor, before the ticket inspector even turned around. First class began at the next carriage of the long train, and Mr. Arthur Byron Williams was determined to pay his respects to Mr. Frederick Albert Warren.

§

The prospect of the most romantic capital in Europe seemed to provide Ellen with relief from the nausea she had developed as a result of shipboard overindulgence, the angry

Channel and an increasing sway in the coaches as the long train gathered momentum on the rails. For a moment at least, Ellen became the woman George admired. She moved close to him and murmured, "We ain't been together quite like this before. It's nice."

She had her mind on one thing as the cure-all. George was not imperceptive.

"Do you still feel sick?" he asked delicately.

"It don't matter," replied Ellen, lips moist, eyes glittering.

"Then what say you . . ." said George softly, "if"—he pulled down the blinds on the corridor side of the compartment—"we make ourselves at home?" he finished.

Taking Ellen in his arms, he bent toward her.

"Oh, George," giggled Ellen delightedly.

George's lips were a hairsbreadth from Ellen's when the loud knock (of what was in fact a silver-topped ebony cane) on glass resounded in the compartment.

"Damn," exclaimed George. "Who is it?" he asked loudly after a pause.

"Williams," came a voice above the noise of wheels on rail and rattling carriages of the speeding train. "Williams, sir—of the cane, sir!"

Ellen was wonderful (George had discovered) when confronted with an emergency or the unexpected. "George," she said, suddenly weak, "I feel sick."

"Well . . ." began George to Ellen.

"Wait a moment!" he shouted to the unknown Williams outside.

"Oh, George," said Ellen, believing George was requesting her to wait, "I can't!"

In one movement Ellen had swirled to her feet, reached for the door and opened it.

"Pardon, I'm sure," said the startled Williams, momentarily blocking access to the corridor. He stepped back, and Ellen staggered out to make her way toward the communal toilet, somewhere on board.

"Well?" asked George ominously, now on his feet.

"I was looking," said Williams, his eyes fixed on George, "for a gentleman of my acquaintance." He paused, looking around the compartment behind George, then up at the number. "In Calais they said he had booked—ah, yes—*numéro deux*." Williams found the correct digit; then, "Are you perchance sharing the compartment with another gentleman?" he asked.

"No, I am not," said George emphatically, unaware that Williams' gaze had also found the portmanteau.

"Then 'ow, sir," said Williams accusingly, " 'ave you another gentleman's portmanteau above your 'ead?"

There was as yet no answer George could think of. He said nothing.

"George," Ellen interrupted, shouting from the end of the corridor, "I can't"—she was obviously crying—"open the door," she finished in a sob.

"If I may be so bold, sir," Williams began imperiously, suspicions fully aroused, "George . . . *what*, sir?"

At that precise moment, for George, at least, the world seemed to stop. As if at a slower pace than normal, Williams, the man in front of George, disappeared sideways exactly as the regular roar of wheels on rails changed rhythm to a crescendo; then it was as if all were silent. George began to pivot, slowly and uncontrollably; the sliding door came across the entrance to the compartment at a strange angle as all the glass cracked, splintered, then shattered everywhere.

George remembered being pressed almost upside down against the floor of the carriage by some tremendous unseen force as all the luggage fell toward him from the rack above the seats. Instinctively his arms went up to protect himself—and only then did he realize what was happening. The train had left the track and was in the process of becoming a holocaust.

Paris

GEORGE Bidwell regained consciousness in almost total darkness. All about him he heard babbling Frenchmen as the more active passengers aboard the Calais–Paris Express clambered from the wreckage.

For some, their hour had come, and they had gone on to better things—or worse. For others, the pain of injury or the sight of an open wound allowed their fear, now relieved somewhat by sheer survival, full vent. Screams, shouts and sustained wailing added to the chaos of overturned carriages; smashed compartments; smoke; steam; flames and sparks, rushing into the sky to become wind-borne red and yellow stars—they died before reaching the low, fast-moving night clouds. As a bonus to the survivors and village locals, struggling to help as they clambered onto the overturned carriages, fate threw in an extra: it began to rain heavily.

George took the hand reaching in to him from a man shouting in the French Channel dialect and thankfully scrambled out onto the shattered carriage side. Standing on the words CHEMIN DE FER DU NORD, George shook himself, to discover all was working: apart from a crack on the head and

bruises everywhere, he appeared to be fine. At that moment
the rain made its mark on George, for his feet slipped on the
wet surface and he found himself falling between two large
wheels onto the track.

George hit the gravel and sleepers of the track hard. This
brought him to his senses fast; he cursed loudly and realized,
for the first time, that Ellen was not with him. He got to his
feet and began to run along the track, estimating where she
would have been before the crash. Praying, he leaped between
the twin axles of the front wheels of the carriage and clambered back onto the carriage side. He straddled the outer
door, which was beneath his feet.

To the right and left of him, people scrambled through windows and open doors as if the train were on a time fuse to ex-
plode. Shouts for help came from all around. George wiped
the wet hair out of his eyes and crouched, again trying to open
the carriage door. It was stiff and heavy, but once the catch
was released George was able to lever against the frame so
that it opened to vertical, then slammed back against the
carriage, obscuring the 1ère digit painted boldly on the door
beneath its window.

George jumped down into the corridor and found himself
again straddling a door—the toilet. He closed his eyes and
prayed just the once, feeling the rain pouring in over the exposed interior. George again leaned in and attempted to pull
open the much lighter door. Releasing the handle, he realized
it was locked, so he kicked the door hard. It crashed open inward, just missing his beloved, who lay spread-eagled across
the toilet seat. She was a sight. Dignity is not the first requisite
for a survivor of any tragedy. Ellen's legs had never been
more attractive to George; her dress was ripped, her ample
bosom exposed to the rain, which poured in. George jumped
into the small compartment, standing on the washbowl fixed
to the wall.

"Ellen," he said gratefully as her eyes opened.

"Oh, George," said Ellen, "I was sick."

§

A gray morning arrived in the town of Marquise. On the

platform of the station, on stretchers or beneath shrouds, were the victims of the night crash. Doctors from the district hospital and local practices ministered to all in need. Others, who had had the luck to escape without injury, were crowded into the canteen, bar, restaurant (if it could be so called), waiting rooms and offices. George's nerves were now showing the effects of the crash, and coffee he had been given was slopping out of a cup which he held two-handed.

Ellen ate heartily from a plate before them on the table containing sandwiches and confections. Officials had arrived to oversee the event, quash as much bad publicity as was possible and ensure the well-being of their stranded passengers.

In America, as George recalled, despite its being the "glorious and free" place he knew and loved, the killing or mangling of a few persons, more or less, was of no particular interest to anyone beyond the friends of the victims—least of all to the railway magnate or his subordinates. But in France at this time, an accident that resulted in injury even to a single passenger was a very serious matter. The officials always hastened to take full responsibility. For even minor incidents a strict juidicial inquiry was convened, presided over by a high official of the state, and compensation was awarded proportionate to suffering and generous to a fault.

As a first-class passenger, George was high on the list for personal apology and offers of aid as the official concerned approached the table where Mr. Warren and his accompanying passenger were sitting.

"M'sieur," he began, "all your luggage is saved. It is most—unfortunate . . . most . . ." The official gestured helplessly and shook his head as the French best know how. George merely looked at him and said nothing.

"Sir," the official continued, "we of the Chemin de Fer du Nord extend to you our official apologies and are instructed by the president himself to ask you to demand of us anything that—"

"M'sieur," said George slowly, "we are at this moment grateful to be here as we are; there are some poor souls who are not." George had spent several hours dragging out the dead and injured, together with an army of helpers come from the surrounding countryside.

In the hot, gas-fired room, crowded amongst others from first class; wet; covered by a blanket; shaking with fatigue and nervous reaction; watching his disheveled sweetheart eating happily, mindless of her narrow escape, George was not in the mood to discuss blame or accept official sympathy; he just wanted to be dry and asleep.

"Of course, m'sieur," said the official quickly, "I understand—but it was the wish of our president that we of the Chemin de Fer du Nord—"

"Who?" interrupted George.

"The Chemin de Fer du Nord."

"No," said George, "your president."

"Le Baron," said the official.

George tried to remember; in his befuddled state it was difficult, but somewhere deep down he had the knowledge from some financial paper, read perhaps months back, that one of the many companies belonging to . . .

"Le Baron Rothschild insists that if there is anything . . ." The official stopped as George fixed him with a look, then smiled—in a most charming way, the official remembered.

"There is . . ." said George, ". . . perhaps . . ." he continued, suddenly wide awake and fully alert, ". . . one small service . . ."

"You have only to ask," assured the official.

"Your offices," said George: "are they in Paris?"

"Of course," the official replied, almost indignant. He heard George mumble something, but caught only the word "coincidence." He did not quite understand, but spoke all the same.

"It is not by accident, m'sieur, that all roads in France lead to Paris." He beamed at George, happy now that the man had responded to conversation.

George nodded to the official, who bowed and went on to the next group.

Oh, but m'sieur, George thought, it is most certainly by accident. He looked out through the long windows, partially misted with condensation, and saw the gray sky, now considerably lighter. He had never really believed in fate before—superstitions he left to Mac; yet—well—he called it luck, and *that* he always hoped for. George smiled wryly to himself. "Give a little—take a little," he said softly. The rain had stopped.

§

Some hours later, an express arrived specially to pick up passengers from the accident and take them to Paris. George and Ellen checked into the Grand Hotel; had a hot bath, which they shared; and went to bed, where they both slept for twenty hours, until the morning of the following day.

§

Bismarck's unification of Germany had presented a problem to France. Napoleon III knew that his country would be eclipsed as the leading power of the Continent if, at its heart, were such a dominant threat as Prussia's confederation. War was inevitable.

Bismarck engineered a quarrel with France over the Spanish succession. Napoleon's fears of German ambition proved well founded. Prussian victory in the war of 1870 was achieved despite the French superiority of manpower and equipment.

Overconfidence and inefficiency amongst the French undermined their chances in the eventual conflict. By the beginning of September 1870, the Germans had routed one big French army at Gravelotte, shut it up in Metz, the famous fortress capital of Lorraine, and captured another, led by the Emperor Napoleon III himself, at Sedan.

The French were beaten. Paris was surrounded and besieged. The city suffered badly. Privations were added to by the abortive uprising of what was known as the Commune, a socialist extreme element, which destroyed large sections of the capital.

Surrender was agreed on January 28, 1871. The German Empire was proclaimed with the crowning of William of Prussia in the Hall of Mirrors at Versailles. The peace, which concluded an ignominious collapse of military France, the terms of surrender for Paris and the future role of French power, was made in Frankfurt by representatives from both sides. Negotiation was tough, and a man who had much to say

in the final presentation of the document was one whose
background—born in Frankfurt, prospering in Paris—made
him the perfect go-between. His name: Baron Alphonse de
Rothschild.

As George Bidwell was to find out, Le Baron Rothschild
did not shake hands often. The hand that had shaken Bismarck's was seldom used and then, with few exceptions,
solely when the gesture had real meaning; the only concession
he made to French adoption was with intimate relations: they
received, on each cheek, a kiss.

Rothschild

DURING the sixteenth century, houses of the Jewish Quarter in Frankfurt were not numbered; instead, each door was distinguished by a sign or shield of a particular color. The "red shield" the family gave first—as is recorded, to Isaak Elchanan—the name Rothschild.

In 1755, Meyer Amschel came into a small inheritance when he lost his parents. A young Jew in the midst of Christian neighbors, he developed the vigor, industry and resilience at first to compete with, then to supersede his rivals. At the age of ten, several years before his father's death, he had been employed by his father, converting gold and silver coins into the appropriate amount of copper—the so-called common coin.

Germany was in a chaotic condition, divided into small principalities, cities and jurisdictions. Each had its own currency system; thus the business of money-changing obviously offered magnificent opportunities for profit. Each potential traveler was compelled to call on the services of an exchange merchant before undertaking even the smallest journey. Business prospered.

Meyer Amschel's interest in coins developed. He became an

expert numismatist. He entered the firm of Oppenheim in
Hanover and met General von Estorff, also a keen coin collec-
tor. Through this man, Meyer was introduced to Prince
Wilhelm of Hesse, of the small state of Hanau. The Crown
Prince was already an interested numismatist, and in a short
while Meyer Amschel became the official Crown Agent of
Hesse-Hanau. The business relationship that grew en-
compassed many aspects of finance and control.

Amschel married and in time created a large family—five
sons and five daughters. Come of age, the eldest sons proved
a blessing: instead of recruiting strangers into the expanding
business, Meyer Amschel utilized the skills of his offspring,
thus retaining the various secrets and subtle experience he had
to offer exclusively within the family. By the end of the century they were worth a fortune.

The family business expanded throughout Europe. Nathan,
Amschel's third son, became an outstanding figure in English
finance. Anselm continued in Frankfurt, whilst his brothers
Solomon, Carl and Jacob, known as James, created great
reputations in Vienna, Naples and Paris. All five sons were
made barons by Francis I of Austria.

Vast financial favors—loans organized by these influential
men—bought them power and influence. Eventually the
family name became synonymous with wealth—Rothschild.

§

Having spent the first day, which consisted mostly of afternoon wandering with Ellen in Paris near the Ile St.-Louis,
where they drank wine in the sunlight, seated outside a
brasserie; Notre Dame, where they prayed, and along the Rue
de Rivoli, where they had their photograph taken (which
became Ellen's most cherished possession), George alone, on
the second day, walked, still a little unsteady, into the Rue
Lafite to the palatial Maison Rothschild. The various offices
opened onto a courtyard; the architecture suggested the
residence of a head of state or nobleman, rather than a financial trading center.

As George mounted the steps with difficulty, bandaged in
excess of requirement and leaning more heavily on his cane

than was necessary, he reflected upon the vast amounts of money owed to this building, together with the more immediate compounding interest payments accruing, and shook his head in wonder.

He entered and encountered huge rooms; then he made his way from one lackey to another until finally he stood in the English department. The Manager arrived filled with concern at the information George had conveyed to an underling. George had produced his ticket and explained that here was a survivor of the wrecked train. The Manager frowned a moment at George's request, then disappeared for five minutes. He reappeared with a smile and the corroborating passenger list in his hand. George was ushered down a corridor into one large room, a second, then to a mahogany door, which was opened for him, and the Manager, having insisted George sit, left him alone, closing the door quietly. The taste of the furnishings was impeccable, if a little old-fashioned. The room represented only one thing—that which can afford taste: money.

A door opened beside the large fireplace and a slight, sallow man in his mid-forties entered; he wore an out-of-date stovepipe hat and a shabby-looking gray-brown suit. George stood up hesitantly, then sat again as the new arrival came and perched on the desk in front of his visitor. Both men took off their hats.

"M'sieur," said the arrival, "you are a lucky man."

"And you," said George, now certain, "are Baron Rothschild."

"I am . . ." began Rothschild, ". . . sorry," he finished.

"Cuts," said George with a rueful grin, "a leg wound, crack on the head and nerves." He paused to make the point: "You have lost a train."

"You shall have my physician," Rothschild began; "he is the best. There shall be no charge."

"I have already paid a doctor, sir," said George firmly, playing the injured party to the hilt, "for bandages—and to be told that I was in a train crash. If that is the extent of your Paris medicine men's experience, I would rather save you the expense."

Rothschild smiled slightly with his eyes only.

"My own physician," he said, "insists that I see him once a week to confirm that I continue in perfect health."

George smiled now, careful not to lose his advantage; they were getting along famously—for the moment.

"Consultation . . ." Rothschild continued, ". . . is the practice . . ." He hesitated a fraction, but got it right. ". . . Mr. Warren . . ." George nodded as befitted his alias. ". . . but conciliation is the norm—wouldn't you say?"

George nodded again, then spoke up.

"Your obvious concern for my distress is ample compensation, sir. I shall say no more of the matter, be assured."

"Mr. Warren," Rothschild cut in smoothly, his English perfect, "as I am, so are you, I am told, a businessman. If there is one thing I am able to do to assist you—please. You have only to . . ." Rothschild obviously awaited George's grateful interruption and immediate request. It did not come as he had thought, and when George spoke it was, again, firmly. "I am . . ." he began, ". . . indeed in business, but at the present time I am unable to practice."

"Of course," said Rothschild, "but—"

"Thus, I believe," George went on, "that the best course is to return and await my regained health."

"To England?" asked Rothschild.

"Indeed so," George replied.

"I hope, sir," said Rothschild with now a full smile, ". . . by train?"

The two men laughed. George was almost there. He nodded again—as Frederick Albert Warren, of course.

"Oh," said this Mr. Warren, "I am carrying rather a lot of French money and am unable to return without a bill on London, for its amount—for safety reasons—I'm sure you'll understand." George paused; then, "I wonder if you would be so kind . . . ?"

"What is the sum?" asked Rothschild brusquely. This was business.

"The equivalent of six thousand pounds sterling," said George—he hoped not too fast.

"Then you wish six bills for immediate payment?" asked the Baron.

"I may have to make my return slowly," said George. "Can they be ninety-day payments?" he asked.

"It is not normal for us to make out time bills," said the Baron Rothschild firmly.

"Nor, sir," said George, equally firm, "is it normal for me to be in such a—helpless—state."

The two men were eye to eye for a moment—George sprawled in the chair, bandaged and an obvious victim of fate; the Baron perched atop the desk, swinging a leg loosely, master of all he surveyed.

"Then," he said, "I shall make an exception."

George swallowed.

"Six bills of ninety days." Rothschild said it as though the deal were done. It was not.

"One," said George.

"I am sorry?" Rothschild was genuinely surprised.

"It has always seemed to me," began Mr. F. A. Warren, hesitantly, "unreasonable to create so much work for so little money. *If* "—George emphasized the word—"it is in your power, sir, one bill, if you please."

Rothschild now scrutinized his visitor. He had offered assistance and knew he was in no position (being the head) to refuse this request now made of his company. George knew it too. He had phrased the last sentence so that at the very least, should he fail, Rothschild would lose face. The Baron was a proud man.

"I see," said the head of the Maison Rothschild—remembering, as he reviewed George's condition, that he was also president of the Chemin de Fer du Nord.

Mr. F. A. Warren now took out of his voluminous side pockets three bundles of money.

"Fifty thousand francs each," said George, and placed the money on the desk beside Rothschild.

"I have no doubt," said the Baron, and pressed the newly installed electric buzzer beside him.

Barely a second passed before a servant entered and crossed to his master.

"Where are the blank bills?" asked the Baron.

Silently the servant opened a side drawer in the large desk at the rear, took out, and placed beside the Baron, a blue bill of exchange. He then took up the three bundles, unbidden but knowing the process required, and went out of the room quietly.

"It is . . ." began Rothschild slowly, taking up a pen, ". . . within my power—Mr. Warren—and an exception shall be *added* to—as is your wish." Here the Baron fixed George with a look that told him it would not happen again. Having written the six and three noughts, he put in the date, then signed his name, *Alphonse de Rothschild*.

"Here," he said, and offered the bill to his visitor.

"Thank you," said George, controlling the urge to grab the bill and run. He had the blue paper in his hand and was about to pocket it when the Baron spoke.

"Wait," he said, and took back the bill. George was stunned. He wondered how fast he could get out, if indeed that was possible.

"It will first have to be countersigned by the Cabinet Minister of Treasury," continued the Baron.

"Oh, then, if . . ." George interrupted; even this close to his goal he was willing to quit in sight of trouble.

"We have no stamp . . ." Rothschild went on, ". . . of sufficient denomination—for the tax." He paused, seeing Mr. Warren's sudden consternation, then by way of explanation concluded, "Internal revenue, you know."

"I apologize for causing so much . . ." George did not finish.

"On the contrary—it is I who must take responsibility for causing so much . . ." He paused, mimicking George's faltering voice. ". . . to you." Rothschild watched George closely. "Don't worry," he said; "the Cabinet Minister . . . is my cousin."

George stood up, now stiff with cramp and tension.

"I shall send it this afternoon to . . . ?" Rothschild paused, indicating the bill.

"The Grand Hotel," replied George.

The Baron had again pressed the buzzer, and a servant appeared at the open door behind Mr. F. A. Warren.

"Baron," asked George, "do you believe in fate?"

"No," answered Rothschild. "I *depend* on abilities, but I *believe* in—perhaps the word is—luck."

"It is," said George.

"And *that* a man can only be given." The Baron looked at his visitor and thought of the train crash. The visitor looked at the Baron and thought of the bill of exchange.

George extended a bandaged hand to offer his thanks and by way of illustrating respect. The Baron ignored it. He took George by the shoulders and bent to the tradition he had assumed.

George left Maison Rothschild, and the Baron sat down, more properly, at his desk. One had solved a problem, the other eased his conscience. Had they been asked, both would have agreed, visitor and Baron, that George was privileged: he had received, on each cheek, a kiss.

Explanations

BACK at the Grand Hotel, George was lying on the chaise longue in the lounge of his suite, almost asleep, when a light knock on the door to the corridor reversed the falling process. Head propped on a pillow, chin resting on his chest, when he opened his eyes what George saw was the blue bill, still in his hand. Again the knock sounded, louder this time.

"George" came a woman's voice. "George," it repeated in a demanding tone. Ellen was obviously irritated. George turned slightly, reluctant to awaken fully, and looked toward the bedroom, where the voice came again, strident now, from the adjoining bathroom.

"Open the door," she shouted. George could see the bathroom door ajar and could hear the bath taps running, so he reasoned Ellen would still be dressed. George closed his eyes. The knock came again, twice, loud. The taps were turned off; George heard a rustling of robes. He relaxed again and began once more to enjoy the lazy afternoon. The final knock coincided with Ellen's rushing out of the bathroom into the bedroom and then her striding across the lounge to see George seemingly still asleep.

She muttered to herself all the way to the corridor entrance and opened the door of their suite.

"Yes?" she asked (demanding the errand of the obviously intruding servant). "Oh!" she finished, recognizing that the man's purpose was obviously to enter and that he was most certainly not a servant. She was new to George's friends and had so far met only a few.

"I am sorry, madame," the man began; "I was looking for my brother. I am Mr. Warren," he finished loudly.

"Who?" asked Ellen, perplexed. A lady followed the man into the room—elegant, beautiful and quite obviously, as Ellen could not fail to notice, class.

She clasped the robe about her, remembered her hastily piled hair and blushed.

"This," said the man, referring to the lady, "is the Countess . . ." he did not finish.

"Mr. Warren" came a voice quickly, and George stood up in one movement, crossed from the chaise longue and shook his brother Austin's hand.

"Why, Mr. Warren, sir," retorted Austin (with a wink), "I heard you were—"

George interrupted Austin with the one word "lucky." It finished the sentence. George was frowning, but Austin grinned happily.

"George," he said turning to his lady, ". . . this is Elizabeth. The Germans kicked her out of Wiesbaden." She smiled. "She's to be my wife," he finished.

Austin had maintained his liaison with the Countess Elizabeth in a series of letters to her, all addressed to Wiesbaden, from Frederick Warren, London, Poste Restante. Eventually they had agreed to meet—opportunely, as local pressure for her to relinquish her involvement in the Casino, now that her erstwhile husband, François Blanc, had gone to better things, was making it difficult to manage a concern that in principle was hers, but in practice presented only her associates with what little profit remained after many of her husband's loans and interest thereon were covered. In short, she was a beauty but no businesswoman.

It was suggested by the group that they run the Casino and pay her a guaranteed sum; thus she would be free of responsibility. They had also tactlessly pointed out that such an action would relieve them of the burden scandal continued to present (this they cited as reason for the dwindling throngs since Blanc's death) and provide the wherewithal for a new life and possible husband for the still-young woman.

Elizabeth had again met "the boy from Brooklyn" in Wiesbaden—Fred-er-ick, as she called him, spelling out the word as she spoke—and remembered the period they had enjoyed together, putting time and distance between them and their fateful introduction. She associated the American with her freedom from a constricting life; the analogy became, in her mind, one of prince and damsel. Several days later the couple—as they enjoyed the countryside, wrapped beneath blankets in an open coach—despite the weather, or because of it, began to feel more than affection for each other.

They fell in love. And as that particular sensation is normally brought about by two people both developing the same needs at the same time, with complementary requirements, they were ideally suited. Elizabeth became a part of Austin's dream of the future, and he (handsome, charming and above all amusing, not to say successful in his slightly mysterious business) was a welcome compromise in the unstable world of Elizabeth's self-reliance. Austin became the object of his woman's affection, and as women do, Elizabeth set about turning this into a deep, passionate and possessive love. When Frederick confessed to his deception and revealed his true identity, she had only laughed and loved him the more.

One week after their arrival in Paris, only the day before they presented themselves (two floors below their own rooms) at George's door in the Grand Hotel—complying with the message George had left for their return from Versailles—they had become engaged. As Bismarck's empire had been declared, so had Austin's commitment of love to Elizabeth: in the Hall of Mirrors. It was all very romantic.

Elizabeth smiled at George, the brother of her future husband, intrigued by what she had heard and not at all sure yet how he should be addressed. Her own humble beginnings and constant machinations within her previous formal marriage, together with an increasing love for her madcap American, made the woman a willing conspirator. So she did what assumed breeding had taught her and said nothing.

"I'm Ellen," came a voice. George's lady curtsied, so Austin kissed her extended hand.

"Pleased, I'm sure," Ellen said, rising and looking the man directly in the eyes. She turned to the Countess, but Elizabeth was too fast for her.

"Are you running a bath?" she asked, looking Ellen up and down.

"Half in, half out, you might say," replied Ellen—in turn looking at the Countess, from peeping shoes to pinned *chapeau*.

"Perhaps it is inconvenient . . ." began Austin.

"No," said Ellen decisively, and turned to her man with a sharp look. "George will look after you." She then went into the bedroom, closed the door and, presumably, proceeded to have an excellent bath.

As George bent to kiss the hand of the Countess—a lady he had already heard much about—Austin caught his brother's eye and winked.

"George, I've a surprise for you."

"Another?" asked George genially.

Austin turned, looked into the corridor, coughed and made a sign. A man appeared, his head wrapped in bandages under a precariously placed hat.

"The man with the cane!" exclaimed George, dumbfounded. It was Williams.

"It seems," said Austin, "that you've met."

"Do not speak, Mr. Williams," said George. "After the last time, I feel that if you do, this hotel might come down about our ears."

"I am sorry for the misunderstanding, Mr. Warren, sir," began Williams. "Er . . ." He paused, uncertain, then found Austin's familiar face and went on, "Mr. Warren, sir, your brother, has explained it all."

"He has?" said George, doubtful. He had not quite put all the pieces together, and for a moment (delicate as it was) the situation was beginning to take on the semblance of a French farce.

"Very determined is our Mr. Williams," said Austin —"brother George," he finished for the benefit of the tailor's assistant. "I found him playing detective below in the foyer—incognito . . ." Austin winked. ". . . in four feet of bandages." He referred to the bandages around Williams' wrist and one on his ankle besides those around his head. Williams grinned amiably.

"I wonder, Mr. Williams, if you would be so kind . . . ?" said Austin.

"Come, Mr. Williams," said Elizabeth quickly. She smiled at George and ushered the young tailor's assistant away down the corridor. Austin closed the door.

"Who the devil . . . ?" began George seriously.

"A very bad coincidence—corrected," Austin said. George stepped back and sat down heavily on the chaise longue.

"Are you hurt?" Austin asked.

"I survived," George replied.

Austin saw the blue paper beside his brother and pointed. George took it up and held it out with a smile. He said only the one word: "Rothschilds'."

Austin read the amount and saw that the paper was a time bill. Both realized its value to their scheme; Austin whistled.

"Mac's idea," said George.

"Impossible." Austin was transfixed.

"Exactly," said George. Then Mr. Williams flung open the door. For a moment the scene was a tableau. An audience would have roared with delicious, nervous laughter. In fact, Williams was obviously too far away to see the object of interest. All he knew was that his Mr. F.A. had a brother, and it would be pleasant, should the gentlemen so wish, to share a jar or two before his late departure.

"Pardon, I'm sure," began Williams, "but knowin' that you—Mr. F.A."—referring to Austin—"'as rooms at the same 'otel as your brother 'ere, sir—Mr. Warren, sir," he said—referring to George—"I was wonderin' like, it bein' near the evenin' hour like, whether you—I mean you both, sirs"—he smiled with studied charm—"would be doin' me the honor of havin' a drink with me down in the bar?" He paused.

Austin and George exchanged a look, as noises from the bathroom told all in the suite's lounge that Ellen was quite happy by herself.

"I appreciate you lettin' me leave my luggage for the few hours, Mr. Warren, sir . . . but—"

Austin interrupted, for George's benefit. "Mr. Williams has apparently been delayed on his journey and was unable to remain at his own hotel this morning, so I . . ." Austin finished with a helpless gesture.

"You were looking for me?" questioned George. Williams blushed.

"And you found *me*," replied Austin in Williams' defense. "There is only one *Grand* Hotel." He emphasized the word and winked at his brother.

"Are you going far, Mr. Williams?" asked George.

"Berlin, sir—at midnight," he said.

George had smoothly, seemingly with no concern whatsoever, pocketed the Rothschild bill. He looked at his brother and merely nodded.

"Then," said Austin, "we shall drink to your success, Mr. Williams."

"And to yours too, sir—I mean you both, sirs," said Williams, and remained immobile in the doorway.

"Then run along, Mr. Williams," said Austin firmly, in the character of Mr. Warren, F. A. He indicated the black ebony clutched in the young man's hand. "And take your fine cane with you."

"Thank you, sir," said Williams, touching his hat.

"My rooms upstairs," said Austin, "are at your disposal, to . . ." He looked at Williams, obviously overheated—overdressed in the hotel, which was gas-fired throughout and, as warmth was synonymous with wealth, extremely hot. "The Countess," Austin continued, "will provide you with whatever you need."

"Only ablutions, sir," said Williams, helpfully. He had at least begun to back out of the door—if slowly.

George was exasperated now; he had much to talk about with Austin. "Then go, Mr. Williams," said George through bared teeth, "and ablute!"

Williams went. George and Austin waited in silence for the young man to remember the open door; return quickly; apologize profusely; then slam it. They waited until he must surely be gone before truly relaxing. Still they said nothing.

From the bathroom, noise continued as Ellen, heedless that the sound carried, was busy proving to all who could hear that she would never be a singer.

Outside and below, the distant clatter, rattle and rumble of horse carriages to-ing and fro-ing faintly carried into the room, now dimly lit from a fading late-afternoon sun. It was a sanctuary, in which to review the many events they had encountered which had brought them this far. Sitting together, staring at nothing, alone with thoughts and premonitions, George and Austin were becoming aware of what they were now ready to undertake.

Austin's head was resting on the back of the chaise longue, George's on a corner pillow.

"Explanations," he breathed quietly. It was both question and statement. Austin began. When George understood for whom Williams worked, he went pale.

"He recognized the portmanteau from his shop and—until he saw you—thought you to be 'Mr. F.A.' original." Austin paused. George was staring at him wide-eyed.

"Yes," he continued grimly, seeing the message sink home.

"Did you say anything—anything to him?"

"No," answered George with a long sigh, "thank God."

"For many things," nodded Austin.

George lolled back, shaking his head at the now fully understood second near miss, then began to describe the rail crash and his coup at Rothschilds'.

That evening the three men had a fairly pleasant two hours, with exceptions. George, once, almost forgot that he was supposed to be Mr. Warren, the barman having to address him twice. Austin, alerted by this, realized with a start that he was registered at the hotel in the name of Horton. This fact immediately precluded further drinking.

"I'm afraid we'll have to leave you, Mr. Williams."

"Of course, Mr. F.A., sir," said the tailor's assistant drunkenly, and stood up. "Mr. G., sir," he went on, shakily extending a hand to George. With slurred farewells, Williams left the hotel at nine thirty, almost blind drunk, and was put into a cab, which Austin instructed, in passable French, to "take His Honor to the Berlin train!"

The two brothers returned to their respective women, now

pampered and prepared for public viewing. Austin swore Elizabeth to secrecy in regard to his brother's adopted name.

"Warren and Wilson!" Elizabeth laughed delightedly. "Oh, how intriguing it all is!" She kissed Austin and (when he had explained the English expression to her) agreed to "keep mum."

Thus the several references Ellen made later to "my Mr. Wilson" (in a whisper privately to Elizabeth) passed uncontested. George impressed upon his "Mrs. Wilson" the need to accept the name Warren whilst in France.

"There is a measure of danger in the business in which I am at the moment engaged," he announced quietly.

Astonished and not a little excited, Ellen became (precariously, in George's mind) Mrs. Warren for the duration of their journey; but it was, as Ellen complained, all very complicated.

The quartet went out on the town.

The two brothers and their women talked only of the inconsequential and drank further quantities (nothing if not substantial) until the following dawn. It was, after all, as George said—referring to many things—by way of a celebration.

Parting

FOR George and Austin several days in Paris were enough. Their respective women were soon in disagreement about most things, so they decided to embark for England and, although to the same city, different destinations. The Christmas holiday was approaching, and the four Americans' plan was now almost complete. First the bill from Rothschilds' had to be dealt with by Austin.

The day after their arrival in England, the two brothers went to St. James's Place to see their friend. Mac had returned to his lodgings from May's rooms and found Miss Green in bed with a cold, desolate that a key had been lost by the young Captain.

Mac patiently heard the woman out, then fell in with what George had obviously invented, consoling Miss Agnes with the thought that the other key must turn up. He unlocked and entered his rooms with the key George had left him before his Continental departure, then watched the daily maid, who had now arrived, dust and clean for more than an hour. After she had gone, Mac took out his work and began, refreshed by a week with May, to scrutinize all he had done to date.

It was in this attitude that George and Austin found their friend. Franz Anton Herold ushered them in soon after six in the evening and pointedly, it seemed to George, explained that his mistress was confined to bed. George sent his sympathies, then went in to see Mac, who had already been joined by Austin.

Mac could hardly believe what he heard and then only when he saw the bill. Austin had taken it to St. Swithin's Lane the previous day and presented it to the English House of Rothschild; there, as all could see, was the second signature, in thin violet ink: *Accepted, Antony de Rothschild.*

The three men sat around a newly stoked fire and began to talk of their future. For the moment it seemed that they were fortune's favorites, and who could deny them that—then? Austin was, like Mac, feeling the cold and had decided to travel southwest to the Caribbean (against George's advice) on completion of his part in the scheme.

"Listen to me, Austin," George said: "do as I say and go to New York. Mac and I will hold the first bills until you arrive. After you check in to the best hotel in the city and are seen about, go upstairs at Delmonico's to 'our' table—" at this there was a flurry of reminiscences but George continued: ". . . inform Irving of your presence, all public and aboveboard. Only then will we start the bills from Birmingham."

Austin began to argue that recognition might lead to discovery and proof positive that Warren was, quite obviously, out of Great Britain and, more especially, Birmingham. George thought recognition unlikely, especially if Austin checked in as Bidwell—this would be essential, as he was known in New York, and would therefore establish definitely his absence from the scene of the crime when the time came.

"But it's so damn cold in New York, George," Austin argued. "I hardly see the difference—anywhere abroad will do, surely. In any case, who is to associate me with a bank thousands of miles away when I have a house in the tropics?"

"Extradition, boy," George said. "Not only will there be

not a single particle of evidence against you, but even if there were, the British would never get you out of the U.S. with Irving behind you."

Austin fell silent. Mac interrupted to convey in detail his problems with the bills, and the point slowly was lost amidst involved conversation, hot port with lemon, and cigar smoke. The fire dwindled. Mac decided to retire for a few hours before attempting to start work on his copy of the Rothschild bill; and the visitors quietly left 7 St. James's Place. Outside, it was pouring with a steady rain from the heavy night sky. Austin looked up at the building for the last time. His sentimental reflections were interrupted by George curtly.

"If you want to stand in the rain—good night."

Austin shook his head. "I'm coming," he said softly.

The two brothers walked to the end of the street and parted. They had a dismal journey back to their separate destinations. Both were noticeably without the Christmas spirit.

That night Austin went back to his only consolation; the Countess was already between the sheets. Even so, when he awoke in the morning, his first thought was: I shall never have to go to the Bank of England again. Then, remembering the night that had passed, Austin looked lovingly at the woman beside him. He rose from bed at the Grosvenor Hotel, London, in a suite they both now occupied, registered openly in the name of Bidwell. Austin left Elizabeth with a kiss on her cheek. She returned to sleep in blissful ignorance of what was about to take place.

§

It was almost ten thirty. As had been arranged, the Rothschild original was waiting in a sealed envelope, delivered by hansom cab at ten o'clock from St. James's Place to a Mr. Bidwell, Grosvenor, Victoria, London. Twenty-eight minutes later, Austin Bidwell transformed himself imperceptibly into Mr. Frederick Albert Warren, stepped from his carriage and entered the portals of the Bank of England.

Farley met him. They went into the office of the Assistant Manager. Fenwick was glad to see his valued customer, and Mr. F.A. prepared himself for a final confrontation with

Colonel P. M. Francis. He was ushered into the "inner sanctum" at three minutes past the hour of eleven. A handshake, a few words of greeting, an exchange of financial news and a brief discussion of the joy and sadness of the recent American elections began the meeting.

General Grant had been re-elected, but the strain of the campaign, it seemed, had been too much for his opponent. On the twenty-ninth day of November, Horace Greeley had passed away.

It was very sad for the entire American nation. Nevertheless, Congress had reconvened on December 2, and life, for most but Horace, went on. Austin smiled at the drift of the conversation and agreed with Colonel Francis that stability in life was an excellent goal and a satisfying achievement. He presented the Rothschild bill just as Colonel P. M. Francis was getting into his stride once more on the merits and otherwise of Great Britain's "young cousin" America and of her financial sons, one of whom, Austin decided, he himself was, in the Manager's allusion.

Rothschilds' blue paper silenced the Colonel; a time span of ninety days surprised Peregrine; most certainly the amount in question, clearly written, shocked and delighted Madgewick, and the signature of a London acceptance gave credibility to Francis that here was an important document, let alone bill of exchange.

"Antony de Rothschild," he whispered, and looked up at Austin.

"I think unique, sir," he said. Then he saw the Paris treasury signature for the tax of an equivalent thirty-seven dollars, or one hundred and eight-seven francs—too large a sum for a ready-made seal stamp.

Peregrine Madgewick sat back in his chair and gazed at the bill.

"A Cabinet minister," he said in a hushed voice. "Mr. Warren—you are making history."

"We Americans," said Austin, "need every bit we can get." He paused, then, as he watched the bill placed carefully on the desk, continued. "I hope that paper will be good enough for you?"

Slightly embarrassed at the obviously sarcastic remark,

Colonel Francis laughed, then clasped his hands and, leaning on the desk, asked earnestly, "How is the—er—'plant' is your word, I think, for ours 'the factory'?"

"Prospering," said Austin. "Indeed, I shall be for some time in Birmingham henceforth to supervise. I would appreciate your continued co-operation in handling what may appear to be considerable sums in the next months, while I am absent, Bills of Exchange of course."

"Oh!" began the Manager. "Then how can we—?"

"By post, Colonel Francis," Austin cut in, "registered from me to you—direct." He smiled charmingly.

"I see," said Colonel P.M., frowning slightly. "And where will you reside in Birmingham?" He took up a pen and reached toward his small note pad.

"For that," Austin said, "you may write, 'of no fixed abode.' "

The Colonel looked up immediately, disturbed.

Austin continued smoothly: "I shall be constantly moving in the area."

"Then how—?" Colonel Francis began again.

"Your excellent postal system," Austin went on, "inclines me to suggest the post office there, as a firm contact. I shall, of course, correspond to keep you informed of my progress."

"I see" was all Colonel P.M. could say, and he put down his pen.

"I trust you find that satisfactory," said Austin, and held his breath.

"If," said the Colonel, "it is the only way . . ." He paused, uncertain a moment, then thought of the excellent record of business in Mr. Warren's file. "Of course," he finished, "if you go to the trouble of sending the Bills to us, the least we can do is aid you at this obviously most important time."

"Thank you," said Austin, and stood up.

"As the Pullman cars I am making are completed," Austin said, walking to the door, "I am naming them after history's dignitaries—a good idea, don't you think?"

Colonel Francis joined his valued customer. "Excellent. What will be the name of your first?" he asked, offering a hand to Austin.

"Why, Colonel Francis," said Austin, taking the plump hand. The moment was portentous; here was Austin at the very core of English, or perhaps the world's, finance. He savored the words: "where history's dignitaries begin: the first will be, of course—George Washington."

Both men laughed politely, and Austin left the room, his reputation maintained as something of a wit.

Seeing the bill, as he turned again to his desk, Colonel Francis lost his momentary reaction to the American side of his customer, of which he was not overfond, and extended, in his mind, all the good will in the world to this young man who in many ways was, he thought, as he resumed his seat for the next appointment, of the stuff that had made England great.

The list of Mr. Warren's qualities after drive, ambition, shrewdness, intelligence, business sense and charm began to revert to the negative, so dispelling any further speculation, Colonel Francis pressed his buzzer to find out what Fenwick had for him next.

Outside, Austin stepped lightly along the corridor. He looked around only once as Mr. Fenwick came out of the adjacent waiting room, poised at the Manager's door and bade his Mr. Warren "Good day."

Austin waved cheerily, and just before Farley took him along to the foyer (where he paused only a moment, before stepping into the street and walking briskly to Garraway's), he saw the great door open and close. The Manager's name was clearly etched in Roman lettering, and the gold lion, rampant, roared in silence, frozen as a beautiful doorknob. He was never to see it again.

§

Garraway's was bedecked for the Christmas festival. Austin took time to absorb everything as he entered: the familiar bar to his left, and before him, down a short flight of steps, the huge dining area, behind which lay the series of alcoves. Mac saw him first and beckoned Austin across. Leaving his coat with the doorman, who spent as much time within as he was able (the cold outside being intense even though the day was now clear), Austin crossed through the crowded tables and made his way to the alcove occupied by his friends.

He sat down as George gestured for the waiter. They ordered lunch and two bottles of claret, along with some water in a jug. They ate lamb, after fish, with fresh vegetables, mostly potatoes and some cabbage. They talked of their experiences, and slowly Austin revealed that all was as he had expected. The final piece was in place. A heavy pudding in the English style completed the meal; Noyes and Mac each ordered a brandy. The Waiter arrived with coffee for George and Austin, closed the curtain, then left.

Outside the alcove, the bustling restaurant was gay with the approaching holiday; inside, once more, there was silence. The four men within, although not somber, looked at each other until all eyes fell upon Austin. A pause lasted, charged with some emotion, until George spoke.

"This will be the last time we are together like"—he faltered—"this," he finished lamely; but it was a statement all knew to mean the beginning and an end.

"I've booked," began Austin slowly, "to leave the day after tomorrow."

"Mac?" questioned George.

"The first batch of bills are ready," he said.

"Noyes?" George asked.

"I have an appointment with the Continental Bank this afternoon to draw out most of what is now in the Warren account. I have the check with me Mac's written to Horton."

"Good," said George. "Should anything go wrong—even at this late stage—at least we'll have what's left of our original capital." He took out his wallet. "Here are the tickets for Mac and me to travel to Birmingham"—he looked at Austin—"the day after tomorrow." George lay back in his seat against the wall. "One hundred thousand pounds, boys—each!" He spoke quietly, as if it were already theirs.

"Two million dollars," said Edwin Noyes in a hushed voice.

"At the end of sixty days," said Mac, in a tone that carried a warning.

Austin fumbled with a sheet of paper in his pocket, then put it on the table before them all. It was plain white, large and, but for the creases, unmarked. He took a pen from the inside of his jacket, paused only a moment, then wrote the signature *Frederick Albert Warren*. He put down the pen. Mac's eyes were alight; he looked at Austin, then took up the pen and wrote the same name beneath—a perfect copy. They repeated the procedure for *C. J. Horton*, with the same result.

"Money," began George, "will be sent directly to you, Austin, as soon as it is withdrawn."

Austin nodded. George put out his hand, and Mac took from his wallet two blue paper bills. They appeared to be from the Paris House of Rothschild. And indeed George, whilst still in France, had found a printer with a stock of the particular paper used by Rothschilds'.

Mac looked at the others: they appeared to be waiting. He gave the two blue paper bills to George, who looked at them only a moment, then put them down near the piece of white paper with only the four signatures written clearly on it. Mac took up his pen once more and wrote quickly, *Alphonse de Rothschild*. The copy from the bill was as perfect as the eye could detect.

"Are you sure," asked Austin, "that you made the copy from the original as well as . . ." He stopped. Mac looked hard at him.

"We're all in this, Mac," said George gently; "we have to be confident that—"

"I'm sure," said Mac decisively. He put down the pen and leaned back.

George gazed at Mac a moment without moving. "It's the biggest, Mac—what you asked for—and being so, is perhaps the most dangerous."

"Why?" asked Mac. He was angry that his abilities were in question.

"Because it's unusual," replied George.

"They were happy enough with it at 'the Old Lady,' " said Austin in Mac's defense. "Colonel Francis called it a 'document.' "

"That," said George decisively, "is what will get it looked at all the more."

All eyes now watched George as he reached into his side

pocket and took out a small, translucent sheet of paper. On it
was scribbled a name. George placed it carefully first over the
signature on the copied Rothschild bill, then over the newly
written signature Mac had put on the white sheet. It fitted
almost exactly. Mac's eyes blazed.

"I copied it from the original on this tracing paper, Mac,"
said George. "We had to know for sure." He gestured to the
others. "All of us." He looked at Austin and Noyes, who
were obviously impressed. "We can't afford mistakes,"
George finished softly—"this time."

Mac began to smile, then laughed openly at the test to
which George had put him.

"Do I pass?" he asked.

George said nothing, and that was everything.

Austin stood up as George took the two blue bills of exchange. "See you, boys."

"Take care," said Mac, eyes suddenly moist.

"Good luck," said George impassively.

Austin reached for the end of the cigar he had put down after coffee. Ash fell on the tracing paper as he put the still-
burning tobacco to his lips.

"Where are you goin'?" asked Edwin Noyes.

"The Caribbean," Austin replied.

"So it's to be the sun, eh, Austin?" George said, badly concealing the conviction in his mind that it was the poor alternative.

"Nothing will go wrong," said Austin quietly.

"Tell me in ninety days when we're with you," stated Mac
with a grin.

"It's a place where money buys anything," said Austin,
"and we're going to have plenty of what buys!"

"Why not?" said Mac, looking at George.

"It's your own decision, brother," said George.

"It's a big place," said Noyes. "Where've you a mind to
settle—exactly?"

Austin took time to answer; he looked at his cigar as if
seeking inspiration, but the tickets, bought already, belied
this. "Havana," he said, "Cuba."

Hands were shaken. George threw a feint at his brother's
chin and ducked beneath the return he'd taught Austin. They

clasped each other tightly a moment, then stood apart. A pause lasted of a duration none of them could afterward honestly define, and suddenly Austin was gone. It was a beginning; and that was the beginning of the end. Outside the alcove, through now half-open curtains, the three men could see the boisterous group who had begun to sing loudly a Christmas carol.

God rest you merry, gentlemen, let nothing you dismay.
For Christ was born our saviour, was born on Christmas Day.

The three men in the alcove were no longer an invincible force about to test a great institution. They were three individuals, separated, alone, solitary and afraid, aware of their mortality and dwelling on the punishment should they fail, rather than the pleasant vision of rewards from success.

The carol faded away as port became a more attractive alternative for the majority of brokers at the large table in the center of the dining room.

Glad tidings of comfort and—joy.

But there were none for the trio in the alcove, and suddenly, even though gas-fired, Garraway's was very cold.

Smiles between the three men were not enough, and already, to George, it seemed that he had not merely bidden *au revoir* to Austin: but that he had lost his brother. Goodbye, he thought quietly, but spoke words of a different meaning to Mac and Noyes. "Here we go, boys," he said. They were committed. This time a toast was made with coffee, and never more apt: from here on, they would have to be fully alert for any eventuality.

§

Two days later, in the evening, the night train for Birmingham pulled out of Euston Station, slowly gathering momentum. The first bills would be dispatched before Christmas, along with a cordial letter to Colonel Francis, R.S.V.P. to Post Restante, Birmingham, written by Mac. Before the

New Year they would know if all that had been planned was
to succeed. If otherwise, they must be prepared to run immediately.

In the compartment where Mac and George lay back on the
long seats with only two oil lamps above for comfort, silence
was created by mood. As the train, now moving fast, began to
leave the suburbs, Mac looked out the window and wiped
away some of the condensation. Outside, were the lights of
London—the last they would see until several hours later,
when they would reach Birmingham, and the Queens Hotel,
for the night. Mac began to smile.

"What is it?" asked George eventually.

"More important things" was all Mac said. He was
thinking of May.

George thought only of Austin and wished him *bon voyage*,
as he would to them all when the time came. He was soon in
an unsettled sleep, full of fears from childhood.

Mac continued to look for the evening star.

§

The French steamer *Martinique* was sailing to Mexico,
leaving Liverpool with a port of call in Lisbon. The first stop
in the Caribbean was to be St. Thomas, eighteen days from
Europe; then on to Cuba.

Austin and Elizabeth boarded early and were seated,
waiting to dine, as the ship pulled out of harbor. Long blasts
from the ship's horn faded into the night over the cold water
toward the City.

Observing lights to port and starboard, the pilot eased his
ship through a deep channel, then out into the open sea, where
the little fog lying low on the water was thinning out. A half
moon was up, and stars sparkled. It would be Christmas
aboard unless the ship made Lisbon in good time, but not for
the pilot: Liverpool was home; eagerly he jumped down into a
following pilot cutter, whose small steam engine raced and
took the last Englishman not traveling away into darkness.

The *Martinique*'s engines went to full ahead, and movement was felt throughout the ship. Austin and Elizabeth
gazed at each other with every indication of anticipated joy to

come. They kissed in candlelight as the first murmurings of a waiter asked their "desire." Elizabeth's mind was full with only Austin and the future. Austin, even with this beautiful woman of his heart before him, could think only of the immediate past: his friends and brother—George, Mac and Edwin Noyes.

His mind raced over possible problems ahead or mistakes made; he could find none. He hoped he had done his part well. Suddenly confidence flowed into him, and he consciously dissolved his analysis and projection of the setup. He was here and now. And besides, he decided, as he smiled at Elizabeth, the plan was—perfect.

Winter

1873

The Final Play

ON the ninth of January, 1873, Prince Charles Louis Napoléon Bonaparte—the third Emperor of that family name—died at Camden Place, Chislehurst. His death was caused by the painful illness of a stone which had been undermining his constitution for several years. The Emperor's determination to rid himself of this debilitating affliction had driven him to accept surgery. The operation of lithotrity had apparently proved successful.

The night had passed in uninterrupted sleep. When Napoleon awoke, he was refreshed and apparently strong. That morning, he was able to rise from his bed; he was hopeful and well satisfied. The Emperor was visited during the morning by his medical attendants, who saw nothing in his condition to excite any sort of apprehension. Arrangements were in progress for the administration of chloroform at noon, in order to complete a final operation to remove the last particles of that which had been the cause of so much distress.

The Empress paid her morning visit as she had done throughout the whole illness; her attention had been constant and her solicitude unceasing. Just before half past ten, as several visitors were being ushered into the chamber where Napoleon lay, a sudden change became apparent. The man's pulse, which had been at eighty-four, rapidly fell; the action of his heart started to fail; he became prostrate and began to fade.

The Empress was instantly summoned and came to her Emperor's bedside, but he did not appear to recognize the woman; he was fast sinking, notwithstanding the small doses of brandy prescribed; immediately administered, they produced only a momentary reaction. The Empress ordered the young Prince Imperial and the Abbé Goddard of Chislehurst to be brought at once.

The Empress, the Duke de Bassano, Viscount Clary, Count Davillier, M. Piétri and Mme. le Breton were kneeling by the bedside when the priest arrived to administer the last sacrament to His Majesty. Nothing could be heard in the bedroom but prayers of the priest and the sobs of those present. As the religious ceremony terminated, the Emperor appeared to give some signs of consciousness. His Empress approached for a final embrace. The movement he made was slight—an indication that he wished to give a last kiss to his wife; after which he heaved two deep sighs and expired from this earth. It was exactly a quarter to eleven.

§

Unaware of the great and tragic event that very moment taking place some miles away at Chislehurst, the Assistant Manager of the Bank of England looked up to receive Farley with the morning beverage.

"Tea, Mr. Fenwick?" asked Farley as he always did, quite needlessly.

"Yes, Farley," replied Mr. Fenwick. It was their ritual. Fenwick opened a large buff envelope, part of the morning's post on his desk. Inside he found six bills of exchange. He looked them over and checked the date and signatures of each.

Fenwick paused a moment, his thoughts (quite genial and without suspicion) directed toward the young American

whose name was scrawled at the bottom of the short accompanying letter. Farley was about to leave.

"Credit these to Mr. Warren's account, Farley, as I did the
first batch."

Farley took the bills and buff envelope. He looked at the
postmark. "From Birmingham, Mr. Fenwick?" He was
clearly perplexed.

"Colonel Francis has made an arrangement with Mr.
Warren," replied Fenwick tartly. "They're ninety-day bills,
so store them in the vault, and with the receipt reply the
usual—'Hoping you . . . et cetera.' Bring it to me for signing.
It is to go to the Post Office, Birmingham, Poste Restante."

"Yes, sir," said Farley, and as instructed, went into the
outer office to prepare a reply of acceptance. To Mr. Fenwick
it was just another part of the morning's business, as, that
day, dying had been for the Emperor of France.

Fenwick, humming to himself, unaware as yet that with this
second batch of bills from Birmingham accepted, he had committed himself to be part of something great and tragic also,
began to open several other letters as he took a first sip of hot
tea.

It was exactly a quarter to eleven.

§

On the return trip to Birmingham at the beginning of the
New Year, George and Mac had discovered from the letter
Colonel Francis sent on receipt of the bills, which arrived after Christmas, that they had indeed been accepted. The letter
was cordial in tone and hoped that Mr. Warren was
recovering from any effects of the fall from his horse, and
that he might have the pleasure of seeing him in London
soon—he remained, dear sir, Yours faithfully—P.M. Francis.
It had been signed by a Mr. Fenwick on the Manager's behalf.

It was impressive. For the first time George realized how
well Austin had behaved as his alias.

When Mac read the letter, he smiled at George, sharing his
now soaring confidence. Mac's inventiveness had added the
horse in a letter accompanying the bills sent before Christmas,

mindful of the injuries George still displayed. It maintained
the human touch that Austin had assured them would be well
received and continued the personal aspect of the relationship
Austin had established.

The second batch went in and were received on the ninth
day of January, as the next receipt and accompanying letter
stated—now written by Mr. Fenwick and countersigned by a
Mr. Farley. At this the trio's jubilation was difficult to contain. Acceptance of the first dispatch might well have been a
singular favor to her valued client, Mr. Warren—but "the
Old Lady's" crediting of the second batch of bills indicated
strongly that the process—long planned by George; set up by
Austin; prepared by Mac and served by Noyes—would work.

George, Mac and Noyes were now absolutely sure of themselves, and they set their timetable: sixty days. So it began.

§

On January 21, Edwin Noyes stepped out along Lombard
Street (the Wall Street of London, as he liked to refer to it).
Just before twelve o'clock, he entered the Continental Bank
and walked over to the teller, now of his acquaintance, to
make his demands—with charm.

Mr. Richard Amery had taken to short chats with Mr.
Noyes, wherein he learned a good deal about the feelings of
"our cousins across the sea." He knew Mr. Noyes to be the
confidential clerk of Mr. Horton and, as his business appeared to be booming since Christmas, was suitably impressed.

"Well, Mr. Noyes, what'll it be today?" said Mr. Amery.

"Good morning to you, sir," greeted Edwin cordially.
"Four thousand pounds."

"A deal of money," said Amery.

"To go in," smiled Edwin.

"Ah, we are always pleased to hear that," smiled the teller,
reaching under the grille to accept the Bank of England check
now on the counter.

Edwin watched the man stamp the paper. He looked up and
shook his head.

"From Mr. Warren again? That's good business Mr. Horton has, I'd say."

"Yes," Edwin agreed, "and two thousand to go, in gold, if you please." Edwin had decided not to beat about the bush.

Gold would, of course, take several moments longer than paper currency—the bags would have to be checked and weighed—but Edwin was prepared for this. He leaned on the counter and watched the rest of the large bank continue about its business.

"There's the rich, an' there's the poor . . ." the teller behind the grille began to say, as if confidentially, to his financial equal, ". . . isn't that so, Mr. Noyes?"

"There is indeed," replied Edwin sagely, maintaining his role.

"An' never the twain shall meet," said Mr. Amery wistfully. He handed over the two bags; they were heavy.

"Oh, I wouldn't say that," said Edwin quickly. He signed for the gold in four places in the required spaces of the form presented to him, bade Mr. Richard Amery a pleasant good day and left the Continental Bank soon after twelve fifteen.

Finding a cab into the West End took time, as the traffic was congested from the river to Trafalgar Square, so it was past one o'clock when Edwin Noyes finally got transport. He had walked some distance with the two bags weighing more than fifteen pounds each (not too dangerous a thing to do, as during the day the City area was well stocked with policemen, dissuading any street robbery); then, when he left his cab—stuck in a St. James's Street jam, where a heavy beer dray had overturned—he walked again down St. James's Place, to number 7.

Edwin upended one of the Continental bags, and gold spilled onto the table. George and Mac were visibly moved. It was not the first, nor would it be the last, amount they would see, and there would be larger to come; but two thousand gold sovereigns, tangible evidence of all they had worked for, gave them good cause to be stirred.

Edwin was cold, and George handed him a glass of mulled wine from the fireplace, where flames were roaring brightly. Edwin told George, in detail, of the atmosphere he had encountered in the Continental, and George affirmed, with a smile at his joke, that he too was now "content at the Continental." They turned to Mac, who was writing at the table.

"For deposit," he said quietly, concentrating still. He had just signed Mr. Frederick Albert Warren's name with a flourish. "Eight thousand pounds," he continued, "for Mr. C. J. Horton's account." The check was on the Bank of England. Taking a different pen and changing the angle of his hand, Mac again wrote, on a clean sheet of paper, *Make payable to Mr. Noyes the sum of six thousand pounds—cash*. He signed the note with Horton's signature. It looked totally different.

For each withdrawal Edwin made on the Continental, whether attached to the ingoing check or presented by itself, there was a note, authorizing his clerk to collect, signed by Mr. C. J. Horton—written, of course, by Mac.

George took up his black leather bag and moved to the table. Edwin Noyes watched the ink dry on the paper before Mac. George began piling the sovereigns in stacks of ten.

"I'll take these," he said, "to buy bank notes; you'll have them tomorrow, Ed, to order the U.S. Bonds from Jay Cooke."

With notes numbered from the Bank of England it might be possible, George assumed, to trace their passage in the City. Thus, he always cashed notes for gold, or exchanged gold for notes, whichever Edwin drew out of the Continental. Only then would George allow Edwin to collect United States Bonds—currency in themselves—from Jay Cooke, McCulloch and Company.

George, Mac and Noyes had enjoyed a pleasant entry into the year of '73, with prospects of a new life never more real. They gave themselves until the end of February this New Year before their need for flight became acute. That would be the end of their sixty days. This was the plan. With thirty days before the first bills came due, they would have the entire world in which to get lost.

George stopped counting out the sovereigns as he remembered once again the date. This was their twenty-second day.

"Know the weight of ten thousand pounds in gold, Ed?" said George with a wink to Mac.

"Not yet," replied Edwin, falling in with the exuberant mood that had developed.

"Austin had a baby getting it out of Rio," laughed George.

"I ain't had that good fortune," said Edwin.

"Yet," finished Mac for his friend.

George, a powerful man, concealing his strength with graceful movement, lifted Edwin Noyes (who weighed all of one hundred and fifty pounds) effortlessly off his feet.

"Thirty days more on English tripe and onions," George laughed, "and he'll be about it, Mac."

"Put me down!" shouted Edwin. He was more astonished at George's ability to sweep him from the ground so easily than he was at the obvious obstacle so much gold presented.

"Okay, Ed—okay," said George, and with a quick bone-breaking squeeze dropped Edwin to the floor.

"Leave him be, George," said Mac quietly. Edwin made a mental note to engage a trusty porter when the time came to move greater sums than those he had handled to date. As he adjusted his clothes, he looked at Mac.

"Are *you* that strong, Mac?" he asked. Mac, a tall man with a formidable eye, only winked at Edwin, then looked steadily at George.

" 'With a mind *and* muscle'—isn't that correct George?"

George smiled slowly. " '. . . a man will go far,' " he replied, then looked at Edwin and indicated the table. "Let's finish," he said. And they did, counting out the sovereigns into small sacks, which George then placed in his large black brief case.

He arranged a rendezvous the following day with Edwin, bade Mac farewell, then stepped into the corridor. Franz Anton Herold let him out the main entrance door with the information that Miss Green was still "holidaying" on the coast at Eastbourne with "relations." There were implications in the way he said it that spoke of more, but George ignored them and stepped out into the cold sunlight.

Through Mac's windows that fronted onto St. James's Place Edwin watched George walk down the street. He said nothing, but grunted to himself. Mac looked up from the papers on the table.

"What is it?" he asked, for a moment concerned.

Edwin turned around, obviously still cold. "I don't like tripe and onions," he grinned.

The two men burst into laughter. Outside, Franz Anton Herold sniffed haughtily at the hilarity coming from the Captain's rooms, certain that if the laughter was the result of a joke, it was at his expense.

§

January moved steadily toward February. Some days passed quickly; others (especially for Mac, scrutinizing details, concerned always with the bills) seemed to contain more hours than a month.

All the while, the Birmingham run was being done now by either George *or* Mac. No longer traveling together, they alternately stayed one night at the Queens Hotel; sent from the post office more bills and a letter, ostensibly from Mr. Warren, hoping Colonel Francis was . . . and the "plant" was coming . . . et cetera; then collected from Poste Restante the reply and accredited accounting of the previously posted bills. Mr. Warren's credit at the Bank of England was growing to enormous proportions, and it seemed that "the Old Lady" was quite happy about it.

The bills obviously looked good—especially the repeated Rothschild "blues." Mac's continuing industry created in him a tension and fatigue. George's journeying to Birmingham and sense of responsibility, now, for the "project" added daily pressure to his own constant fear of the unexpected. Only Edwin became relaxed. He was growing into his role.

For him, it was all exhilarating. Edwin's confidence increased with every transaction successfully concluded at the Continental, the Bank of the U.S. Bond brokers. It was as if each week he exorcised the nightmare of his past betrayal and incarceration in America. Thus he entered the offices of Jay Cooke and McCulloch without a qualm—bent on trying what, he had finally convinced his friends, would work. It could be, as he put it, *his* contribution to the scheme. Besides, as he'd successfully argued, time was getting short, and the more they could get . . . ? George and Mac had agreed.

Alfred Joseph Baker looked first at the check, then slowly

up at Mr. Noyes. He spoke slowly—eventually.

"Twenty thousand pounds?"

Edwin replied tersely, "A Mr. Warren of the Bank of England, it seems, has done excellent business with Mr. Horton, and the latter, who, although you have yet to ask, is in good health, wishes me to order U.S. Bonds with it—direct."

Baker chewed his lips and mused, still observing Edwin Noyes. "The check will have to be cleared first before we can part with so large a number, Mr. Noyes," he said.

"Oh, come, sir," said Edwin. "The City deals with over seventy-five million pounds of bonds each year. That"—he pointed at the check, almost with contempt—"is only twenty thousand." This, on the part of Edwin, was sheer bravado.

Both men knew it was a very large sum. Edwin had been meeting this pompous little clerk (as Austin had described him) since "Mr. Horton" had gone abroad. Now, in February, the two men were accustomed to each other. Edwin had suggested to George and Mac that he could buy direct from Jay Cooke with a check for Mr. Horton from Warren. The accompanying letter, written by Mac (as Edwin's employer), was composed convincingly, and no problem was anticipated other than the normal formalities. With these Edwin was prepared to cope. This, after all, as he had stated, was *his* particular part of the scheme.

"Twenty thousand," said Mr. Baker in his high-pitched, affected, English "gent" voice, "is one hundred thousand dollars, Mr. Noyes—a not inconsiderable sum."

" 'S all numbers to me," said Edwin, seeing that humble pie might bring this prig off his high horse. "I'm only a three-hundred-a-year clerk—even though I assist Mr. Horton in every way," Edwin could not help adding.

"That's a good salary, I'd say," answered Mr. Baker.

"As I do myself," said Edwin brashly.

"There will, of course, be no problem if this Mr. Warren"—Baker almost spelled it out—"is good for it."

Edwin had anticipated all this. He stood up and brusquely indicated the check.

"Then clear it first. I'll be back tomorrow."

He was about to stride out, maintaining his image and

hoping that what be believed of the Bank of England would come to pass, when the obvious improper tone of Baker's remark settled on him. He turned quickly as he buttoned his coat against the cold outside. Good for it? he thought, as he looked at the podgy face before him. The man was all merely "assumed" confidence. In his "position." Baker would never have "money"—he'd never know it as he, Edwin Noyes, would, inside twenty days now.

The bonds, gold and notes already deposited at Durrant's, at the Cannon Street Hotel and in a trunk at Mac's lodgings (all this due to "Mr. Warren") amounted to over . . . Edwin stopped himself and the figure appeared in his mind. He waved an admonishing finger at Alfred Joseph. "If Mr. Warren's good for it!" he exclaimed. "I don't know the man myself, but there's one other thing I would say. My Mr. Horton's a gentleman, and I'm bettin' this Mr. Warren's much the same as him." He softened his voice as if confiding privileged advice: "Aspersions don't make for promotion."

After Mr. Alfred Joseph Baker discovered the reaction of the Bank of England in providing, with great speed, a personal guarantee for its substantial customer Mr. Warren, he was, the following day, almost a simpering wreck as he asked Edwin (who had arrived to "ascertain Warren's credit") all kinds of nonsense about trivialities the young American might have encountered in London, inquired of Mr. Horton's health several times and spoke of his hopes for more future business—direct—from Mr. Warren.

The impression Edwin felt he had left behind as he walked out of the company offices on that second occasion, with a bundle of U.S. Bonds in his leather bag, was one befitting his role. As with the Continental, so with Jay Cooke, McCulloch. Edwin was, for the moment, "content." Nineteen days to go, he remembered. His head lifted, his stride quickened and Garraway's approached faster with every step.

What exactly he would do with the money when they'd all got out Edwin did not yet know, but it would not be the squandering life of New York that had almost destroyed him. Edwin had decided one thing, at least: apart from a few friends, even in some faraway place he would become a very private person.

Private Lives

THE success of the concept was now clear. As fast as the bills were prepared by Mac and taken to, then posted from, Birmingham by George, they were accepted and credited by the Bank of England with solicitous well wishes that Mr. Warren would continue to prosper. It seemed inconceivable, as the letters of receipt arrived, that it could all be so easy; but the preparation had been long, arduous and thorough.

George Bidwell constantly explored their situation in his mind, looking for a mistake and finding none.

Austin was gone; Noyes with an alibi (the *Times* advertisement and the public interview at Durrant's); Mac and himself unknown. The three men now remaining in London attempted, when they could, to relax in their own way.

Mac with May; George had Ellen; Edwin Noyes, less successful than his friends with women, cursed with a shyness from upbringing, found solace in drink. Never so much as to impair his daily duties or affect his role as Horton's clerk; but George had cause to notice, more than once, on the few occasions they all dined together, that Edwin "enjoyed his tipple."

Mac had suggested the Gaiety to him at the turn of the year, and Edwin grew to like the atmosphere of that well-known public house, where, for the hours he spent and money he poured down his throat, he could lose what were unmistakable signs of more than worry, and less than fear.

They were all gambling now—and knew it. Sense spoke quietly to them all individually, cutting through the bravado of Noyes, the unquestioned experience of Mac and the pervading calm of George; for each of them, the nightmare of unforeseen disaster lay in every hour of the days that passed.

As these days became weeks, the mood among them fluctuated wildly. To Mac, George was always late, and then ill mannered or insensitive and sardonic; Noyes became a slow fool rather than the charming country boy Mac had always thought a friend. To George, Mac had become an irritable, un-co-operative companion. Edwin thought George too smug by half, resented Mac's prima donna behavior and now, with all Mac's accomplishments and obvious education, saw his friend as an aggressive superior, constantly intimidating the young man from Hartford, until he fell into a sullen attitude. None of the three, by this time in February, could detach himself long enough from the building pressure of each day to find words to relieve the tension. Separately, they now retired into a prison of their own making. What mattered most had emerged *with* the initial success—endurance.

Mr. Warren's balance at the Bank of England stood at a massive sum—six figures. Baring's, Blydenstein, Morgan, Rothschilds'—all the major financial houses were now represented on credit at "the Old Lady" to Frederick Albert's account.

The brisk business with Mr. Horton at the Continental had increased dramatically and, now, dangerously; in the rooms of all three men were large quantities of notes, gold and bonds—hidden as yet, but soon to create a problem as the thought of imminent flight grew fast into an immediate necessity.

The evening Edwin arrived at 7 St. James's Place with a large package, he was ushered in by Franz Anton and greeted with a smile. Now an occasional visitor, the young American had made a better impression on Herold than had George.

"Cold, Mr. Hills?" the manservant asked.

Edwin shivered and nodded an answer, enjoying for a moment the alias he used specifically, at George's insistence, for Herold's benefit. "Mr. Wilson is within, sir." Franz Anton indicated Mac's door.

George was already waiting when Edwin entered Mac's rooms. Sitting beside the fire, George watched Edwin cross to the table and lay the package down. If Mr. Noyes, he began to think, became, albeit unfortunately, a *cause célèbre*, then his association with "the young Captain" might eventually come to light; but then, if a full investigation began, how many clues existed that could trap them? George was disturbed suddenly; premonition or foolishness he did not know, but now he wished Noyes had never come to Mac's. Yet he knew that Edwin always changed his circuitous route and never came direct to St. James's Place. So even if he were caught, who could trace his movements? Edwin almost always (on George's instructions) went first to the Terminus Hotel on his way from the City, to leave a message for "Mr. Horton" in the suite to which he had access. There Edwin added the sum withdrawn from the Continental to a column of figures in the ledger predominantly displayed on Mr. Horton's desk.

This practice served to strengthen the business association with his employer. On the occasions when he did not do this, the excuse would be that a rendezvous had been set somewhere "in town." Even then he would return to the hotel, to leave a further message to the effect that the meeting had been a good one and he hoped Mr. Horton would have a pleasant journey, et cetera.

The reason for these notes: that they might provide further evidence corroborating Edwin's role as personal employee. This arrangement continued (in Horton's absence) with instructions to the hotel that all communications should be sent after three days to the Victoria post office. Here they were collected at the end of each week by "Mr. Horton's clerk" Edwin Noyes, presumably (only if questioned) to further them to a Continental destination.

George censored his thoughts. It was tight as a drum; what other precautions were there? He sighed deeply, recognizing that he had become a dismal character recently, as Ellen constantly reminded him; but he could do nothing about it. In any case, it was the immediate leads from which he, George, sought to protect Edwin in the event of . . . No one could connect Noyes with Mac but Herold—and to him Edwin was Mr. Hills.

Only an identification line-up would ruin Edwin; even then he could say perhaps that the alias was an instruction of Mr. Horton's, that this particular business partner was . . . In any event, how would the authorities find 7 St. James's Place? On the evidence they would have, they could never charge Edwin. Anyway, if . . . George screwed up his eyes tight.

"George?" Edwin asked pleasantly, genuinely worried. "You all right?"

George opened his eyes and looked long at Edwin, who was a certain and trusted friend. His heart warmed as the young man smiled. "You want some port?" George asked.

"I'd better not," replied Edwin, glancing at Mac, "after what you two were saying" (remembering—guiltily—their criticism of his drinking). "After all, it's only—"

"Seventeen days," Mac interrupted. He sat back in his chair and rubbed his eyes. Ink stained his fingers, and his brow was furrowed.

"Have you finished?" asked George.

"See for yourself," said Mac. George crossed to the table. *Alphonse de Rothschild* was still wet on a last bill beside the others; the buff envelope, already addressed, together with the accompanying letter wishing Colonel Francis well. George shook his head in wonder, looked at Edwin and spoke kindly.

"Open the package, Ed."

Noyes took off the string, unfolded the brown paper and revealed one hundred thousand dollars' worth of United States Bonds.

Mac took the pocket watch from his waistcoat. "You've only thirty minutes to make the Birmingham train, George."

George was about to retort harshly when the front-door bell rang. Only Mac was not startled. Silence held in the room as they heard the outside door opened and a female voice speak out clearly to Franz Anton. Edwin began quickly to gather up the U.S. Bonds.

"Mac," George began quietly, "I thought we agreed?"

Mac merely looked up at George, his face tired and flushed, his eyes strained, anger curling his lips. Edwin crossed to the trunk and dropped the hastily assembled package inside. Taking out a folded bed sheet, he came back to the table, then threw the sheet so that it fell over all four corners.

"She can't read, George," said Mac.

The door opened, and Edwin (already there in haste) let May into the "office," as she knew it to be. He closed the door. Mac stood up and indicated his friends. "May," he said, "these are business associates—er, Mr. . . ." he looked at Edwin.

"Hills" said Edwin, and shook May's hand; she curtsied.

"And this is . . ." Mac stopped as George crossed quickly to the woman, a smile on his face and the one wish in his mind that she should get out as quickly as possible.

". . . Wilson," said George smoothly.

"How beautiful she is . . ." he began, then looked quickly at Mac. "Get your coat Mac; I think we should all go for a drink." Turning to May, he went on, "Mac has told me so much about you . . ."

"Let me give you a lift to the station," offered Mac, reminding George of his errand.

"I'll get a later train," George answered quickly.

"Mr. Hills." George gestured to Edwin, who once more opened the door and ushered the bewildered May out again.

Mac moved fast, now angry, pulling on his coat. George stopped him at the door and started to turn down the gas lamp on the wall. Shadows began to jump from the light of the fire. Mac was straining to follow May. George was firm. "Ellen is outside, in a cab. I never allow her in, and neither will you allow May. Do you understand?" George's eyes were brilliant, aimed at what remaining sense Mac could now muster.

"Austin's out; Ed has his alibi; I've got an alias; but you"—George paused—"you are wide open."

"Listen, George . . ." Mac knew he was ineffectual.

George grasped Mac affectionately about the neck with a strong hand. "Never both together," he said; "always separate—it's too dangerous."

Mac pulled away, but was held.

"Never," said George; "understand it now. Business is work, and private lives—is pleasure."

Silence between the two men; fire roaring in the grate; a light laugh outside from May. A slight cough sounded faintly from upstairs. George looked up, then slowly back to Mac. "For us all, Mac," he said; "remember."

"Seventeen days," nodded Mac.

"Lock up," said George with a grin.

Franz Anton Herold closed the door firmly after the two men. He paused, listening to young Mr. Hills bid Mr. Wilson good night, then turned round to return to the warmth downstairs. He glanced at the young Captain's door as he passed. Since Miss Agnes had lost the master key he had been unable to enter the downstairs rooms, unless they were occupied—just to check, of course. He hoped all was in order; after five years in employ, he'd become attached to number 7. He tried the handle of the door, sniffed disparagingly with the thought that the Captain wasn't a proper toff the way he used to know 'em and went belowstairs.

§

The cab was not a hansom, nor was it a carriage. It carried four people in less than comfort and, with a surly driver, hardly created the fabled atmosphere of foggy London nights. But it would arrive at its destination, and for money, the driver, despite his ill-mannered impatience, would wait, move or stop at the beck of his fares; it was merely the prerogative of tradition that he grumbled.

His horses cantered, galloped and sidled through the evening traffic in light rain that added wetness to the heavy yellow fog all around; only gas lamps breathed noxious fire to light their route.

To Mac, faraway places had never seemed more attractive. He longed to be elsewhere. Ellen had met May, Mac had shaken George's woman's hand and then only the rattling wheels and outside cries of the night city interrupted further thought.

The two women eyed each other suspiciously as Mac fell

into a semiconscious awareness. Life, for the moment, became a dream, and only the fixed stare of George, the glittering eyes of Ellen or a jolt and shout at a crossing brought him back into the cocoon of the vehicle and a dim perusal of his situation. He was exhausted.

The cab stopped. No one moved for a moment, and Mac peeped out the small window.

"We've arrived," he said.

"Not yet, Mac," said George pointedly, "not yet."

The cab continued, how long Mac did not know—all he could feel was May's warmth beside him. The cold outside was dangerous and predatory, as if wishing to invade the small compartment and envelop the group. Mac shivered and shook himself fully awake.

"Euston," said George. The cab was stationary.

"Have a good journey," said Mac.

George climbed out, helped Ellen down from the other side and made sure that their overnight cases were taken by the porter from the cabbie.

"Where's Ed?" said Mac suddenly, realizing his friend had gone without a farewell.

"He took a hansom," said George.

"Where to, sir?" asked the porter. The rain was laying a film on his shoulders, and tip or no, he wasn't going to risk his death waiting for the likes of these gents.

"Birmingham," said George.

The porter wheeled the bags away. The gaslights of the station were just discernible in the background.

Ellen began to follow; George, stern-faced, merely waved a hand, and the group disappeared into the fog. May giggled. Mac looked at her clear eyes and happy smile, drew the woman toward him—and was interrupted in an embrace.

"Where to, sir?" was repeated now by the driver roughly, through the open trap above the pair inside the cab.

"The Gaiety," answered Mac, looking up.

"With the lady, sir?" The cabbie, knowing the place, was obviously offering a warning.

"Yes, cabbie," said Mac, as he gazed long and affectionately at his woman, "with the lady."

The trap slammed shut, and horses jerked the cab away into the wet, yellow shroud of a cold London night. To the two lovers it was all lost in a kiss.

§

The warmth of the Caribbean was balm to tortured imaginings Austin Bidwell could not, even with overwhelming optimism, exclude from his mind. Now that he knew the operation was under way, even thousands of miles behind, his nerves needed strict discipline. He had lost, in the first week out from a last European stop at Lisbon, the boyish exuberance that Elizabeth had become accustomed to, yet she made no attempt to scold or return Austin's mood in kind; she merely waited, always affectionate, willingly sympathetic, until Austin finally confided that business problems had been troubling him.

Privately, he hoped that the New World would provide overwhelming distractions—sufficient at least to relieve his increasing anxiety. It began merely as a wish, but the morning Austin awoke to the first breath of Gulf air, it became fact. Soft trade-wind clouds, floating above a warm, clear blue sea and distant vessels, under billows of sail or with a thin stream of smoke, on the horizon, as they rose and sank beyond vision, became as if a dioramic dream. Islands appeared to float by until the reality of their first port of call, St. Thomas; rich, luxuriant vegetation shading white sand beaches and a colorful shantytown below the more settled colonial houses of the harbor brought home to Austin forcibly that here was another world and it was, if he chose, his.

After a late lunch on the second day out from St. Thomas, the Captain of the *Martinique* informed first-class passengers that soon the highlands of Cuba would be in sight—the Pan of Matanzas. Although it was still clear overhead, a mist lay along the southern horizon. At about four, the undulating coast line became visible, though the ship was still sixty miles from Havana.

Westward along the northern shore the fertile land came right to the sea, rising inland to hills above which lay galleonlike clouds, peculiar to the Caribbean. The turquoise and myriad blues of the water were ornament to the pale wash of sky, sun-scorched till dusk.

At the rail of the *Martinique*, Austin and Elizabeth leaned forward, as did all others aboard, pointing excitedly as the capital of Cuba emerged from the fading day. There, right ahead of them, was a city on the sea, seemingly without harbor or bay; jutting across it, the Morro, a stately hill of tawny rock, rising vertically out of the water; walls, parapets and towers; atop, flags and signals flying, whilst just in front of its outer wall was a tall lighthouse, commanding the sea all around.

As *Martinique* slowed to make her approach, all her passengers could see the narrow harbor entrance between the Punta and the Morro; beyond appeared a mass of innumerable masts and funnels. The loud horn of the *Martinique* bellowed across the water and received a flash of light from the tall tower before the Morro.

A deep, resounding shot was fired from the Citadel and caused all aboard to look first ashore, then westward as the sun dipped below the horizon. It was the sunset gun, now followed by trumpets echoing over the water from the fortifications. It was too late to enter port, so the Captain reluctantly went about and turned north, full ahead, to find sea room for a night anchorage.

Darkness fell quickly, but still Austin and Elizabeth lingered on deck. The slow rise and fall of the sea beneath a sky full of stars, the Southern Cross just above the horizon, two streams of light on the sea—one of gold from the Morro, one of silver from the moon—created an enchantment that made decision easy for the two travelers staring toward the shore.

Austin had whispered to his lady, relinquishing the idea, grown and nurtured during the voyage, of continuing to Mexico and taking a hacienda near Vera Cruz; in a word he had created the future: "Cuba," he had said. Elizabeth had only sighed.

Blood and gold, the yellow-striped flag of Spain flew over the towers, guns and signal poles of the Morro fortress as a first glow of dawn revealed Havana to the several passengers already on the deck of the *Martinique*.

The morning gun thundered out, and a "leave to enter" signal was run up on the Citadel. The ship pulled its anchor and, at full ahead, bore down on the channel into the harbor. Blue, white and yellow houses with red-tiled roofs; the quaint old cathedral towers; continuing lines of fortifications and seeming endless masts and "stacks" of shipping, densely assembled at the quays and docks below an already azure sky, only traces of sunrise remaining, framed with the backdrop of luxuriant hills: all this, was, to Austin, a reminder of Rio; but here was civilization and—perhaps—home.

The *Martinique*, as she slowed, was besieged by boats to load oranges, bananas, water, supplies or to take off the passengers going ashore. Austin had determined already; the bags had been waiting since the first light—of blood and gold.

§

After several days at the Grand Hotel (not quite up to its name, but at least a tropical version of service and cleanliness), Don Fernando, the proprietor, offered Austin his large villa built on a hillside above the Gulf, with superb panoramas and cool protective surrounding vegetation. Austin agreed to the price and moved in with Elizabeth.

Here life became a series of outings, dinners, parties and dances: the colonial ideal; the heaven-on-earth. Austin soon became acquainted with most of Havana Society, and his personality established him as an excellent guest and generous host. Via the telegraph to the United States, thence Europe, Austin had communicated his whereabouts to George, Mac and Noyes. Thus, when the middle of February had passed and, in the north, raged still—the blizzards and winter storms—in Havana, at Customs, Austin received the first of several packages. No report was recorded or seal damaged, but several Customs officers were able to add substantially to their civilian wardrobes.

On the evening of February 21, Austin and Elizabeth drove along the Paseo de Ysabel Segunda. It was the custom before supper, between five and dusk, to ride here or the Campo de Marte and then along the Paseo de Tacón, a beautiful double avenue, lined with trees, which led two or three miles into the countryside from the sea.

The tropical day turned slowly to night: above, the clear moon in a blue field of glittering stars; all about, the pure, balmy air with its myriad aromas and hum of crickets, flash of firefly and soaring swallows. The English-style carriage, with two servants in livery on the box, took Austin and Elizabeth to the rise from which they were able to look back on the city. In the distance, oil lamps and gas burners danced with fireflies that were all around the stationary carriage.

Austin's cigar smoke wafted into the air, where, from overhead, the stars arced toward Havana until all the twinkling pinpoints of light—moving insect, stationary man-made and infinite glitter—became one, as if gems thrown on soft purple velvet.

Elizabeth felt the relaxation in her man, with whom she now lived as "wife."

"Europe seems so far away," she said thoughtfully.

Austin did not reply.

"Are you glad we remained here?" Elizabeth asked.

"Instead of Mexico?" replied Austin.

"Yes," said Elizabeth, lying against his shoulder, looking up into the night.

"We'll go there, eventually," said Austin slowly.

"Why?" asked Elizabeth, mildly troubled that they might now be disturbed from the pleasure they'd found.

"Reasons," said Austin, and then was quiet.

Elizabeth knew that something had again come to trouble Austin; she had thought that they had left the past behind.

"The only time you become agitated is when the New York papers arrive. Why?" she asked.

"Because they're already a week into history afore I read 'em," said Austin and drew on his cigar—now, after several years of smoking them in many countries, bought from source at the very place where they were rolled.

"The large package," Elizabeth began after a while, "that arrived the other day . . ."

"What of it?" Austin spoke lazily.

"It was cleared through Customs unopened." Elizabeth wanted an explanation.

"A *douceur*," Austin said with a smile at his woman, rubbing his finger and thumb by way of illustration, "buys co-operation."

The two people relaxed a moment longer; then Elizabeth rustled her dress and took something from her purse. She unfolded the paper and wafted it in front of Austin.

"It contained a fortune in U.S. Bonds," she said decisively, and smiled. The paper was self-evident—a bond. Austin was at first startled, then angry, but the woman beside him only began to laugh at his consternation.

"I will explain . . ." he began.

Elizabeth stopped him with a kiss.

"There is no need." she said, then looked away. "Besides," she went on softly, "it will give our little visitor—security."

Austin sighed and signaled to the driver. Eventually he would have to tell Elizabeth the truth, when the storm broke: as it would—inevitably.

"What visitor?" he asked absently, and leaned back to look up into the infinite depths of night; there was not a cloud in sight.

"I've been to the doctor," said Elizabeth.

§

The two men walking briskly down Bond Street hesitated at the intersection of Bruton Street and decided to turn left toward Regent Street. Once again, halfway along, one changed his mind and, remembering that the small jeweler's they wanted would be closed for luncheon, decided to walk directly to St. James's Place, where a rendezvous had previously been set, for which both men were already late.

Thus it was that George Bidwell and Edwin Noyes found themselves walking down Savile Row at five minutes past one on the twenty-second day of February 1873.

"One more week, Ed," said George.

"We're late for Mac," Edwin replied, noting that George had lengthened his stride.

"St. James's is not far," George said, his warm breath misting in the cold air.

The day was bright, an overcast of light cloud diffused the sun, but it was still quite definitely winter. The voice, sharp, and directed at the owner of the name it uttered with such surety, stopped both George and Edwin dead.

"Mr. Warren, sir!" it cried.

George turned slowly, prepared for anything.

An eager young man ran up.

"I was just returning from an errand, sir," he said to George. "Mr. Green's, sir!"

Edwin remained puzzled.

"Mr. Williams, sir—of the cane."

George knew instantly, but nodded slowly. "Mr. Williams," he said laconically, suppressing a scream of anger. "Well met." They shook hands.

"Indeed it is, sir." Mr. Williams pumped George's hand. "Indeed it is," he repeated with pleasure.

"My . . ." George paused as he referred Williams to Edwin with a private glance. ". . . brother's—tailor," he said.

"Pleased to meet you, Mr. . . . ?" Williams had taken the initiative.

"Hills," said Edwin, and shook hands with Mr. Williams.

" 'Ills, pleased, I'm sure," said Williams. "What a night we 'ad in Paris, eh, Mr. Warren?" he said, looking directly at George. "How is Mr. F.A.?"

"Well, Mr. Williams, well," said George quickly. "I am afraid we are in rather a hurry. Perhaps some other time we could . . ." George faltered.

"It would be my pleasure to buy us all a noggin," said Williams with a smile.

"I'm sorry." George tapped the watch he'd taken from his pocket and, with a forced smile, shrugged.

"Another time, then," said Williams, a little despondent. " 'Ere, Mr. 'Ills," he continued, taking one out: " 'ere's me card."

"Good day, sir," said George. Edwin took the small rectangle of card, pocketed it absently and, as he turned sharply, instantly forgot Williams. The two men walked quickly away.

At the end of the street Williams thought he saw George wave (it was, in fact, a gesture at a small beggar boy out of sight). He raised his arm and waved back enthusiastically.

Williams went into Mr. Green's with a smile on his face. "A nice coincidence, he said to himself." As he closed the shop door he caught a glimpse of the sky, which had darkened just in those moments outside. It began to rain.

"Lucky, that," he said to one of his colleagues as he took off his coat. "I was almost caught out in it."

Omission

OF all the papers concerning medical science read before the British Association at the beginning of 1873, none was more important than that of Professor Ferrier on the localization of the functions of the brain. From the time it had been established that the brain, as a whole, was the organ of feeling, of thought and of voluntary motion, it had become more than probable that each of these functions had its especial seat in the nervous tissue and that their partial operations might also be localized in a similar manner.

Ferrier, experimenting with induced electric current, had established the constant and definite results that stimulation of the same part of the surface of a hemisphere always produces the same movement, not only in the same animal but in all animals of its species. Thus when the conductors touched one portion of the brain, a front limb was moved in some determinate direction; when they penetrated another, a hind limb moved instead. In this way a great variety of actions were illustrated with absolute certainty.

Ferrier deduced from this that the cerebrum had a proper reflex action of its own and that this action was exerted unconsciously, so that a connected series of cerebral modifications could take place, of which only the results came within the sphere of consciousness as ideas or emotions. As to the question whether the centers of the movements were also the "organs" of the ideas or emotions which called forth those movements, Ferrier expressed himself more doubtful. It was as well!

Religious groups did not react in any other way than characteristically to the publication of such phenomena and interference with God's instrument on earth. The spark of life was the soul, it was religiously and forcibly declared; and where, it was asked, in Dr. Ferrier's experiments, had he established that soul to be?

The enraged eye and pointing finger of numerous sermons in divine flight, that Sunday after the revelation had been made public, gleefully emphasized that these devilish experiments were doomed; for if man was made in God's image, would the Almighty await discovery in the body of man at the hands of a quack scientist with a galvanic battery?

In the main, the religious hysteria had missed the point. Ferrier indeed established what *was* in man, and conceded, perhaps disturbingly, that even in so doing he might have established what also, in man, *was not*.

§

In the late afternoon of Thursday, February 27, 1873, in the rooms of "Captain" MacDonald at 7 St. James's Place, George Bidwell and Edwin Noyes were at the end of their task, counting out the sizable amounts of U.S. Bonds, gold and Bank of England notes taken from the large trunk.

Mac stoked up a fire until the flames roared with heat, intense even for a cold winter day. The blinds were drawn. Outside, it was becoming dark already.

"One last trip, George," Mac said, "and we can clear out."

"What's remaining?" asked George, pausing before a final count of the sheaf of notes on the table. All three men were in their shirt sleeves.

"Four on Rothschilds'," said Mac, taking the bills of exchange from the table, "and two on Blydenstein."

"That's one hundred and forty thousand dollars!" exclaimed Edwin Noyes, incredulous.

"And that touches our 'two,' George," said Mac quietly.

A silence gripped the men in the room as Mac's words went home. Two million dollars! The gas burners hissed loudly; the fire crackled. St. James's traffic passed by in the distance.

Four hundred thousand pounds. George sat down slowly on a chair at the table. He looked from Edwin to Mac.

"For a man who's talking in millions, he's very calm—eh, Ed?" Edwin merely smiled at George's rhetorical question.

"I'm tired, George," said Mac.

George nodded and saw in Mac the tension in them all. It was finished. The sixty days they had prescribed were over. They would have the thirty days remaining (until the first bills were due to be presented at their issuing house) to disappear. George pointed at the Bank of England checkbook on the table.

"Write the checks, Mac," he said. "One for Jay Cooke, an' we'll take bonds direct; Horton's to endorse it on the back." He paused. "Ed"—George turned to Edwin Noyes—"you order for one hundred thousand dollars' worth tomorrow."

Mac began to write.

"The other check make out from Warren to Horton again—that will be the final one to be credited at the Continental." A thought occurred to George as he looked at Edwin. "Your rent all paid up, Ed?"

"Yeah," said Edwin, still counting sovereigns, "by Mr. Horton."

George looked at the checkbook in front of Mac, who caught his eye.

"One more blank," Mac said, indicating the last unused check.

"We'll leave it," said George, and began counting the bonds again. Edwin Noyes looked up a moment, saw Mac writing, then continued counting sovereigns. It was so hot now, all three men were sweating.

Mac finished the two checks as George came around the table; he looked at the six bills, still incomplete.

"I'll finish 'em this evening," said Mac. "Pick them up at

Holborn on the way to Euston Station.''

"Okay," agreed George, after a pause. He looked at the roaring fire, Edwin's now expectant face and the pile of wood blocks, seals and reject paper they had accumulated in a heap at the fire grate. He nodded to Edwin Noyes.

"Let's get rid of all that will burn," he said. "The rest goes into the River Thames—tonight." He looked at Mac, who smiled at the words and began moving toward the fire to throw into the consuming flames the instruments of fraud. George's relief was obvious.

"It's over," he said.

§

In May's lodgings, above the Red Lion at Holborn, Mac was seated at a small table near the window, and May was where Mac could see her, through the open partition doors to the other room—in bed.

"Mr. MacDonald," she said slowly. The name was allure in itself, for she spoke it with love. Mac moved the oil lamp nearer his pen, then turned briefly to see the outline of his woman beneath the covers, her head against a pillow at the headboard. Mac looked again at the six bills laid out on the blotting pad. A letter he'd written to the Manager of the Bank of England was already folded, put to one side.

The small table was a pull-out extension of a chest of drawers, with a corrugated roll top. A metal arm that swung on a hinge allowed Mac to insert an oil lamp and guide its light to the precise spot he needed to see the signatures he was putting on each bill.

It was more the feel of the hand and the preparation than was actual writing of the name that took time: a confident flourish was achieved only when the hand rested in the correct position and the pen had the right angle, the arm dictating the exact pressure. Mac concentrated, then wrote, *Alphonse de Rothschild* and the date.

The bedclothes rustled in the other room, and soft footsteps crossed the space between bed and table. May kissed Mac on the cheek. He looked at his pocket watch, open on the table.

"He's late," said Mac.

"I left the door unlocked," answered May, and kissed Mac again.

"Good," replied Mac, and absently kissed May in return, indicating in the kindest possible manner that he, as yet, was not finished and wanted no interruption. As May moved away, a knock sounded out below. Mac swore. "Damn!" The pen was poised again.

May quickly took her robe from the bedroom, wrapped it around herself and crossed back to the hall door, which was ajar. Footsteps could be heard clearly as she opened the door wide and looked out. Mac wrote again, a signature and the date. On the landing outside, George saw May. He shook her hand formally. "Mr. Wilson," she greeted. "May," George rejoined, then entered the room. He was wet.

"It's raining," he said. Mac only grunted.

"Would you like something to drink?" asked May.

"I've got a cab waiting," replied George. He stood a moment, surveyed the cozy rooms, then walked the few paces to Mac. He stood by the window and looked into the wet night.

"It's cold out," he said.

"Mmm," Mac muttered, and wrote again.

George looked down at the table top beneath the oil lamp and in the circular pool of light caught sight of the last bills—the four completed on Rothschild and two from Blydenstein.

"Two more?" George asked quietly.

"I've done the Rothschilds'," said Mac, "and the letter," he finished, indicating.

"You've done," said George warmly, "a good job, Mac."

He looked at the four blue bills closely. They were perfect.

"Garraway's?" asked Mac as he leaned toward the two Blydenstein bills—a different pen, different ink and shaping a different hand.

"Saturday," said George. "I'll be back from Birmingham tomorrow, but we're going to the opera in the evening."

"With Ellen?" asked Mac absently.

"I'm educating her," replied George with a smile.

"She outside?" May smiled as she spoke, holding the robe to her. There was a draft from the stairs, so she crossed nearer to the small fireplace.

"Ellen is all right," said George; "she's wrapped in rugs and a fur." He hesitated, then found the right words. "She doesn't like climbing stairs at night; she's afraid of her ankles," he finished lamely.

Mac looked up and across at May, who smiled beautifully; then he caught George's eye. It was a weak excuse, and Mac was becoming sick of deception. May didn't understand the need to keep "private" lives separate, as George had always insisted. She thought that Ellen was too grand to enter a "slum" and, although not showing it, was obviously upset at this false pride.

Mac looked about the rooms, putting down his pen. He was irritated now and stared long at his friend. George became uncomfortable. He swallowed.

"Cozy, eh, George?" Mac said.

"Yes," George replied honestly, expressing his own first reaction.

"They belong to May," Mac indicated with a gesture. Involuntarily George took in the rooms, then smiled at the lovely woman by the fire.

"Assigned"—May pronounced the new word in her vocabulary with real pride—"to me."

"Look, Mac," began George, "I'll go down and bring Ellen up if you like. I just thought the bills would be . . . Besides, we don't have much time for the train; if I'm to catch tonight's mail, I . . ." He stopped.

"George," said Mac softly, "you don't have to say a thing." He turned back to the table, signed both bills carefully and put the date on the top corner of one of them. He dipped his pen in the ink a final time; the metal on glass sounded quite clearly in the silence.

May, a little embarrassed, spoke out. "True 'uns is rare," she said looking at George but speaking for Mac's benefit. The words went home and took the poison from Mac's mind, as they did the pen from his hand. He put it down on the blotter and turned to George, memories of their adventures flooding his mind, overwhelming his emotions. This was a friend, and he wished him no harm. Mac stood up and grasped George by the shoulders.

"Nice to 'ave, 'ard to keep," said Mac, mimicking May's London accent.

"What?" asked George, puzzled.

"Friends, George," said Mac: "you and Austin and Ed."

George caught the welling emotion and embraced Mac affectionately. Mac smelled rain on the coat and felt his face wet on George's shoulder.

"Halcyon days, Mac," said George thickly.

"And Helicon nights," Mac added with a grin. The two men remained locked together a moment longer. Then George coughed, and they parted. He looked down at the bills.

"Finished?" he asked.

"Yes," replied Mac, looking at May with love.

Tears were in her eyes as Mac embraced his woman in an altogether different way than he had his comrade and friend. Here were lovers.

George gathered up the six bills and short letter for "the Old Lady's" Manager, then put this last of Mac's work in an envelope, which he placed carefully in his pocket. Kissing May good night, and shaking Mac's hand farewell, George went. Footsteps on the stairs, a pause, a slam of the outside door; then, through the window, the sound of a whip, a rattle of wheels and the whinny of a horse. George was gone.

Mac and May went into the bedroom. The rain outside had become heavier and spattered on the window louder. The flame in the oil lamp jumped, bringing May back to the small table a moment from the bedroom. The soft light, as she turned out the lamp, made of the pale curves of her flesh an artist's dream. The lamp out, only a shadow flitted back to the waiting arms in her bed. Of the table and its blotter, nothing at all could now be seen.

§

A daily postal service was a positive boon to business, reflected Mr. Fenwick as he entered his office at the Bank of England, precisely as the chimes from several of the City's clocks struck the hour of nine. Already on his desk were a

number of buff and white envelopes, come from several of
England's cities. The railway was making its mark on
civilization in numerous ways—not the least, continued the
thoughts of Mr. Fenwick as he eased off his coat, rubbed his
hands by the gas fire and took the first of many glances out of
the window that day; not the least, he repeated to himself, in
aiding the developing sophistication and, above all, reliability
of the postal system of Great Britain.

The door opened and a head popped through.

"Morning, Mr. Fenwick," came the bright greeting. "Tea,
sir?" the voice asked.

"One morning, Farley," Mr. Fenwick replied quickly, "I
might say, 'No.' "

"Only were the earth to turn about, an' the moon to fall
into the Hatlantic Ocean, sir," Farley finished cheerfully.

"Very graphic, Mr. Farley," went on Mr. Fenwick, sitting
at his desk, "I prescribe less fantasy, more study and two
spoons of sugar." Mr. Fenwick felt quite cheerful himself. It
was a fresh morning, and the brisk walk from Westminster
had warmed his bones; since his early rising in the dark had
been to discover that his "woman who did" was ill and he
had no provisions, this morning—especially—tea was most
welcome.

"Well, go along, Farley, go along," said Mr. Fenwick.
"I've a deal to do, and you've to be more than tea boy today
by the amount of work on your desk."

"Yes, sir," said Farley, and went, closing the door quietly.

"Now," said Fenwick of the Bank, to himself, "to
business." He began to open the mail.

§

Some moments after ten o'clock, still with his gloves on,
Colonel Francis, Manager of the Bank of England, reached
out to the calendar on his desk and changed the day to Friday,
February 28, 1873. February was damnably cold this year, he
thought as he went directly over to the open fireplace, where
flames pleasantly threw out their warmth.

Peregrine Madgewick began to prise off the gloves from his
still-frozen fingers. His face remained red from the cold air

outside. The short walk he had promised his wife to take every day was becoming shorter by the month; damn his constitution and circulation, did she want his limbs to fall off? Brusquely he shouted at the timid knock that always indicated ten o'clock, or thereabouts.

"Well, come in, Fenwick!"

Fenwick entered and stood as if it were his first time in the office. Colonel Francis, still prising at his gloves, pointed, two-handed, toward his desk.

"Well, put them down!"

Fenwick crossed to place the already opened mail on the leather surface.

"What have we this morning?" asked Francis.

"Well, sir . . ." began Fenwick hesitantly. "Ah . . . well . . ." He began to look at his notes.

"Well, sir!" exploded Colonel Francis. "Well?" he repeated loudly. "Must you always enter this office with the night's fog in your brain?" He pointed a now naked, admonishing finger. "Mr. Fenwick, a little less tannin in the blood and you might think clear and fast."

"Tannin, sir?" asked Fenwick, puzzled.

"The cocaine of the addicted tea drinker, Mr. Fenwick." Colonel Francis sat down heavily. "Come, to business. I warn you, I am in a brisk mood."

At that moment the fire crackled, as if to corroborate the fact. Mr. Fenwick inched around the desk to offer guidance on the mail.

"Ah, Mr. Warren, sir . . ." he began. "We have six further bills, posted yesterday evening."

"And how is he?" inquired Colonel Francis.

"Well, he assures me, sir—the . . . er . . ." He fumbled over the word. ". . . the 'plant' progresses, due he says to the hardworking abilities of our British workmen."

"Splendid," said Colonel Francis with a wide smile. "See that he receives my best regards and hope of continued success. How does his account stand at present?" he asked Fenwick.

"Er—large, sir," said Fenwick. "At the moment."

"What do you mean?" asked Francis absently, already looking at another letter.

"A messenger from Jay Cooke came again, sir, not ten minutes ago, to request clearance on a check to this Mr. Horton, of Mr. Warren's acquaintance."

"For what sum?" questioned Francis.

"Twenty thousand pounds, sir," said Fenwick.

"Mmm," mused Peregrine Madgewick, "we have done this before, have we not?"

"We have, sir—several times," answered Fenwick.

"Then why ask me?" said Francis.

"Well, sir—it is procedure," replied Fenwick.

"Quite right," said Francis after a pause. "Well, then, see to it."

"Yes, sir," said Fenwick.

"Next?" questioned Francis.

"Ah, the bills, sir—Mr. Warren . . ." began Fenwick.

"Well, credit them and deposit the bills as usual in the exchange vault, if they are the normal three-month—are they?" asked Francis. Fenwick replied in the affirmative.

"Well, then, do it, Fenwick, and return my regards as instructed; must I explain procedure after sixteen years?"

"One of the bills," said Fenwick, "is undated—sir."

Colonel Francis rubbed his hands, thought of his wife, stood up, crossed again to the fire, wished lunch to arrive sooner than the prescribed hour, thought of mulled wine and said, "Well . . . er . . . undated?" It was unusual but not unknown.

"Might I suggest, sir," said Fenwick, "that we return it to have the . . . omission . . . corrected?"

"Whose is it?" asked Colonel Francis.

"Blydenstein," said Fenwick.

Colonel Francis put his head back as he turned around at the fire, opening the vent of his long coat to arouse chilled buttocks.

He closed his eyes and sniffed away the beginnings of a cold.

"We've a messenger tomorrow morning, have we not?"

"Yes, sir; always on a Saturday we deliver bills come due—it clears the week." Fenwick was explaining common knowledge; Francis became irritable.

"Someone of trust, I hope?" he said.

"Yes, sir, absolutely," answered Fenwick.

"Who?" asked Francis, rocking on his heels as he opened his eyes to fix Fenwick with the look his wife said frightened children.

"Me, sir," replied Fenwick, not a little proud.

"Really," said Francis, genuinely interested that Fenwick himself would cross the City to add work to his load of the sixth day of the week—not realizing that Fenwick actually liked walking.

"Then you, Mr. Fenwick, will do, as will tomorrow, to inform Blydenstein of their mistake," he said.

"Omission, sir," said Fenwick, correcting the word for the sake of manners and the touchy temperament he knew the clerks at Blydenstein to have.

"Can we get on?" asked the exasperated Manager with a grimace at his assistant.

"Indeed, sir," said Mr. Fenwick.

The rest of the meeting had nothing whatsoever to do with Mr. Frederick Albert Warren. Fate had already taken charge.

"Change Alley"

SATURDAY morning the first of March 1873, in London was a day from the gods. Crisp air, clear blue sky and an unmistakable but indefinable smell of spring on the slight breeze that blew until early afternoon. It was a day when even the hopeless and desperate majority gave way to speculation—anticipation that what was to come must be an improvement on what had gone before.

It almost never is, of course; for civilized man, existence with hope offers only the ever-distant promise seemingly fulfilled always by others.

That morning, stepping out of the Jay Cooke, McCulloch and Company offices in St. Swithin's Lane, Edwin Noyes knew with utter certainty that he was one of "the others"—the chosen in life; he was at the threshold of all his dreams, at the portals of a New World. He could hardly suppress his spirits, which lifted with each step he took, despite the bulky black leather case he carried. He wanted to tell the world that he was one of fortune's favorites, to sing an aria to fate, to bless chance, to offer up praise for luck, to thank God for his endurance. Never to return to Jay Cooke—what a thought!

He skipped a pace and reached the cobbles beside his waiting four-wheel, four-seater "growler"—the large cab he had taken solely because the cabbie had the hoods down and it was open to the bright morning sunlight. He climbed in; tipped his hat to Alfred Joseph Baker (still waving through the window of the Company offices), who had just given him one hundred thousand dollars' worth of U.S. Bonds; turned to the cabbie and, as he settled back in the seat, dropping the leather bag at his feet, said, with a light heart and an open smile, "Continental Bank, my man."

If the cabbie did not, his horses caught Edwin's spirits, and the growler took off with a lurch.

At the bank, Edwin paid in the check from Mr. Warren to Mr. Horton; signed for notes he took in a package from Mr. Amery and, bidding him good morning, left the Continental Bank—never, he hoped, to return. Outside, his spirit surged again, and one word was enough to set the cabbie in motion.

"Garraway's," he said, and the growler moved off once more.

§

Coming from opposite ends of "Change Alley," Mac and George greeted each other with an exuberance accumulated throughout the morning when each had realized what it meant: that the scheme was over. Months of tension now dissipated in the crisp air as sunlight found its way into the narrow alley and bathed both men with momentary warmth as they clapped each other about the shoulders. To the idle onlooker, they could have been brokers successful in a morning's coup or City speculators informing each other of an improving market.

They stamped their feet to improve circulation, blew warm breath into the cold air and smiled in anticipation of Edwin Noyes's imminent arrival. The rendezvous time had been strictly set. It was eleven thirty.

§

The four-seater growler was unable to enter the narrow alley, so Edwin Noyes alighted at the southern end and, taking the leather bag in one hand and the package from the Continental Bank in the other, began awkwardly to negotiate the increasing pedestrian traffic that flowed to and fro from Cornhill and Lombard Street.

Dogs chasing a cat almost took Edwin's feet from under him, and four urchins ran by, knocking into him, one of them depriving the gen'lem'n of a loose handkerchief from his side pocket. Edwin's nose was running and he was irritated by the time he saw George and Mac. Their laughter at his condition and disheveled appearance did not soften Edwin's mood; after all, that morning, it was he alone who had completed the operation.

But it was just that thought which went home to Edwin as George and Mac relieved him of the bag and package, then indicated the warm, inviting interior of Garraway's with sympathetic smiles. Just as the awkward weight had been lifted from his arms by his two friends, so the burden of the past weeks dissolved in his mind; thus a smile was on each of the Americans' faces as they entered Garraway's for the last time.

§

The rush and bustle of "Change Alley" continued as the City went about its business. An old man of modest means, waiting in a solicitor's office, adjacent to Garraway's entrance, with a view down the Alley, saw two small chimney sweeps pass; a gypsy seller of lucky heather; two beggars—one legless—who always seemed to be about the area, one dragging the other on a makeshift cart. A pair of well-to-do ladies, veiled against recognition, passed, clinging tightly to each other, chattering excitedly, moving beneath their voluminous dresses as if on wheels, rolling rather than walking. A window cleaner, farther down the way, was washing the bow front of a gentlemen's-accouterments shop. The numerous bank messengers ran up and down, clutching their satchels. Three soldiers of a Guards regiment sauntered by, pausing beside the cleaner at the gentlemen's shop before merging with the crowd.

As the old man shifted in his seat and checked his pocket watch against the ancient clock on the dark interior wall opposite, he took his gaze from the Alley for the first time in some minutes and so missed the emerging figure, moving slowly, coming up the narrow public way as if in a state of shock—ashen and distracted. He was jostled continually but appeared not to notice.

The old man signed loudly, then coughed, in the hope his solicitor, through the closed door, would remember an appointment already well overdue. He pocketed his watch and again squinted out into the busy Alley, to catch the first sight of a man who, he noted, looked decidedly ill. As the figure stepped slowly into sunlight out of shadow, the old man confirmed his first impression, but then forgot the Alley altogether as the door opened and a clerk beckoned to him from the inner office.

He went in to his solicitor, rallying arguments to support his important business. He would not pay out more money under any circumstances. It was his opinion that he had been duped. The door closed; the room was empty; the sole, vaguely concerned witness to Mr. Fenwick's physical state, gone. It was eleven thirty-nine.

§

Fenwick felt the need to lean on something the moment he sensed sunlight on his face. He was faint. He put out his hand and steadied himself against the wood support of a doorframe. He could feel warmth from somewhere, but could make no sense of his surroundings. Thoughts merged with voices. He was unable to decipher reality from the fearful imaginings that inundated his mind.

The one word at Blydenstein, not twenty minutes before, had destroyed Fenwick's world.

The door beside Fenwick opened suddenly and several men came out; with them, the warmth of the interior and a babble of conversation. Fenwick smelled alcohol, and the one clear thought of a strong brandy for a moment checked his growing confusion. At eleven forty, Fenwick entered Garraway's.

"Yes, sir?" asked the young man behind the long bar. Fenwick merely gazed blankly at the face before him. "What'll it be?" the young man questioned again, now with less politeness. Fenwick remained dumb. "Drink?" the young man said in contempt, thinking his customer already drunk. There were others at the bar, and he had no time to fool with the likes of this man. He was about to take another order, and could see one of the waiters signaling from the center of the dining room, already crowded, that drinks would be required, when Fenwick spoke.

"Brandy," he said, barely audible.

The bottle was put beside a glass on the bar top and left for the man to serve himself.

Instinct alone poured the large measure, and only smell guided the strong aroma to Fenwick's lips. Need, not greed, forced the liquid down his throat in one gulp.

The barman returned to Fenwick; only now did he register the pale face and shaking hand of this customer in a more sensitive light and so added to his experience, that morning, something that was the foundation of the excellent landlord he hoped to become. His previous dismissal of the man before him turned to genuine concern.

"Something wrong, sir?" he asked Fenwick.

The man's eyes stared blankly at the barman as laughter came from the far alcove and three American voices faded once more into the general hubbub of the place.

"The earth . . ." began Fenwick, to himself.

"What, sir?" said the barman.

Seeing the barman for the first time as the warm brandy found its mark, Fenwick became flustered. He turned around and surveyed the throng in the large dining room.

Across the seated crowd, in one of the alcoves, three men (as unfamiliar to Fenwick as he was to them, yet as inextricably bound together in the next sixty minutes as brothers of the blood) gave a toast, whose words were lost in the din of Garraway's, then drank down the dregs of the first bottle of champagne, before one reached for a second and another pulled the curtain to shut them off and create privacy.

The perfect Assistant Bank Manager stared into space, stupefied by the turmoil of his mind.

"That'll be twopence," said the barman, gently.

Fenwick took out some money and faced the young man, whose furrowed brow showed continued concern.

"The earth," repeated Fenwick, "has turned about."

Resolution flooded Fenwick as the brandy went to work, relieving the Assistant Bank Manager of some of his extreme anxiety. Fenwick was gone in the moment it took the young man to reach down for change of the sixpenny piece. Garraway's door slammed shut, and as the young man could see through a small side window which gave on to the alley outside, his erstwhile customer actually began to run.

§

There is a gulf where thousands fell,
Here all the bold adventurers came,
A narrow sound tho' deep as Hell,
Change Alley, is the dreadful name.

Mac began to read from the Swift poem printed beneath the name, GARRAWAY'S, on the daily menu. The three men had decided on an early lunch, commencing with the champagne already opened. George took up the second verse, blissfully unaware that a middle-aged man, moaning to himself in anguish at the thought of what he must reveal to his superior in a matter of moments, was reaching the intersection of 'Change and Cornhill, still on the run.

Subscribers here by thousands float,
And jostle one another down,
Each paddling in his leaky boat,
And here they fish for gold and drown.

Edwin Noyes began the last verse just as Mac decided on the duck, George on the lamb and Fenwick mounted the island pavement in front of the Old Lady of Threadneedle Street.

Meantime, secure on Garraways cliffs,
A savage race by shipwreck fed,
Lie waiting for the foundered skiffs,
And strip the bodies of the dead.

Edwin burst into laughter and chose the lamb. Mac filled

their champagne glasses. Three empty stomachs tentatively accepted more of the cold bubbling nectar. Noyes, still suffering from the effects of debilitation during his sojourn in New York custody, became almost immediately "slightly the worse for wear." But this was a celebration. Even George thought, as he observed Edwin's already glazed eyes, What the hell!

"I am never . . ." began Edwin unsteadily, ". . . to go . . ." he continued loudly, then muting his voice, finished, ". . . to the bank again. Come shake on that." He extended his hands, and both George and Mac reached out and shook enthusiastically. A waiter appeared through the curtain, bowed to the three men and asked their choice of lunch. They began to order.

§

Sometimes, Colonel Peregrine Madgewick Francis did not come to the Bank of England on a Saturday. Sometimes he went to the country with his wife and remained there until early on Monday morning. Along with dinners, conferences, the occasional journey abroad or to other parts of Great Britain (all of which were duty, despite the pleasure they more often than not provided), the long week end was a "perk" of office.

It was as well that March 1 brought a slight fever to the Colonel's wife, cancelling plans to vacate the City in search of first signs of spring in the country.

Some minutes before midday he was in his "inner sanctum," as he always referred to his office, when Fenwick, unheralded, even by a timid knock on the door, walked in and, unbidden, began talking fast.

It took several minutes to communicate sense to Colonel Francis, as information and trivia seemed to issue from Fenwick's mouth at the same time. He babbled. His superior made no attempt to stem the flow; his ears merely reacted to the single word, repeated, it seemed, with every sentence Fenwick uttered. Finally the man stopped, or rather petered out, as the face behind the desk gradually changed color and its mood became quite visibly dark.

Peregrine Madgewick rose to his feet slowly and crossed quietly to the long window facing out onto Threadneedle Street. As he put his hands behind his back, first clasped, then locked, his entire body appeared to Fenwick to become rigid. The clock's ticking, the fire's crackling and the muted street sounds lasted almost as long as Fenwick's impromptu speech before anything issued from the lips of the Manager of the Bank of England.

When it did, it was only the single word, spelled and forced out slowly with increasing volume, so that it finally exploded in the room, leaving no reason to question the might of Empire that lay behind the retribution that would be dealt out to criminal folly. Colonel Francis bellowed.

"FORGERY!"

§

Farley was in Mr. Fenwick's office when his superior ran back down the corridor from the Manager's office and burst in. He crossed straight to his desk, ignoring the young man.

"Tea, sir?" asked Farley.

"No!" shouted Fenwick, slamming the open drawer where he normally kept current accounts' queries. "Bring me the Warren file—immediately! Check on all his transactions of the last few days. Send a messenger to Jay Cooke and . . ." He paused, suddenly helpless, leaning against the desk as the horror of the impending scandal dawned upon him. He was almost in tears when he said, ". . . and go—yourself, Farley—to Scotland Yard and bring back . . ." He paused again, screwing his eyes tight, his head swimming, ". . . bring back . . ." He could hardly say it. ". . . the police—at once."

"But . . ." Farley began, quite perplexed, ". . . the file, Mr. Fenwick?"

"Send it in to the Colonel," Fenwick shouted hoarsely. "Now—go!" In fact, it was he himself who left the room to run directly back to the "inner sanctum."

Farley hesitated a moment longer, quite at sea, then went through into his own adjoining office. As he entered, so did a girl from the corridor leading out to the general offices; she carried a tray on which were milk, sugar, teacup, saucer, spoon, teapot and a jug of steaming water. She knew something was wrong the moment she saw the young man's face.

Farley looked at the pretty woman and began to reassemble himself; speculation he would leave for the journey to the "Yard," for now he had his instructions. He pointed to the tray and then his desk; he'd take a sip of tea today himself before leaving the building.

What was in the wind he had, as yet, no idea. That it was something big he had no doubt; that it was a disaster of sorts he was already correctly guessing; but what he did know was what he said to the girl as he indicated she should leave and reached for the teapot.

"The moon, girl," he said, " 'as fallen into the Hatlantic Ocean."

§

George, Mac and Noyes ate luncheon. By ten minutes after one o'clock they had finished. The plates were cleared. Noyes ordered yet another bottle of champagne. It arrived quickly, the waiter anticipating the need.

"Speculation and success," said George amiably, and gave the waiter a sovereign. The waiter went, partially drawing the curtain.

"We're out," began George to his friends, "clean and un-detected."

"And our only loss," Mac laughed softly, "fifteen thousand pounds." He lifted the glass to his lips.

"What?" said Edwin. He was, despite ample food and sobering conversation over luncheon of plans to travel fast and far, quite drunk—and dangerously at that, for he did not appear to be; neither did his companions criticize his condition, being much the same themselves.

Mac patted the black bag beside him, then touched their package from the bank.

"It's the balance in the Continental," he said.

"Then that," George said, "John Bull shall have."

"Indeed," Edwin Noyes said, "he shall not."

George took no heed of this and merely sipped his drink as Mac mischievously produced the Bank of England checkbook, his two pens and the small vials of ink to which they were attached. He laid them out ceremoniously.

"We've got that one check, George," he said.

It had always been policy, agreed upon by them all, that no money would be withdrawn from the Continental without money's being, at the same time, deposited. It was the human touch to maintain the confidence of the bank, to allay suspicion that, even for a moment, the traffic of money had become one-way and to facilitate a speedy transaction when the clerk (more often than not knowing Noyes), aware that the Horton account was good and seeing more going in than being withdrawn, would not even leave his window to complete the required procedure of checking the balance.

It had been precisely like that during the morning: the withdrawal Noyes had made from the Continental had taken only as long as his signatures on the receipt form and the packaging of the notes he had received. Because of this, the implication in Mac's statement of the one check remaining was obvious to both George and Edwin. George's laugh prompted Edwin further.

"Write it out," he said to Mac. "Warren to Horton, say—for five thousand pounds." Edwin took another sip of the delicious stimulant from his glass as Mac winked at George, then complied, as if obeying an order.

"It'll do us as pocket money," Edwin said, watching Mac endorse the back with a second signature and the other pen. "I've been once today already, and we've got . . ." He paused, took out his pocket watch and saw the time. ". . . fifteen minutes before the banks close for business." He wafted a hand.

"All's well," he grinned at George.

"That ends well—as it has," said George. "Forget it, Ed." He turned to Mac. "Now tear it up," he said.

"I was just about to," replied Mac with a laugh.

"Don't!" cried Edwin, and snatched the check.

Completely sober, George would have stopped Edwin.

Totally drunk, Mac would not have been able to write the check properly; but as the very reason people are prepared to buy expensive champagne is to achieve that exquisite state between reality and oblivion, so the mood in that alcove of Garraway's attested to the fact that if this spirit was the goal, money had been well spent.

Edwin stood up, moved out of the alcove and bumped against the table. Taking his hat, he said, "It'll be nice to have." He crossed the dining room, negotiating the crowded tables admirably, and was out the door before either Mac or George could make any serious effort to stop him. He was gone, and so, suddenly, was the mood between the two remaining men.

Instinct provided George with adrenaline, and that sobered him fast. He looked hard at Mac.

"I know it sounds stupid, Mac—but I've got a feeling . . ." George faltered, faintly embarrassed.

"It's not stupid at all, George," said Mac, already on his feet. "Let's go!"

Indicating to the waiter that they'd be back, and for him to look after their possessions in the alcove, the two men left Garraway's without ceremony.

§

One glass too many and champagne sours to the taste. Cold air on blood warmed by alcohol, drunk in convivial surroundings at a pleasant temperature, sobers or increases the sensation produced by excess. Edwin Noyes, at the steps of the Continental Bank in Lombard Street at one twenty-seven, had a bitter taste in his mouth and not a little regret that he had decided to return one more time. He hesitated a moment; then, knowing the transaction would take only a few minutes, entered the bank. It was no longer busy, and in fact, Mr. Richard Amery was already closing. Edwin arrived at the grille.

"Hello again, Mr. Noyes."

"Mr. Amery," said Edwin, "one I forgot." He took out the check and handed it to the teller. Mr. Amery looked at the clock.

"You just caught me," he said with a smile, and took the check. "Five in, Mr. Noyes?"

"And five out," said Edwin.

Mr. Amery frowned. He had almost completed cashing up in the hope of an early start home.

"Could it not wait, Mr. Noyes? I'll be glad to see to it first thing next week," he said.

"I've my instructions, Mr. Amery," said Edwin.

"I see," Amery replied. He paused a moment; looked at the check, then into his open cash drawer, all neat and stacked tidy. The clock's minute hand, on the wall, ticked to one twenty-nine. "Right, sir," the bank teller said. "I'll just check the balance."

"Now, why is that?" asked Edwin, vaguely irritated.

"Twice in one day is why is that," said Mr. Amery pointedly. "I've my instructions too."

He began to move away; if he was to be inconvenienced then, what little he could do to reciprocate he would, just to remind his customer not to take liberties in their established business relationship.

Edwin's mind, even before it could begin to worry, was put at ease by Amery's parting remark.

"Will you be wantin' hundreds or gold?"

"Hundreds will do," said Edwin thankfully.

The two men knew each other well enough now for Edwin to merely sign on behalf of Mr. Horton's money. Enough letters of "request to pay" had passed between them and been eventually dispensed with; the balance check was an occasional irritating formality, which Amery normally did only when the Manager, Stanton, was "out front" amongst his staff.

Edwin turned around and leaned on the long counter at the grille, watching the few customers remaining complete their business or file past the guard, now stationed at the double doors. In ten minutes he'd be back at Garraway's with George and Mac—for coffee, he remembered. No more champagne. The minute hand of the bank clock dropped to the half hour.

§

George's stride was long and fast; Mac, despite the fact that they'd left overcoats and hats at Garraway's, was warm enough to perspire.

"Why in hell are we walking up a sweat?" Mac asked, sobering irritably.

"Mac," said George, his voice taut and harsh, "when Ed walks out of the Continental I'll apologize for your exercise."

"Okay, okay," said Mac. They both turned into Lombard Street and onto the crowded pavements where early starters were leaving the City, which was closing down for the short week end.

§

Mr. Farley, Mr. Fenwick and four policemen pushed past two customers coming out of the Continental as they entered. The guard, recognizing police uniforms, stepped back to allow them passage. Inside the bank, only a few people near the door noticed the group; then, as the entourage crossed toward the access gate to the bank proper, more heads turned in mild curiosity.

Edwin's back was to the group. Mr. Amery was counting out money on his side of the grille. He looked up casually, saw policemen and indicated the diversion to his customer. Edwin turned around. His entire system reacted, as a man's must at the final drum roll before execution. Mr. Amery was again counting. "Two thousand . . . one hundred, two hundred, three hundred . . ." Edwin saw the access gate open at the end of the long counter and, through the glass, the Manager's door, first ajar, then pulled back wide. Mr. Stanton was behind his desk as two of the men stepped into the office almost sixty feet away from Edwin and the teller.

"Three thousand . . ." Mr. Amery continued, ". . . one hundred, two hundred, three hundred . . ."

Edwin looked quickly at the still-open outer doors of the bank. The guard was interested in the distant group, but remained unconcerned as customers continued to file out. "Seven hundred, eight hundred, nine and four thousand . . ." said Mr. Amery, ". . . one hundred . . ."

Edwin looked around, his brow now beaded with sweat,

and saw Mr. Stanton, through the glass, rise from behind his desk; he was shaking his head, but the two men continued talking furiously. The four policemen had entered the bank proper and lounged, seemingly unconcerned, looking about at nothing in particular.

"You all right, Mr. Noyes?" came Amery's voice.

Edwin brushed his brow and coughed quickly. "Cold coming, probably," he said harshly. "Have you finished?" His voice broke, and he coughed again to hide it.

"You'd better take yourself a hot toddy and then to bed, Mr. Noyes," said Mr. Amery pleasantly.

"Just count," said Edwin; "please," he added plaintively.

Very slowly, now deliberately, with that look universal to bank tellers, no matter whether they hold your money or are refusing you credit, Mr. Amery began to place final notes on the pile heaped behind his grille.

"Four hundred, five hundred, six hundred, seven hundred . . ."

Hunched over the counter, Edwin caught only a glimpse of Stanton, seemingly on his toes, looking around him, beyond the crowded filing cabinets and along the counter to the only teller still paying out.

"Four thousand eight hundred, nine hundred and a thousand—that's five, Mr. Noyes," Mr. Amery said impassively. At which precise moment, in the distance, Mr. Stanton pointed and said something to the two men beside him.

The only immediate clue to Mr. Frederick Albert Warren was in the most recent transactions, according to Bank of England records, with his long-term business acquaintance at the Continental Bank, a Mr. C. J. Horton. Thus Mr. Fenwick had been advised to try there first. As the Bank had been open still when the police, brought by young Farley, promptly arrived in Threadneedle Street, it was decided to waste no time and begin inquiries immediately.

On their arrival at the Continental and the Manager's office, Mr. Stanton had informed the group, obviously agitated (but with the very best credentials which one of them produced on request), that the customer they sought had been absent some while in person, although indeed his account had an excellent record. But his clerk was a frequent visitor and had, in fact, been in that very morning, he was informed—for further information perhaps, Mr. Stanton suggested (and at that point had risen on his toes to begin a survey of the bank above the level of desks and file cabinets), the teller with whom his clerk did business might be of some help; here he found and pointed to Mr. Amery, who was just finishing business, as all could see, with a last customer.

As luck would have it—Mr. Stanton smiled at Mr. Fenwick—Mr. Amery (as he now realized) was in fact, at that very moment, dealing with the man whom Mr. Horton had introduced as his personal clerk—a Mr. Noyes.

Electricity had literally shocked the Victorian world. The increasing uses of this instant transmission of, to the majority, a mysterious force were making reality of the incredible. Soon a switch would (some believed) provide light; now, a button provided sound. No one quite remembered who pressed it that early afternoon in the Continental Bank, but he was excused as what immediately followed was duly unraveled.

Edwin was dumbfounded at Richard Amery's suddenly open mouth; saw him instantly pull shut the security bars of the grille with time himself only to move his fingers, reaching for the bank notes; heard what must have been the slamming of the great doors behind him; felt perhaps with only the hairs on his neck—or more probably, perceived with the peripheral vision of his left eye—blue uniforms detaching themselves from the distant group.

His own legs would not move, but everywhere was the sound of running feet, and above it all was the electric cacophony of bells which clanged with a harsh, reverberating ting-a-ling. For one person alone, they were truly the bells of Hell: they rang especially for Edwin Noyes.

Oranges and Lemons

WHILE the alarm bells were going off inside the bank, where hell truly broke loose was outside. Instantly the entrance to the Continental became congested as voices rose in the throng, shouting all manner of things. Into this madness George and Mac pushed their way; all eyes were on the closed doors as they slowly began to open.

George and Mac were the only pair in the crowd who did not have to guess the source of such panic. Mac was beside himself. Even had the discovery happened, as it obviously had, hundreds of men could have answered to Noyes's description had he not been there in the flesh for all to see. His two friends could have shipped off the only recognizable face to any destination; remaining themselves unknown to the authorities. But with Edwin taken, what might happen now? Mac looked desperately at George.

"His story's solid, George—isn't it?"

"He'll never betray us, Mac," said George grimly.

"We've got to do something," said Mac helplessly.

At that moment a roar went up from the crowd as the great doors of the Continental opened wide and Edwin Noyes was escorted out. Shouts went up in the throng, packed tight, and not all were out of sympathy with the fellow who appeared to be a culprit.

The police began to force a way through the crowd. In sheer desperation, Mac pushed to within feet of Edwin, but was finally restrained by George. There was a moment, amidst the clamor, when Edwin saw his two friends as they caught his eye. He shook his head almost imperceptibly and appeared calm, as if resigned or confident—which, neither George nor Mac could perceive. He was dragged off. His eventual destination: Newgate Prison.

"Mac, we've got to leave him," said George. "They don't even know we exist, and they're not likely to, if we go now. We've still got time."

"In a week, George," pleaded Mac, almost in tears, as the crowd surged past them. "It'll give us time to clear everything, send off the last of the money and . . ." He faltered. ". . . and see what happens to Ed. We've got to help him," he finished.

"Nothing can be proved," said George emphatically. "With no evidence they can't charge him, let alone hold him long. To the world he's a dupe of some man who's disappeared. They'll have to release him."

George took Mac by the shoulders and shook him. The crowd, now full of rumors, jostled past; running feet and cries of "Forgery," "Bank of England," "Millions lost" were all around them. Lombard Street had never witnessed such a scene. Mac looked in the direction in which his friend had been taken, and almost sobbing, partly to himself, partly to Edwin, he said, "Stay cool, Ed—stay cool."

§

When the two men returned to Garraway's, that too was in an uproar. As they collected their belongings from the waiter, paid the bill and began to leave, the young barman said to them excitedly, " 'Ave you 'eard of the Great Bank Robbery, gentlemen?"

George nodded for Mac's benefit and led his friend from the very place that had spawned their entire scheme.

"Nice to 'ave, 'ard to keep," said Mac as he stepped into the cold air, the building already denying sunlight to the Alley, which was dark and dismal. The day was waning fast.

"Mac," said George—consoling, if he could, his friend—"Ed ain't lost yet."

Then, the two men themselves became lost in the pedestrian throng of Exchange Alley.

§

In the middle of a large room quite bare of decoration—gas lamps on the wall, furnished with solid chairs and a single table—Edwin Noyes, now disheveled, sat quite still and calm, watching his inquisitors mill about. The detective sitting opposite him, only feet away, repeated the same questions once more.

"This Mr. Horton employed you as his clerk, you say?" came the voice again.

"He did," said Edwin calmly.

"And you answer to the name Edwin Noyes?" the man asked. Edwin nodded, then spoke.

"Why am I arrested?" he asked.

The detective paused and looked at several of the other men moving about in the background, as if to corroborate his statement. "Conspiracy to defraud," he said firmly.

"Is that a charge?" asked Edwin.

"It will be," said the detective.

"Have you evidence to substantiate that?" asked Edwin pointedly.

The detective shifted in his seat uncomfortably.

"You are, at present, aiding our inquiries."

"I see," said Edwin.

"Now . . ." began the detective again.

"Is it voluntary or obligatory?" asked Edwin.

"What?" said the detective, a little put out by Edwin's calm.

Edwin Noyes had long since decided to play to the hilt the only card he had: innocence. He was doing it superbly, confident that the precautions previously taken to ensure his safety and release should this very thing—the unexpected—occur would be sufficient to procure his freedom.

"Am I arrested?" asked Edwin.

"You are—aiding our . . ." began the detective once again. He was not overly intelligent, but he looked the part and acted it well, provided he kept his voice low, his face stern and the questions he put fairly simple.

His height and his background as a sergeant in the Army, with if not a distinguished, at least an adequate record, had also contributed to his promotion. From police uniform to plain-clothes detective had been achieved with the aid of a large moustache and sideburns that, at forty, with some added weight around his midriff, gave him the solid appearance of law and order.

Although he was now an inspector, his imagination was limited, and his intelligence was—well, he got there in the end, but it took time and patience, both of which, as the world knows, a policemen has aplenty.

"If I am *aiding* your . . ." Edwin emphasized each word. ". . . inquiries," he continued, "may I make a request?"

The detective inspector looked across at the other men in the room. Mr. Fenwick was a taut nervous wreck, but Farley, beside him on another chair, watched the whole procedure fascinated.

"What is it?" asked the detective of Noyes.

"I would like a cup of tea," said Edwin. Across the room, Farley involuntarily burst into a quickly stifled guffaw. Just as well, because at that moment Colonel Peregrine Madgewick Francis marched in as if John Bull himself.

He strode directly up to the detective inquisitor—who stood up to greet this new arrival—and looked long and hard into Edwin's face. Nothing could now shock Edwin, so he merely smiled back pleasantly.

"My name is Francis," said the Manager of the Bank of England. "The man is American?" he continued.

"We believe so," said the detective.

"Then I want American detectives in on this," Francis continued. "I want a full report of your intentions."

"The usual precautions have been taken, sir," began the detective sergeant sonorously. "All ports and stations are full alert. Major cities—er—roads, main routes, are being watched. We have already cabled the United States of America and, come morning, the relay will have instructed even Australia of what information we have at the moment.''

"And what is that, may I ask?" said Peregrine Madgewick.

The detective shifted uncomfortably on his feet now, wishing he could relax with a pipe, alone, to think this whole thing out. "Well, sir," he started, "er, nothing—yet, sir."

Colonel Francis swallowed and by sheer effort of will retained his composure. "My office, I hope," he said, looking across at both Farley and Fenwick, who actually changed color to a pale green, ". . . has been . . ." continued Francis, ". . . co-operative?"

The detective nodded. The Colonel continued.

"Then when can we expect what must be a speedy arrest of this man"—he paused at the name and spoke it with hate—"Warren?"

" 'Ard to say, sir," said the detective, decidedly uncomfortable.

"But you have before you—" began Francis, now losing his patience altogether.

"A man," cut in the detective inspector firmly, now utilizing his authority and what little information he did have at his disposal, "with a completely acceptable story, who is probably a perfect dupe and will shortly be set free—unless . . ." He looked at Edwin, then again at Peregrine Madgewick and shrugged.

"He will most certainly not be released," said the Colonel.

"It is the law," said the detective inspector.

Colonel Francis barely managed to control himself in damning the entire institution of order, in all civilized countries, with a few choice words. He swallowed and spoke tersely before leaving.

"I too, sir, have already cabled—America—for more than information." With that (and his contained fury) he left the room.

The detective seated himself again. A policeman brought in a large tea tray full of steaming mugs. Milk, sugar and the stewed Indian brew of British prison beverage arrived for all in the room. Edwin had his first taste of what was to become familiar. The only one who choked on it was Fenwick.

§

More than a week passed for the police, with nothing to show at the end of their investigations but a mass of proof favoring Edwin Noyes's innocence. As he stressed continually, there was nothing to conceal, and if co-operation would speed his eventual release, then these guardians of law to whom he spoke daily, his inquisitors, had only to ask—politely.

They went to Durrant's. Indeed Mr. Noyes had been a resident, and apart from a few late-night arrivals, with perhaps a lady visitor and a little too much to drink, he had been an excellent occupant of two rooms for several months.

The Manager remembered, quite distinctly, the interview with the Mr. Horton described by detectives, and commented on Mr. Noyes's pleasure at being accepted as his confidential clerk. The newspaper clipping, among Edwin's effects, confirmed the fact that he had solicited for the job in a quite normal way on arrival from America.

Edwin's introduction to Mr. Stanton at the Continental Bank had been through an official business appointment, and he had been accepted by the Manager solely on the recommendation of his excellent depositor Mr. C. J. Horton. There was not one shred of evidence to prove that Edwin Noyes was anything but an employee of the man, and in no way could he be connected with any nefarious dealings that it was, even now, only assumed had been conducted between Horton and Mr. F. A. Warren.

Edwin, of course, denied ever knowing Mr. Warren, other than by the checks that came to him via Mr. Horton personally, or were left at the Terminus Hotel. This was amply corroborated by the receptionist, who had grown accustomed to Mr. Noyes and had seen nothing unusual in the employer-employee relationship observed between Mr. Horton and his confidential clerk.

Alfred Joseph Baker at Jay Cooke, McCulloch and Company confirmed the business transactions with Mr. Noyes and added that it was his opinion that Horton's clerk had little knowledge of F. A. Warren; their conversations had established that they had indeed never met. ''Don't know the man myself" was his direct quotation of Noyes reluctantly taken down by the police. The fact that a description of Warren exactly tallied that of Horton was, Edwin assured his inquisitors, as much a surprise to him as it was to the authorities.

The London press overflowed with headlines and columns; the dailies, weeklies and even monthlies speculated with amazement that an impregnable system could be so easily breached and that the fraud could remain undetected for such a length of time. The consensus was that Mr. Edwin Noyes was an innocent dupe and should be immediately set free. Only continued pressure from the Bank withheld liberty from the young American. It had become a scandal and was beyond all law and justice, it was declared.

Sympathy poured in for the young man; daily it became more difficult to provide adequate reason for his detention. Even his American "record" (discovered through diligent inquiry and cabled from New York) merely prompted cries of "Victimization!" Edwin remained remarkably cool, impassive to bribes, threats and the continuing inquisition. He merely repeated his answers to much the same questions until even the police were embarrassed by the situation.

Unshaven, unwashed, poorly fed, confined in solitary and with daily visits from aggressive officials, Edwin should have felt his spirit drain away, knowing that the might of a pompous Empire was determined to break him. It was almost as if Edwin's guilt, or innocence, had no bearing on the case: by his very presence, as the only link with the great fraud, he must be found guilty no matter what the evidence.

But by the tenth day Edwin felt certain he would be set free, and the rigors that continued no longer had any effect on him. Even in his abject state he smiled at authority and was polite to all. Murmurings even from his warders filtered back to the Bank of England, and it was declared that a question would be raised, on his behalf, in the House of Commons at the earliest opportunity.

George and Mac read all the editorials and determined to stay on in London until they felt certain that Edwin's freedom was imminent. They used the time well. In various names, the remaining money and U.S. Bonds were packaged, placed in trunks containing clothes or English merchandise and consigned (in different names) to America. Thus they disposed of their vast booty. The receipts were divided. Some they kept. Others were posted in separate envelopes to New York's Central Post Office to await collection at General Delivery.

They did not forget Austin in Havana, nor Irving, who received a further considerable sum, as a gift, should he be needed in the immediate future for protection against investigation across the Atlantic.

On the tenth day, both George and Mac decided it was time to leave. The whole affair had grown out of all proportion, exceeding even their worst imaginings, and they felt that should they remain in the capital city longer, they would be tempting fate. So it was agreed: America, New York and Irving's "cloak," which would conceal them until they could emerge in Florida with new identities as members of the Four Hundred.

The trouble was, the affair had in no way cooled as was expected; if anything, it had become hotter; so even getting out of London might prove a problem. Here their worries were well founded.

May arrived at Euston Station just after seven in the evening of the twelfth with a heap of luggage that was stacked near a barrier at the platform from which the train for Liverpool was to depart.

Her instructions were plain; she was to rendezvous with Mac at seven thirty.

Mac, in his rooms at 7 St. James's Place, told Franz Anton Herold he was leaving for a two-week visit to Europe; communication of the date of his return would be by mail. Miss Agnes Green bade farewell to Captain MacDonald, wished him a pleasant voyage and retired to her rooms and the company of a new male lodger.

At seven fifteen, May became unduly anxious. The carriages were already at the platform, and several passengers had begun boarding for the journey; departure was at twenty minutes to eight. In the station there was a great bustle of activity as the last trains of the evening prepared to leave for their northern destinations.

Passengers crowded past barriers onto the many platforms

to embark; they pushed, jostled and shouted, knowing that there were not seats for all and that unless adequate reservations had been made, half of them would be standing between seats or lying in corridors of the new carriages.

May looked up at the great clock suspended from the huge area of grid-and-glass roof. Nervously she began to watch the time tick away. She was obviously agitated by seven twenty, even to uninvolved onlookers, of whom there were many: a beautiful woman, alone, will always draw eyes.

Detectives had been watching May since her arrival, and several had already established that she was to travel not only to Liverpool, but onward to America. Stuck onto her luggage were the "pretty" labels she had found with the tickets Mac had given her; these indicated a vessel and shipping line—the *Java* of Cunard.

In fact, May had informed her landlord of the public house that she was to go to Europe for a holiday with her gentleman friend, and actually had no idea that it was not truly her destination. She had never before been out of England.

The detectives now awaited the companion for whom she was obviously waiting. At seven twenty-three, with loading still to do—inconsiderate as he had already proved himself to be by leaving this attractive woman alone—he was cutting it fine.

"Oh, Mac!" said May to herself, tears welling in her eyes, "please!"

§

"Euston was it, sir?" asked the cabbie through the trap in the hansom.

Inside, Mac, looking up, nodded. The trap slammed shut and the cab jerked forward. Outside, London passed by for the last time. How, Mac wondered, could it rain without clearing the thick yellow fog that seemed always to settle heavily as the sun went down? Depression suddenly swamped the excitement he had concealed all day that here was the final move. He tried to sum up London, his impressions, memories, dislikes, as he knew he would never return. Cabs; always it was cabs. Hansoms, growlers, his occasional hired brougham. A voice came to him: "With 'er, sir?" He remembered that first night with May. "Claridge's," he'd said.

He smiled and settled nearer the window to catch a last glimpse of the tall terraced houses in the narrow streets, the dim gaslights picking out what few pedestrians dared venture abroad. "With the *lady*, sir?" came another voice: the night he'd gone to the Gaiety with a very different woman—a beauty—in love. He blessed May's innocence and promised himself that she should have only the best—soon.

"It'll be nice to have." The words came chillingly—a recent voice: the last sentence spoken directly by his friend—Ed. Suddenly Mac shivered. Damn the cab; now he wanted only to be out of this place, this city, this country; it was almost seven thirty already. "Nice to 'ave, 'ard to keep." The delicate voice spoke with the remembered smile; May finished the quotation: "True 'uns is rare."

Mac closed his eyes tight as the memories flooded into his mind. Time enough later, he thought angrily: a world of time for reflection—later; now he had only to get to the station and be gone. "Is it always goin' to be like this—now?" asked May of Mac, as if she were actually in the cab with him. He was startled at the clarity of the voice and opened his eyes wide to see her. There was only the blackness of the lumbering interior. "Perhaps," he said aloud, as if she were with him; "perhaps," he repeated softly.

He was suddenly ice-cold; the hair prickled on his neck, and his eyes sought frantically for the lights of Euston Station as the cab entered the main thoroughfare.

§

The night fog and rain outside the long window of the "inner sanctum" of the Bank of England, where the draperies remained open, were only background to an unfinished painting—by Turner, perhaps. Within the room it was warm; the fire in the large grate beneath the Adam mantelshelf burned bright and crackled as the logs, brought by Colonel Francis from his country orchard, dispensed their aroma to the gentlemen gathered about the fireplace. The voice that spoke first had crossed the English Channel to be at this rendezvous, late as it was, and although it was enunciating English perfectly, the edge of authority it carried made it quite clear to the listeners that patience had its limitations.

"Here," it was saying, "I believe, and correct me, please, if I am wrong . . ." The voice remained soft and beguiling, wooing its audience. ". . . it is law that the man cannot be held indefinitely."

The pause that followed was deliberate on the part of Colonel Francis as he looked slowly at the speaker.

"He must not be released," said the Colonel.

"Law," continued the voice from across *la Manche*, "is not necessarily justice, Colonel, for either the plaintiff or defendant, but it is something we must eventually accept, even though our personal interests are perhaps not always served. Without it we would have anarchy, and for such as we . . ." The voice paused, its point made. Baron Alphonse de Rothschild had no more to say with words; his eyes surveyed the group and spoke clearly to Colonel Francis, Mr. Fenwick and the young man Farley.

The detective inspector, uneasy in the company of a man who represented untold wealth (and whose intellect was so apparent as to make him nervous when the man merely smiled), coughed loudly and ventured a few words himself.

"Well, sir, our inquiries indicate strongly his . . ." The detective paused, looking at Colonel Francis, but finished for the benefit of the visitor, ". . . innocence."

"We shall see, sir," said Francis vehemently. "We have not even one reference on this 'Warren' "—he almost spat the word; "only a recommendation from his tailor." Here he looked viciously at Fenwick, who had grown accustomed to trembling at the implication over the past few days. "The only clue is his connection with a Mr. Horton—and this man Noyes is, or was, Horton's confidential clerk!" He paused dramatically. "We shall see, sir!" he finished, and propped a foot on the brass guardrail around the grate for emphasis.

The Baron's soft voice was unperturbed by bluster. "I have not traveled as far, or as speedily, as our expected guest," he said, changing the conversation to the immediate reason the group had gathered that night; "nevertheless, if he is unable to arrive at the stated time I shall have to bid you good evening. I do not like to dine late."

A clock in the room chimed the half hour of seven thirty as a knock sounded at the door. Fenwick crossed quickly, grasped the lion rampant and pulled the door wide open. The man revealed was imposing and made his entrance accordingly. He stood a moment, took in the entire room at a glance from cold eyes, then stepped two paces forward, allowing the door to be closed quietly behind him by Fenwick.

"Gentlemen," said Colonel Francis pulling himself upright and raising his voice, "Mr. Robert A. Pinkerton."

The visitor said nothing but absorbed every detail of each man gathered before him.

"Sir," Colonel Francis continued, "this is the Baron Rothschild." The two men nodded to each other. "These are my employees—Mr. Fenwick, and Farley," Francis indicated cursorily, "and this . . ." he said, indicating the plain-clothes English policeman, ". . . is the man into whose custody Edwin Noyes was delivered and who has carried out all the investigations to date—Detective Inspector Spittle."

Robert A. Pinkerton looked at the Englishman, who shuffled under his gaze. He wetted his lips and slowly spoke the first word since his arrival at the Bank of England. It was onomatopoeic.

"Spittle," he said.

§

Totally unaware of the danger George was approaching, Ellen had begun to prattle the moment a hired brougham, bearing them both and substantial luggage, pulled from the entrance of the Terminus Hotel, London Bridge, for the last time. Distracted, George had been unable to stop the voluble flow of inconsequential nonsense from his woman by polite requests for silence, but his curt "Shut up" had done it. Not only quelling conversation, George had initiated in Ellen an ominous black mood.

It was in this manner that they passed under the famous Greek arch and arrived at their destination—Euston Station.

A porter brought a trolley and began loading the luggage from their brougham, whose driver George paid off handsomely. The porter, sensing an equally rewarding tip, went to work with a will. George was unable to control his nervousness and continually looked about, staring into the fog; inside, his instinct was sounding out loud warnings.

Ellen paced up and down, developing her anger. The porter indicated the station entrance and shuffled off pushing the loaded trolley. Ellen followed, swirling toward the light as if making a stage appearance. George hesitated a moment, his thoughts of poor Edwin Noyes and that unfortunate's continuing incarceration. He prayed for news of the man's release.

"Ellen, I'll just find an evening paper."

The woman (already distant) ignored George, but the porter shouted back helpfully, "Late edition's sold round the west side, sir," and he pointed.

"Thank you," said George; he began walking and was swallowed by the fog.

§

Steam escaping from an engine, along with shunting sounds and belching smoke, was prelude to a long whistle blast that echoed throughout the night station. It startled May, who was now on the brink of tears, as she could see plainly that it was seven thirty-three and Mac was late. She began looking about, searching for her man, praying that his face would suddenly appear and with his smile the world and her fears be put to rights.

It was not Mac she found, but Mac's friend George's woman—the lady she'd been briefly introduced to—Ellen; her luggage was on a trolley, pushed by a porter; the two crossed with it toward the Liverpool train's platform. For a moment it seemed as if she saw May, but if so, she made no attempt to give any sign of recognition.

Ellen stopped and turned around. For a moment she was obscured by a crowd now surging forward for third-class accommodations, from a queue that had been held back until the last few minutes. Ellen now seemed as agitated as May had

become, which was immediately observed by the numerous
detectives who were converging on the area around a ticket
barrier to the last train that night for Liverpool. May could
withhold her emotions no longer; she burst into tears.

§

In candlelight, ignoring the softly falling rain, George Bidwell looked over the front page of London's evening paper
fast. Nowhere was there anything relating to Edwin Noyes.

"I'll take an early edition also," he said quickly, "if you
have one remaining."

"Here somewhere, sir," replied the news vendor. "I've
already put back what's left." He patted his little boy, who
was sitting happily on a box with a penny whistle in his hands,
humming a nursery rhyme.

"Now you look after the gentleman, Georgie," he said,
taking a single candle, "and I'll go look inside." He read in
his customer's face the urgency that drove him speedily into
the rear of his makeshift shed to search among stacks of paper
tied with string.

George Bidwell looked at the child, who was instantly
silent. He gave the boy sixpence, which was accepted with
wide eyes that glittered in the light of the remaining candle.
George touched the young boy's face gently, thinking of a
similar young child years before in another city thousands of
miles away: despite time and distance, poverty is indelible.
George closed his eyes only a moment as events of three
decades began to crowd into his mind. The voice that came to
him was from this other "little Georgie" as he began to sing:

Oranges and lemons, say the bells of St. Clement's.
I owe you five farthings, say the bells of St. Martin's.

"I got one, sir!" shouted the news vendor from the back of
the shed. George's eyes opened quickly, memories fading
rapidly.

When will you pay me? say the bells of Old Bailey

went on the child earnestly.

> When I grow rich, say the bells of Shoreditch.

"Here we are, sir." The man had reappeared and offered the paper.

George Bidwell paid him and began to search the front page and Courts Section for information of his friend in custody.

> When will that be? say the bells of Stepney

sang the little boy in his high voice.

> I'm sure I don't know, say the great bells of Bow

he finished.

The father saw the sixpence in his son's hand as the lad took a deep breath trying to remember the final verse.

"You lucky boy," said the news vendor. "Thank you kindly, sir," George smiled quickly.

The two men looked at the innocent face of the child, involved with his nursery problem. In that moment both George and the tradesman searched themselves for that quality they had long since lost.

George suddenly realized he had only minutes remaining to catch his train. He started to leave.

The news vendor, intent on his son, held the flickering clue closer that the boy might finish his rhyme. "Here comes a candle . . ." he prompted.

> . . . to light you to bed,

the child immediately began.

> And here comes a chopper

he shouted enthusiastically,

> to chop off your head!

George stepped back as though physically struck. If instinct had done nothing else, it had given him this last opportunity to decipher intuitive feelings that something was definitely wrong.

"Well done," said the news vendor, again patting the boy, ignoring his customer. As he looked up to see that the gentleman had gone, a light gust of wind blew out both candles. The man swore. Instantly his son began to wail—fearful of the swirling fog, sudden darkness and harsh voice of reality.

§

George Bidwell walked cautiously toward the end of a dark passageway where it opened out into the station. The narrow access on the west side gave out onto the road where George had bought the papers. He stopped dead. In front of him, his nightmare was beginning. Two detectives sidled through the crowd and reached the porter who was with Ellen. They ignored her and spoke only to the man. Ellen's temperament, volatile in anger, exploded at their impertinence. George could see that she had become imperious and indeed might well carry the day.

He now had a choice. Now—and only now—he could walk onto the platform, explain his search for the news vendor, apologize to his woman and bluff it out with these police. One of them appeared to be asking Ellen's destination; the other had taken out some sort of badge. The view across the large, crowded area in front of the platform barriers suddenly became filled with a group of passengers running for a train. A moment later, George saw Ellen seated on the luggage, ashen-faced, near to tears, with both men now bending over the woman, unconcerned at her emotional state. One was talking; Ellen listened without saying a word.

George leaned against the cold, damp wall of the station in shadow. There was no panic in him yet; his mind was already racing over alternatives. Euston, Ellen, Liverpool; the situation before him. Police George had expected. That traveling to Liverpool at all (even with the women as cover) was a chance he knew; that getting out of London—or, indeed, England—would be a problem he accepted; but this . . . ! No one appeared to be above suspicion; and now two unaccompanied ladies awaiting their beaux, unable to give adequate answers to simple questions as to destination or even their lovers' business . . .

George swore. He should have arranged it differently; now it was too late. If he crossed to Ellen and brazened it out, he would have to rely on her—could he? The question he asked himself was rhetorical; he already knew the answer. George stayed a moment longer, watching three more detectives approach the weeping May; wished both women all the luck of the gods, and turned back into the passageway leading out onto the road.

§

Mac's luck was immediate; as he stepped down from the cab, stumbling over his bag in the rain, scrabbling for money to pay off the cabbie, his arm was gripped firmly by George, who shouted up to the driver, "We'll take it on."

"George," said Mac, recovering from the shock, "I can't . . . May . . ." He didn't finish.

"Does May have anything of yours with her, Mac—anything?" George asked, even now considering a reversal of his decision. Perhaps they could join the women and survive an inquisition.

The rain, on a wind that had risen, whipped into George's face, and all around him, seen under gaslights, the fog began to swirl and eddy as if it were the murky waters of an estuary at turn of tide.

Seizing Mac, George shook him and repeated his question urgently.

"Of course," said Mac, straining from George's grip.

"Money?" asked George.

"Come along, gents!" shouted the cabbie.

"Two thousand pounds in gold sovereigns," whispered Mac hoarsely.

"Then get in," said George.

"But . . ." began Mac. Then it was too late. Both he and George saw the horse-drawn "Black Maria" police wagon as the fog thinned outside the station entrance. Strange shadows danced under the gaslights as Ellen passed beneath them, escorted by two uniformed policemen, others carrying her bags.

"May's taken too," said George quietly in Mac's ear. Mac

stared into his friend's eyes, rain dripping from the rim of his hat, with an expression of despair. The screams that came from the station entrance tore Mac apart as he turned to see May being dragged physically toward the Black Maria. The scene was as if from some grotesque act in a play of horror. Mac would have collapsed or cried out had not George supported him and clapped a hand to his mouth.

"Mac," said George, fast and urgently, "we've got to run like no one has, ever."

"Where'll it be, gents?" shouted the cabbie again—now impatient.

"If we get caught, Mac, then we're done." George let the words sink home as they watched May pulled forcibly into the black horse-drawn van with the words METROPOLITAN POLICE on the side. "There'll be no mercy," finished George harshly.

"Come on, gents," bellowed the cabbie, huddling up in his exposed position against the increasing rain. "It's comin' on cats an' dogs."

"Where can we go?" asked Mac brokenly.

"New York," said George. "New York, where we've got Irving's protection. We've been paying his New York City Police long enough. Now they've got to earn their money."

Mac dropped his head and shook it, almost in tears.

"Besides," said George quietly, watching the "Black Maria" disappear into the swirling fog, "it's the only place." His arm around Mac's shoulders attempted reassurance.

"When we get there, I'll buy you dinner—upstairs at Delmonico's," George whispered with a forced smile. Mac spun on him.

"Easily said," he sobbed with anger. "New York is a world away."

George picked up Mac's bag and bundled him into the cab with it. As he climbed in after his friend and the cabbie jerked them away, he slammed the half door, slumped down beside his shattered comrade and said grimly:

"But it's home, Mac—home."

Spring

1873

Scent

PINKERTON'S National Detective Agency had been founded by Allan Pinkerton in 1851. He had originally come to the United States to avoid arrest in Glasgow, Scotland, where, a cooper by trade, he had become, as a member of the Chartist Movement, a part of the workingmen's revolt against the political power of wealthy landlords.

A timely warning had allowed him to escape with his newly married wife, and he had sailed for Canada, eventually reaching Chicago, where he settled outside the city in a small town named Dundee. Sharp-eyed and observant by nature, Pinkerton began helping the local sheriff in his investigations. He became a special agent for the United States Post Office, leaving his cooper's business to be run by a foreman to whom he eventually sold it, lock, stock and, of course, barrel.

When Chicago established its first regular police force, Pinkerton became a member—as a detective. In 1850 he resigned and "went private" in company with a partner. He dissolved the relationship a year later and became independent. Thus the Pinkertons began.

His two sons, Robert and William, became a part of the
organization, and the Agency's services, as its worth became
apparent, were called upon increasingly. Close contact with
leading lawyers, financiers, bankers, businessmen and
politicians elevated Pinkerton's National Detective Agency
until its future and pre-eminence were assured. Their confidential files, knowledge of the underworld, appreciation of
criminal techniques, dogged tenacity in following every clue
until an arrest had been effected, created for the Pinkertons a
reputation that was without equal.

They were revered by law-abiding citizens and feared by
petty crooks and criminals. By 1873 the name had become a
myth in America, as Sherlock Holmes became in England; the
difference being that—as many who were caught by them
could attest—the Pinkertons were real.

§

Edwin Noyes had been allowed to wash—less, he thought,
out of consideration for his own personal hygiene than
because the animal smell of decomposition that exudes from
any human being after a certain period was affecting his
warder's sensibilities. The razor with which he was also
provided had been blunt for the last man, let alone for Edwin,
so after a single attempt, when he gashed his chin, Edwin let
the razor be and continued to sport a thickening growth of
beard.

Bread, water, the indescribable tea, porridge, a minute
amount of (mostly fat) meat and potatoes had been the sub-
stitute for a staple diet. So it was a gaunt young man with a
dark-jowled face, soiled clothes and faint aroma of carbolic
soap about him who once more entered the familiar
inquisition room of Newgate Prison in the early evening of the
twelfth of March. Outside, it was raining.

Edwin sat down opposite a man behind the table who was
referring to notes. He looked up and presented a new face; the
others, Spittle and his assistants, Edwin knew well. He smiled
at the man, but received only a long stare in return. Eventually the man spoke.

"You're a Hartford boy?" he asked.

Edwin became immediately uncomfortable: the new arrival was obviously American. He nodded an answer.

"And an ex-con," said the man.

That was no longer a secret, so Edwin nodded again.

Spittle noticed the subdued attitude of the young man as he responded to the American voice across from him. His confidence seemed to ebb somewhat. After Spittle introduced the visitor, Edwin's tide began to turn.

"This is Mr. Pinkerton, Noyes—from the United States." He waited for a reaction.

Edwin's eyes narrowed and his teeth bit tight into his lower lip, but he said nothing.

"Why . . ." began Pinkerton, seemingly to the large room in general, ". . . is this man still wearing his own clothes?"

"Well, sir," said Spittle quietly, "he's held like, but not—yet—charged."

Pinkerton actually rounded on Spittle, his eyes wide. "For more than a week?" he questioned.

"Er—yes, sir," said Spittle, embarrassed.

"They appear . . ." said Pinkerton, now to Edwin directly, a slight smile on his face, ". . . over here, in England . . . not to practice habeas corpus, Mr. Noyes."

Edwin moved not a muscle. Spittle shifted about on his chair.

"It's the Bank," he was now saying. "They won't hear of Noyes's release, sir, and we can't—"

"Empty his pockets," said Pinkerton quietly, ignoring Spittle.

"We 'ave, sir," said one of the other policemen beside Spittle. He indicated a buff envelope on the table. Pinkerton reached for it, weighed it a moment, then emptied everything inside onto the table top. The contents fell with a clatter—nothing unusual: pocket watch, a clasp knife, coins, folded paper, tickets, a wallet, calling cards.

Pinkerton sorted through the effects slowly. Edwin could hear steady rain pouring down outside, along with the hissing gas. It was the only other noise but for the breathing of the men in the room. Pinkerton handled each article he saw before him. Edwin watched him take up a small card and look at it, front and back.

"This card says, 'Green and Sons, Savile Row,' " he stated.

"We been there, sir," said Spittle. "Mr. Green is very astute, knows all his customers—personal. He knows no one of Noyes's description."

Edwin felt a wave of cold envelop him like an outer skin. His face remained impassive, but he knew what was coming. Pinkerton referred to notes on the pad beside him.

"Mr. F. A. Warren," he read aloud. Then: "And—the Bank of England." He looked up slowly, staring at Edwin. The beginnings of a smile played at the corners of his eyes and mouth.

"A recommendation from a tailor, I have written down here, Mr. Noyes," he said, indicating his notes. "What might that mean, I wonder." Pinkerton paused again, looking directly into Edwin's eyes.

Spittle, beside the American detective, was quite lost.

"In the light of what we know of Mr. Warren," said Pinkerton, turning pointedly to Spittle, "did this"—he indicated the card—"not seem strange to you?"

"A coincidence you mean, sir?" said Spittle.

"I do," replied Pinkerton, waiting for an explanation.

"He"—he nodded at Edwin—"Noyes, sir—said his Mr. Horton recommended the tailor and that's how he got the card—but he never took up the advice."

"So, the card was from Mr. Horton," Pinkerton said.

"Yes, sir," said Spittle.

"And on the tailor's books was there a record of a Mr. Horton?" Pinkerton asked.

"Er—no, sir," said Spittle.

"And still you did not suspect anything out of the ordinary?" continued Pinkerton to Spittle.

"Well, sir, it seemed logical that if these two men was in cahoots—Warren and Horton I'm meanin', sir—then, as Noyes 'ere suggested, one would 'ave given the other his tailor as a . . ." He faltered. ". . . recommendation."

"But you have established in your inquiries that from their descriptions, Horton and Warren are so similar that they are almost certainly one and the same, Mr. Spittle," Pinkerton said, "have you not?"

Spittle only nodded.

"Then it is possible that Mr. Noyes could have received this card directly from a Mr. Warren, is it not, Mr. Spittle?"

Pinkerton was not supercilious; he merely spoke slowly, then waited for an intelligent reply. Spittle was lost.

"Well, I suppose it is, sir"—he hesitated—"if you say so."

"I do, Mr. Spittle," said Pinkerton, exasperated, "I do." He looked at the young man before him and breathed deeply.

Edwin said nothing.

"Does your family know you are here?" asked Pinkerton, suddenly genial. "I mean, here in England?"

Eventually Edwin spoke. "Yes," he said, and coughed.

Pinkerton's smile faded. "And here also—in Newgate Prison?" he asked harshly.

This first barb from Pinkerton hurt. Edwin's thoughts were immediately of home; his mother, sisters; the Connecticut countryside. Suddenly tears appeared in his eyes. Edwin coughed again, then wiped his nose obviously, and his eyes surreptitiously. He did not answer the question. Pinkerton observed him silently.

Finally, when Edwin's eyes were clear and he was glaring defiantly at Pinkerton, the man spoke again; and when he did, his voice was hard and cruel.

"I think, Mr. Noyes, you are going to be here at Newgate quite some time. Do you not agree?"

Edwin said nothing, but his heart missed a beat.

"I think you understand me, Mr. Noyes?"

Pinkerton's gaze seemed to penetrate Edwin's innermost thoughts. Edwin hoped with all his soul that it did not.

"Green," said Pinkerton, looking at the card between his fingers. He turned it over and looked long at the reverse side.

"There is a name," he said, "and an address in a place called Kensington printed here." Without looking at Spittle, he handed him the card. "Bring the owner of that name here, Mr. Spittle," said Pinkerton.

Spittle's mouth fell open, and he just managed to stop himself from reaching for his pocket watch; he knew it was already eight in the evening. "Now, sir?" he asked, hoping the answer was no.

"Yes, Mr. Spittle," said Pinkerton. "Now."

Spittle rose and, with one of the other policemen in the room, made his way around the table past Edwin Noyes; across the large, dark area in the center of the room behind the prisoner and through the door into the corridor outside. It would take time to fetch the man, and Spittle had hoped to be at home with his wife for a decent dinner. For a single moment (and it was the only time he associated the two Americans together), Pinkerton and Noyes became one in Spittle's mind, as in Pinkerton's were Warren and Horton. He cursed them both heartily under his breath; under his belt, his empty stomach agreed noisily.

Eighty-three minutes later, Pinkerton was leaning back in his chair, hands clasped behind his head, watching the two English policemen slowly pacing beneath the gas lamps. It had become quite hot in the room during Spittle's absence.

Pinkerton heard the footsteps first. The policemen stopped pacing. Edwin continued to sip a second cup of tea, but he too detected sounds in the long corridor outside. They became gradually louder, then stopped. A door opened. Spittle and another man entered the large room and crossed respectfully to the table.

Pinkerton nodded at the man with Spittle, then, again with his head, indicated the prisoner.

"Do you know this man, sir?" he asked.

Mr. Williams of Green and Sons, tailors of Savile Row, took a long look at Edwin Noyes, frowned, then smiled with surprise, forgetting for a moment the surroundings and situation.

"Why, it's Mr. 'Ills, isn't it?" he asked.

Edwin said nothing.

"Does he know," began Mr. Pinkerton, "and answer only if you are sure, a Mr. Warren, for whom I believe you tailor?"

For all others in the room the moment was actually only a second or so, but for Edwin it was a great deal more—he was fully occupied with all the years of his life as they began to flash in front of his eyes. Then Williams spoke.

"Mr. Warren? Why, yes, sir—he does." Williams paused, then continued, snapping Pinkerton fully alert. "But not Mr. F.A. You're acquainted with Mr. G., sir, ain't that right?" He looked at Edwin, but again it was left for Pinkerton to speak.

"And who is Mr. G.?" he asked.

"Why, George, sir," Williams said, "whose uncle once owned this very cane I'm holdin' "—he showed the ebony cane to Pinkerton—"as did the uncle of Mr. F.A., from whom I obtained it."

"What are you saying, sir?" asked Pinkerton, confused.

"Why, that Mr. G. is Mr. F.A.'s brother."

Pinkerton relaxed in his chair, pursed his lips, looked long at Edwin, then beckoned to Williams for the cane. He scrutinized the handle and saw the inscription. "What is this 'A.B'?" he asked.

"Arthur Byron, sir—them's my given names." He indicated. "Those is my initials." Williams smiled proudly.

"I see," said Pinkerton. "And the cane was a gift?"

"Yes," answered Williams.

"So you had your initials inscribed here, on . . ." He held up the cane.

"No, sir—not I," said Williams, explaining. "They was there already."

"A.B.?" asked Pinkerton.

"Yes," said Williams.

"From a Mr. F.A."—he emphasized the letters—"Warren?"

"Yes, sir," answered Williams.

"And you thought nothing of this?" asked Pinkerton. "That the discrepancy of the initials was strange?"

"No, sir," replied Williams.

"Why is that?" asked Pinkerton.

" 'Cause A.B. was also in his 'at," said Williams, as if patiently explaining to a child.

"Whose ' 'at'?" mimicked Pinkerton.

"Why! Mr. F.A." explained Williams.

"Frederick Albert?" asked Pinkerton.

"The same, sir," said Williams.

"And—George—Warren: what of him?"

"I just met him, is all, sir," Williams replied to the American detective, "in Paris."

"In Paris," repeated Pinkerton to himself.

"An' a gentleman he was too, sir," said Williams, "like his

brother.'' He paused, then continued loyally, "It's difficult to
believe all these things they're a-sayin' about Mr. Warren,
sir.'' He hesitated. "Fraud?'' he said, and paused. "If
mistakes are made, sir, here's one been done proper, and
that's a fact.'' Williams finished there and then, because
Pinkerton was staring at him with ice-cold eyes.

"It is not a mistake, Mr. Williams,'' he said, slowly and
firmly, "and *that's* a fact.'' Williams swallowed and was
silent. "Now, on the cane and in the ' 'at,' as you say, the
initials—explain,'' Pinkerton said.

"Why, yes, sir,'' began Williams, "Mr. F.A. had the same
'ead like.'' He smiled.

"Come clear, man!'' shouted Detective Inspector Spittle,
who was utterly confused. Pinkerton's eyes blazed at him a
moment, and again there was silence in the room from all the
men but Williams.

"Mr. F.A.,'' he went on, "had the same 'ead as his uncle.''

"His uncle?'' repeated Pinkerton.

"Yes, sir—them's 'is full initials on the cane.'' Williams
pointed, as if to clarify.

"And how did you deduce this?'' asked Pinkerton.

"Why, Mr. F.A. told me,'' said Williams.

"I see,'' said Pinkerton, exhausted but not showing it.
"And the ' 'at'?'' he asked.

"Like I said, sir''—Williams was eager now—"he 'ad the
same 'ead like—a fine 'at it was and a shame not to wear
it—bequeathed, sir, God rest old Mr. A.B.'s soul . . .'' He
paused to cross himself, then continued to all at the table, as if
he were a salesman in mid-pitch: "Ourselves at Green's, sir,''
he went on, "we don't 'ave 'ats, but I've always thought that
one day, perhaps, I might 'ave me own shop—for 'ats like.
That's only supposin' 'avin' me own tailor's establishment was to prove difficult, sir. It's competition, sir, that's
what . . .'' Mr. Arthur Byron Williams paused, aware now of
his digression. He smiled helpfully. "Mr. Warren—F.A., that
is—always gave me 'is 'at, cane and gloves to watch over
when in Mr. Green's, sir. . . .''

Pinkerton interrupted. "And?''

"Well, I always gave his 'at a brush, sir,'' Williams went
on, "and I always looks inside at the labels of good 'ats, sir.

It's only professional curiosity, of course, sir," continued Williams righteously. "The first time he came to us, he 'ad on his uncle's American custom-made 'at, and perfect, if I say so myself." He paused. "A white Stetson." The room was quiet.

Pinkerton repeated slowly: "A white Stetson."

"Yes, sir," Williams said, "with curled sides and a black leather band."

"You remember very well, Mr. Williams." The tailor's assistant nodded.

"I do, sir 'cause he never wore it again. Always fine English 'ats thereafter." He paused, actually considering. "Dark toppers is very distinguished," he said (having difficulty over the words), "but more imposin', to my mind, is a white Stetson."

Pinkerton sighed deeply and looked into Williams' eyes.

"Then the initials we now have, it appears." He paused. "But the names, sir—do you know them?"

"Why, yes, sir," said Williams, and grinned. "They was writ clear inside the white 'at."

"Then tell us, Mr. Williams," said Pinkerton, slow and patient, "just the names and no more."

"Why, Austin, sir, and Bidwell." Williams checked himself. There was complete silence.

"Austin Bidwell," repeated Pinkerton slowly.

"Yes, sir," corroborated Williams.

"The uncle's—full name," Pinkerton said to himself.

"On the mother's side," said Williams helpfully.

"The mother's side," said Pinkerton, disbelieving. Williams was now unsure of himself for the first time.

"As . . ." He hesitated. ". . . I knew him to be, sir," he said.

The English detective inspector leaned on the table toward Williams. "And you never thought to question the veracity of this supposition?" said Spittle ponderously. Williams was now embarrassed.

Pinkerton answered for him with some appreciation of the young man's trusting nature. "He obviously did not, Spittle."

Pinkerton looked, now kindly, at the young tailor's assistant.

"About this man before you, and his associates—Mr. Hills, as you know him to be—we shall ask you to make a full statement. I hope you will not object?"

Mr. Williams shook his head at the turn of events, and his belief in his Mr. Warren began to fade.

Suddenly all in the room relaxed as if their tension had been forcibly withdrawn. All eyes came to rest eventually on the prisoner. For a moment, Mr. Robert A. Pinkerton was actually sorry for Mr. Edwin Noyes. Then the unwanted emotion passed and the steady gaze toward the young man intensified.

"Mr. Noyes." Pinkerton spoke clearly for the record. "You may now take it that you are a guest of Her Majesty . . ." Pinkerton glanced at the dumbfounded Spittle. . . . "officially." He paused. "The thread," he finished, "has begun to unravel."

"Oh, Mr. 'Ills," said Williams, quite distraught at the realization that he might have had something to do with this poor man's incarceration. "I am sorry."

"The name, Mr. Williams," said Edwin, with the resigned calm of a condemned man; "the name," Edwin repeated to the honest eyes of the upset tailor's assistant, "is Noyes, with a Y.E.S."

§

The two women, Ellen and May, were held at Bow Street Police Station. They were kept apart, in separate cells. No official arrest had yet been made, and suspicion was all the police could put forward as a reason to detain them overnight—of what, as yet they did not reveal. The clothes and other contents of their luggage the women had with them at the time of apprehension, the police hoped, would provide some proof; enough, at least to permit them to charge the women, in some degree, with something—officially.

Then they found Mac's gold in May's luggage. Even though she was utterly confused by what had come to pass, she said absolutely nothing; it was as if she were awaiting Mac's arrival, explanations and her instant release.

Ellen, equally uncomprehending, could only think that she

had been cruelly jilted. She betrayed her former lover as soon
as the police maliciously painted crude pictures to her of
George with other women, laughing at his erstwhile love. Of
George the police soon had a full description. She said it all.

The instinct for revenge was strong in Ellen, and she sought
now only to destroy her former love, if love she knew, and
have him entrapped in the net, which for her had already
fallen (albeit upon aggressive innocence and therefore only
temporarily depriving her of freedom).

"It's Wilson, that's the name" flowed from her tongue as if
she were hungrily awaiting thirty pieces of silver and to get it
were determined to please. "Most of his luggage is gone
abroad," she said, "so I doubt you'll find much amongst
mine. You ask 'em at the Terminus Hotel."

The fact that Ellen remembered the name Warren, used by
George during the Paris journey, caused tremors of excitement amongst the Bow Street police. This news was
quickly conveyed to the American inquisitor at Newgate
Prison. The police also discovered that May was known to
Ellen and that she thought the man for whom May had waited
in vain was called Mac; more she could not say, as more she
did not know.

§

Pinkerton absorbed all this information on arrival at Bow
Street.

There Pinkerton and the ever-amenable Williams confronted Ellen—the erstwhile "Mrs. Wilson." She smiled
defiantly. Williams shook his head toward Mr. Pinkerton, as
instructed if he were to find the woman not of his acquaintance. He left the cell. Pinkerton remained—silent;
merely observing the woman. When he felt sure he had her
measure, he stood and began to take his leave.

"Madam," said Pinkerton, and he bowed slightly.

"It is Mrs. Wilson," said Ellen aggressively.

Pinkerton smiled with what George's woman always
remembered (perhaps wrongly) as a cruel expression.

"It is not," he stated simply.

Ellen's face was a vision of surprise.

"The name, if indeed it is yours by legal right," said Pinkerton, and paused, "is Bidwell."

Ellen began to stutter. "What?" she finally managed to say—but Pinkerton was gone, and the cell door slammed shut.

May continued to say absolutely nothing. She cried incessantly for several hours, then became ominously calm and remained utterly silent until Mr. Pinkerton arrived at her cell. He just stood still, feet planted slightly apart, the door behind him wide. Robert A. Pinkerton had time for an assessment of the woman before she looked up at him and stared defiantly into his eyes. The gaze was as strong as Pinkerton had ever encountered: May's instinct for survival was emerging fast. Time enough to relax when Mac returned, as she believed without question he would; whatever this trouble was; now was for coping. She was prepared for anything but what Pinkerton said with a smile.

"We've made a mistake, May; you're free to go home."

This broke the lovely woman, and her tears, now of joy, after she herself had assessed the truth of the statement in Pinkerton's face, brought the man to her side, and she eventually, sobbing, whispered to him the address of the Red Lion, for the cab that would take her home. She was still so obviously upset that Mr. Pinkerton insisted, as a gentleman would, that he accompany her the entire way to her very door—and of course, this he did, overstepping the bounds of propriety only when the door to May's rooms above the Red Lion was actually open and she had begun to light the gas bracket on the wall.

Pinkerton pushed past her. This alerted May immediately to the fact that here was more than manners and consideration, qualities to which she had started to become accustomed. May fell onto the bed sobbing once more; her anguish was that of the dreamer awakened to the harsh realities of a familiar world.

Pinkerton wandered in the rooms. He tried to imagine himself as the man of this lovely and obviously loyal woman. At the rolltop bureau, Pinkerton paused. The oil lamp was still in place on the metal arm.

Absently the American detective reached behind himself and found a chair; he pulled it toward the bureau and sat down. Taking from his side pocket a packet of Lucifers, he struck one and lit the oil lamp.

The lamp they'd used to climb the stairs was beside May on the bedside table. The single gas bracket on one wall which May had lit on entry was the only other light in the rooms; this threw a shadow from Pinkerton's bulk onto the bureau. He pulled out the sliding table and locked the arm beneath it. The jumping flame in the lamp threw a pool of light directly onto the spot below.

A blotter showed up white and unsoiled; no ink stain marked its surface. It was just large enough to be of use to a letter writer. Pinkerton slid back the roll top of the bureau. He found no pen or ink immediately, but a pencil was on hand in one of the drawers. He began to rub the blotting paper lightly with the pencil. May watched as this other American sat where such a short time ago her lover had been occupied creating, as he always said, a new life for them both. Her beautiful eyes were wide and tears still fell, but she saw the concentration of Pinkerton, and instinct told May that he was destroying her—and she could do nothing.

As the white surface darkened with the patterns he made, Pinkerton listened to May's world around him. Holborn at night: the seemingly always falling rain; a distant, out-of-tune piano; voices singing bad lyrics to dull melodies, prompted by cheap alcohol; shouts from below, in the street; the fading scream as from a struck child or woman, the sudden boisterous laughter from a passing group exchanging shouted abuse. A baby started crying across the way; a man roared at his wife or daughter, and she patiently assuaged, with sweet words, a child's fears of darkness; the crying ceased. A cart passed in the street, rattling on the cobbles, splashing in the puddles; feet sounded on boards; urgent calls between several men penetrated the night. Then, suddenly, silence came—but for the steady rain outside and faintly hissing gas within: a background to the soft sobbing of May in the bedroom.

A watchman passed along an adjacent street, and his call was just discernible. Pinkerton's ears did not hear the hour, but clearly spoken came the words ". . . and all's well." He looked down at the dark patch he'd just finished on the white blotting pad.

It was as if a pale spider had trailed spoor over an ebony mantel. There, as Pinkerton peered toward his work of art, were the words, quite discernible, *Alphonse de Rothschild, six thousand pounds, F. A. Warren*—two signatures, one sum of money. Pinkerton smiled.

Outside, a last cry from the night watch—as the "Charley" rounded a corner of the Red Lion—was swallowed; sound shut off by bricks and mortar, as if a door had slammed closed on the man. "All's well," he'd said, "all's well."

Pinkerton stood up, crossed into the other room, then sat down on the bed beside May and shook her gently. She rolled over, stifled her sobs, sighed deeply and propped herself on an elbow, looking at the American with all the signs of warning a woman gives out to a man she believes is about to "take advantage of a situation," without encouragement.

"Read that for me, would you, May?" said the American, continuing in May's mind to be unpredictable. She looked at the blotting pad held before her eyes, under the glow of the bedside oil lamp.

"I can't," said May.

"I know it's difficult in this light," said Pinkerton, angling the pad so that it was better lit, "but look again."

"I can't," said May, and tears began once more at the thought of Mac's attempted lessons to add literacy to beauty.

As the realization dawned on Pinkerton, he smiled, then handed May the pencil. "Write me your name," he asked of May softly. She took the pencil angrily and scored two short lines on the blotting pad, one over the other, at right angles, meeting in the center.

Pinkerton looked up from the cross, his eyes full of compassion for May; her defiance in adversity was to be admired, not fought.

"Do you rent this place, May?" he asked.

"I owns it," May said, after a pause with more than a hint of pride.

"Then where," asked Pinkerton coolly, "are the deeds?"

May's eyes involuntarily turned toward the other room,

where she knew the bureau to be. She concealed the look, a fraction too late. Pinkerton stood up and took the blotting pad back to the occasional table. He sat down again and began opening the small drawers, one by one. Third time lucky, he found the folded document. Opened, it revealed the usual formalities and conditions of sale: the rooms had been assigned to May.

Robert A. Pinkerton was mumbling to himself as he sought for the signature, eventually found it and, without trouble, deciphered it. "Edwin Noyes," he was saying under his breath; "Austin Bidwell, brother George and—whom have we here?" He found the name and compared it with the writing on the blotting pad. It was different, but he'd bet his last dollar that a real expert would be able to make a match. "Writing can't lie," he'd been told; study had proved that a man's scrawl revealed a great deal about his personality, and like fingerprints, to an expert it was unique.

Pinkerton looked again at the signature on the deeds of "rooms above the Red Lion, Holborn, City of London, England," and smiled with satisfaction.

There, of course, written "large as life," "bold as brass," "confident as you like"—whatever the cliché—was the signature of May's lover and benefactor, the highly regarded friend of George Bidwell, Austin's admired companion and Edwin Noyes's loyal *ami*—a son of American soil, of excellent education, quick-witted, talented, knowledgeable, with a natural sharpness and cunning—qualities that would need only the hint of adversity to hone this man into an elusive quarry.

Pinkerton spoke out the name loud: "George Mac-Donald."

"Corked"

THE wreck of the White Star Liner *Atlantic*, on the first of April 1873, was a great disaster. Off the coast of Nova Scotia, fifteen miles from Halifax, the ship ran onto the promontory of Meagher's Head, at the entrance of Prospect Harbour. Almost six hundred people perished, including all the women and children. The cause was, beyond question, an error in reckoning of the distance run and of the course and position of the ship and mistaking of one lighthouse for another; magnetic interference with the compass was not proved.

Though she had crossed the ocean after which she was named according to schedule, it appears that the ship's Captain became worried, in the worsening weather, that the remaining coal supply would not be sufficient; thus a change of course was agreed upon and Halifax made the new destination.

The night of the catastrophe was dark and the sea rough. The ship struck at two in the morning, west of Sambro. The impact was felt several times, and the officers and crew, immediately alarmed, rushed on deck and endeavored to clear away the boats with axes; rockets were fired off by the Second

Officer. Suddenly, not ten minutes having elapsed since her going aground, the *Atlantic* heeled heavily to port, fell onto her beam ends and sank. The women and children who were asleep at the time the ship struck were prevented from coming on deck by the seas washing over the fast-sinking ship. A portion of the rigging remained above water, in which all who were able took refuge.

The Third Officer, Mr. Brady, managed to swim with a halyard to a rock, thence to a second and at last to the shore. Some passengers were therefore able to escape by using the rope as support, but the rising tide and heavy sea made the situation perilous. Many died on the rocks from exhaustion and exposure; others became maniacs and chattered like children.

At about six o'clock in the morning, the first boats from the shore were able to take off those who remained clinging to the ship and rigging.

The Chief Officer had taken hold of the only surviving female and secured her in the rigging, making himself fast also against the cascading seas and flying spray. The day dawned, but it was not until two o'clock in the afternoon that the Reverend Mr. Ancient fought out to the ship with a crew of four men, pulling against the huge waves, and rescued the officer, who was swept from the wreck, numb and exhausted, saved only by a line thrown him by the clergyman. The woman, after bearing up with remarkable strength amidst the surging foam, died moments before the small boat managed to approach; her half-naked body was still fast in the rigging as the crew of the small boat pulled away, holding off from the dangerous rocks over which the sea churned and broke; the woman's eyes protruded, her mouth continued to foam and the ghastly spectacle, it was reported, was made more so by the sight of numerous jewels which still sparkled on her hands.

Throughout America, papers were full of accounts, both of the accident itself and of the reception and hospitality extended to those passengers who escaped. The wreckage was fully documented; the cruel and abundant plunder was not.

Official investigation into the cause of the disaster commenced in Halifax on April 6. Gross neglect on the part of

Captain Williams was declared, and incompetency was the accusation flung at the man whose watch it had been, the Fourth Officer.

In Great Britain no inquiry was made—opportunely, for at least one man. As the registration officer, all records and half those aboard had been lost beneath the waves, and tickets issued for the voyage included one to Mr. Bidwell, George—who could not be found amongst the survivors of the wreck—it was assumed that he too had drowned.

Thus on April 3 *The Times* of London declared quite clearly the demise of said suspected criminal. Alphabetically, he was high on the published list.

It had all begun on March 20. . . .

Mac and George had split up and declared a rendezvous in New York. With the women taken, they felt sure their true identities would be discovered eventually, but not having allowed for the entrapment of their ladies, they had retained only their own—genuine—passports, all others now destroyed. There was certainly no time for Mac to make forgeries; so understanding the chance they took, both men had fled as fast as they were able. Mac to France—first Paris, then Brest. George to Ireland—Cork and Queenstown.

§

Pinkerton's discoveries in England had immediately persuaded him to cable New York.

As the revelation of Edwin Noyes's term in prison had not been difficult for the English police to discover, so for Robert A. Pinkerton with "Uncle" Austin Bidwell and George Wilson, alias Warren, *né* Bidwell. It was confirmed by both their descriptions and their criminal records that the brothers were without doubt the men wanted in connection with the great Bank of England fraud.

The fourth man in the case—one who increasingly began to intrigue the American detectives—was George MacDonald. He proved to have been using his own name in America *and* England, but although he was of respectable background, his immediate past and associations with criminal elements in Manhattan suggested to Pinkerton's New York office that "he should be suspected of presently following a dubious vocation."

This was all Robert A. Pinkerton needed. And thus the hunt began in earnest.

§

At the Hotel Richmond, in the Rue du Helder, Mac stayed only one night before going on to his last European destination. It was long enough for his pursuers. Expense had been swept aside by the Bank of England; thus, repeated cables to Paris, and the cooperation of French police in scrutinizing hotel registers, finally established that an American by the name of MacDonald had indeed been a guest of the Richmond, but had already checked out.

The evening of the night before, on a Pinkerton hunch, Spittle and the American detective had gone over the timetables of all sailings for the Americas—North and South.

"Liverpool and Plymouth have gone, sir," Spittle said, examining the timetables before him. "Bordeaux ain't sailing for six days. Hamburg for three. Southampton went yesterday. We've only the two left—Brest, in France, and Queenstown, Ireland—tomorrow sailing."

Pinkerton thought—correctly, as it turned out—that he understood, at least to a degree (and that was all, if the truth be known), the ingenuity of the men he was up against.

"Spittle," he said, authoritatively, "you take the French ship, *Thuringia*, at Brest. I'll go for the Irish ship."

"It's the *Atlantic*, sir," Spittle had replied. "A White Star liner."

"I know, Spittle," said Pinkerton patiently, having studied the timetable in detail. "I came over on her. Now go, man; you've no time to lose."

Spittle went.

§

The deep note of a ship's horn sounded out loud and long as its gangway was slowly disconnected from the shore. Mac paced the deck of the *Thuringia*, checking his watch minute by

minute. His attention was focused on the shore. As the fore
and aft hawsers were cast off and the steamer slowly turned
on an axis, before making headway out into the Channel, Mac
began to breathe deeply, the sea air of freedom.

The day before, Mac had rushed to the quay, late, waving a
ticket he'd bought at perplexed officials, not waiting for a
reply; but his conversation with the Purser beside the berthed
liner had shaken him.

"This *billet* is now for tomorrow, m'sieur," the officer had
explained; "we sail at noon."

"What?" Mac exclaimed.

"We have been delayed, m'sieur, by one day. Passengers
are staying in the town—there are good 'otels, m'sieur."

"May I cable from there?" Mac asked.

"Of course, m'sieur," the officer replied.

So Mac had the opportunity of informing Irving, in New
York, of his imminent arrival. Once on the ship, apart from
sightings of other ocean traffic, passengers knew they were
cut off from the world until landfall. Thus there was an
urgency to the message. It was Mac's only chance.

§

The delayed sailing regained for Spittle precious hours that
had been lost by cancelled ferries between Dover and Calais.
From the French Channel port to the transatlantic harbor, a
fast coach and six took him through the night to a morning
stop, some miles from Brest, where he was able to hire a
carriage and pair to complete his journey.

Spittle burst into the town office of the French Line in the
middle of a ceremony. Two officials were opening a '56 bottle
of claret with great reverence. Spittle demanded attention.
They ignored him until they had assured themselves that the
wine was still sound. Eventually they found, then began to
check, the passenger list of the only sailing that day for the
United States. Spittle looked at the pocket watch in his
shaking hand. It was just before noon.

"Maas . . ." the official began, as his companion looked
impatiently at the vintage Bordeaux; ". . . Maber, McCann,
MacDonald—George. *Oui*, m'sieur," he said, pleased at the

discovery, "he is sailing." By the time the official looked up, Spittle was gone.

At the quayside, the Scotland Yard police badge meant little to the Customs officer, especially as the ship in question had already sailed; besides, his tour of duty was over until the arrival of an evening liner from Lisbon.

"Noon!" the Englishman was shouting, almost incoherent. "Noon!"

The Englishman (as the Customs officer could not fail to see) was pointing to both hands of a pocket watch that indicated twelve. "Noon!" the man bellowed hoarsely. Obviously confused, the Customs officer said—and indeed, understood—nothing. He retained his dignity and simply walked away. Since the French did not observe Greenwich time, the Paris meridian declared it to be one o'clock; and as a Frenchman, the officer had a more important matter to attend to: his luncheon.

§

George had taken a night ferry from Holyhead across the Irish Sea to Cork and thence to Queenstown, the last port where transatlantic steamers took on passengers.

It was early morning, and George was bent over the basin, shaving, when a knock sounded on the door and a man's head peered into George's cabin.

"It's Cork we'll be landin' at, sor, in a half hour," the steward said with a bright smile.

"Is Queenstown far?" George asked, his face nearly touching the heated water, most of his sideburns and all of his moustache floating on the surface, an inch or so from his face.

"If it's the White Star *Atlantic* you'll be wantin', sor," said the Irish voice, "you've time and half, sor; time and a half," it repeated.

"Thank you," mumbled George without turning.

"New York's a grand city, they're sayin', sor," said the Irish steward. "Is that roight, sor?" he asked, and stepped into the cabin.

George coughed loudly and nodded vigorously.

"Well, good luck to you, sor," said the steward.

Just as the man turned to leave, George stood upright and for a moment caught the steward's gaze in the mirror above the basin.

"An' if you don't mind my sayin', sor"—the steward grinned—"I prefers a man clean-shaven meself."

The steward was gone in the second it took George to swallow and curse all the gods at once.

At the Queenstown docks, George's carriage was stopped at the gate that led to the cobbled roadway beyond which was the point of embarkation. The White Star liner had already begun to embark passengers, George knew, and his urgency communicated itself to the Irish official who was taking a great deal of time, it seemed, to read the very simple information in George Bidwell's passport.

The man paused yet again, and once more turned a page back to the written description of the American. He looked at the driver of the carriage, then at his passenger, and approached the occupant until they were almost nose to nose.

Now clean-shaven, George suddenly realized that it was clearly this discrepancy which was causing the official concern; but the man said nothing, as he compared the description with the man before him. George swore to himself, it was the only time he wished that he had a photogravure depicting his previous appearance in his possession. The official reread the words deemed sufficient to convey George from one country to another, then read further to find his place of origin and occupation: agent of business.

George's impatience was obvious; he was becoming exasperated. Then the Irishman spoke.

"Would you be havin' a five-pound note on you, sor?" the official inquired in a genial manner. "An' the price of the cab back into town?" finished the Irishman in charge of his gate.

"Why?" asked George tersely.

"Well," began the Irish official slowly, "it ain't for me to say, sor, really, but I've an idea that the three gentlemen—two of our Irish, but English-bought, policemen"—he rubbed fingers and thumb together in reference to, in his mind, the Irish turncoats—"and of course, the American gentleman with them—and he does have a particularly gruff turn of phrase—who are waitin' for you by the steamer there . . ." At this he made as if to turn toward the *Atlantic*, partially hidden behind the wharfside buildings; then, thinking better of it, remained facing the gentleman in the carriage to whom he was speaking. ". . . well, sor," he continued with a slow smile, "I'm thinkin' that they ain't exactly gonna present you wid the keys of Dublin City, loike." He grinned at George and handed him back his passport. "I'd only be guessin', o'course, sor," he finished.

George looked wildly toward the docks and confirmed the official's suspicions. Seeing the man's eyebrows saying more than words could, George took out some money—twenty pounds, to be exact—and handed the English notes to the Irishman.

"You bein' an American yourself an' all, sor," the official continued, pocketing the notes, "well, the only good thing about the English, sor, is their money." He looked into George's eyes, directly and with a very definite expression that he should be gone—fast. "Would you not agree, sor?" he questioned.

George nodded, unable to speak.

"It's a Fenian man I am, sor," the official said confidentially, declaring his anti-British sentiments. "An' afflicted wid Cromwell's curse."

"What's that?" George managed to utter hoarsely.

"The occasional blindness," the official said with a wink, "Mr. Bidwell, sor." He touched his peaked cap.

"God bless you," said George.

"He does, sor," said the Irishman, stepping back to allow the carriage turning room. "He does," he repeated, tapping the notes now in his inside pocket.

It took no time at all for the carriage to turn back the way it had come and rattle off toward Queenstown once more. By the time Robert A. Pinkerton discovered a carriage had arrived late at the dock gateway, the White Star Liner *Atlantic* had sailed and George Bidwell had disappeared into the heart of the Emerald Isle.

Sanctuary

NEW York in 1873 was quite obviously a much younger city than its European rivals, its size only one third that of London. Yet there was little doubt that the varieties of color, creed and national origin amongst the "picturesque" population, densely crowded into a series of ghetto districts, produced in these poor quarters, where the land of promise had failed expectation, that peculiar intensity of crime in acts of blood and riot which only the English capital, or its northern port for the West, Liverpool, could equal.

The "dangerous classes" of New York were ignorant of all but their city and the need to survive, more brutal than the peasantry from which they descended; the products of passion, vice, accident, neglect, destitution and misery. The land of opportunity had another meaning for them, and in its greatest city these dangerous classes learned to take, corrupt and destroy as did their fellow citizens give, convert and create.

Europe was a narrow sphere, where a man was born to his "place." To rise above his equals he had not only to make extraordinary efforts, but have abilities and qualities above the average. Thus if a man remained in Europe, it was to work to live or, at most, to arrive at comparative ease; in America a man learned to work to become rich. It was a goal any man, no matter what his background, had the chance to attain; not all men achieved it, but most tried.

From this turmoil sprang many a sharp mind, to whom only fortune dictated and fate decreed on which side of the law it should operate. Many were successful in treading a course equally between the two sides.

The police developed a relationship with both established business and criminal association, and within bounds— however nefarious, clandestine or immoral—it worked.

Political contacts *and* personal liaisons with the underworld of New York put an ordinary detective on the city police staff in a unique position. One who had outshone his fellows in this respect was named James Irving.

A short time after the Civil War ended, whilst the whole country reeled still from the mighty conflict, the position of Chief of the New York Detective Force became vacant. The successful candidate was none other than "Jimmy"—as he became popularly known—Irving. And he survived. Enormous money issued from the government, to shore up the shaken economy, created flush times, and with everything booming, associations were formed in the underworld to promote rackets, vice and fraud on a large scale.

Percentage payments to precinct headquarters and to politicians guaranteed a blind eye. Irving's position made his protection much sought after.

From Spring Street to Tenth, Broadway, full of night games, became the happy hunting ground of New York detectives. Jimmy Irving bought diamonds to wear as rings and pins; he had his own fast trotting horse and rig, which had cost more than a thousand dollars; as his pay was a mere two thousand dollars per annum, it was assumed he was "doing well." Wallack's Theatre of an evening; Delmonico's for late supper; long week ends at Long Island homes; holidays in the South, when Florida's winter weather became fashionable: Jimmy's world was expanding.

To James Irving, the trivialities of administrative police work were the only problem he had to solve. In part he delegated duties to two associates, Stanley and White, who had become cronies in cahoots with most of his schemes, but there was always that for which only he could be responsible and to which his signature must be appended.

The late-March winds, bearing morning sleet, blended night snow and mud together with manure into a nightmare for any horse and owner who wished to negotiate a path from one place to another without being soiled. By eleven, the New York traffic was thick and noisy.

Irving's arrival on Tuesday the twenty-fifth was his first appearance that week at Central Police Headquarters. He was hung over, irritable at having this chore of office thrust on him and angry as hell at the commotion below on the streets, where even he had been spattered with mud.

He burst into the outer office, taking off his gloves and sounding out to the policeman in charge of the desk, who stood up respectfully; the two other men, seated opposite, did not. Irving ignored them all and made directly for his own door.

"Morning, Chief Irving, sir," said the policeman.

"New York traffic's gettin' worse every damn day," said Irving, on the move. "Morning, lad. Well, sit—sit." He continued to the door. "One day they'll invent somethin' better'n horses," he finished, and paused only a second at the door, acknowledging his visitors in a glance.

"Who are they?" he asked the policeman, not recalling their faces, and whom Irving did not recognize in the city of New York—in his mind at least—wasn't worth knowing.

"These two gentlemen, sir," the blue uniform began.

". . . can wait!" Irving finished. He entered his office and slammed the door.

The policeman could only shrug at the two patient and imposing gentlemen.

The cable on Irving's desk had been there since the previous Friday. He ignored it until he had downed a whiskey and settled himself in the large, comfortable swivel chair, his back to the window, high above the street. He opened the cable and read it slowly. It was from George MacDonald. His door was opened cautiously by the policeman from the outer office. He looked up.

"Well?" he asked, still trying to digest the cable.

"They was here yesterday too, sir," the blue uniform said.

"Who?" shouted Irving.

"The two gentlemen," said the cowed policeman; "they been waitin' to see you."

Irving was about to declare a busy morning when one of the two large visitors pushed past the policeman and opened the door wide to allow his companion entrance also.

"Well, gentlemen?" said Irving, respecting their obvious size and evident authority.

"We are seeking the whereabouts of a George MacDonald," said one.

"And an Austin Bidwell," said the other. Both were quite impassive, and their voices betrayed nothing of their character.

Irving looked from one man to the other, remembered his own all-pervading authority and quite without qualm folded and pocketed the cable. "And who are you?" he asked.

"My name," said the one, "is William Pinkerton, and this is my associate, Mr. John Curtain."

Irving and the Pinkertons had different missions in life; they had never met but knew each other by reputation. Irving grinned and made an expansive gesture. "I wish I could help," he said, making it obvious that he either could or would not.

Pinkerton threw the morning paper onto the desk in front of Irving, his opinion of the man badly concealed by the look that came into his face.

"You can, sir, when he arrives," Pinkerton said coldly.

"Who?" exclaimed Irving, leaning toward the paper. Its front page was ominous. He already knew the answer.

GEORGE MACDONALD, screamed the headline, SUSPECT IN THE GREAT BANK OF ENGLAND FRAUD, ESCAPES NET, SAILS FOR NEW YORK. Irving gritted his teeth and looked at the two men, who had seated themselves comfortably opposite; they now watched the New York Chief of Detectives expectantly.

Irving swallowed and wished for another large glass of whiskey. He indicated to the policeman to leave. "Get out,

Jake," he said. "and see that we are not disturbed."

"Yes, Chief Irving," said the policeman, and left the room quietly, closing the door behind him.

§

A thousand-mile voyage from New York Harbor, on the cold deck of the ship *Thuringia* seven days out of Brest, Mac huddled against the davit of a lifeboat and stared long and hard up into the clear night sky, naming those constellations which he knew. He had been at this several minutes when the door on the starboard flying bridge opened some yards away, at the top of a short flight of steps, and the dark blue uniform of the Captain emerged. He leaned on the rail to breathe fresh sea air.

Out of the corner of his eye he saw Mac, who acknowledged his host of several pleasant dinners at the large round table in the dining room. Mac moved nearer, to just below the bridge, and both men, one above the other, looked out into the darkness and shared silently their pleasure in the unique peace offered only by a ship far out in a vast ocean.

At sea, a ship was truly a world of its own, isolated for the duration of a voyage from all but others like it. Only lights, loudhailers and flags served to communicate news, greeting, requests or emergency.

In the distance, an eastbound steamer could be seen, her lights sparkling across the water. One began to flash, in what became an irregular sequence—obviously a message expertly sent. Mac and the Captain watched.

Eventually the steamer passed by, blowing two blasts from her horn in farewell. The sound was muted by distance and faded mournfully. The answering blasts from *Thuringia* destroyed the peaceful surroundings a moment; then those sounds too dispersed across the dark ocean, until the rippling wake of the ship and soft noises from her bowels, belowdecks, provided the only distraction to a night of glittering stars.

"Do you read Morse, m'sieur?" asked the Captain suddenly. He was looking at Mac, seriously but with a kindly glint in his eye.

"Yes, Captain," answered Mac, looking still after the

steamer, now indistinct, merging with constellations on the horizon. "I am afraid I do." Mac's dejection had been observed by the seaman.

"As a Frenchman, it does not concern me," began the Captain, "but it seems, on our arrival in New York, you are going to have"—he paused—"problems, Mr. MacDonald."

Mac sighed and thrust both hands deep into his heavy coat.

"That is the third ship today which has conveyed to me the same message," the Captain went on, "always, mid-Atlantic, we exchange news. After all," he smiled, "while we are at sea, the world might have come to an end."

He looked long and sympathetically at Mac. He had no love for the English or for their boorish colonial behavior. He turned to go back into the wheelhouse. "Can you swim?" he asked with a grin.

"Badly," replied Mac soberly, not appreciating the humor.

The Captain appraised his passenger, and his heart went out to the young man of whom, during the last week, he had grown rather fond. "Then I hope you have friends," he said, and re-entered the bridge.

Mac was alone. He looked up at the stars; the night was suddenly cold and bleak. Tears filled his eyes, not of self-pity, but of compassion for May, as she appeared in his memory with that smile and those eyes he would never forget. Somewhere, he hoped, she too was looking up into the starry sky; perhaps then she would remember what they had almost grasped and—no matter what—forgive him.

§

It is one hundred and forty-three miles from Lismore to Dublin. Lying in an armchair of the lounge in the Lismore House Hotel, George reviewed his situation. Ireland was crawling with police and detectives, all, it seemed, looking for the three Americans involved in the great Bank of England case. George was exhausted, having eluded one detective after another, keeping always ahead of danger with a sharp eye and cunning mind; now, for a moment at rest, analyzing his situation, he felt only a deep sense of despair and—worse —loneliness.

His head was back, eyes closed, his stomach full from a stodgy Irish meal, when another man entered the poorly lit, overly furnished lounge, belched twice, then sat down to read the evening paper. George opened his eyes a fraction and watched the man rifle the paper quickly, read the first two columns on its front page, then turn into the second and third, continuing the lead story.

The photogravure on the front page, without doubt, was from the photograph taken of George and Ellen in Paris. On reflection, it seemed sheer stupidity to have allowed her to keep it, but to Ellen it had been, at least for a while, precious. It made him look older than he was, especially since his clean shave, but the description beneath the picture would (no doubt with Ellen's help, he had sense enough to realize) have rectified that. He had not energy to curse the lady. His eyes found a figure printed below, large enough to read. Five thousand pounds reward!

The stout man with the paper put it down, rubbing his pudgy fingers on a handkerchief, which he then used to wipe his lips, around which the soup from dinner had dried yellow and brown. The large peasant-farmer face broke into a smile as George's eye caught his. The man nodded, gave George a long look and took up the paper as if to leave, but remained in his seat. Unaware that he was staring at George, he stroked his own long sideburns and absently twirled his sagging moustache, referring momentarily to the picture emblazoned on the *Irish Evening News*.

The man obviously was not sure of George—the hasty shipboard barbering had certainly changed his appearance—but there was something in George Bidwell's eyes that was unique; perhaps their pale color or the dark lashes and brows—whatever, the camera in Paris had captured the quality so admired by Ellen. George kept his eyes closed.

Suddenly with a great effort the stout man stood up, broke wind and waddled out of the large room. George took a deep breath; remembered that he had on his person, and in his coat in the cloakroom, all his valuables and lost no time at all in picking up the small bag beside him (his only luggage) which he had, as yet, not even taken to his room and left the hotel.

He could not gamble on passing unrecognized. It was going to be a long night.

The next twelve hours were a discovery for George of what keeps the grass green in Ireland. The rain bucketed down in torrents. He walked for an hour, until at the outskirts of Lismore he found a place with its light on, declaring JAUNTING CARS TO LET. He went round to the livery stable behind a house and found the hostler just uncoupling the harness from a "car." The young man touched his cap when George produced five sovereigns and listened intently as George asked the various routes to Dublin, impressing on the Irish lad the urgency of his journey and that it should begin immediately, not at dawn.

The hostler scratched his head for several moments before speaking. In George's mind it was crucial that he leave immediately; his increasing fears and growing desperation made him feel sure the detectives from Queenstown would not be far behind. The stout man at the hotel must have recognized him, he told himself. Perhaps it was merely pessimism, but to George it seemed that everywhere he went, people stared. A stranger is an immediate suspect; had he red hair and a hunch back he felt they would still accuse him, to gain the offered bounty.

Ireland had become too "hot." In George's mind was now the only alternative plan: to embark for Scotland, then race across England, out of the clutches of those who thought him "bottled up" in the Emerald Isle; over the Channel to Calais; on to Spain; from there to South America; then a slow boat to the Gulf of Mexico and perhaps New Orleans. If his pursuers followed him that far, they deserved his soul.

Despite his situation he smiled at that thought, and the Irish hostler responded, thinking the expression meant for him. He had now worked out a route for the first part of the gentleman's journey, and outlined the road to Clonmel, which was beyond Cahir, a place where Cromwell had once been so stoically resisted by the Irish defenders—"Where brutal retribution was meted out on their surrender," said the lad, now checking his horse's bit. George remembered the one thing he knew of Cromwell's Irish campaigns. "Without mercy," he said with some feeling.

The lad's eyes narrowed and he looked at this gentleman with renewed respect. George had made an instant friend.

"Is it, if you'll forgive me askin', sor, a Fenian man you'll be, sor?" The patriot in the man's heart had been touched deeply now, and any suspicion he held toward his prospective fare was dispelled.

"From America," said George, nodding, falling in with the assumption. "I'm a leader of a group there, who has returned to the home country to see the situation."

"From America!" the lad repeated in awe.

"And it's not entirely a welcoming committee I think I have on my heels," George said, deciding to commit himself to the fervor he'd stirred in the Irishman. He climbed into the jaunting car beside the lad. The one thing real about his new-found status was that George and these Irish Fenians shared a common enemy—the English.

"A Fenian man," whispered the lad as his sleek blood horse trotted out into the torrential rain. The lad looked at George with the passion of youth and patriotism. George nodded.

"For that, sor," he said—then, remembering the money, he grinned—"and your five sovereigns, it's to Hell I'll be takin' you if you wish it."

"Or Clonmel," said George, smiling at the Irish eyes.

"There's what I'd call a 'safe house,' the lad went on, "in that town. There they'll keep you, I'm sure; you'll be able to take the train on to Dublin and even Belfast—if you wish it."

"Then drive on, boy," said George, "to Clonmel or Hell."

"One and the same, sor," retorted the lad, grinning hugely, "one and the same."

The hostler stood up, shouted wildly, cracked a whip over the horse's back, then whistled loud above the noise of distant thunder as the jaunting car began to move. The rain seemed to become even heavier to George as they raced off toward a road that only the lad could make out. For George, who could see nothing but walls of water, it could well have been to Hell he was being taken.

In the jaunting car, the Irish patriot and the American brain behind the greatest disaster the Bank of England had ever suffered galloped at breakneck speed toward the black

nothingness before them and disappeared into the torrential
night.

§

Dawn came, and the sun made what impression it could on
a dull countryside as rain continued unceasingly. George,
exhausted and huddled in the jaunting car, was shaken into
consciousness by the Irish lad. Opening his eyes, he saw
behind the hostler—his coachman of the night—some distance away, two uniformed figures emerging from a house.
Seeing the car, they started to approach. In an instant George
was fully awake. They were police.

"Don't move, sor," said the lad quietly. He turned and
waved to the two men, who, recognizing the lad, bent against
the lashing rain, cursorily returned the greeting, then made
off, swallowed by the deluge.

George was soaking wet, hungry and tired past caring; for
the moment he had become a pathetic figure, and the boy's
sympathies extended toward his "Fenian man." Seeming to
make no impression on him, as if it were sustenance to the
body and soul, the rain fell into the lad's eyes, splattered dark
hair to his forehead and ran from a face that broke into an
honest smile.

"You've not to worry, sor," he said; "they'll be lookin' after you here, sor." The lad sprang down from his seat, ran
across the yard and through the half-open door from which
the police had come. As George watched, his spirits sank and
he wished only to be dry and warm, no matter what the consequences. He no longer cared whether the boy was trustworthy, the building offered refuge. He climbed down stiffly
from the car and squelched across the mud, ignoring the puddles into which his boots slithered. At the door he paused,
gripping his bag firmly. The lad came out, smiling broadly,
and scampered back to his car waving encouragement; then he
climbed up onto the rig. What the hell, thought George. He
turned and stepped into the "safe house."

The room was not empty. A turf fire burned in the grate,
and to one side was a long counter. The clock against one wall
of the room, a grandfather, almost scraping the low ceiling,

showed eleven. It was March 30 and a Sunday, George knew.

Beside the fire crouched a man with what appeared to be an apron round his waist. At one of the two windows stood another man. Both ignored George as he stepped toward the fire. The man from the window crossed slowly to the door, closed it and returned to his position. The man beside George at the fire stood up and faced this stranger. He nodded over at his companion; the man made a sign through the glass, a sign unseen by George, who now collapsed onto a stool at the grate.

There were three doors to the large low room, and in the next moment the two at the rear burst open and fifteen or sixteen men came crashing in boisterously, then, seeing George, fell silent, unmoving. The man beside George at the fire motioned to him to sit again, now with a smile.

"Sunday liquor, sor," he began, "in Oirland is—a delicate problem; 'illegal' is the word." He smiled and turned briefly to the men waiting for reassurance that George was not an intruder. The proprietor nodded; with that they seemed to relax immediately.

"But," the proprietor continued, "if you've an Irish heart, then it is neither an English conscience nor their law you'll be keeping." He bent toward the seated stranger and said confidentially. "Tell 'em, sor, in America, 'tis still the feelin' we have."

He paused as George reappraised the situation, dispelling all his worst imaginings. His relief was as obvious as had been his fears, and the proprietor, in company with several of the men, laughed at his answer.

"I will tell them," said George, "*if* I get back."

"Then indeed you will, sor," said the proprietor confidently, waving a hand to the others indicating that they were now free to cross to the counter, behind which were bottles of potheen, the homemade Irish brew that served to describe his "house" as a bar. "Indeed you will," he repeated, clapping George about the shoulders, "if we have anything to do with it."

George lay back in the alcove of the grate, where the fire now burned with a warmth that his bones received with thanks.

"You are," said the proprietor, "now amongst friends." The words were never better meant or more gratefully received. Although George had no choice, instinct told him he could trust these men. He wanted to weep, but didn't; instead he got quite specially drunk and joined in the singing amidst rags on the floor in front of the fire in the "house of potheen."

> At the sign of the bell,
> On the road to Clonmel,
> Pat Flagherty kept a neat shebeen

were the last words of the song George absorbed, and he silently thanked "the man himself," before succumbing to dreamless oblivion.

§

Irving took up the daily paper to read aloud its news, and discovered on the front page of the *New York Herald* a verbatim cable dispatched from Great Britain. The Chief of Detectives read it out to his two subordinates, standing with his back to the window of his top-floor office.

"Three shabbily dressed men, who from their accent are believed to be Americans, were arrested in Cork, Ireland, this morning, while attempting to deposit twelve thousand dollars in that city. They are, it is thought, the parties who recently committed the Great Fraud on the Bank of England."

Irving looked across at his two assistants, who were sprawled in the "hospitality" chairs. Stanley and White—if not taxed too hard and allowed to exercise their delegated power (sadistically for the one, in bully-boy manner for the other)—were the perfect assistants for Irving. They both grinned.

"So they're done," said Stanley, shifting his thin frame and extending long legs, which he crossed and placed on a footstool.

"Then they ain't our bother no longer," said White. He sat forward, tensing his muscles, elbows propped on the armrests.

Irving walked to his swivel seat and slumped, taking his time to answer.

"Every day a report comes from somewhere that one of the boys is caught; why should this be any different? We know Mac's aboard *Thuringia*, so how do these Irish think they've made a coup with all three? If the boys have sense, they ain't travelin' together, and we know they ain't short of sense." He looked at his detectives, Stanley and White, and shook his head. He fixed them both with a stare of sheer pity. "Jesus Christ!" shouted Irving. The two men sat up quickly. "That Pinkerton 'private' was here tellin' us they've split and are off an' runnin', so how in hell do you think it ain't our bother no longer . . ." Irving stopped, exasperated. "I had to promise 'co-op-er-a-tion' (he spread the word sarcastically as he said it) to that investigator; but," he went on slyly, "I didn't tell *him* for who . . ." Expecting a response, he waited with a grin. This only perplexed both of his associates.

"We know one thing for sure," said Irving, wiping the smile from his face in disgust: "where our money's been comin' from. I ain't heard complaints from you two since you started spendin' it."

The men squirmed in their seats now, uncomfortable.

"You two have to learn something—obligations." He paused to let them absorb the word. "Thirty thousand dollars in bonds, with more due, is for services rendered or help to come, boys—you understand?"

Stanley nodded and looked at White, who made an apologetic grimace at Irving, who spoke again, quietly now.

"Gentlemen," he said, "we owe them for sendin' it—so somehow," he continued after a pause, "we have to get Mac off his ship." He paused.

"Ain't got a clue—have you?" said Irving derisively. The two men coughed, one after the other, as if—like a yawn—it was compulsive. Irving was right: they hadn't even one idea.

"Jake!" shouted Irving. A uniformed policeman appeared at the door. "Bring him in," he commanded.

The policeman went, and reappeared with another man, poorly dressed, cap in hand, the unforgettable face of a city rough, spread with a large grin, showing more gaps then teeth.

"Gentlemen," said Irving to Stanley and White, who twisted round in their chairs.

"A onetime burglar and sometime seaman," finished Irving's introduction—"Johnny Dobbs."

The two detectives appraised the man and could barely manage a nod of recognition.

"I have a plan, and Johnny's going to help us—aren't you, Johnny?" asked Irving.

The man, Dobbs, became mock-serious a moment, utilizing the advantage of being, for one time in his life, on the right side of the law—or at least, under its auspices, which to Johnny Dobbs was the same thing.

"Glad to be of service, sirs," he said.

Irving waved at Jake to be gone; the policeman went quickly.

The Chief of New York Detectives, James Irving, leaned back in his seat, which he swiveled slowly from one side to the other, already deep in thought.

"Well, close the door," he said absently, biting the end of a pencil with which he tapped his teeth, "and sit down." By obeying this first instruction, the ex-convict Johnny Dobbs began working for the New York Metropolitan Police.

§

HONESTY IS THE KEYSTONE OF LAW, declared the small plaque on William Pinkerton's desk. He looked up over this motto of the Agency and watched his excited associate enter with news. John Curtain held up the letter in his hand and give a whoop of joy that caused Pinkerton to frown.

"We've got a locate on Warren!" Curtain said. "I covered Florida down to St. Augustine before I sent a request off to Cuba."

He put the letter in front of William Pinkerton, who took it up and began to read. The peaceful wood-paneled, green-carpeted office was silent, as if it too, for that moment, were in on the discovery. The only sound was a rustling of the letter's three sheets of paper. Pinkerton's face began to set in an expression of triumph before he reached the end.

John Curtain, who could no longer withhold his knowledge

of the finale toward the bottom of the third page, blurted it out.

"It's from a Dr. Houscomb, in Havana. He has a patient by name of—Bidwell!"

"Elizabeth Bidwell," said Pinkerton quietly, still reading.

"And she's to have a baby," Curtain said quickly.

"I read it, John," said Pinkerton, looking up.

"The bill was paid by Austin," finished Curtain lamely. Pinkerton nodded and smiled—he had read that too.

He leaned back in the straight-backed leather chair, reached for a cigar and took his time to light it. John Curtain refused the offer of one and seated himself opposite his superior, breathing fast with excitement.

"Then you, John," said Pinkerton thoughtfully, "got yourself a trip to the tropics."

"Couldn't I wait for MacDonald?" said Curtain, momentarily disappointed.

"I'll see to that," said Pinkerton firmly. "We know Irving, and his reputation convinces me that we should go in, on a private boat, so I'll be taking with me state marshals, lawyers and our best men available here in New York."

Curtain nodded, acceding to Pinkerton's wishes as he saw that he would be unnecessary.

"Austin Bidwell's yours, John," said Pinkerton. "Robert will take George in Europe—of that I have no doubt."

"And you want MacDonald?" said Curtain, stating the obvious.

Determination in Pinkerton's eyes answered the question that was statement.

"The net is out," said Pinkerton, slowly drawing on his cigar; then, leaning toward his loyal and trustworthy associate, he looked him directly in the eye, as if to communicate his own strength to the man. "We will have them all now," he smiled grimly; when he spoke, it was slowly and without emotion: "one, by one, by one."

The Last Supper

To the Editor of The Times.

Sir, So much has been written, both in the British and German papers, against the English Police, that probably a little evidence upon the procedure of the German, and more especially, Bavarian forces of law and order, may not be uninteresting at the moment.

Myself and son, a sub-lieutenant, Royal Navy, made a great effort to reach the grotesque, old city of Nuremburg, on Saturday the 22nd March, arriving there about seven p.m. We were asked to put our names in the strangers' book, as usual, which we did and retired to bed. Imagine our surprise on rising Sunday morning, at receiving a visit from one of the Chief Police Officers, requesting us to "legitimize" ourselves.

I asked him his object for making this demand, he replied that a man named "Horton" was wanted by the English Police. In vain I showed him an old passport and letter addressed to me, showing my name was Hutton; he informed me that I could not leave my room, and placed two policemen at the door.

At one o'clock, I remembered an influential inhabitant of the town, who knew me, and sent for him. He, at once, went to Headquarters and gave bond for me to a large amount, and at six o'clock in the evening myself and son were released.

I have since received, thanks to the strenuous and prompt action of the British Minister at Munich, a very ample apology, in writing, for the blunder that had been committed. It is signed by the Burgomeister of the city and as the intelligence of this worthy, seems to be equalled by his simplicity, he sends me a safe pass to protect me in my further travels, in case Hutton should again be considered the same as Horton.

> I remain, Sir,
> Your obedient servant,
>
> Chas. W. C. Hutton,

Ex Sheriff, London and Middlesex.
Frankfort-on-the-Maine. 25th March, 1873.

Having dutifully read the article, upon the insistence of the two other men in the carriage compartment, George Bidwell returned the paper and murmured with a shy smile, *"Merci."*

Far from hilarious, his reaction (unlike that of the other occupants who faced him on the train he had boarded at a small station ten miles out of Dublin) was one of intense consternation. The two Irishmen, obviously drunk, despite the fact it was before midday, roared with laughter. Even recognizing the humor in Chas. W. C. Hutton's misadventure, George wondered at the astonishing efforts instituted by the Bank of England to ensure the capture of the three Americans still at large.

From Clonmel he had been taken, by the shebeen proprietor's son, to the outskirts of Dublin, where contact was made with a group that spirited this "American leader from the States" (George's money ensuring that no questions were asked) to the railway link with Belfast. At a small country station, George had boarded a train, thus avoiding the dangers of Ireland's southern city; in his pocket a ticket only to Drogheda, to allay any suspicious inquiry as to his reason for journeying to a port of embarkation; in his mind, the sound advice given him by one of the group, along with a French silk hat and matching valise, that he should, if he was able, abandon his American identity and create a Continental character, which might well confuse all who should ask his business in expectation of an articulate reply. George had assumed a meek behavior with the two drunks and appreciated every jolt and rattle of the train with a growing sense of relief, as it took him north to freedom—out of the "corked bottle" (as *The Times* now described his situation in Ireland).

It was only when the middle-aged English governess boarded and seated herself beside George that he had his first moments of panic in the guise of, as his companions insisted on calling him, "this Frenchy." The governess, asked in drunken politeness by the more persistent of the two Irishmen whether or not her education included the language of Napoleon, answered in the affirmative, then turned to George with a penetrating expression and the question *"Vous êtes français, m'sieur?"*

For the rest of the journey, George was the hastily assembled author of obscure poetry, published in his homeland of Russia. He had, he emphasized to the governess, only pretentions to the language of romance, born from a love of France's capital. All the way to Drogheda, George was assured by this woman, endorsed from her ten years' experience of Paris, that it was indeed the most elegant and sophisticated place on God's earth, and that it was unfortunate that the city was not in England itself.

The boy from Brooklyn's mongrel French and English was a marvel, gaining the admiration of both Irish drunks and the approbation of the Englishwoman. She encouraged her fellow voyager to maintain his interest in a language she had mastered as well as her own and perhaps (she ventured) his native Russian tongue would be enriched, as she herself had found even her own most lauded language embellished by the joys of fluency in another tongue!

At Drogheda, she insisted on buying the ticket George confusedly explained he would appreciate, to continue his journey in such pleasant company. George saw several detectives at the ticket office, who were questioning prospective travelers, brushed aside by this magnificent woman as she purchased, with the notes George had proffered, a small punched card that would carry him further to freedom.

Her voice resounded on the platform as she made her way back to the train, leaving the puzzled detectives only partially satisfied.

"He is a Russian, sirs," she replied imperiously (to what she thought impertinent questions), but she did politely wave at two detectives when she saw that they looked after the train as it moved off toward its final destination, Belfast, the embarkation port for Scotland and Glasgow.

§

George arrived on the docks of the northern capital of Ireland at nine P.M. The cab he had taken with the assistance of the governess, a Miss Durrant, transported him across the city with the lady, who insisted on leaving her new-found, and about-to-be-lost, charge within the gates, having explained to her "Russian" the rudiments of negotiating the final hurdle—a short walk to the point of embarkation.

George remembered *"do svydanya"* and wished it with all his heart to Miss Durrant, who caught the sentiment if not the meaning, and with the aid of George's not altogether unattractive appearance, the years seemed to slip away and dreams of her youth were once more fleetingly exhumed.

A Russian poet, with only the Romance language with which to communicate and the mutually appreciated sights of Paris, exchanged throughout the otherwise dismal hours, had created in Miss Durrant a glow that more than surprised her "family" when finally she arrived at the suburban mansion, pink-cheeked and sparkling-eyed. Having changed, she went directly to the library and took down the recently published Brontë book. She was enraptured for several minutes.

"Those burning eyes," she said to herself. . . .

The children were allowed clandestine chocolate cake and hot milk at an "unearthly hour," as it was described the following night, when they made the request once more. Thus George Bidwell—unknowingly—created in a vibrant, albeit aging, Miss Durrant a secret "Cathy," whose daily "embellishments" thereafter of her "Russian" finally lodged George, in her memory, as the facsimile of a young man running across the moors toward the tender embrace of a most willing English governess.

§

"Is it a ticket yer after havin'?" asked the harsh voice of an Irish seaman.

George whirled around to see the sloppily dressed sailor eyeing him from behind several crates, stacked at the foot of a gangway leading up to the ferryboat's main deck. It was dark but for two oil torches placed on either side of the inclined walkway to freedom. George swallowed. *"Parlez-vous français?"* he asked.

"Well, now," said the seaman, cutting a piece of tobacco, slowly, with his clasp knife. "If it's French you're speakin' of, it'll be all of Greek to me." He popped the thick chunk of black tobacco into his mouth and indicated the ship.

"Aboard you'll find the Purser, who'll be givin' you a ticket, if it's a ticket you're after havin'."

"Un billet?" asked George.

"Up there." The seaman pointed, now irritated.

"Merci," said George, and mounted the gangway.

"Mother of Mercy, I'd say as well," muttered the seaman to himself as he watched the fancy man take the incline with the delicacy George had assumed as part of his character.

The Purser's French was poor enough to allow George acceptance as one of "them Frogs," and, emphasizing his fey behavior with much use of eyebrows and limp-wristed gesturing, George bought his passage to the Scottish city port of Glasgow. Eventually he found the communal washroom, to which he was directed by the loud, coarse voice of an Irish seaman.

George took off his hat and coat in the washroom and leaned on the sink, arms locked, head bent. His nerves were strained, as it seemed that every corner he turned brought something unexpected—but he had survived.

§

The ship's loud horn hastened the already fast pace of both Robert Pinkerton and Inspector Spittle. Having come north, they had been tipped off by the Drogheda detectives that there might well be a suspicious character aboard the Belfast train. They had assembled numerous Irish police to check the last ferry that night before they "bottled up" the Port of Belfast.

The men raced up both gangways from the dock. The police boarded aft, along with Pinkerton; Spittle ran on, to the forward cargo access of the ferry, shouting up to the seaman who was already in the process of letting go the gangway. Spittle was on deck in moments, speaking urgently to the puzzled seaman, who indicated, finally, a way down to the saloon and Purser.

Pinkerton was already there when Spittle burst in breathless. The ship was only half full, and few of the male passengers remotely fitted the description of their quarry. The Second Officer, who felt his authority threatened, refused to grant these intruders more than five minutes before sailing to conduct the search they were demanding, unless they had a warrant; they did not. Pinkerton issued fast instructions, and the ship was suddenly filled with running feet and opened, then slammed doors, with no regard whatsoever for the occupants of cabins, bunks or public rooms.

George knew quite well what was happening outside the washroom. His pocket watch, now on a shelf below the mirror, told him, together with a long second blast from the ship's horn, that the ferry was only four minutes from sailing. He sighed deeply, anxious beyond description, as he heard outside the staccato banging of doors, shouts from policemen and the heavy treat of Irish law approaching inexorably down the corridor from which he had entered the washroom.

George scooped water onto his face. Then, as a third and final blast from the ship's horn sounded out loud and long, the door behind him crashed open.

A man stood in the doorway. George raised his face until he could see the policeman in the mirror. Detective Sergeant Spittle saw the silk hat, pretty valise and frock coat of a man at the wash basin, poised in "ablution," as he described it in his official report. "The man turned," the report went on, and said (in a rather light voice, for one whose appearance, stripped down to shirt sleeves as he was, gave a quite solid impression), *"Oui, Monsieur? Vous voulez quelque chose?"* (Spittle's stumbling attempt at quoting, from memory, a language he knew nothing of was finally translated by a better-informed R. A. Pinkerton.) Spittle paused as the apparent

"Frenchy" brushed back hair from his eyes with a wrist and smiled into the mirror, in, as Spittle reported it, "a most telling way."

The shout from Pinkerton outside, beyond the corridor in the saloon, perhaps saved George. Despite the "performance," his nerves were at breaking point, and even vague questions from the intruder would, in all probability, have broken the charade and created a violent confrontation, then and there.

Spittle's head turned as he heard his name. With only a single backward glance, containing the best sneer George was possibly ever given, the detective sergeant was gone. The door slammed shut. George had to hold on tight to the washbowl, as his legs had gone also. He spat thickly into the basin. The footsteps receded; the ship's engines started up. The ferry was about to depart.

Once the police had reassembled on the docks, lines were released fore and aft and the night packet boat to Scotland was under way. George looked at his watch on the shelf, caught a glimpse of his white face in the mirror and, feeling the strong vibration of the ship beneath his feet, allowed all the tension to flow from his body in the heartfelt retch, the residue of which fell into the half-filled basin. As he had eaten little in the past twenty-four hours, it was mostly pain and effort. Tears of strain clouded his vision before he opened wide his eyes and saw floating on the brackish water a last taste of Ireland. What had issued from his mouth and continued to drip into the bowl could only be described as phlegm, or bile—or perhaps more properly, spittle.

§

The trails and clues that had led Pinkerton and the English inspector to believe George Bidwell would make an attempt to leave Ireland from Belfast finally petered out on the city docks whilst they watched lights from the packet boat they had searched, as she plied out to sea, disappear slowly into the night.

Both men were dejected.

Spittle was away from his wife and, consequently, missing the comforts and considerations of a marriage partner; the English detective was unhappy.

Pinkerton, a dedicated man of law, was disappointed with the outcome of what he had felt would be the "denouement."

That night Spittle broke his vows and joined Pinkerton in several stiff brandies. During the evening, over dinner and whilst they discussed the case, an admiration arose for George which prompted rueful remarks from both men. *When*—they used the word with confidence—*when* George arrived he would certainly be in for a surprise.

The two detectives agreed that they had moved so fast that almost certainly they were ahead of their quarry. They went to separate hotels, single beds, nightmares of chasing elusive game, and with them they took the decision, made over a last brandy—they would wait.

§

Two days later, in the shipping office at the docks, where each morning and evening both Spittle and Pinkerton were to be found, posters arrived. The photogravure from Ellen, corroborated by her description, bore a very passable likeness of George Bidwell. Instructions had been given that the posters must be distributed to all public buildings in the immediate area.

A refurbishing of the shipping office, planned months before, had created mild chaos; now drop cloths covered what valuable or delicate objects the clerks had around them, and a smell of white enamel paint was strong to the nostrils.

"Thank you for your cooperation," Pinkerton said, directly before leaving for lunch. "These posters will make our task easier I am sure." The shipping clerk nodded in agreement.

Spittle took one of the posters from the pile and decided to begin with the wall opposite, on a portion that had been painted the previous day.

"I would like them," Pinkerton continued, "to be put in all places to which the public has access, as Bidwell may well try to . . ." Pinkerton's voice droned on as Spittle pressed pins into both top corners of the poster and came face to face with a likeness of the man he had sought hour after hour, day in, day out, for, what was it now? . . . He had begun to think exactly how long he had been chasing George, in company with Pinkerton, when he caught the look in George's eyes, an expression that was strong, penetrating; exuding danger and intelligence. . . . Somewhere in Spittle's mind the tuning fork that set the tone for the sound of anguish he was to make sounded out loud and clear.

His hand, as if prompted by another mind, reached out to the discarded brush, settling in a pot of paint left by the decorator, already at lunch. He put a temporary pin into the center of the bottom edge of the poster to hold it down, then slowly used the white enamel paint to extend the bright background of the photogravure resembling George Bidwell across the image's upper lip and, with two further strokes, up to the hairline in front of each of the American's ears, obliterating both moustache and sideburns.

When Spittle opened his mouth, Pinkerton was already looking at him, as was the clerk, who had furtively indicated to the detective from the United States that his English counterpart was behaving in an abnormal manner.

"Mr. Pinkerton . . ." began Spittle hoarsely. He turned full around, seeing Pinkerton with glazed eyes, his head still only inches from the confident portrait of George Bidwell. "The Frenchman, sir . . ." Spittle trailed off.

The noise that Pinkerton made was matched a moment later by Spittle, but both, as the clerk later attested, seemed "very put out," and Mr. Pinkerton's fist, he would have sworn, had cracked the edge of the office desk. Pinkerton actually said something quite different, but history records the words, spoken at a volume remembered to have been penetrating, as "Damn him!"

§

Toward the end of the first week of March, Austin Bidwell, without Elizabeth—who preferred the tranquillity of Havana's civilization—departed by one of Cuba's only railways to San Felipe, from which he and his friends Don

Andrez and Don Alvarez, with a wealthy Savannah-born
American named Gray, took horses on to the southern
seaport town of Cajío.

It became obvious to Austin, judging from the reactions of
the town's inhabitants, that his self-effacing, humorous and
loyal friend Don Andrez was treated by all who came under
his auspices as a person of great distinction.

The eastern part of Cuba—Santiago and Puerto Príncipe,
together with Pinar del Rio, to the extreme west—was held by
rebels who were determined to fight for *"Cuba Libre"*—to
create a national state from Spanish oppression. As Austin
and his party passed through the port of La Playa de
Batabanó, evidence of the insurgents' abilities was dis-
gustingly apparent. It was the other aspect of colonial occupation. Houses had been burned and bodies left to rot; a
massacre had been committed in the name of freedom, and it
had taken a week for the Spanish authorities to hunt down the
terrifying band of rebels who had marched inland, burning
houses, killing the landowners and calling upon slaves to join
their cause.

At San Marcos, Spanish soldiers had shown no quarter to
the enlarged group they eventually surrounded. The desperate
fight ended in a government victory and butchery, for which
the legions of Spain, in any century, have always been in-
famous. The ashes of fires kindled to consume the bodies of
the slain and mutilated gave pause to Austin and the entire
party, and each reflected upon private thoughts thus
stimulated. For Austin, the power and ruthlessness of
authority had never been more clearly illustrated. His shiver
caused Don Andrez to laugh at his dear American friend's
concern and reassure him that he would always be protected
by the elite amongst Cuba's aristocracy, of whom he—
Austin—was now a warmly accepted member.

The twinkle in Don Andrez' eyes stirred Austin's instincts
and he smiled his appreciation with a steady look, which Don
Andrez held without flinching.

"It is terrible" said Austin.

"It is history, my friend," replied Don Andrez, "which
cannot be concealed." His amusement had nothing what-

soever to do with the scene before them. Austin became uncomfortable.

"There are some of us who would prefer that the past retain its mysteries," he said slowly.

Don Andrez, leaning from his horse, clapped Austin about the shoulders and said conspiratorially, "Good feelings between men are bigger than their bad histories, and all of us, my friend, have something"—he paused, indicating the ashes with a gesture, his eyes unwaveringly on Austin—"something we might wish as easily buried."

To Austin, as the private moment held between them, it seemed that Don Andrez read his mind and saw everything. His eyes fell, and Don Andrez roared with laughter, warm and truly reassuring.

"Come, my American friend," he said—then, softly, "with the English suits."

He turned to the maudlin group surrounding the pyres and pressed his horse into a canter, making off toward the dense tree line ahead.

"You are women," he bellowed, laughing over his shoulder. The party's hearty shouts of rebuttal accompanied them as they did Don Andrez, into the silent tropical forest.

It took the rest of the day before they emerged from the thick vegetation into a balmy Caribbean sunset.

The party came out onto a white sand beach. Their horses pawed, nostrils flared against the sea breeze of evening. Palm trees spread far along the shore; coral reefs lay beyond dashing foam that edged blue water.

In the distance, small islets were topped by more palms which lazily swayed in the moving air; glowing colors on the horizon were a background to magenta-and-gold clouds which, with Promethean skill, became substance and form to the imaginings of all the party, who, now hushed—still as Medusa's victims—sought to catch last rays of warmth before the sun finally dipped beneath an ocean as azure as was, high above these men, the sky's zenith.

Suddenly, as in the tropics it will, the sun was gone and twilight shrouded them all. Don Andrez took out his pocket watch, declared the hour and indicated with a laugh to the still

mesmerized men that in twenty minutes they would be at the
great mansion whose oil lamps could now be seen farther up
the coast. There they would rest.

The party moved off along the darkening beach, their talk
and laughter quickly lost across a great expanse of ocean to
their left and into the dark tropical forest on their right.
Horses' hoofprints, dogs' paws and slaves' bare feet in the
sand marked the trail until at first purple shadows, then sea
foam, brought higher onto the shore with a night wind,
searched for, found, obscured, then obliterated the only
evidence that man had passed by.

§

On the north shore of Cuba, in the harbor of Havana, a
ship that had just beaten the sunset gun was already unloading
cargo and with it New York papers, containing newly cabled
headlines from Great Britain as a result of the discovery in
London that Frederick Albert Warren was the name of a man
wanted by the Bank of England throughout the world.

§

Several days later, on an open-decked ship, the group from
Havana, with twenty black slaves, four turtles, hunting dogs,
fighting cocks and a large snake that had the run of the vessel,
set out into the Gulf of Matamano, on a sea that was so clear,
over a white sand bottom that was so brilliant, it appeared to
Austin Bidwell that they were flying. This impression was further confirmed by the hot sun and numerous tots of port
which, despite the midmorning hour, were served to all from
casks broached by colored slaves.

Those who were not required to work the passage of the
ship lay on deck and peered down at the teeming marine life
with a wonder akin to that of childhood. A fine sea breeze
filled sails set by an excellent captain, and rushed the vessel
through the water at a great rate. The seventy miles to the pier
of San José was interrupted only once (flocks of sea birds had
risen excitedly on their arrival), when the ship lay to for an

hour at the uninhabited islet of Cayos de Tana, where turtle eggs were sought and found.

In the twilight of a glorious day, Don Andrez' ship ran slowly alongside the small town's jetty, and the group disembarked on the Isle of Pines, to a wonderful welcome; shouts, cheers, songs and gunshots went up into the soft evening air from almost one hundred gaudily clad slaves.

Their uninhibited joy was perhaps aided by rum, liberally distributed—a gift of the caretakers who ran Don Andrez' local plantations; also fact was that the only day "free" for slaves was Sunday. Nonetheless—as Austin observed without cynicism—there was as much natural as stimulated excitement amongst the assembly in celebration that their master, the island's Caesar, had returned with his friends.

§

The two weeks Austin remained on that island were perhaps the best of his life; yet still, a small part of his mind prompted unwanted memories of Europe, England; more exactly, the Bank in Threadneedle Street and specifically, created images of Colonel Francis, Fenwick, George, Mac and Edwin Noyes. Only these thoughts, which came especially during long morning swims within the safety of enclosing reefs and occasionally to disturb a night's sleep, sullied an otherwise idyllic situation: shark fishing far out on the ocean by day; tipping turtles on the moonlit sand in the evening; the never-ending spectacular battles between fighting cocks at the village pits; hunting game in the jungle; by night carousing over exquisite dinners, prepared and served in the huge Spanish-style dining room, as if for ambassadors in a palace.

Cigars, brandy and eventual sleep came often, for all the group engaged in animated, then philosophic, conversation, lying in woven-grass hammocks swinging gently beneath the roof of a long patio that fronted onto the southern ocean. Watching phosphorescent waves rippling and breaking on the beach under the light of a full moon, listening to distant childlike songs of the colored slaves (allowed their freedom of the estate, for which their loyalty and love were now obvious),

Austin felt almost totally at ease. Almost.

As his final night on the Isle of Pines passed through the late evening into the early morning of the following day, stories from dinner mixed in Austin's mind with anxieties for the morrow; he had decided to sail back to Cajío, to meet, at a rendezvous, his servant from Havana, whom he had instructed before leaving to carry with him pistols and a rifle, as an excuse to bring all the American papers of the past weeks.

The world outside the Isle of Pines would have news for Austin, he felt sure, and he wanted to know just how much of a furor he had caused, and to what extent he was involved, albeit with an alias. He had plans to construct, and they all depended on news. Before his eyes closed on a last, dream-filled sleep, he remembered Cayos de Tana and the turtle eggs, unearthed from the sand, found, heaven knew how, by the colored boys; then images of the poor turtles staked out in a shallow pond near the island house came into his mind, their soulful eyes staring up at his—prisoners, to be devoured at will. As it was custom, Austin was unable to complain, but he had been sickened by the helplessness of these magnificent creatures from another age, out of a tropic sea.

"Man's homage to his own stomach," he had said after dinner, "will destroy us all, eventually." His remark prompted a humorous but cautionary story from Don Andrez' manager, Señor Mondago. As Austin looked across at the tropical forest fringing the long curve of bay, Mondago's story took on a significance to him. He looked above the delicately swaying palm trees and stared into darkness beyond, where hills and valleys concealed the raw, harsh existence of thick jungle.

"A missionary," Señor Mondago had related to his expectant audience, "who arrived on an island much like this in the South Seas inquired of the 'boss cannibal gentleman' where his predecessor might be sojourning. He was promptly informed," continued Mondago, with mock seriousness, "that he had 'gone into the interior.'" The group laughed loud and long, Austin included, then; but later, thinking of a strange shore, seeing the dark forest, he felt a chill in his bones and blood, despite the warmth of friends, their hospitality and the luxuries that accompanied civilization.

Austin had been suddenly flooded with disturbing premonitions. For a moment humor was replaced, and he knew the fear of that missionary in the story. The apprehension that stirred in his mind was never more strong and, as events proved, never more justified.

These thoughts had been dispelled by Don Andrez, who had then mentioned that although it was not the season, the local inhabitants predicted a hurricane. About such things, he'd said, he was skeptical, but the old man concerned had been brought to him and was adamant, in which case, he had decided, with his whole plantation at stake *and*, he continued with laughter, his friends' well-being to watch over, it was a warning that "might well brook some consideration."

All at the table had observed Don Andrez' seriousness a moment; all agreed he was right. They had then risen from their dinner and with much humor repaired to the long patio.

§

A resolute, trustworthy and devoted servant is rare; Austin was lucky. As his ship nosed toward the little bay of Cajío, he could see the man he had instructed in Havana waiting for him, then, catching sight of his master, wave enthusiastically. It was almost sunset when Austin set foot again on the mainland of Cuba.

A letter from Elizabeth told him that all was well at home and became, toward the end, a loving plea that Austin return as soon as he was able. His feelings toward his lady in Havana were as hers, and suddenly he longed to be with her. The New York papers confirmed to Austin the direction in which he must travel.

At Don Andrez' hacienda near the beach, by the light from an oil lamp, in the twilight of a tropical island, Austin Bidwell began to read with amazement of the storm brewing in Europe over the Great Bank of England Fraud, of Edwin Noyes's untimely arrest and his incarceration and of the world-wide hunt for the mysterious F. A. Warren.

Then, worst of all, the paper stated, in two editions, that the Pinkertons, who were working on the case in "exclusivity," had discovered the true name to this obviously "false alias," Warren. No details would be released at this date, it went on, as it was felt the culprit might well be "utilizing" his real name, and therefore be unknowing of the imminent arrest "now expected." "Our reporter has been reliably informed, by an English detective, working on the more trivial details of the case, that the first two letters of the alphabet might well be identical to those of the villain's initials."

Mr. "A.B." put down this latest edition and momentarily felt the unfamiliar sensation of total panic, as if the whole world knew the mystery and were looking at him alone. Then Austin's mind began to dissect the information, coldly. Now he knew plans must be made—and quickly.

He was fortunate to be alone, because he was unable to speak for several hours. He lay on his bed, as the twilight turned to darkness outside, watching insects endlessly circling the oil lamp on the bedside table. The wind in the palms of this remote place slowly picked up, until rustling in the vegetation had become a steady noise, as if it were the mur-murings of a great crowd beyond huge doors that Austin was steadily approaching at the end of a long corridor.

Although Austin trusted Edwin completely and believed, as some of the papers wrote, that he would eventually be released, he felt the time had come to leave Cuba and create a new identity. The night passed in an anguish of dissolving nightmares. The enormity of what he had done was now inescapable. As wind in the darkness outside plucked at trees and roared at buildings, Austin, sleeping fitfully, walked always nearer to the huge doors beyond which lay all his fears. The unseen crowds became louder and raucous. Although in-decipherable, their conversations were harsh and aggressive. At the moment he was about to enter—even as he seized the doorknob in the shape of a lion rampant with blood dripping from bared teeth—he awoke. The wind was only a whisper, and dawn had broken.

Without the presence of Don Andrez to inspire action in naturally lethargic natives, Austin's return to Havana became a slow, frustrating journey. It took three days before he arrived at his villa outside the city.

Elizabeth looked into Austin's eyes after their long kiss of greeting, and eventually she said, slowly and softly, "You should have told me before." Austin was unable to speak; if Elizabeth somehow knew, where could he begin?

"We are to leave?" Elizabeth went on. "Where?"

"To Mexico," said Austin finally. "I must change my name; only then will I be free and beyond . . ." He was about to say "justice" but stopped himself, knowing that Elizabeth, despite her feelings for him, would not let the issue pass uncontested. ". . . the reach of English law," he finished.

"When?" Elizabeth asked simply.

"Perhaps a week," said Austin; "not more."

"But our friends . . ." Elizabeth began. "I have arranged a dinner party here for Thursday . . ." She stopped.

Austin's gaze was kind but firm.

"If the steamer leaves as usual, we sail to Vera Cruz on the fourth."

"But that is the following day!" exclaimed Elizabeth.

"Then it will be a farewell dinner," answered Austin harshly. "Spare a thought, if you can, for Mac and George—for them it may already be too late."

Elizabeth dropped her eyes before his formidable gaze.

"I will explain everything—later," said Austin. "You have time enough to pack."

Elizabeth paused and saw the worry and strain in her man's face; she smiled warmly and said softly, "We . . ."

Austin kissed her with a passion he had thought long lost.

§

On the night of April 1, a Tuesday, the French ship *Thuringia* was something less than two hundred miles from New York Harbor, her dining room full, one table, reserved for Mr. George MacDonald, now occupied by the gentleman and two guests.

Mac had made several acquaintances on his voyage, but none (apart from the Captain perhaps, whose wit and anti-British sentiments appealed greatly to Mac's intellect) were more agreeable company than his two dinner companions. Four empty wine bottles on the table had created an ambiance Mac found most convivial. It certainly enlivened his guests, both ladies, who giggled as Mac waved at the Captain, across the room.

He returned Mac's salutation and indicated that he would join his passenger shortly.

"French!" Mac exclaimed, "and not used to wine?" He leaned toward one of the ladies with a mischievous grin. "An impossibility, I would have said." He reached out for the chilled bottle of champagne in the bucket beside him. The ladies appeared to like the dessert course, a delicious *gâteau*, baked by a chef who must have also been a master pastry cook.

"Too cloistered a life you must have led," said Mac as he poured champagne for the ladies, pink-cheeked and happy as they had not been for some time.

"A last supper aboard the good ship . . ." Mac forgot the name.

"Thuringia," said the Captain, who now stood at the table.

Mac indicated to the Captain a vacant fourth chair.

"I came to inform you that owing to the head winds we have encountered, should they continue into the morning, there remains somewhat less than twenty-four hours before our arrival in the Americas." He bowed to the ladies, who nodded bashfully.

"Enchanté," said the handsome French officer, with a charming smile. Mac had poured a glass for the master of the *Thuringia* and offered it to him.

"To these lovely ladies, sir," Mac said, referring to his companions, dressed much alike, as if sisters of the blood, their dark apparel very becoming in the candlelight of the dining room. "To these lovely ladies, sir," repeated Mac, "who—whom—" he corrected himself, feeling again the pang of sorrow that memories of May evoked. Tears appeared in his eyes, thereby instantly evoking compassion from his innocent guests, ". . . whom," he repeated, "I've convinced of the pleasures o' life and . . ." He paused, touching his nose confidentially, articulate, but definitely drunk. ". . . who have convinced *me*," he emphasized, "o' the damnation o' the hereafter."

He held his glass high and touched it to the three others. The Captain smiled at the two nuns, Sisters of Charity, bound eventually for New Orleans and, perhaps, the French Captain observed, an incarceration not much different from that for which this gentleman was destined. That, at least, they shared; so the Captain drank his champagne, wishing all three happiness in the freedom they enjoyed at present but of which most certainly, within hours, they would be deprived.

"You know, Captain . . ." came a whisper in the officer's ear. He bent to catch the hushed words, given in confidence. ". . . before I—pop off," Mac went on, "there is one thing I'd always promised myself I'd do." The Captain could only raise his eyebrow to discourage the thought, spoken with a candor he envied—the thought had, he must admit, not been a stranger to his own wishes at one time in his young life. He looked at the two nuns, who were most attractive physically, and in view of their inebriated state, what Mr. MacDonald was suggesting, he could see, was not inconceivable.

He coughed, censoring further images, stood up and took his leave, bowing only to the single lady beaming toward him; the other was too concerned in adjusting her habit to relieve a hot flush.

Mac had already begun reaching out a hand across the table, earnestly addressing the woman before him who now so reminded him of May.

"I am a worthless fellow—squandering my life in the service of greed and pleasure—instead of—higher things." He smiled into the young nun's eyes, and as she quite obviously responded, the Captain could bear to watch no longer. He knew that the two nuns were simple, unsophisticated, and under such circumstances as travel, when they were thrown into the world, religious rule was allowed suspension. For the duration of the journey, they were able to live—so far as food and drink were concerned—as did those with whom they associated. But the ways of the world only begin in a public dining room; aboard ship, as the most delicate heart knew, anything was possible.

The Captain strode purposefully across the room, nodding right and left to those diners still lingering. After all, he thought (before the image of a hot toddy, warm bridge and blast of cool night sea air came to him), in all probability (and as a result, one had to forgive the young American's intentions) this would be—in civilized surroundings, at least—Mr. MacDonald's last supper for some time to come.

What Mac did that night, history has not revealed, but beneath his large brass bed, which was secured firmly to the cabin deck, a middle-aged Irish cleaner, some hours after *Thuringia* had docked, found what might, she thought, in the light of the gentleman's being "wanted an' all," have been a valuable piece of evidence. A clue of some sort, at least: a bodice garment that was used to strap down large breasts— with a French marking! The Irish cleaner finally decided to say nothing to the authorities. She realized what Mac had discovered, and the original owner knew well enough: that the "find" was too useful.

§

All day on Wednesday, April 2, in New York it had been clear sky and bright sunlight but cold, with a biting north-easter blowing hard. For anyone—venturing out for pleasure rather than necessity—who was well wrapped with thick coat, boots, scarf and firmly placed hat, the freshness of late after-noon (when the wind abated somewhat) could certainly have been described as healthy.

At sea, some miles out from her destination, soon after five o'clock with the day fast fading, the sun low in the west, *Thuringia* was emerging from squalls that had marred her journey for several days, and now the duty watch on the bridge strained to be first to catch sight of New York's un-mistakable skyline. The long blasts from both foghorns rever-berated in the ship, creating excitement, anticipation and, for some, apprehension.

Thuringia had been passing the long shore of New Jersey for several hours. On the horizon a steamer from the South, perhaps Carolina or Florida, was making smoke, also in her final approach as was *Thuringia*, engines racing as if eager to be inshore and at rest. A fishing fleet was sailing eastward, where twenty or thirty miles out to sea the crews would lay nets for the night's catch, to be inward bound again, come morning, for the markets of a great city.

Some small but powerful tugs idled low in the water,

breathing out clouds of steam. One by one they hooted briskly at *Thuringia*, obviously in need of no assistance as she cut through the smooth swell, her wake churning out foam that splashed the gunwales of the compact little ships. Already showing, despite the early hour, the twin lights from the heights of Neversink twinkled seaward. With these astern, at a fair rate of knots, in only a matter of minutes the white spit of Sandy Hook came abreast, and here the *Thuringia* cut to half ahead as a fast steam pinnace, bobbing up and down in the sea swell, ran in alongside to deposit the agile pilot, who leaped onto the hanging ladder and pulled himself, hand over hand, to the deck.

Overhead, sea gulls wheeled, mournfully demanding (in the first American cries some of the passengers had heard) sustenance against the bitter wind in which they swirled, above a sea that was hardly more inviting. The clear sky belied sleet and the last snow (remaining from some lost winter clouds) that had fallen in the city on previous days. As the great harbor entrance appeared, all the passengers who had decided to brave the cold of the deck saw white patches against the dark land mass.

The Narrows' channel was negotiated with the confidence of an experienced pilot, and the *Thuringia*'s master again blasted on the horn—a noise echoing across the expanse of water to the small homesteads either side. Staten Island could be seen clearly; the Heights of Brooklyn and a distant view of the Hudson River's densely populated outskirts spread now in all directions.

Hats clasped against the wind; excited smiles; arms extended, fingers pointed at the broad bay and its numerous tributaries to the north and east; then the tall spires and lofty warehouses of the city itself. To all points of the compass were the close-packed hulls, entangled masts and elegant smokestacks of shipping from all over the world.

Bells rang throughout the ship. In the wheelhouse the clang, clang of slow ahead sounded out, and *Thuringia* began to lose speed. More blasts on the horn indicated to all, ashore or aboard, that destination was made and with thanks to God's mercy, a ship had arrived in a port many called home.

Mac lay on the bed in his cabin, propped against a pillow,

looking out the porthole, nervously exhaling smoke from a cheroot. The *Thuringia* went from half to slow ahead; he felt the change of speed, and as the horn's blast sounded out across the cold water, Mac shivered in anticipation of just about anything—and none of it good.

§

Johnny Dobbs squinted into the distance from the pier at the foot of Robinson Street, crowded with drays and drivers. The slush and mud was well trodden by thousands of ill-clad local inhabitants, all having discovered that it was here that the *Thuringia* would finally dock.

The New York papers had made a field day of the single passenger whom the gathering crowd had come to see. For many, this American was already a hero (those in poverty seeming always to accept the loss of others' capital without sympathy). Many were expecting to leave quite hoarse with cheering, and shouts of anticipation began as the *Thuringia* came into sight.

Johnny Dobbs pushed his way along the quay until he was free of the packed masses and began walking quickly along to the small jetty with steps leading down to a sleek steam pinnace thirty feet long, mahogany and brass gleaming in the shafts of sunlight that fell on the wharfside through gaps in the tall buildings.

A carriage was waiting at the head of the steps beside two bollards; seated within, Irving, Stanley and White said nothing, but Johnny Dobbs grinned and wished them a good afternoon—no more. Then, tipping his hat, he stepped gingerly down into the steam pinnace and made preparations to cast off.

The carriage jerked away and, turning in a slow arc along the north side of the wharf, clattered away over the cobbles, threading between derricks and cranes in the direction opposite to the waiting crowd. The carriage was making for the dockside where, in the distance, a large steam tug, paid for by the detectives, was straining at her hawsers. The rendezvous, her Captain had been told, was with the approaching steamer from France—*Thuringia*.

§

At this season in Cuba, such intense humidity in early evening was unusual, as all twenty of Austin's guests knew quite well. What little movement of air there was only added heat to the atmosphere, whose heaviness was more akin to that of October storms. Normally April had a delicious balminess, warmth, relieved by cool sea breezes.

Austin's staff had become lax in his absence, and what Elizabeth had planned as an early dinner was fast becoming a supper party, the several hours' delay compensated for by alcohol. Drinks were served constantly by two servants, dressed in livery, chivvied along by Austin, whose nerves could be calmed only by constant champagne. Although *he* was not, by eight in the evening (late when the usual hour for dinner was between five and seven thirty) most of the assembled guests were not merely hot and garrulous, but drunk.

Austin, alone in the large dining room, walked down first one side of the long table, then the other, checking the seating arrangements and name cards. On the Gulf side, six huge French windows were opened onto the wide balcony that ran the length of the villa. Their diaphanous lace curtains billowed slightly as the breeze strengthened to a light wind.

Austin stood for a moment at the head of the table, where he would sit, and surveyed the tableau before him, lacking only his guests—all, as Elizabeth said, "brand-new best friends." He smiled and, for the first time in days, relaxed completely. Ahead lay a new life, to create as they wished. The one word—Mexico—was now, in his mind, full of the promise he had anticipated of Cuba; if Elizabeth and he could live even half as well elsewhere, he knew, they would remain happy.

Austin stepped away from his tall chair, high-backed and superbly carved; then, taking a Havana cigar from the inlaid silver box atop a Spanish oak sideboard which stood against the wall between two large doors, he walked the length of the other side of his lavishly laid dining table, made of dark polished rosewood, but covered this evening with an intricate lace cloth, almost twelve yards long and four wide, that fell in exquisite folds nearly touching the floor.

Austin moved toward the adjacent French windows of the
side wall of the villa, high over the sloping garden that fell
away below. He lit his cigar and stepped through the open
doors onto the small curved balcony. This side it was not
joined to the long balcony that ran the length of the hacienda
on the Gulf side. Looking over the darkening vegetation and,
beyond, to the western lights of the city, he breathed deeply.
By God, he thought, I'll miss this place.

Austin beckoned to the four Cuban musicians waiting in the
garden below to come up, then stepped back into the large
room. He would put them, as Elizabeth had suggested, here,
he thought, looking immediately about him. In front of these
windows at the end of the table, where I can catch their eye if
they become too loud, he mused. Austin put the cigar firmly
between his teeth and used both hands to close the windows
and lock them tight. It will throw the music into the room, he
decided as he turned the key; besides, the breeze is becoming a
wind, he went on, knowing that although the northern Gulf
side was protected, a south wind would blow right into the
room from the west wall. He checked the French windows
once more to satisfy himself that they were secure, then went
out of the room by one of the large carved oak doors and
closed it quietly. He had thereby made one mistake that
evening which would afford few others.

§

In downtown Havana, John Curtain looked at his pocket
watch and replaced it in his waistcoat. He was a civilized man,
and the last thing he wanted to do was ruin a dinner party. He
rose from the bar in the small hotel run by an American lady
and went into the foyer, where his four associates stood up
immediately.

A rare combination, John Curtain; he was both likable and
easygoing, yet commanded respect with a glance: "A good
man to have working for you," Pinkerton the elder had many
times told his sons.

The group—Curtain and four New York Pinkerton employees—began walking the short distance from their hotel to
a building which housed both the police and the local militia.

It had become familiar to all of them these past twenty-four hours, and the "speedy" issue of a warrant for arrest had been a grueling business.

The five men entered the building at ten minutes after eight o'clock, exactly as Austin Bidwell, in his villa above the city of Havana, stood proudly at the head of his table. His admiring guests, cooler now on the upper floor of the hacienda, saw the obvious effort in the magnificent display. They murmured approval.

Austin indicated to the Cuban quartet that they could begin, snapped his fingers at the six servants in attendance and with a smile to the assemblage, poised now, all having found their allotted places, said simply, "Please—sit."

G·A·M·E

EDINBURGH was built on seven hills near the sea. From the esplanade beneath the famous Castle, perched on its dominating rock, to the palace of Holyrood House, past St. Giles Cathedral, John Knox House, Cannongate tollbooth and the Abbey Church ruins, the direction is straight; this is known as the Royal Mile. Above this rise the romantic buildings of the old town. Below, beyond what was once a loch, drained to create Princes Street Garden, lay (spreading north) the neo-Georgian "planned town."

Here George Bidwell had decided to lie low. Having eluded his hunters, and whilst, he believed, they backtracked in Ireland to discover a clue overlooked or discounted, George began to relax; slowly he regained his confidence and nerve, which had been tried to breaking.

On his arrival in Scotland, the dismal city of Glasgow (shrouded in rain) had made a poor impression. George had taken a train to Edinburgh, stayed one night in a temperance hotel, maintaining his French identity; the following day he had taken a room in a lodginghouse for medical students, at 22 Cumberland Street. George had declared to his landlady,

Mrs. Laverock, that he was not in the best of health and would like to be disturbed as little as possible.

Mr. "Coutant," although foreign, appeared to be an agreeable gentleman, and Mrs. Laverock assured the "Monsieur" that she would do her utmost to see him right. Their brief conversation was on April 2, two days after George had departed Belfast.

That afternoon, George walked to the intersection of Cumberland and Dundas streets, turned south and continued almost to Northumberland Street, crossing Great King Street, until he arrived at the news agent's, where he bought the London and Edinburgh papers from an old man with half glasses on his nose, little hair on his head, hardly any light in his shop, but with a canny look in his eyes.

His sycophantic smile and almost unintelligible language decided George on the least possible conversation between them. He had come for the papers, nothing more, and if he wished to repeat this each day he remained in Edinburgh (the shop being, Mrs. Laverock had assured him, the "only place for a mile or more"), George would start as he intended to go on.

He paid the man, grunted a farewell and left the dark little place, stepping out into sunlight breaking through heavy clouds that lowered over the city. George had spent an entire day scrutinizing a street map of Edinburgh, so he decided to test his knowledge and walk the long way back to his lodgings, along Northumberland into Howe Street, passing the Royal Circus entrance into Vincent Street and thence Cumberland, with a right turn.

George glanced at the front page of the day-old London paper, which revealed "the death of the White Star Liner *Atlantic*." Astonished, he became impatient to read more; he quickened his pace and was back at Mrs. Laverock's inside ten minutes. His narrow escape from the shipping disaster added amazement to the tone of a letter he began to write to Austin, recounting his adventures in Ireland. George smiled as he wrote his signature, then addressed it to Austin Bidwell in Havana. He sealed the envelope and stood up—about to make his way to the post office when he was shaken by his own stupidity. He sat down heavily. He crossed out *Bidwell* and had actually begun to write *Warren* when he threw down his pen on the small table. What was he thinking of? In buying a stamp and mailing the letter, he would have provided the vital information for the capture of both himself and his brother. Dumbfounded and aware now, more than ever, of his total isolation, he sprawled onto his bed. Physically he was exhausted, mentally in turmoil. Only at dusk did he fall into a troubled sleep.

§

Last rays of sunlight danced behind the tall buildings of New York City, then were there no longer, leaving only ominous silhouettes against a pale and lifeless sky—sunset colors of the day's end drained away as if blood from a severed artery.

Mac, on deck of the French liner *Thuringia*, could not share the exuberance of all those around him, clad in furs and heavy topcoats, leaning on the rails, hand luggage beside them, watching buoys below in the dark waters pass by slowly as the ship negotiated her way nearer to the Robinson Street pier. Finding himself at the davit where, far out to sea, he and the Captain had shared a moment of peace and the fateful message in Morse, Mac looked up.

The Frenchman was again out of the wheelhouse, standing on the flying bridge, binoculars about his neck. A seaman came out of the wheelhouse, buttoned his short winter coat tight about him, then pulled across the iron gate at the top of the short flight of steps to deny access during the delicate docking procedure.

The Captain turned around and saw Mac. The seaman went quickly back into the wheelhouse. For a moment Mac and the Captain both observed the iron bars that now separated them. The Captain saluted Mac lazily, as if in distant farewell to a friend. Mac responded with a smile and, with the tips of his fingers, touched the brim of his Homburg.

§

United States marshals, lawyers, armed State Police and

William Pinkerton with several private detectives from his New York Agency crowded forward on the cold foredeck of the lumbering police boat that, belching black smoke into the darkening sky, was churning toward *Thuringia*, still some mile and a half distant. The faces of these men were impassive, but beneath the tobacco-brown trilby (for the perceptive to discern) there could be made out, in Pinkerton's eyes, a strong glint of triumph.

Had Pinkerton not insisted on so many men he could have used a fast launch, but they were necessary for an immediate and thorough search of the ship, and should George Mac-Donald make a break, they ensured that he'd have no chance. Pinkerton felt he had covered every angle; his quarry was trapped aboard a ship whose starboard side he had in sight. Impatiently he cursed the speed of his large but slow vessel. Bellowing against the sound of throbbing engines, he demanded the estimated time of rendezvous.

The police boat's master pulled three fast hoots on the steam whistle, gauged the time of crossing the *Thuringia*'s bow at inside ten minutes and shouted back his reply.

Approaching fast from the port side of the French liner, Johnny Dobbs opened up his steam pinnace beyond half ahead to run along parallel to Irving's tug. He saw the detective waving. Both vessels were approaching *Thuringia* on the blind side to the crowd, the docks and, more important, Pinkerton's official police boat. Irving had chosen well; his craft was capable of almost twice the speed of the police boat.

Irving's tug pulled away from Dobbs's sleek mahogany-and-brass pinnace. New York's Chief of Detectives James Irving waved a final signal; Dobbs understood and flashed his lamp back to the tug before stepping up the throttle once more so that his bow lifted several degrees. What light remained was fast fading. Johnny Dobbs swore and peered ahead trying to make out figures aboard *Thuringia*; all he could see was her shipboard illuminations. He swore again as he hit the swell of the fast tugboat's wash.

"This ain't gonna be easy," he muttered to himself. But words were lost against the noise of a racing piston rising and plunging, driving a shaft that propelled Johnny Dobbs's steam pinnace—Mac's only hope of escape.

The Captain of the *Thuringia* had correctly anticipated a
delay in disembarking on arrival in New York Harbor. Irving's fast tug demanded, by Morse light (once identification
was given), that the French liner stop and let down both
gangway and loading pontoon for immediate access to her
deck. The Captain, not unduly surprised, gave the necessary
orders. He then issued instructions that the second police
boat, approaching slowly from the starboard side, should be
told to come to port, where her party could board—as had
also been requested by the flashing Morse light. He was confused by the duplicated messages and the need for so many
State Police officials and private investigators on the one side
and New York detectives on the other, merely to arrest one
man; but in foreign waters he was obliged to comply. Mr.
MacDonald was not *his* problem.

§

As Pinkerton's police boat crossed the *Thuringia*'s bows,
all on board (apart from those who, armed, were checking
their weapons) saw ahead, floating beside the ship at her
water line, the loading pontoon and a gangway leading from it
at an incline to the French liner's deck. Another vessel was
already hove-to.

Pinkerton leaned over the gunwale of his boat, peering into
the gloom of twilight toward suspended oil lamps which
Thuringia's sailors were placing at the rails. "Hell!" he exclaimed. At that moment the police boat began to go about,
turning from the French liner. Pinkerton spun around.
"What the . . ." he began, then shouted at the skipper, "what
are you doing?"

"Orders from the Frenchy, sir!" the captain yelled from his
open bridge. "We have to stand off until the other boat, the
tug, has cleared the pontoon."

Pinkerton could see the Morse light flashing still from
Thuringia. "I'm ordering you, man . . ." bellowed Pinkerton
hoarsely, "get back on course!"

Now the captain of the police boat was confused. Torn between his own sea sense and a landlubber's directives, he
started to turn the wheel.

Pinkerton looked back at *Thuringia* and caught a glimpse of four figures making their way gingerly up the gangway, aided by several of the French liner's sailors. He thought he recognized one of the four men as he reached the deck and was caught in the glow of several lamps: the Chief of Detectives in New York City—Jimmy Irving. Pinkerton's anger exploded. "Damn and blast!"

§

Mac saw the stout detective, red-faced from cold and effort, pushing his way across the crowded deck as all heads turned after him, Detectives Stanley and White and Jake the policeman following close behind. The four men burst out of the passenger throng which now backed away from Irving's imposing bulk. Mac, seeing him in the gloom under a flickering glow of oil lamps, was undecided which he read in Irving's set expression—friend or foe; he hoped the former, and gave New York's Finest a wide and open smile.

The detective remained impassive. His hand reached out to Mac's shoulder, and a gasp went up from the crowd.

"George MacDonald?" Irving asked loudly.

"Yes," replied Mac.

"You have a cabin aboard this ship?" Irving boomed.

"I have," responded Mac, equally loud.

"Then I must ask you to take us to it." Irving paused. There was absolute silence on deck. "By the authority vested in me by the City of New York . . ." He looked menacingly into Mac's face, as all the crowd could see. ". . . you are under arrest," he finished.

Mac's heart sank. So he'd been betrayed. There was no choice but to go belowdecks.

§

In Cuba, at Don Andrez' mansion on the Isle of Pines, the hurricane warning, given almost a week before Austin Bidwell's dinner party, had been accompanied by winds of unusual strength for the time of year. They blew hard for several days, abated, then petered out altogether, to leave each subsequent day so perfect that mild concern was expressed by Don Andrez' group on the second day of calm (after an inebriated lunch) at the single white-and-gold puffball cloud that slowly passed on the distant horizon above a glittering sea. It dissolved, finally, away to the east—as, in their separate rooms, did the mood of the gay party, who, by late afternoon, had all become aware of an increased heaviness in the air, creating an eerie stillness.

The birds stopped singing; insects were strangely muted; no sounds came from the slaves' village and although the sun shone and waves rippled on the white sand, the suffocating oppression of the atmosphere was affecting even Don Andrez.

That evening, he placed his glass on the large table in the center of the patio and stood up from his wicker chair, taking a last look out to the western sky, afire with a sunset that now played on fast-building pillars of cloud, creating shapes to stir even the most apathetic imagination.

Interrupting a joke being drawn out by the American, Gray, Don Andrez clapped his hands twice, loudly, and achieved silence from the assembled group.

"We will leave," he said seriously.

Not one man demurred against the decision. By eight o'clock, under a three-quarter moon and full sail, the group, clustered on the deck of their ship, were cutting a fast course to the mainland. The wind that blew them was by no means light and increased in strength with every hour that passed and each nautical mile that brought them nearer to Cajío, San Marcos, the railway at Felipe and home—Havana.

On the night of the third day since their departure from the Isle of Pines, they were asleep in their own beds, with only a whispering wind again mocking their temerity. Hearing that his friends had returned to the capital, Austin at once sent them invitations to his (as yet undisclosed as a final) dinner party. Thus Don Andrez, Alvarez, Gray and even Mondago not only swelled the numbers but added warmth to the assemblage.

§

All the guests came in from the patio overlooking the Gulf

of Mexico, assembled in the dining room at Austin's superb table and sat down. The melodies of an old culture, played on Cuban instruments, enhanced the delicacies of a gourmet cuisine and the already established convivial atmosphere.

Only the wind rising outside caused an occasional anxious glance to wander to a window or seek the draft that seemed with increasing frequency to catch each of the splendid candelabra in turn and waft the candle flames until they resembled palm trees bent over in a storm of great force.

Laughter and explanations came from Mondago and Gray of their reasons for leaving the southern shore of the island—only, as they said, looking along the table, bowing with smiles and raised glasses, to be in the presence of such beauty as Elizabeth represented and to partake of the best offerings on the island. The conversation was rich, trivial, political, inventive and never dull. Whether thanks to alcohol or because the meeting of schooled intellects provided wit and humor as tools with which to utilize knowledge, the guests were making—as was the exception rather than rule—of (as it was remembered) "Austin's supper" a magical night, rewarding the efforts even of the servants, who caught the atmosphere and whose smiles told equally of enjoyment and of quantities of cooking wine illicitly consumed in corners of the large kitchen along the wide corridor outside the glowing dining room.

"Let's not think of Mexico, Austin," said Elizabeth softly. She put a hand on his arm, smiled a moment across at Don Andrez and looked down the length of the table to the far end, where, to one side, Gray—the pleasant Savannah-born American—was being taught correct Spanish by one of the ladies amidst peals of laughter. Elizabeth looked back at her "Señor Bidwell."

"These are your friends," she continued to Austin intimately—then, with a smile, "our friends," she emphasized —"who are privileged and influential." She paused a moment, trying to read in Austin's impassive face some reaction to her obvious wish not to leave. "Wherever you go in Cuba you will always be welcome, and I feel sure if it were necessary . . ." Again she paused, now to place the word carefully. ". . . protected," she finished.

Austin understood quite well what Elizabeth meant. He was about to speak when she put a finger to his lips and with moist eyes and that soft mouth Austin knew so well, moving delicately over white teeth of indescribable perfection, she said the words he would never forget—words that sustained him in what was to come: "And I will always be with you wherever."

As Austin leaned toward this woman of his love, heart full and eyes concealing nothing, he could hear only the wind, blowing now in strong gusts, as if isolating the two lovers from the world outside. His lips touched those of his loved one. Austin's guests, seeing the gesture, began to applaud loudly, some standing as they did so, the women smiling—instantly tearful at the exhibition of emotion. For a moment Austin was oblivious to everything but the sensation of a lover's kiss. Then his ears alerted his mind to a sound they detected in a short lull between the strengthening gusts of wind outside: running feet.

Suddenly, ten or fifteen armed men burst in from the six tall windows behind Austin's guests. The long lace curtains billowed around them. Both large oak doors to the room were thrust open. The dinner party was stunned into a shocked silence. From the outside corridor, in rushed armed civilians, police and soldiers, surrounding the table. The flurry of movement subsided.

A young American stepped into the room, not much older than Austin himself. He surveyed the seated group, and his firm gaze came to rest at the head of the table. The candlelight flickered across the host's face, creating expression where in fact there was none.

"Austin Bidwell?" asked the young American.

Austin stood up slowly and nodded his head. A blast of wind came around the house, howling from the darkness outside as if in protest, before plunging into the surrounding vegetation to tear at the leaves and roots.

"My name," stated the young man in a clear voice, "is John Curtain, of the Pinkerton Force. I am sorry to disturb your dinner party but am forced to tell you that I have in my pocket a warrant for your arrest, on a charge of forgery upon the Bank of England."

A murmur of protest began at the table, but was silenced by the unspoken command in Curtain's eyes as he glanced at the soldiers on either side of the table. The loading of a first round into almost twenty rifles is a sound that communicates even to the most imperious.

All eyes were on the host. For some reason he could never afterward explain, Austin, outwardly calm (although he had become pale), hearing only the tempest outside, looked directly at his cigar box on the Spanish oak sideboard behind Curtain and thought of the beautiful craftsmanship represented by the intricate silverwork inlaid to such perfection. It was an astonishing reaction to adversity. But Austin's voice, when he spoke, was clear. "Mr. Curtain, will you come into the other room?"

Austin's arm made a gesture indicating an adjoining room behind double doors: the "smoking room," as Elizabeth called it, which Austin used occasionally for a study and for his gentlemen guests, who always enjoyed retiring to it for port and brandy.

"Certainly," replied John Curtain.

"Excuse me, ladies and gentlemen," said Austin to the expectant faces, all awaiting Austin's instant dismissal of this ludicrous accusation.

Austin walked around his chair to the double doors, opened them, ushered Curtain in, entered himself and closed the doors behind them both. The dining room remained as if a box photographer were silently counting out seconds to the assembled mass in the hope that an unmoving tableau would produce a sharp and distinct photograph, recording the event.

Every person gazed fixedly at the smoking-room doors, the only movement and sound coming from uncontrolled currents of air which now swept unhindered through the tall windows, informing the majority who had survived hurricanes before that there was no longer any doubt of what was to come.

§

"Is our Edinburgh air makin' ye feel any better, Mr. Coutant?" asked the Scottish voice of George Bidwell's landlady.

"Non," muttered George. ". . . *malheureusement*, Mme. Laverock," he said with a forced smile.

Looking the man up and down, she decided her lodger was right. In the fading light of late afternoon she could make out what looked like two days' growth of beard.

"Well, if you're after yer evenin' paper, you'll find one at the station—Dundas Street is early closed today." She had correctly guessed why George was venturing out.

"Merci," said George. *"Sank you."*

She watched George walk toward the corner of Cumberland and Dundas.

§

A gentleman who had been in the habit of visiting Mr. Anderson's dismal little news agency had been, for several years, in the employ of Messrs. Gibson, Craig, Dalziel and Brodies, and unlike George, he enjoyed the occasional conversation with his fellow "canny Scot." They talked mainly of the trivialities men exchange in such situations, but as the Great Bank Fraud continued to be a focus of national speculation, it was not unusual that the regular conversations of the past month had dwelt upon this topic—especially since the gentleman in question, who worked for "Messrs. Etcetera," as Anderson was wont to call them, was in fact himself (once removed, of course, he modestly admitted) an employee of the Bank of England.

Mr. Anderson needed his half glasses only for reading. His distant vision was better than good; it was, in fact, exceptional; and, unfortunately for George Bidwell, people were Mr. Anderson's life: his hobby, as he often said to whosoever asked, was the observation of character and habit. Eyes fascinated him! And the photogravure on the front page of paper after paper that he sold, day in and out, morning and night (as he later rambled on to Pinkerton and Spittle) had shown him a likeness, said to be good, of the wanted man in the Great Fraud case. It had presented him, Mr. Anderson, with an indelible image of George Warren, alias Wilson, alias Bidwell.

In his mind there had been no doubt whatsoever that the owner of those eyes in Ellen's once-cherished photograph was the man who had come into his shop for a paper and passed himself off as foreign. Gossip provided the fact that he was staying at young Mrs. Laverock's. This information—"for what it's worth," he'd added with a glint in his eye—Mr. Anderson had imparted to the gentleman from "Messrs. Etcetera," who in turn informed the partners of his firm, representatives of the Bank of England in Scotland. They cabled Threadneedle Street and received instructions to await the arrival of the police and Mr. Pinkerton.

Thus, when Pinkerton and Spittle arrived in Glasgow and cabled their whereabouts, they received a copy of the telegraphed instructions to Messrs. Gibson, Craig, Dalziel and Brodies in Edinburgh, to be examined for what it was worth to them. To Pinkerton, R.A., a hunch was as good as a clue; as his father always said, "When you ain't got nothin', you only got this," and he'd always tap his head. This time Robert A. Pinkerton threw away a lifetime oath and bet Spittle any price that they had their man.

§

George, at the end of Cumberland Street, saw in a backward glance that his landlady was still watching him. He waved quickly, as she did in response; then he was around the corner and gone. Mrs. Laverock walked up the small front garden path, climbed the five steps to her front door and only then, as she had been instructed, turned around, pointed to the end of Cumberland where it intersected Dundas Street and nodded her head vigorously.

The house across the street was suddenly full of movement. The front door burst open, and six, then a seventh man ran out into the middle of the street. Mrs. Laverock's neighbor opposite and her two children now rushed out themselves—having been physically constrained to silence whilst they had watched (along with the police) "Annie" talking to the "Frenchy."

"Well, Mr. Spittle?" asked Pinkerton excitedly, buttoning

his suit coat tight. He threw off his topcoat, which was caught
by the old man, who, though he had half glasses on his nose
and not much hair on his head, had retained the penetrating
Scottish look of canny insolence, along with a burr which the
American detective had barely been able to decipher in his impatience.

"Thank you, Mr. Anderson," said Pinkerton.

He knew his quarry now, and the clean-shaven description
from Anderson corroborated for him, as did the sight of their
man through the upper windows of Mrs. Laverock's neighbor, that he was theirs for the taking. They had finally run
George Bidwell to earth, and if the rogue did not come quietly
when apprehended, that was exactly—literally—what Pinkerton was prepared to do.

The American private detective at the center of the group in
Cumberland Street looked about him moments after George
had rounded the corner into Dundas. Pinkerton was trying to
ascertain whether these hastily assembled Scottish police
detectives were up to what they were about to undertake.

"M'Kelvie?" The man nodded. "I'm told you've got legs
on you?" The man nodded again. "Then if he runs . . ."
Pinkerton paused. "I'll get him," said the dour Scot quietly.
"Good man," said the American grimly. He took in the
whole group.

"You all saw him?" he asked quickly.

They nodded. "And you'll recognize him?" he questioned
again. They all nodded. Spittle hastily finished doing up the
bottom of his coat and pressed his hat close to his head.

"Okay, then, boys," said Pinkerton, and began walking
fast to the end of the street, followed by the others.

"We've got him."

All six men broke into a run. Half of Cumberland Street
came out to watch them go. Only Mr. Anderson remained
outside 22, holding several topcoats. He smiled and thought
of what he would do with five thousand pounds.

§

"Now, listen, Mac," said Irving urgently, looking quickly

at Stanley and White, who were already going through Mac's luggage to create the impression of a thorough search. "We ain't got ten minutes. So here's what to do. . . ."

The public image of harsh law and inescapable justice had fallen from Chief of Detectives James Irving as easily as he had turned the lock of Mac's cabin door. He had stationed his uniformed policeman, Jake, outside to guard it. Now he gave Mac the details of his plan, which he hoped would get him off the French liner and lost in downtown Manhattan before William Pinkerton's police boat could pull in to *Thuringia* and lie to long enough for its occupants to board her.

It had been made clear to Irving's tug captain—and a substantial bribe had persuaded the man—to remain hove-to against the pontoon at *Thuringia*'s water line and deny any approach, should Pinkerton ignore instructions from the French liner's bridge to stand off until access to the gangway became clear.

The commotion on the police boat as marshals, armed State Police and Agency men shouted angrily at Irving's tug, was added to as they began to throw lighted torches across at the other craft. It all created a marvelous diversion for the passengers aboard *Thuringia*, and now, as she swung around on the tide in the cold, dark harbor water with the tug moored to her side, it provided a spectacle for the crowds gathered ashore.

As the anger of the police and their confusion became apparent, a huge derisive cheer went up from the wharfside, penetrating the darkness. Pinkerton was desperate; he watched his men flinging the burning shafts into the sky toward the tug. He hoped these torches would provide more than light. If the fact that those aboard the official police vessel were determined to board *Thuringia now* had not penetrated the skull of Irving's tugboat skipper as the oil torches roared overhead onto his decks, then what the hell, thought Pinkerton, we're going in anyway. He bellowed orders to his own captain, and the standoff was over.

The heavy police boat smashed against the tug, knocking the crew still aboard off their feet. Fighting broke out between Irving's men and several of Pinkerton's conscripts. The others, led by Pinkerton, some with torches held high, leaped over the tug, scrambled onto the loading pontoon and raced up the gangway to the main deck of *Thuringia*.

§

"Will you have a glass of wine?" Austin Bidwell asked John Curtain quietly. The two long windows in the room were secured and locked; thus the rush of wind outside was muted, and a comparative calm had fallen. Austin indicated one of the deep, soft leather armchairs. Warily, John Curtain sat down, first perching then sinking into its enveloping comfort.

"I never," he replied with a faint smile, "drink anything but Clicquot."

"But that is champagne," said Austin, poised at the drinks cabinet. He raised his eyebrows and turned slowly to face Curtain.

John Curtain nodded, taking in the room at a glance, communicating to Austin that he might well be susceptible to the temptations wealth could offer, as his taste already illustrated.

The several oil lamps and single candelabrum on the center table, surrounded by glasses, added brightness to what otherwise (the wood paneling being darker than in the adjoining room and the colors dull) might have been a somber place.

Austin rang the small hand bell, whose clear note passed through the double doors for all in the dining room to hear. The nearest servant entered his master's study cautiously. He listened to Austin's request, hurried off and returned with a bottle of champagne already chilled—one of many awaiting the long-delayed dessert. He opened it.

"Clicquot," said Austin. He took two cigars from a large, plain humidor on the table against the paneled wall and offered one to Curtain.

"Thank you, no," said Curtain, but accepted a glass of champagne.

Leaving the bucket in its stand, Austin's servant nervously went, closing both doors with great care.

From the dining room there was no sound. Only gusting wind outside the study competed with what little noise the two men made as they calculated every gesture, eyes locked on each other. Austin smiled; cigar held lightly, he reached for a drawer in the table.

"Cutter," he said amiably by way of explanation.

Curtain relaxed slightly.

Austin indicated the champagne. "You have good taste," he continued patronizingly.

"I know yours," said Curtain, and raised his glass. Austin pulled open the drawer, reached in and took out the cutter under the hawklike gaze of Curtain.

"Inquiry produces information," Curtain said. "You are now in our files, Mr. Bidwell."

"I am flattered," said Austin, and looked for a moment at his cigar before snipping the end expertly.

"If I were you," said Curtain, "I would *not* be."

Austin responded, feeling the cigar in one hand, the weight of the cutter in the other, "You are in no position to judge my feelings, Mr. Curtain."

"I am in the best position, if you will reflect a moment, sir," said Curtain confidently.

Austin, moving unhurriedly, crossed two paces to the candelabrum and leaned toward the flame to light his cigar. He held it above the point which leaped to the rolled tobacco, then turned the cigar in his mouth until it was aglow. He faced John Curtain again and slowly crossed back to the table with the cigar cutter.

"You know the power and value of money, Mr. Curtain?"

Curtain smiled and said nothing.

The two men scrutinized each other.

"As you are aware," said Austin deliberately, "I have a fortune." He paused. Curtain was impassive. Austin drew on his cigar, then, with his lips slightly parted, let the smoke escape. When he spoke, his face was without expression.

"Sit where you are—ten minutes; say nothing; do nothing; raise no alarm and fifty thousand dollars is yours."

To judge by the wind, his offer had been accepted, if not by Curtain then by the surging air outside, for at that moment the tempest rattled the shutters as if attempting to break into the room and seize the proffered bounty.

Curtain reached for the champagne, poured more, replaced

the bottle, then drank down the contents of his glass, putting it empty and inverted onto the ice in the bucket. He looked steadily at Austin Bidwell.

"Why, sir, that is five thousand dollars a minute!" he exclaimed in a low voice.

"Indeed it is," said Austin with nonchalance as he replaced the cigar cutter in the drawer.

"But I will not be bought," said Curtain. He put a hand into his coat, where, hanging loosely under his left arm, was the first of many—a brand-new single-action Colt "Peacemaker"; as he grasped its butt, he began to rise from the deep armchair. The bargaining was over for them both.

Curtain's eyes caught the slight change of course as Austin's hand in the open drawer sought the cool metal of his own pistol, a Smith and Wesson thirty-two-caliber rimfire.

The Pinkerton man pushed himself up from the chair. His face showed fear as the new Colt snagged in the fabric of his waistcoat.

Austin Bidwell fired point-blank. The noise exploded in the confines of the study. The impact knocked Curtain across the armchair. "Damn you," he exclaimed. Clutching his side, he fell to the floor.

Austin was already moving. Four paces took him to the double doors, which he kicked open; then, leaping into the dining room, he knocked aside a chair and crouched like a cornered beast.

For a moment the crowded scene remained frozen. Then it was as if the box photographer, who had kept the entire group mesmerized, finally pressed the shutter release and flashed his pan. All hell broke loose.

§

William Pinkerton jumped onto the polished deck of the French liner *Thuringia*, amidst shouts of indignation and screams of surprise from the passengers, crowded to view the spectacle below. Behind him, lighted torches held by his men, the marshals and armed New York police led the way for lawyers, who followed more cautiously. Angrily, the official

representatives of civil order, state law and federal government pushed their way among the panicking throng, yelling
for passage and impeded in their progress to the bridge by the
fact that, like sheep, the passengers, rather than parting,
merely surged in front of them.

Pinkerton ignored the loud protests of those aboard.
"Cover the ship, men! Spread out and seal it up!" he ordered
in a voice that carried above the melee. "This is the port side.
Port, man!" he shouted at his own associates, one of whom
was already fighting to gain access through the cabins.

"Get over to starboard!" bellowed Pinkerton. "Starboard!" went up the cry, relayed from mouth to mouth; but it
did little to stir the packed throng. If anything, they merely,
hearing the word, moved that way themselves, shouting,
screaming, now fighting and kicking against the brutal ruf-
fians who were oblivious to the sensibilities all on board had
built up during almost two weeks of sedate sea voyage.

Mac ran along the upper deck until he could go no farther.
Before him was the flying bridge; below him, on the main
deck, was, he could hear, a surging, panic-stricken crowd. He
looked about him frantically, then over the side of *Thuringia*,
and saw, beside the pontoon, Irving's tug and the police boat
locked together. Fighting still continued aboard.

Beyond the torch lights he could see indistinctly the skyline
of New York Harbor in deepening darkness. Mac swore. It
was freezing cold, and the air was misting fast; soon it would
be impossible to make out anything. Nowhere was there any
sign of what might be his only chance of escape—Johnny
Dobbs.

Suddenly the door of the wheelhouse opened and the Captain of the *Thuringia* strode out to the rail; megaphone raised,
he was obviously about to deal with the chaos on board.

"Which is starboard?" shouted Mac hoarsely.

"In all conscience, Mr. MacDonald," replied the Captain,
looking down at Mac before lifting the loud-hailer to his lips,
"I am unable to give you assistance." He paused a moment;
then, before bellowing orders down at his men in the crowd,
he said quickly to Mac, "But if it is of help, I am here to quell
a riot on the port side of my ship." Mac thought that the Cap-

tain might have winked, but he was never sure, for he was already running back to the access passage in front of the funnel.

William Pinkerton was first to find a stairway to the lifeboat deck and shouldered his way between a large passenger and a State Policeman grappling with him to grab the stair rails, then climb up, until, knocking open a barred gate, he reached the space above. Finding no one, he bellowed for his men to follow and began to run back toward the funnel. From the upper deck, the Captain, on his flying bridge, was still using the megaphone, issuing instructions in French to his men that they should calm their passengers and aid the officials.

Mac leaped down onto the metal walkway in front of the funnel; throwing off his coat, then three more steps to the starboard lifeboat deck, where he began running close to its rail, searching below desperately for a sign of the steam pinnace Irving had described.

Suddenly, behind him, Mac heard shouts; he turned his head and saw William Pinkerton and several Agency men jumping down onto the deck from the funnel passage. The few oil lamps of the ship and several torches in the men's hands gave just enough light for the pursuers to realize that here was their quarry.

§

Johnny Dobbs kept losing sight of *Thuringia*'s decks as he circled in the thickening mist of the harbor on the starboard side. To port he could hear all sorts of commotion. High above, the night was still clear, but the damnable mist was hanging low over the water, so that it was difficult to maintain a sense of direction. He began to shout up to *Thuringia*, "Mac! MacDonald!" It was this which Mac heard.

§

Several of the passengers had managed to fight their way out of the furor, through the public rooms and to the comparative peace of the starboard side of *Thuringia*—amongst

them two nuns who were being looked after by several
gentlemen of questionable heroism, who had in fact successfully used these ladies first as a buffer, then as a pass to
safety. Now their loud complaints stopped as they saw Mac
running toward them. In that moment Mac heard his name
shouted from below, somewhere in the mist over the rising
swell.

He yelled back once and leaped onto the railing. Grasping a
lifeboat's davit, he peered into the gloom searching for
Johnny Dobbs. The water, he knew, would hardly be forty
degrees Fahrenheit, he was already frozen and worst of all, as
a country boy brought up inland, he could barely swim.

Still on the run, Pinkerton shouted, "Stay where you are!"

Immediately Mac stood free of the davit, teetering on the
rail. In the distance Pinkerton halted, crouched, raised his
revolver and took careful aim. One of the nuns screamed; the
other prudently crossed herself.

"Dobbs!" Mac screamed into the night. "Johnny Dobbs!"
Arms fully stretched, Mac brought his hands together above
his head, and as all who dive know, that first disconcerting
sensation of lost balance came to him. For Mac, it was unique
and terrifying—so he jumped.

§

George Bidwell crossed Dundas Street to its west side and
stepped into shadow. Last rays of sun caught shop fronts on
the opposite corner, where several groups lingered to talk as
the emporiums closed for the day. George stopped a moment
to look into the small JEWELLERS AND REPAIR window. HIGH
CLASS TO MODEST OBJECTS—ESTIMATES FREE, declared a
sign above.

George stared intently at several rings and a long pearl
necklace—represented as GENUINE but, if so, inadequately
guarded, there being no bars on the window, which was one
sheet of clear glass kept always highly polished, as were the
articles on display. Reflected sunlight—almost pure orange
color—came from across the street, giving luster and sparkle
to several of the diamonds; as a result, George could see that
they were real.

He shifted his gaze and thus his focus, and in that fraction of a second, George saw two men opposite staring at him. He looked quickly back the way he'd come (still in the reflection) and saw two more men crossing the road from the corner of Cumberland Street; and then—there—unmistakable in the shaft of sunlight, stood the policeman he'd seen on the ferry in Belfast.

George became immediately cold and clammy. How the hell . . . ? Slowly he turned from the window and began walking down Dundas Street, his mind racing. Where could he go? What now? The whole of his experience presented itself to him in the next few moments as he examined possibilities: action, obviously, but what? He lengthened his stride, and his pace quickened. Behind him the two men passed several women gossiping on the street and began to approach fast.

In the distance George saw, as he turned sharply to cross the road, that the man he'd seen aboard ship—Spittle, in fact—was accompanied by another whom he recognized from a photogravure in the papers: it was Pinkerton.

George, now on the opposite side of Dundas Street, having avoided the two drays carrying Scottish ale to a public house in Airlie Place, was about to continue down the roadway as if making for Queen Street Gardens when the first decision fell into place—as did the entire plan of his escape. In his mind was the whole area studied from the Edinburgh map he had been examining since his arrival.

He had always kept himself in exceptional physical condition and was still damn good on his legs, he knew; he smoked only cigars and therefore never inhaled, so his lungs and breathing had not suffered in the years since his youth, when he'd run everywhere in Brooklyn. During the Civil War, out of the Reb town and after he had jumped Pender's train, his escape had been made over rugged country on foot. The past weeks had cleared his system of any delights he'd indulged in during his London sojourn. Thus his condition was excellent for what was to come; and with the aid of the natural energy adrenaline gives the sighted quarry, George was about to become formidable game.

George buttoned his coat, slowed his walk on the corner of

Great King Street, then suddenly, instead of crossing, ducked around left and began running toward Drummond Place. George was grim now that he knew the chase was on and in earnest. He increased his speed, passing startled pedestrians who barely managed to avoid him.

His hunters let up a shout and themselves broke cover. They were already into Great King, perhaps one hundred yards behind him and gaining. George hit Dundonald Street, traveling at speed, leaped off the pavement over two huge water-filled holes in the cobbles and raced across into Drummond Place.

The first of his pursuers, unable to stop, careened into one of the deep puddles and fell heavily onto his wrists. The second man, M'Kelvie, leaped over his companion and just caught sight of George entering the north road of "The Place" on the Scotland Street side. He swore; tugged at his coat, which, close-cut, was hampering him; threw it off; yelled to the policeman still sprawled on the ground to "See ta ma coat" and sprinted over the cobbles, guessing that George was in fact after London Street, on the curve of "The Place" that would put him into the alleys of Bellevue or Broughton.

M'Kelvie had been a Scottish Police "Harriers" man before his wife had had a baby the previous year, so instinct now began to regulate his breathing and dictate a pace. "I'll get 'im," he swore under his breath, and then was out of sight of his fallen companion, who pointed after him wildly as two other Scottish detectives, then Spittle and Pinkerton, who now appeared, followed fast.

George reached the second curve of Drummond Place—an oval garden within a square, four streets dividing buildings on each side. Flat out, he sprinted around the garden until he was out of sight of M'Kelvie; then, instead of turning into London Street, George continued on until he hit Dublin Street. At the corner beside a Baptist church he recognized from the map he'd studied, George turned again, breathing heavily now from the effort, hoping that he had become lost to whoever was directly behind.

George had begun running down Dublin Street Lane when he was suddenly faced with what looked like a cul-de-sac. The map as he remembered it had shown no blocked exits here; he swore and slowed a moment, looking over his shoulder. There was the "damn Scot" running for all his worth. George saw before him that perhaps the road did not end but curved again farther along where it became narrow. There, if he was right, a terraced row of houses should begin—but he could not take a chance of becoming bottled up.

He stopped and leaped for the wall beside him, perhaps nine feet high, that sealed off a terrace from Dublin Street Lane. George pulled himself to the top and stood a moment. Behind him, M'Kelvie was himself almost at the wall, steeling his body for a flying jump; to *his* rear the others (some way apart now, with Pinkerton in the forefront and, surprisingly, Spittle close up) shouted at M'Kelvie to "Get him."

George looked down from his position, then crouched on the wall and cursed nervously; he was using every second to regain his breath, for he could see, as his pursuers could not, what lay ahead. Parallel walls, each perhaps five feet high, stretched for several hundred yards into the distance, each enclosing the small, narrow garden of a two-up, two-down drab, though newly built, terraced house.

It was a nightmare. Even the light was going now, making what was in the distance hazy, but George thought he could just make out the high wall of an adjacent terrace. He jumped down into the first garden, strode four paces, leaped for the wall, swung over into the second garden and again ran for the next five-foot wall.

M'Kelvie, with great effort, scrambled up the nine feet of end terrace wall. Atop, he saw, as had George, the formidable obstacles.

"Dear God in Heaven!" he muttered, breathing heavily, feeling his lack of condition. His strength was beginning to ebb, as before his marriage it would not have. "Soft life," he panted to himself.

Behind him, Spittle leaped for the wall, grazing both hands and his face as M'Kelvie leaned down to help pull him up.

George was over a third, then a fourth wall as Pinkerton hoisted himself up the nine feet of bricks and mortar to join his two associates.

"We'll get him!" the American shouted from his vantage

point, slumping a moment to regain breath. He gestured at the two others below. "That way," he breathed. "Around!" he exclaimed, and indicated the curving road that did indeed lead through to the front of these terrace houses.

The two men ran off. Five thousand pounds, even shared, was a huge sum and a fair spur to them all. Spittle and M'Kelvie leaped for the first low garden wall together. Each had a wife who continually emphasized the value of money, and neither wished to have less than the whole reward. Both men swung over the wall, swearing with anger and some pain; Pinkerton, close behind, jumped, gripped the top and was over and into the next garden with the two others, who already were striding for the second wall.

Determination and will fueled the men; they ignored their bodies' pleas to stop. All three leaped for the next wall together.

George reached the fifth wall—flagging now, but heartened that his pursuers must be in the same condition. He glanced back and saw them coming, two gardens behind; he leaped, again swung over into the next squalid little backyard, where, taking first strides toward the opposite wall, he halted just in time. Bottle glass, jagged-edged, fixed into the brickwork atop the wall ahead made it an impossible obstacle.

He spun round desperately, looked up at the pitched roof of the building and in the next moment had run to the half-open back door of the terraced kitchen. He took a deep breath and plunged into the house.

The woman at a gas stove preparing her family's meager supper screamed as an intruder burst into her kitchen. George smashed through the swing door to a small hallway, grabbed the handrail and ran up the stairs two at a time. At the top, on the landing, several children, playing, shouted in amazement as George jumped between them, yelling for the kids to move.

He entered a small front bedroom. Unable to avoid the bed which took up most of the space, George leaped onto it and kicked out at two hands that reached for his ankles. He was already at the sash window, pulling it up, as the rudely awakened man fell groaning from the bed, holding his jaw.

George, at the open window, was about to jump into the

SPRING 1873

street when he saw the two Scottish detectives, who had come around to the front of the terrace; they saw him and shouted, breaking into a run. No way down, George could only go up.

Downstairs, Spittle crashed into the kitchen of the terraced house, M'Kelvie close on his heels, Pinkerton trailing. The woman, already shocked by George's forced entry, collapsed against the side dresser sobbing.

Pinkerton uttered a harsh apology before following the others up to the landing and front bedroom. A man on the floor was shouting through blood and broken teeth; his several children, in tears, were screaming, the noise added to by Spittle, who was yelling down to the two policemen below. They were pointing up to the roof.

Pinkerton leaned out the narrow side window of the bay and craned his neck. A slate fell. Their quarry was up there. Spittle, first wiping the sweat pouring from his face, eased himself out the main window as M'Kelvie squeezed out the other.

"He'll pay for 'is whistle now," rasped Spittle, and hauled himself out and up onto the roof's edge; his blood was racing and he felt there was no stopping him.

A narrow tiled pathway ran the length of the terrace. It had been conceived by an architect to accommodate sweeps, who could carefully negotiate the path, inspecting chimney stacks set to one side or the other of the pitched roof. Almost two hundred yards distant was a wall rising above even these roofs, which apparently backed onto another terrace, with an additional third floor.

George saw two of his pursuers pulling themselves onto the roof. Below in the street, one of the detectives had pulled out a pistol and was shouting something unintelligible to George. He looked again along the spine of the terrace roof, filled his lungs and began to sprint.

Spittle could hardly believe his eyes. "The man'll walk on water next!" he bellowed hoarsely up to M'Kelvie as, bent over, the man carefully made his way up the slate roof. Spittle staggered and fell heavily. M'Kelvie turned around to see his companion's plight, immediately lost his footing and slid down to the guttering with a shout of fear.

Pinkerton could see the disappearing figure of George fifty yards away—sixty—seventy, as Spittle clambered back to the roof's edge where M'Kelvie was now propped, still breathing heavily, determined even now to attempt a second ascent.

"Damn him!" exclaimed Pinkerton. "Well, follow him!" he shouted down to the two detectives below in the street. They took off down the road. At the end it became a cul-de-sac where the rear of the other terrace formed a high wall. They could see that here George *must* come to a halt.

George was tired and bleeding, but raced the final yards to the back of the three-story terrace that rose above the roof he was on—not knowing how he would get over. In the cul-de-sac below, the two detectives stumbled toward the end of the street still shouting hoarsely. George, his breath rasping, blessed the architect of the pathway: planning ingenuity, consideration for the sweeps had also provided an iron stepladder that gave access to the next terrace roof. George grasped the rusting metal, pulled himself up the eight rungs panting—exhausted, but by no means finished. In his mind was the one place: Waverley—the railway station.

The two detectives in the street were joined by Pinkerton, Spittle and M'Kelvie, who ran up from behind. People from the terraced houses had come out to see the source of commotion, and all of them peered above into the fading light to catch sight of "a man on the run."

Bricks and mortar three stories high, not one window relieving the imposing terrace wall, confronted the five pursuers. Facing its rear to right and left was a narrow lane which led along the back of the terrace. Pinkerton quickly indicated to the two detectives to go in one direction whilst he, M'Kelvie and Spittle followed the lane the other way—out of the cul-de-sac—hoping to get around into what M'Kelvie said would be Broughton Street.

§

George slid down the terrace roof that faced Broughton Street, and in so doing gashed his leg on the guttering. He swore in agony, but with no time to assess his wound, he jumped onto the portico of a house doorway and dropped into communal gardens which ran along the front of the terrace.

George raced across the road to Broughton Place, then turned into Hart Street. He seemed to have lost his pursuers, so thankfully slowed to a jog as if only a man in a hurry. The light had almost gone from the sky, which, with not a cloud in sight, gave George the uplifting feeling he needed. He turned right into Forth Street—which for him was wrong: he had come full circle back to Broughton Street and disaster.

A shout went up from behind, and George spun around. Several passers-by looked also. They had found nothing particularly unusual about George, disheveled and sweating though he was—it was not an uncommon sight in the poor district—but more shouts focused their attention. They came clear and cold from several voices and from men who looked as though they had the authority to mean it: "Stop him!"

It was George's heart that stopped—almost. There, not sixty yards away, were his pursuers. Physically, they were in a condition admittedly worse than George's, but now their voices, at least, were full of renewed vigor.

George guessed that he was less than half a mile from the station; every yard would count. He began to run even more strongly than he had before. With an increasingly powerful stride, George's legs propelled him as if no longer his own. It was a race for life, he well knew. Even if he made the station, he had only a slim chance of freedom—but he had none at all on the streets.

"Fear lends wings." George remembered the saying and proved it true. He felt his feet flying over the cobbles and pavement squares. If he did nothing else, he'd make that station.

Within sight of St. Mary's Cathedral, George swung right, crossing the street in front of cabs, broughams, a sweep's cart, several horses (whose riders shouted obscenities), two torch-bearing watchmen and four or five young ladies who should never have been out in the chill of evening.

George's feet were firm and sure; his heart was steady; his body moved obediently to a rhythm set by steely determination. His stride was long, creating a pace hard to match.

Behind, it was M'Kelvie who was out ahead; Pinkerton, following close, was now running on his last reserves of energy; Spittle had begun to stumble, but with gritted teeth remained at the heels of his American associate. The two other detectives were wheezing slowly to a standstill, aware that somehow they would arrive at the destination Pinkerton had correctly guessed. He rapped it our hoarsely, but loud and clear:

"He's makin' for the station, boys!"

George had entered Albany Street fast. Blood from the deep gash in his flesh was seeping through a long tear in his right trouser leg. His face was cut. Dirt and grime soiled his jacket. His soft leather shoes had split along their cross seams and begun to cut into his feet—but still he kept up a relentless pace.

He ran down a lane to within sight of St. Paul's, turned sharply into York Place and crossed the still-busy thoroughfare. Ignoring the shouts both behind him and from the startled horse-drawn traffic, he entered Elder Street, leading down to the Royal Bank of Scotland.

George burst out of the narrow street onto the intersection of Leith and Princes streets at Waterloo Place; there to the right of North Bridge was the entrance to Waverley Station. Through sweat-clouded eyes he could just make out the clock above the entrance. It was almost seven. George took Way Steps, the stairway beside Edinburgh's Station Hotel, two at a time. Behind him, the shouts of Pinkerton, Spittle and M'Kelvie were lost in the noise of traffic.

George leaped off the steps, ran across the station foyer and broke through a crowd at the ticket barrier onto the platform area, shouting something to the inspector at the gate as if he were late for a train. George, breathing heavily, saw that a throng of people were making their way up the steps of a bridge across the tracks. He swore. It would be impossible to pass them, so he took the only other course of action and jumped from the platform edge onto the rails.

He had already seen his goal—the third platform. A whistle blast echoed throughout Waverley Station as billows of black smoke were accompanied by released steam. The *Southern Express* for Carlisle and beyond had begun to move out.

George scrambled up onto the second platform as, behind, his pursuers burst through the ticket barrier.

Milling crowds awaiting the arrival of the Birmingham express packed the platform as George, oblivious of obstacles, careened into them. He knocked several people aside, sent one man sprawling and kicked into a pile of luggage, which fell across some old women, who screamed loudly. Reaching the edge of the second platform, he leaped down onto the rails. In his mind, a single thought: the departing train, one track away—one platform to cross. George was talking to himself now, almost delirious.

He shouted in alarm as a huge engine—the Birmingham express—whistle screaming in warning, thundered down on him. George leaped for the platform edge ahead and pressed himself to it. Carriages rattled past as the train slowed, approaching the buffers of its destination.

Smoke and steam billowed all around. George could hear clearly that the *Southern Express*, across this final platform, was beginning to draw away. He pulled himself up, staggered out of the swirling smoke and pushed through the crowd of well-wishers waving their last good-byes. He tried desperately to shoulder his way between them to reach out for a moving carriage door. The momentum of the *Southern Express* was now building quickly; George was forced to run faster.

Again he knocked into someone. The breath rasped in his throat; his legs were numb; only will power drove him forward. Square on, George hit a man who tried to stand in his way. He hurdled an empty porter's trolley, punched out at a heroic "buck" grasping toward him, kicked the head of a man attempting a flying tackle; suddenly he was through the final cordon of startled young women, out from under the enclosing roof of the main platform.

George had thirty yards more to make his bid to board the *Express*. Shouts went up from behind as his pursuers burst onto the third platform and themselves began to run parallel with the train, threading their way fast through the crowds.

M'Kelvie gritted his teeth; Spittle swore to himself; Pinkerton bellowed harshly, "Hold him!" An earsplitting shriek from the *Express*, as steam was forced out of its whistle, cocooned in noise all witnesses to the final moments of George Bidwell in Edinburgh on Waverley Station.

§

In Newgate Prison, Edwin Noyes was drowsing against the wall of his damp cell when his heart suddenly lurched. It brought him to alertness. Edwin stood up. He crossed several paces to the four vertical bars firmly inset at the window. His hands found the two on either side, whilst his head fell against those bars in the center. He remained in this position, feeling the chill of evening. Fear for the future seized both his mind and his soul.

Thinking of his lost friends, dissolving ambitions and the abortive attempt at riches; absorbing the hopelessness of his situation; having before him not the four pillars of a great gateway through which he could enter to join the Four Hundred, but the bars of a British prison where he must surely rot, Edwin Noyes did two things he had not done in all the time since first he had been incarcerated: he burst into tears of self-pity and began to pray for salvation.

§

In New York Harbor, a few yards out from the *Thuringia* at the water line, Mac hit the surface of the water hard—to experience the immediate darkness of submersion in a cold, black sea.

The impact knocked all breath from his body. Instinct sealed his mouth; fear flailed his limbs as, hopelessly, he tried to regain control in a world that no longer had gravity or direction. He sank deep. Gasping for oxygen, he found only the all-pervading icy fluid which began to fill every space, flooding ears, nostrils, throat and lungs, dragging him farther down until agony made a nightmare of reality and his fragile senses recognized that all of life was now merely a fading dream.

Johnny Dobbs had heard the splash as MacDonald hit and immediately cut the motor of his pinnace. Mist swirled about him; he could see nothing. Above, from the *Thuringia*'s decks, he heard voices babbling, but his ears waited for another sound: on the surface of the harbor, where he judged it would come from, of a man in the water, panicking. He gripped his boat hook tightly, knowing he would have only seconds to grab Mac before he sank again.

"He's gotta rise once," he muttered to himself. "God in heaven—give him the once," he whispered gravely. And—patiently—Dobbs waited. And waited. And waited. And . . . suddenly . . . he thought . . . for a moment . . . that he had heard . . . the noise of a man drowning. He thrust the boat hook into the mist toward the sound on the water.

"Mac!" he rasped urgently into the darkness. "Mac?" The boat hook was almost wrenched from his grasp and immediately sank beneath the surface. Instantly Johnny Dobbs's powerful hands seized it more firmly, and he began to pull with all his might.

§

No one in Señor Bidwell's dining room—no one in the entire assemblage—ever forgot what he or she then saw take place that night. The host of the evening leaped onto his dining table, scattered plates in all directions and attempted to run but, constrained by a mass of obstacles, began stumbling through the elaborate preparations, crashing into candelabra, dishes, cutlery, flowers, glasses, bottles, platters, food—everything assembled to pay homage to sophisticated demands of the stomach; all of it went right and left, spun into the air, was knocked aside—kicked away.

Although the time it took could have been counted in seconds, Austin seemed to continue down that table for minutes on end, his face frozen in an expression of utter desperation.

Only Elizabeth, from the corner of her eye, saw a figure stagger out of the smoking room brace itself against the doorframe and take clear aim down the center of the table, arm outstretched, squinting along the barrel of a large, cocked Colt revolver.

Curtain bellowed, "Bidwell!" So Elizabeth did the first

thing that came into her mind. She stood up—effectively obscuring Curtain's target.

"Damn you!" he yelled, but the invective was lost amidst the noise of many scraping chairs, as on both sides of the long table the gentlemen who were not already standing—as a reflex of manners, despite the madness of the moment, seeing their hostess on her feet—immediately stood to join her. At the far end of the table, Austin launched himself toward the locked French doors behind the cowering quartet of Cuban musicians. . . .

It seemed that the soldiers, reaching out between the guests, would seize him; that the Cubans could not move in time; that the distance from the table was too great; but there was no time for speculation. All in the dining room saw, without question, the man responsible for the great Bank of England crime falter in mid-air, then crash through glass and wood, which slivered and broke.

With debris that fell beyond the balcony, as Austin's momentum took him out into space, went his shout at the pain of impact; then came a cry of fear as he began to fall. Light streamed from the villa interior into the darkness. A thousand pinpoints glittered on slivers of glass that danced momentarily in its glow; then the raging tropical wind swept them away, and with huge noise—obliterating all else—at full force the hurricane struck.

§

A shrill whistle; billowing steam; the cacophony of pistons, wheels and belching smoke engulfed George Bidwell's exhausted senses as, running flat out with a last effort, he reached toward the fast-moving carriage parallel to him and now pulling away. For a fleeting moment, he saw an astonished face at the window of a door; then his hand gripped a bar beside the handle, which immediately dragged him off his feet. He reached out with his other hand, desperately seeking to secure his hold.

Screams filled the station. All on the platform saw George Bidwell strain to hang on, reach out a second time, fail to grasp the handle he sought, lose his grip—and as the train

thundered out of Waverley Station, a hundred pairs of eyes
saw him slip, begin to fall, then plunge between the platform
edge and the scything wheels of the last carriages. The night
express roared off south into darkness.

Pinkerton, Spittle and M'Kelvie came to a standstill
amongst the anguished witnesses to the horror. The *Express*
was quickly out of sight, gone into a tunnel. Distant sounds
indicated that it had emerged again beyond, so that smoke
rose once more into the dark sky. The southbound train
rounded the rock above which rose Edinburgh Castle, then
plunged into the second tunnel beneath King's Stables Road.

For all in Waverley Station, alarm had turned to shock. All
three pursuers, especially M'Kelvie, were stunned by the
tragedy. Slowly Pinkerton and Spittle walked toward the edge
of the platform, their faces taut, mouths pressed, tongues dry;
both men were sickened at the prospect of what would be
before them. They became the eyes of the crowd, who now
waited with bated breath.

Spittle suddenly felt squeamish. Unable to face the sight, he
looked away—unlike Pinkerton, who, without a qualm,
peered over the platform edge to find the mangled body of
George Bidwell. The crowd saw the American detective stare
down at the rails; a murmur rippled amongst them as they
watched him sag a moment, obviously in anguish. He shook
his head from side to side.

George knew about wheels and rails, suspension bars,
coachwork, bolts, axles and generally the underwork
mechanics of a railway car. The world over, they were much
the same, and years before, he had learned the hard way:
hanging beneath the coachwork and above the wheels of a
Reb train until it had carried him out of town—eighteen
miles; had he relaxed once . . . He certainly knew all about the
power of wheels on rail. His face had been inches away as tons
of wheel and carriage ground dust to powder. . . .

"All you ever need," George always said, "is confidence,
expertise, imagination—and, of course, a little luck."

Slowly Pinkerton looked up into the darkness, put hands on
hips and, despite his exhaustion, began to sob with uncontrolled laughter. What he already knew the crowd on
Waverley Station were about to discover. He'd seen for him-

self, and that was proof enough. George Bidwell was not there.

§

Upstairs at Delmonico's, on the corner of Broadway and Chambers Street in New York City, the boy come to clean was already at work. Dust was suspended in the sunshine as brilliant shafts of light penetrated the morning gloom of the restaurant.

Harry McCann inverted the last four chairs one by one and slammed them down atop the corner table. He crossed to the bar area, opposite the windows, to sweep away the sawdust. Without the stoves alight it was damn cold, but at least fresh compared with the nights; then he worked carrying crates up from the cellar and serving wine—although he was never allowed to take orders. Harry stood for a moment behind the bar, spread his hands and leaned toward imaginary customers. Beyond, where the restaurant was laid out, in the corner, he saw the four chairs on the best table. The papers still headlined the men who had used that table and tipped him better than any before or since. The papers said that they'd planned the whole thing right here in the restaurant. Harry shook his head; the papers said a lot of things. They talked only in thousands, and he'd known only forty dollars a month top.

Harry McCann stared at the table across the room. Five hundred each, the papers said. "That's"—he paused to work it out, slowly—"one thousand years of my life." He stopped himself and swore, then burst into laughter.

He remembered their faces, each one. Since he was fourteen he'd worked here; he'd known 'em then and wouldn't forget—kindness in the rough—sticks. They'd befriended him: that was what counted. Harry took the long handle of the mop, dunked it in the bucket of water and suds and began to swab beneath the tables. Mac had taught him to write his own name—an accomplishment of which he was mighty proud. George had advised him to think lucky, and Austin had given him his first glass of champagne. Mr. Noyes hadn't been around much after the first year.

Harry dunked the mop again. He shook his head and swabbed under the corner table: "their" table he called it still—privately.

He stood upright and then leaned on the mop's handle staring at the inverted chairs. How could it have been so long? Why, it seemed like only yesterday . . . But if it meant traveling to get what the papers said George, Austin, Mac and Noyes had pulled off—then at nineteen years of age, Harry McCann was going places! Five hundred—*each* . . . !

New Yorkers on the corner of Broadway and Chambers Street stopped momentarily to look above the restaurant signs as the contagious laughter of a young man issued forth from open second-floor windows of what was obviously upstairs at Delmonico's. . . .

```
G  *  A  *  M  *  E
E     U     A     D
O     S     C     W
R     T     &     I
G     I     ?     N
E     N  O  Y  E  S
```